THE BOOK OF EMILY

(REQUIESCAT IN PACE)

THOMAS DAVIS

Fourth Edition

Copyrights © 2024 By Thomas Davis

All rights reserved. No part of this book may be reproduced or transmitted in any form by any means, electronic or mechanical, including photocopying and recording, or by any information storage and retrieval system, except as may be expressly permitted in writing from the author.

Dedication

With love and gratitude this book is dedicated to Anthony Brown & Katasha Smart who sat through pages and pages of drafts and ideas always encouraging and always believing in all the unpublished books I sent them. This first one is for you!

Chapter 1

Living in the suburbs has its benefits. I was raised in the city amongst the concrete and mortar. My parents made an exodus to a county that promised better schools, better neighbors, and a better life. Immediately, there was a change in the family. We were one of the first Afro-Americans in the suburban neighborhood. I was the oldest of three, and I was the hardest to adapt to the different lifestyle.

Education has become not a chore but an opportunity. I fought to keep myself changed to city life, but soon, it offered nothing as I watched my friends, who remained entrenched in the environment. Dual in residential upbringing, I could now blend both in the black urban community and function in the whitewashed county. It has made me bi-cultural. I can merge with the ghetto and thrive in the multicultural world. It was these same behaviors that became survival skills in either dichotomy.

My story begins in Baltimore City. The connection with the city never leaves you. You are its product, and its lure beckons at every opportunity. The call of the city, and its rustle and bustle, screams to you like a banshee siren. Although I was successful at escaping its blight, it meant nothing if I didn't return to it to remember where I was from. It had a bond in geographical romance.

It was this romance that leads my story. As an adult, I frequent the city limits as a ritual. I still have friends who open their homes for me to stay in when I want extended visits. Mark was one of those friends. We had planned a day of just talking, eating, watching movies, and usually, more laughter than we could handle. We have been friends for more than 30 years. Throughout our lives, we have lived with each other, and there is nothing that we wouldn't trust each other with. Good old friends to the highest definition.

Mark lived adjacent to a huge park that was as beautiful as any forest, complete with trees, a reservoir, running paths, and a multi-culture of people that use its scenic beauty to walk their dogs and exercise. The plan was to visit the city and stay at his apartment until he got off from work. He left the key at the door for me to retrieve from the front desk to get in. His building was well secured since it was located in a dead center in the hood. I got the key that the desk held for me and went to his 6th-floor apartment. It was a modest apartment with large windows antiquated windows overlooking the park. The plan I had was to change clothes while finishing some business on the phone and go to the park to get a light workout and some sunshine.

The park was only a couple blocks away, but I had stayed on the phone too long dealing with business, which distracted me from the original plan. It was close to dusk when I finally made it out of the apartment. A beautiful day, nonetheless. I decided to not go into the park at this hour. I would have to go deep into to get to the area I like to work out in. It was easier to work out in a small park that was closer- only a block away. Warm breezes from the park were refreshing and invigorating as I walked and talked on the phone with my friend Tony. I hate enjoying this beautiful day on the phone. At times, it can take over my life, but Tony seemed like he needed to talk. Besides, I could do the light workout and talk with him simultaneously.

We spoke once or twice a day, and today, he was a little more talkative.

Normally, Tony is a very put-together person in all aspects, but today, he seems distressed.

"You know, Ty, I'm tired of Ricky doing disrespectful shit to me. We were supposed to be going out to eat this evening, and I haven't heard from him." He said calmly on the phone. " I have had it with young ass mother fuckers!"

As I listened, his normally calm voice and personality escalated to anger. The more he talked about it, the more extreme his anger got. It made me stop working out and just be the ear to let him vent his frustration. Tony is a great guy in his mid-50s and is retired. The young man he is venting about is in his early thirties and has no respect for others' time- lately Tony's.

Fiery dusk was brilliantly washing in with an eerie feeling from pumpkin orange to violet skies crowded with dark bilious clouds that changed what was a beautiful day to a creepy nightfall. I thought it best to head back to the apartment before total darkness set in. The neighborhood is safe during the day, but after dark, it transforms into a treacherous, shadowy danger zone. In my youth, it wouldn't have been an issue. It probably would have been a thrill to go into the park at night. In my older age, it wouldn't make sense to put myself in danger.

I calmed Tony down on the phone and was backtracking back to Mark's apartment when I saw what looked like could be my lighter on the sidewalk. Its bright blue color caught my eye. It was on the sidewalk that I came on, but on my return, I am walking in the street to avoid the rats that run the sidewalks at night. Rats big enough to be a cat! They are a city's pets. They walk freely in alleys and bushes. Street paths are always safer.

    I checked my sweatpants pockets to see if it could be mine. To my astonishment, all the pockets were empty. Cigarettes, lighter, keys, wallet, and more. Panic sank in. I not only lost my belongings but Mark's apartment keys, too. Without ID, I wouldn't be able to get in. My wallet has about $80 in it with credit cards, ID, insurance cards, and all the important documents a man carries in it. I picked the lighter up from a crack in the pavement behind me and peered in both directions for other lost personal items. Dusk was falling and completely transforming into a threatening night in the hood. The side street to the playground where I was, cast in a desolate shadow by streetlights that were flickering on in pinpoint, erasing shadows. I didn't want to use my phone to light up the search because it would leave me exposed to the night's predators but there was no choice. Item by item, things scattered along the outstretched sidewalk, all but the keys and cigarettes. Shadowy figures were lurking on the corners, and better common sense said to end the search. I could see them closing in in curiosity. My hastened steps sped faster and faster as I approached the corner to the safety of streetlights. Fences on both sides of the street were ladened with detailed ironwork at least a century old and coated with layered coats of paint. They were to keep people from intruding, but the feeling of keeping me out was overwhelming. An escape plan would be to hurdle over them onto the abandoned property if I got cornered. I don't often make bad decisions, but this classifies as one of them.

    Turning the corner as if I were out running greyhounds in pursuit, my heart was pounding, and my senses were on full alert. I didn't feel safe until I did. The high fences and bushes didn't allow me to see what I was running from, and I ran directly into a large guy who got to the corner at the same time I did from the opposite direction. He was solid like a statue, and I pummeled into him bouncing off him like a lightweight, but he caught me by my shirt. I knew he could see the desperate panic on my face, but his face was expressionless. I didn't know if I was rescued or captured. He said nothing.

Without a word, his eyes said that he was not one of the hunters I was fleeing from. He had a stillness that eased the panic. He held his gaze longer than most guys and didn't appear to be flirting or hunting. Just staring. There was something odd about him, but he released me, let me go, and turned to watch me pass. He said one line,

"Sorry, I didn't mean to scare you. Are you okay?"

My senses are confused, and I still don't have the lost keys to escape, just feet into the building ahead. Out of nowhere, Mark walks up and startles me out of nowhere, but I didn't want to show the panic of the moments just before. He didn't know that I had lost his keys till we got to the entrance of his building. His only reply was nonchalant and calm.

"Let me hold your phone." He said, taking my phone and dialing. *"Tell the front desk that two people are about to try to get in."* He said in a direct and chilling way.

No identification.

No explanation.

We walked in, and it was as if they knew we were coming, although he left no message in his phone call. As we walked into the high-ceiling marbled lobby, our footsteps echoed against its historic walls. Years ago, this must have been a grand building, but now it's only a fossil of what it was at one time. The ceilings were arched and beveled with 1900-century moulding. Columns reached to windowed skylights that framed a looming night panorama.

We had no problem at the plexiglass desk getting a pass key to his apartment. We wove in and out of hollow halls that vibrated in whispers, voices I couldn't explain nor hear where they are coming from. Most were feelings of complacency, and a few were subversively maleficent. I always got relief when I came here just getting from the main lobby to the ninth-floor apartment. The building itself has a soul that breathes to the sensitive.

Luckily, Mark had a spare set of keys in his apartment, and we spent the evening laughing and talking about old times. We had a really relaxing time until we changed the direction of the conversation to old memories that Mark was sharing about things that he and I did together. I don't remember too much of it. He confessed that he, too, has been having problems retrieving the memories, and it is okay. I still have my writing and the business that keeps me happy, and these memory lane recalls can make me feel exhausted. It got a little stressed and silent, and we eventually ended up watching television. We chose a game show that had the premise of deciphering encryptions. Mark finds it so entertaining because he and I love to battle wits. One problem: I can't remember a lot of stuff that used to be what made the battle fun. My opponent is noticing that I am not as mentally agile. I couldn't help but cry a little about not having it anymore, to Mark's surprise. I seldom cry, so he knows and draws the encryption on a pad for me to at least try to figure it out. (It was about 5-6 words that letters were jumbled.) The key was to figure out the sentence by figuring out some of the words. Mark couldn't figure it out and urged me to try. This only made me more emotional underlining the progressing handicap. I confessed that besides my memory fading, so was my sight. Opening up about it just made me burst into uncontrollable tears. Mark couldn't calm me down, so we decided we needed a cigarette because I never found the ones I lost. We left to go to the store, engrossed in our conversation about how I was feeling inept. As we walked and talked, we looked down for any possible items I might have missed. The only thing we found was the cigarette box, and I thought it was empty until I opened it and found one damp one left in it. The store was in the opposite direction, so we gave up the search and went back to buy more, not paying attention to the surroundings. The shadowed knuckleheads were closing in on us like lions on two deer. Just as we noticed that we were being hunted, we ran and split up in the run. Something inside me said to concentrate and fly! It sounds crazy, but I had nightmares about the ability to fly. To think of something so crazy at this moment is insane, so I closed my eyes, focused on my inner self, and tried to do what the dreams did when I flew.

    To my surprise, it was working! I could feel my weight feeling lighter with each tingling step. It also slowed my escape, but if I focused more, I might be able to elevate off the ground. It wasn't going to be fast, and it took all the energy and focus I had to make it happen, but it did not feel unusual. The hunters were just about to be close enough to grab me when I got both my feet off the ground about an inch, still running, still being chased. I could feel that I was getting an inch by inch in my focus to do it. My pursuers didn't notice that I was treading on air now just an inch off the ground. The amount of concentration is draining me to do just an inch. By two inches, I was near the corner to safety, but they were still closing close behind me. Don't know how, but fear seemed to magnify my concentration. I was just two inches off the ground and starting to get the hang of it when suddenly I felt a hand pull me down. All that effort. All that focus has not saved me. The teeth of the hunter have me grounded. I was left with my natural devices to fight, and I turned to face the threat and saw that it was Nate again. The time is not by accident. He pulled me down mid-air from my strenuous attempts of flight, and the hunters growled in dismay and scurried away. I stood there grounded in Nate's strange grip to see why he acted like he knew me again. Again, he said nothing. He just stood there, weighting me to the ground with me trembling. How is this guy always around? He keeps popping up. He was not saying anything to me again, but his gaze was on the pursuiters who were returning to the shadows slowly. He pushed me behind him and scowled into the darkness. When he turned back to me, he kissed me right on the street with them not far off to witness it. His lips were moist and soft as mine pressed on his. No inhibitions. No insecurities. His eyes are closed, and he is saying something without saying a word in a language that is unfamiliar. The anger riled up hunters, and they yelled gay obscenities from a distance, but it was obvious that Nate was one of them, and his scorn none of them wanted. I didn't resist the kiss, but I didn't commit to it either. It felt like a familiar kiss from an old acquaintance. It was just a full peck that was slow and awakening. The weakness I was feeling from trying to lift was gone away in the kiss. Refueled somehow, it made me lightheaded in its invigoration. I opened my eyes after it in surprise and apprehension. This never happens to me. The swirling in my head felt like I was going to pass out, and I did for a few seconds. I didn't fall to the ground but went limp, and the only thing that had me upright was a tight grip Nate had on my arm.

He was dark-skinned, about 200lbs, with a fat round face and a thin moustache that was manicured tight.

"You don't remember me, do you Ty?"

I was still shocked, not just by the street kiss but by the fact that Nate knew my name and knew about my hampered memory problem. How else could he know that?

"I'm sorry, I don't. I don't remember a lot of things lately, but I remember enough not to resist you." I said. "Thank you for helping me."

Perhaps I should have resisted him. After all, I don't think I know him, or I just can't remember.

I don't understand what just happened, where Mark ran to, or how Nate knows so much about me. The things he said in a voice not spoken intrigued me with fear and curiosity.

Nate escorted me back to the building with the hunters still lurking. I have never felt so confused and helpless, but somehow, Nate feels like someone I know and can trust. Whatever I did or told him that I can't remember, I am glad I did, but something is not right. Somewhere in the lost memory is mischief and danger, and only Nate can tell me what I can't or don't want to remember. As we approached the entrance, Mark came out shaken and glad to see me.

"Where did you go?" He asked worriedly.

"I ran like you did, and Nate came and helped me. He..." I turned to point to him, and he was gone. Vanished.

Mark's face said it all. He looked at me bewildered, as if I was incoherent. I didn't hallucinate him.

"He was just right here, Mark. A big guy with a black hoodie on. You had to see him! I'm not crazy!" I emphatically exclaimed, looking up and down the empty street for him. *"He walked me back here from the corner."*

Mark is still looking at me as if I was insane.

"Chile, I watched you walk up here alone. There was no one with you. Come in here and get yourself together."

After Mark and I got upstairs to his apartment, we had a glass of wine and relaxed before talking about the whole incident. I have known Mark for years, and we live in Baltimore, where we have had this happen to us more than once. We pride ourselves on being street-savvy in each situation like this one, and we have navigated our way through it. It doesn't happen to everyone, but when you are a night owl and put yourself in harm's way, ignoring sensibility, it happens a lot.

The evening was winding down in stories of near catastrophe escapes we had in our youth in Baltimore with the criminals and the police when Mark summoned up the courage to ask me about Nate.

"Tell the truth, Ty, there was nobody with you." He said, examining me. *"I would have seen someone with you. I went up

to the apartment to get my knife because I thought I would have to go out and find you."

"You think I'm lying, don't you? I'm telling you, Nate was with me, and he showed up just before they caught me."

"Who is Nate, and how do you know him?" He questioned in doubt.

It dawned on me that he never told me his name, yet I knew it. Things are getting stranger and stranger as I replay what happened. Nate verbally said very little to me, but in telling Mark about him, I knew more than I should. I told Mark that he is from around this area, and he used to live in this apartment building.

How did I know this? I described this to Mark in detail, which only pointed out how much I gathered in such a short moment. I tried to explain that he told me things without telling me, and it just sounded crazier as I tried to. Just then, the phone rang, the doorbell rang, my cell phone rang, Mark's cell phone rang (and his service was off), and there was a knock at the door. Mark said it had to be one of his neighbors because you must be buzzed in from the lobby otherwise. I reluctantly answered my phone in the confusion.

"Hello?" I said. The number was blocked in the ID.

"*Ty, stay away from the door.*" The man's voice on the phone said.

Before Mark could get to the door to peep out the hole, it crashed open. It was Nate and three others. Two men and a woman. Mark was screaming and running for cover. Nate kicked the coffee table over and grabbed me off the sofa by my arm.

"No time for questions. Come with me. If your friend is coming, tell him to shut up and come on!" Nate said, stooping to avoid view from the window.

He looked different in his panic. Earlier, he was calm and stern, while now he is animated and disturbed. The gentle, unspoken words I heard from him early were now hollering in many voices, all distressed and shrilling.

"Mark, we are leaving with them. Shut up bitch and come on." I said to him.

"I'm not leaving with them. They just broke down my fucking front door, and you want to go with them? You know them?" Mark asks while holding a knife in the kitchen.

"This is Nate. The guy I told you about earlier. Something is not right, and I think we need to just go with them and ask questions later." I said as Nate dragged me to the front door.

"I'm not going a damn place." Mark defiantly said.

I grabbed the threshold, holding on to plea once more to him. My hand has a fuzzy glow around it as I one-handedly stop Nate from dragging me before I convince Mark. Nate's grip feels hot, pulling on my arm, but I won't let go.

"Tell your friend that if he stays, he is dead!" Nate said to get me to let go.

Mark heard what Nate said and still said no. I let go of the threshold and let Nate's hot-to-the-touch grasp pull me down the long hall outside of Mark's apartment. Mark ran to the doorway, yelling that we were going the wrong way to the elevator. His voice bellowed against the antiquated marbled walls. The four led me down the cavernous hallway to a dead end that opened to a secret room. I could still hear Mark screaming.

"*Tyyyyyyyyy....*"

Once we crossed the secret door, it slowly groaned back closed, sliding from left to right. The last thing I heard was blood-curdling screams from Mark. Something was viciously attacking him. I have never heard him scream in that kind of terror before. I broke free and tried to make it through the last couple of inches before the marble slab door closed. I almost made it, but the woman grabbed my collar and yanked me back, saying that there was no helping him.

I heard the marble slab door slide smoothly to a seal, leaving us in darkness. Nate was moving around in it as if he could see me, whereas I was frozen in the shock of Mark's screams behind the wall and the nebulous darkness that surrounded me. One of the other guys lit a gas light fixture across the room. This room must have been built when the building was built about a century ago. As they lit each turn of the century gas light, the room glowed in peeling wallpaper and cracked plaster. The ceilings were high and were lined in over-painted molding trim. In the room, there still was a chimney and old furniture covered in dusty plastic. The room smelled stale and was cold. Wooden floor boarding has buckled and warped over time.

"*I am Navasha. Over there is Simon and Benoit. You have met Nate. Just do as you are told, and you will be fine.*" The woman coldly said, pulling me from the closing door.

She was taller than me, with a grip that was twice that of a man. She wore a faded old black dress that looked about from the 1920's. Her hair was tied back in a tight bun parted in the middle. She had smooth, dark, ebony skin with deep-set eyes that seldom blinked as she spoke. Simon was tall and lean, wearing a blazer and a colonial-fashioned shirt beneath it. His face was thin, sculpted, and chiseled with beady darting eyes that stayed on alert like a century. Benoit was thick and rotund with sideburns that framed his cherub-shaped jawline. He wore a three-piece mismatched suit, his vest complete with a watch chain. I tried to talk, but the terror of what has happened to Mark has overwhelmed my vocal cords. I could only get choked sounds from my throat.

"You got just a couple of minutes to explain to him, Nate. We are jeopardizing a lot to be here. You should have let them have him. He is a dead weight to us. He doesn't even have control. Do it now!" Navasha said, walking away from me in anger.

The tension in the room is thick. What is it that Nate has to tell me? At this point, I am at their whim. I don't know any of them, and they act as if I should. Nate drops what he is doing and comes over to me while the others whisper on the other side of the strange room. His walk is cocky, with a gait that is confident and strong. For the first time since the apartment, I noticed that he was jingling with gadgets, ropes, and weaponry. This is starting to feel as though I have been kidnapped by a militia squad. I backed into a corner, realizing that I was in danger. The smell of death and gunpowder reeks as he gets closer- or at least, that is how I am now interpreting his once-calming scent.

"Ty I am going to need you to calm down. We are not going to hurt you. I need you to trust me." He stopped just a couple of feet from me in the corner. *"Just breathe".* He said. And reached his hand out to me.

I hadn't realized it, but I was not only in the corner, but I was in the corner's ceiling, balled up in an embryonic curl, flailing in the shock of it all. His outreached hand pulled gently on my ankle, and I passed out. All I can remember is waking up on plastic that was on a chez in the corner of the room and Simon sitting across from me sharpening a sword.

"You okay?" He said. His voice was deep and raspy.

I was foggy and very lethargic. More questions than answers have left me in a confused state, and looking at Simon's sword didn't help. I sat up and looked around the dusty room, realizing where I was and what had happened. Besides the old furniture that was covered with plastic, there were paintings still hanging on the wall. Old painting. People in eighteenth-century clothes and poses with haunting stares, melancholy, and staunch.

How long have they stared into a room locked away in secret?

Some of these paintings could be lost treasures and worth a fortune. Despite the dust that accumulated on them, the oil paintings are still haunted with beautiful colors and brushstrokes. One in particular, had the familiar landscape of the park that was across the street from the building. It was different in the surrounding architecture that surrounded it, but it was the same park. I would know it anywhere.

Another glance around the room, and I saw Nate sitting staring at one of them. It was a painting of crops and fields being tilled and harvested in front of a huge plantation with the residents in full regalia and servants on its lawn.

"Hey Nate, your boy is awake now," Simon said, yelling across the room to him.

Nate didn't stir. His gaze was fixed, staring at a pastoral painting. Simon walked across the room to break his concentration and repeat what he had yelled. They whispered some indistinguishable exchange, and Simon joined the others across the room. Nate seemed sad and immersed in thought. I hated to interrupt, but he was the only one of the four that I thought I could get some answers about what was going on. He didn't hear me come across the room, and I walked very timidly to him, but he must have sensed me. He spoke without glancing behind him where I stood.

"Many moons ago, in a time that is rich in memory and scarred in regret, I was happy. Time has moved on and left me like this painting. Frozen and captured. This painting, this building, those guys over there, and you have usurped Chrono's grasp and lay fast in the burden of a past that many have forgotten. I have seen much, and I have seen little. My friend, you have so much that you cannot betray in your soul. It will be a task, but it is not one that you will welcome." Nate continued and wiped his moist face, still without looking in my direction. *"I know you don't remember me, and though I know why, it pains me to see it in your eyes. Nonetheless, I have to prepare you for what is to unfold in the near future. Some answers will lie only in your heart. Some will be easier to understand, and many will peel in time's own duty."* He stopped to look at me as

if he needed to see that I understood what he was saying, although it was cryptic and almost poetic in the way he spoke.

What have I gotten myself into? I didn't ask for none of this. It was a normal day, in a normal way, and it all was going too fast and not fast enough. I can feel fear, and yet I am searching for more. It has been like that my whole life. It is a resolution in knowledge of something I can't explain or understand. In that, I am afraid.

Nate was waiting for me to respond to what he just so eloquently said, and I could only nod my head for him to continue.

"Give me your hand." He demanded, and I did. *"You are connected to us, and especially to me."*

His hand was on fire, and in our connection, the grasp glowed from a twinkle to a radiance, and I snatched my hand free from his.

"You cannot be afraid, Emily; I mean Ty. Fear will be your demise."

Freudian slip or not, who is Emily, and why did he call me her? And why my demise? Who says demise? I have so many questions. I don't know where to begin. Nate has returned his gaze to the painting.

"This painting is from 1890. That's me in the front holding the pitchfork. It was for the Lee family. In the pic are Miss Sara and Mr. James Lee. They were kind folk to us. The work was hard, and you succumbed to scarlet fever and died in the summer of 1892. I mourned your loss and almost died myself. If

it weren't for the children, I probably would have." He sobbingly said.

"I was born in 1968! You think I am somebody else. According to you, I would be well over a hundred years old!" I tried to explain that he had me mixed up with a family that I knew nothing about.

"Be still, and I will tell you things you do not know. That is, you in the painting holding the infant. You were my Emily, who I adored more than the ground I tilled and walked on. You came from an auction in Jamestown, and Mr. James purchased you when you were just 12 years old. Your hair was long and wooly, and I can still feel it between my fingers. Your eyes shine like they do now. Full of whimsical flecks of joy and naive. Your breasts stood firm and were supple even through three kids. I married you when you were just 15 years old. We had three kids named John, Rebecca, and Isaiah." The words were emphatic and flowed from his lips in pride and pain.

"I don't believe you. No disrespect." I said so as not to insult his reasoning.

"Before you discount me, I have so much more to tell you. Find the patience to listen and open your mind, and it might come back. This must happen fortnightly. My penance is to awaken you. To push back the veil of normalcy and unleash what beseeches you. Allow me to guide you to your destiny, and I will uphold all that is true, whether it be pain or joy. There is little time, and the dogs of time trudge the complacent." He almost pleaded.

Somehow, he makes everything sound like a dire situation. His rhetoric sounds reticent of another time that I am unfamiliar with. My face must be showing it because he is speaking slowly as if talking to a child. I have to admit that I feel like one is interpreting what he is struggling to explain.

He went on to tell me of his connection to the building and the painting using less antiquated speech as he went on. It was as if he was tapping into my thoughts and untangling them with an oral command that was responsive and reading my mind, recalculating how to talk to it at each step. In his eyes was a fire of passion and conviction that I could see was not encoded by me and nonetheless real and silently raging in restraint. Whoever he thought I was, he loved more than his and his comrade's safety and was fighting something that made me cringe at the thought of what would make him so distraught. Fright doesn't seem like one of his characteristics, but I could feel his fear for me.

"I am confusing you, and it is not my intention, Em. Forgive me for my urgency. I come from a time you cannot remember. It's a place you can't forget, a symbiotic connection that has endured through tide and juncture. It may sound like riddles and folklore now, but I can only try to amend in a short time all that befalls you and us. Memory loss and amnesia are a result of your coming of age in recollection, your inner essence fighting to dominate the unconscious. You will lose more and subsequently gain more and more if you can't control it." He said, staring back at me menacingly.

The more he told me, the more I was lost in comprehending it all. He stopped when he saw that I was getting more bewildered. He continued, pulled his sleeve up, and opened his forearm for me to inspect. It had a branded tattoo on it that had to be done with a hot iron that seared his flesh, a circle with two lines through it. As I stared at it, he looked away.

"You only know me as Nate in your one-dimensional thought. The time before this, you knew me as Nathaniel. And before that, as Jonathan and Elnathan. In another, you knew me as many other names that I won't bother to exhaust you with. Just know that I have seen your birth more times than you can remember. In each birth, you are just as magnificent, no matter whether it be a man, woman, black, white, Hispanic, or any other race. In each, you lose more recollection. It has been twenty-three of them. In all, I have been there with you, some of you were aware of it, but most of you were not. In each, you followed a light I was not allowed to shape or deter till now." Nate sounds mournful and disheartened, and it is in his tone that fear is growing more and more. It was making me angry hearing him speak as if he was sad that it hadn't happened. Or it has happened so many times that he is reaching for an inescapable fate.

"Aw, hell no! I don't believe none of this shit! You show up in strange places, and each time you do, something tragic happens, and you expect me to think it is something else besides you to blame. Do I look that stupid? Tell me why I shouldn't think that you are the culprit behind everything. Fuck you and your peeps over there. I ain't scared of none of you!" I was panicking and pacing, which brought the attention of the others on the other side of the room. They were on full alert and had swords drawn, rushing over to me. In my anger, I hadn't noticed that my entire body glowed in blue radiance that was blinding them. Blinding enough to force them to shield their eyes but not blinding enough to deter them from drawing their weapons.

"Em, calm down. You are going to hurt yourself and others.

Look at me, Em.

Look at me and focus. They are not here to harm you, but they will if you can't control yourself. Damnit, Em, I can't lose you again!" He cried.

"We told you he wasn't worth it. Again, she has betrayed you!" Simon shouted.

I looked down at them with my arms outstretched and my body elevated off the floor. Light is spewing out in shooting rays that have me paralyzed in mid-air ablaze.

"Oh God, help me!" I pleaded to Nate.

"You've got to calm down, Em. It's the only way I can." He shouted.

He was shielding his face by curling up under the painting that captivated him. As I listened to him, the painting figures moved. I hung there transfixed as I saw the figure of Em carrying the infant, walking from one side of the mansion yard, and pointing to what would be the park. Her haunting gesture was accompanied by a few faint words,

"Seek the path of dead and forgotten and travel to Edison's edge. There you find what others trodden and bid love's eternal pledge." is all she said. I couldn't believe it as I watched her walk into the woods behind the mansion with a child in hand and return childless to her original position in the painting.

I looked down and saw Simon and Benoit getting closer with their swords drawn and in the air above their heads, only a couple of feet away.

"Nate, please!" I cried again in fear that I would die like a crucified martyr for crimes I will never understand.

Nate somehow summoned the strength to grab my foot and sling me behind him into the wall where the painting hung, thus snuffing out the energy within me.

"You shall not harm he that is destined." Nate bellowed in a thunderous roar that shook the entire room and knocked the painting off the wall. It crashed and fell, striking me in the head, and that's all I could remember. When I awoke, I was in a janitor's closet, dazed and bleeding from a gash in the back of my head. A flashlight was in my face.

"We got a live one, Chief!" An indiscriminate voice shouted.

"I need a paramedic down the hall from the crime scene in the maintenance room. Head trauma."

CHAPTER 2

The medics stitched the gash in the back of my head with gauze and tape. Although it was not that large, it was deep. Crimson blood decorated my shoulders like a horror movie scene. My head throbbed with hammered pounding. I was disoriented and weak.

"Do you know where you are?" Asked the medic. *"Follow my finger!"* He said.

I tried to follow his finger, but I was more interested in where I was, looking behind his finger as he panned back and forth.

"I'm in the secret room behind the marbled wall." I said. *"Where are the others?"*

The medic called for an ambulance, saying that they might have a possible concussion and blood loss. The face of the medic looked worried and patronizing as he tried to stop me from getting off the gurney. We fought and tussled with him, trying to strap me down like an insane patient.

"Where's Mark? Where is Nate, and Simon, Benoit, and Navasha? What happened to the room with the paintings? Let me go!" I was screaming, jumping off the gurney, and running down the hall to Mark's apartment. The door was completely gone from the frame and draped in police tape with police officers on each side of it. The paramedics were in pursuit as I ripped intravenous tubes from my arm. They might have been able to restrain me if it weren't for the saline solution sprouting from the tube and wetting the checked marbled floors. I heard

them fall on one another as I got to the doorway. I couldn't believe my eyes. Mark's apartment was tossed as if it had been in an earthquake, and there were streaks of long splattered blood on its walls. What ever happened was so gruesome and violent. Mark must have fought hard. The kitchen floor had a pool of blood on it and a knife he must have been trying to protect himself with. But from what?

"Where is Mark?" I screamed in tears and panic, trying to get through the threshold. The amount of blood everywhere made me sick to my stomach, and collapse to the stained carpeted floor. It was there the paramedics caught up with me and tugged to get me out of the horror scene. The two burly paramedics strapped me in the portable gurney, reattaching the saline drip and administering a sedative. I couldn't stop screaming and crying hysterically. The evening has over saturated my sense of composure.

A detective came out of the apartment and tried to ask questions that I had no answers for. He was a small framed Asian officer chewing gum and a nose clip in his nose. The smell in the apartment was abhorrent and repugnant. It smelled of death like a butcher shop does- distinct and sickening.

"Hello. I am Detective Choo. We are going to get you to the hospital, but first, we want to get as much information as we can from you. Do you understand me?" He paused while the medics were checking my pupils.

"What is your name, sir? Do you live here? How did you get injured? Are you listening?" He spat off the questions so fast that I didn't know where to begin to answer. I listened as he addressed the medics asking them was I lucid enough to answer

questions. The medics rifled through my pockets to find identification and found wallet.

"Mr. Tyson Williams? Can I call you Tyson, Mr. Williams?" He politely asked in an overly calm tone. *"Says here you live in Baltimore County. Do you know Mark?"*

As he asked more questions, and I wasn't sure if I was being interrogated or making a statement. The warn wetness of blood was running on the back of my head. The medics were forcibly trying to push the gurney around the detective, but he wouldn't budge.

"We need to at least get him to the ambulance." They insisted while elbowing the persistent detective out of their path.

All I could think of is, *"What happened to Mark? What happened to Mark?"*

The hallway to the elevator was long and filled with onlookers peeping from the safe doorways. Some of their expressions were ones of disbelief, while other's faces were repulsed at the sight of me. I looked down at me hands and shorts and saw dried blood and dirt intermingled. I can see why their faces would look as they did.

With one sharp turn, we were in front of the elevator. The neon lights of the old ceilings were flickering and buzzing as we waited. I could hear the elevator's gate open and close on the floors below, getting louder and louder as they got closer. The old building moaned and creaked as the antiquated elevator reached the 6th floor. As the doors opened slowly, the medics looked worried about the rickety car that thumped to a stop. As the door opened fully, we could see a dark figure in the corner. The lights on the elevator made it difficult to see who. These old elevators are wood paneled with what probably was a precious mahogany that has been painted over and over. The residents and their guest have scratched their names into its grain.

Terry loves Joe

1966

Big Will, aka Chinaman

JT + KG 4 ever

1957

Black Power

Fuck you!

The one that struck me as weird and out of place was,

گریه حال در بسته بار یک ما رفتن راه به چشم

I reached over to run my fingers across it. Unlike the others that were ripped into the wood, this one was uniformed and beautiful. Someone took some time to engrave it into the old mahogany. It looked ancient, and my thoughts could sense that it may have said a lot of things, although I couldn't decipher it, unlike the others.

The figure in the corner stirred and spoke the words as he could see my curiosity in them. He said the words with reverence as if they were ones that were personal to him.

"*Eyes walk where closed ones weep,*" he said without turning. "*It's Hebrew. It means that you must see what is for you to see or perish in ignorance.*"

He had a large overcoat that hid most of his face. The coat was worn and tattered on its sleeves, designed in rugged stitching and age-stressed material. Its smell was musky yet pungent with scents that I had smelled before. With the medics hovering over me, I could steal glimpses in between their triage. Their glances where cautious for good reasoning. The elevator descent with a gurney and, paramedics, and a bleeding patient would have diverted most people's eyes to at least lookup. The figure stayed pressed on the button panel, never looking up.

5th floor, 4th floor, 3rd floor, the elevator whiz past in its descent.

Just on the 3rd floor, the stranger in the car hit the emergency stop button, and it stopped mid-floor, sounding off alarms and flashing lights. He turned and said,

"*This is where we get off Em!*"

It was Nate. Seeing his chiseled cherub-like face reminded me of where I knew the smell from. It was Nate's scent, almost reminiscent of ceremonial incense like myrrh. He grabbed the restraint bars in the gurney and pulled it away from the medics who fought courageously to secure it with them, but his strength was twice theirs. He threw one into the wall with ease and knocked him out. The other cowered in the corner, using the gurney to put between him and Nate. His face was frozen in fear, while Nate, although forceful, was calm and impassive.

"Be still." Were the only words he said after the scrimmage. He wedged his large fingers in the door and pried the large doors open with some struggle. The sound of forced metal on metal screeched with each inch. His coat on him budged and swelled as his body contorted to finally slam the doors completely open, revealing a floor between floors lit with touch lights and laced with dusty spider webs.

"No, no, no! Leave me alone! Why won't you just leave me alone. You and your spooky henchmen. I don't have anything you guys want. And stop calling me Em!" I beg him. I can't take another weird encounter with these guys.

"Em, I mean T, you are not safe without me. I could leave you in this elevator, and you perhaps will suffer the fate your crimes did, or you could summon up the courage to seek answers to the questions you want to flee. You must come with me on your own, or they will take measures that not even I can preclude." He said.

"You know me well. You were once my sole reason for existence. I beseech you to find me in your mind, and you might find comfort." I saw what was coming. He reached over and grabbed my blood-dried hand and said to trust him. In his eyes were dancing embers of fire that fueled into rampant flames as I stared into them. Past the fire was a campsite with children playing around it, singing, and laughing. The younger Nate was there too, waltzing in the background with a woman immersed in each other's slow steps. In the young Nate's face was happiness. His face looked as it does now, but with less of a furrowed brow and a glowing smile of content. His partner, a slender woman with an apron and gingham summer dress, stared into his eyes with equal content and love. Her eyes, brown as her deep, tanned skin and full of happiness, were fixed in his. But there is a sadness in his ocular flames. The sedate crackling of flames fireside in the front yard of a cabin crackle into screams. Hickory smoke and gunpowder's stench smother the flames, and the woman's voice cries Nate's name out and fades. I snapped out of his gaze to feel his forehead in my hands, and he was sobbing. The memory or insight in his eyes felt confusing and hazy. Images were speeding, intertwined in love and anger.

"Forgive me. My selfish idle last tore you away from me. Please forgive me, Em. I won't lose you again. Not after Savannah, Elizabeth, Frederick, Sven, Josiah, Cadan, Rose, or Neb. All that you are and were, I have failed in time. No more. Come with me, Em!" He said, lifting his head up out of tears and surrender.

Within those wet, remorseful eyes lie hidden answers to truths I am not sure I want, but the cataclysm of emotions, faces, and names I have either forgotten or locked away are loud and haunting to be called. As I look past Nate's head in sorrow, I can see the torch-lit hall behind him with the webs blowing in stale air into it. The gentle wind sounds like a whispered voice as it gusts in the elevator car, cold and stagnant.

"Seek the path of dead and forgotten," echoed down its corridor.

I have made my choice. Maybe not so much a choice, but more as if I could hear the beckoned voice that was now palpable, chasing fear and indecision aside.

"I will go with you if it will end the pain. Whose pain, I am not sure of." I said, loosening the constraints and sitting up, staring down the tomb-like passageway. *"It can't get any worse,"* I said, looking down at my blood-marbled clothes and hands.

We had been traveling through a labyrinth of halls that were arched and constructed behind various walls that muted the sounds of the rooms behind them. How could these secret corridors be kept secret when each one winded through and behind the apartments in the building? As we approached a wooden stairwell at a dead end, I was beginning to second-guess the whole excursion. Wooden shaky steps descended, staring down, zig-zagging bordering against the original brick foundation.

"There has got to be another way. These steps don't look safe. I think I'd rather go back to the elevator and take my chances with Detective Choo."! I said in resistance. The steps seemed to be a poor after thought in architecture.

Nate just laughed. He was amused at my expense. He had a laugh that resounded within the clandestine halls, echoing into each other. I didn't think that anything was funny and turned to go back the way we came. I could see at least 200 feet of hall and torches. In the settled dust, I saw our footprints on the floors. Perhaps we were the only ones that have been back here in decades. At the far end of the hall in the back, torches were being snuffed out one by one.

"Em, I'm sorry, let me explain. More than a hundred years ago, you said the same thing at the same place. I wasn't laughing at you, but laughing at how ironic time is. I remember

it as if it were just yesterday." Just then, he grabbed me and pressed his lips against mine in a swallowing embrace. I fought initially, although he feels familiar and strong. His arms were tightly locked around me, and his eyes were closed in confidence. I wanted to push his forward advances in my own defense and throw him down the shabby popsicle stick steps. He exhaled in the kiss, and it felt assuring, although I didn't want him to know it. In the corner of my eye, the extinguished torches were getting closer. The lit passageway was shrinking in darkness. Something was coming.

"Alright, you two, break it up!" A voice said from the luminous closing in darkness. "We don't have time for this. You just don't care, do you, Nathaniel? We could sense you a mile away. Why did you bring him into the tomb and unsheathed? He lacks no control. No instinct. He is like a tracked GPS, and we can't throw eons of work and leverage in sacrifice cause you have a thing for Em. She cost us a setback we have yet to fix. I don't care that she is "The Vessel"; she, her predecessors, and him are going to get us exterminated." Navasha said, emerging from the shadows. She threw a package wrapped in brown paper tied with parcel string to my feet.

"Get those bloody clothes off. They can smell the blood from afar." She said.

The stringed package contained a crimson full-length light weight coat, a yellowed cotton shirt, and pants that were tailored to a handmade fit. I looked around as if to look for a corner to change in, but there was no place to hide. Benoit chimed in from the shadows, saying they didn't have time for modesty. Nate nodded in concurrence and turned his back as if he was trying to ease my apprehension. The others stood and watched; almost out of enjoyment of the discomfort I felt.

"Come on, come on! We are running out of time. Nobody is paying attention to you. Take off them damn bloody ass clothes and be done with it already!" He said.

"Leave him alone. You see this all too much for him." Nate said, turning just as the last of the old, stained garments were removed. He stood there and stared at me from head to toe. The chill of the cavernous tunnels sent prickly goose bumps before, but now the chilled dampness was unforgiving. I don't know which was more humiliating, the taunting stares of Navasha, Benoit, and Simon or the seemingly lustful inspecting stares from Nate.

The team gathered the clothes, put them in a satchel, and burned them. The new ones made me feel like a renaissance cavalier and fit like a glove on me. There is no way that I could've walked the streets of Baltimore in them except on Halloween, but somehow, I don't think I will see the streetlights again. Where they are taking me is a realm that I am unfamiliar with.

We traveled down, down, down till we reached a platform that had two torches at each side of a double wooden latched door. I could sense the anxiety ebb away as we reached it. Simon led as he twisted the torch on the right at a ninety-degree angle, and a latch clicked on the other side. He pushed the heavy double doors opened with ease. They had to be more than 200lbs each. It cracked with light that revealed another room, warm and full of incense. As Simon closed it behind us, I could hear the wooden steps far above us creaking, first like a faint storm far away, but the feeling of impending malevolent pursuit was coming from a place within me.

"Let's stop here and regain our breath. Clymythious will meet us shortly," Nate said.

In the distance, someone was playing music. It was faint, but its melody was enchanting. It flowed and moved through arrangements and would stop at one part. Maybe the sheet music was missing, or maybe the player was writing an original song; either way, it was beautiful and dark in a B-flat arrangement that had a moody feel and enchantment.

The others made themselves comfortable in the beautiful, embroidered chairs that surround a hearth. Its flames stroke high, surrounded by a marble mantel piece that was carved from marble with depictions of cherubs and goddesses frolicking around it. The team was at home in this refuge. Their weapons were stacked on a table by the fireplace, and they were centered around a round table drinking wine. Whoever stayed here made sure that the accommodations were abiding.

Nate removed assorted weapons from his person. He had an antique dagger in its sheath, a silver sword strapped across his back under his coat, and a utility belt full of ropes and gadgets. No wonder he jingles when he walks. After the removal of a metal meshed vest and leather vest, he looked smaller but still statuesque and large. He had a large scarf wrapped around his neck. It was woven in raw silk with vivid watercolor painting designed in it. He saw me admire it and, removed it from around his neck and unraveled it to show its workmanship. It depicted a knight on a stallion reared, and the knight had his sword drawn in a charge. Upon closer inspection, it resembled him.

"*Is that you?*" I had to ask.

"*It's supposed to be, but it is very old, and I think it has seen a better day. You keep it. It is warm, and it's cold where are going.*" He said, wrapping the scarf around my neck. "*Come with me. I have more to speak to you about before Clymythious arrives. Now is good as any time.*"

He walked around the table of his friends while they sipped wine and laughed with each other. He led me to a panel and pressed one of them, and it swiveled open to another secret room. This room was smaller and had a bed and dressing table in it. It was someone's sleep quarters. It was colder and darker because there were no torches in it.

"*Stay here for a moment.*" He said while he meticulously lit turn the century gas lights that were on each wall of the room. As he turned them on, the room transformed into a decorated chamber with regal furniture and paintings that adorned its velvet wallpaper walls. Side tables were cluttered with small carvings of Grecian depictions and clocks that were still telling another time. The bed was huge and unmade. It was covered with layers of quilts and comforters that were gold and stitched in threaded gold threads. Adjacent across the room, Nate was starting the huge hearth with a fire to warm the hidden bedchamber. His focus was on stroking the flames to a chaotic roar, never looking up at me.

"*You look beautiful in those clothes. They fit as they once did in a time since gone. They belonged to you. Then you were young Frederick Von Henson. He and I, or rather you and I, enjoyed a brief time together in this room. His heart controlled his fanciful mind. Like you, he had no control over his gifts. He was a mere 17. Much younger than you. Ricky was about your height but fairer in complexion. He studied in England as a boy and returned here during the war. He died at nineteen in the country's honor in a mutinous attack on the manor. I tried to stop him, but he was cocky and arrogant. He believed he was immortal."* Nate stopped and peered up at me. *"Remove your clothes and bathe. The water soon should be hot. We need to wash the dried blood off of you. There is a basin on the table and fresh linen bedside. If you prefer, I leave, I could return but make haste."* He muttered at the door with it ajar.

I could hear the others in the other room singing what must have been an old English or Welsh song. Through the secret panel's crack opening.

"'Twas las this time of wind and sail,

We cast no iron upon hills trails

To victory's blood and country's glen fighting side, gallant men

Thrash in brave tried virtue tithe

My heart's Valor lies in

Drink to thine eyes blue

Drink to fair maiden's mane

Towering in gallant fame

Land of my love and you

Hark the winds of waiting for harbors seeking

The Book of Emily

O'er hills through bunkers leaping

Land and ocean's rivers keeping

Mine eyes from far maiden's weeping

Longing for England's shores"

"*Don't leave. There's something that is weird that I can't put my finger on. There are periods in my life that I remember seeing you around. Could that be possible?*" I questioned as I disrobed my borrowed shirt in front of the hearth. I knelt in front of the basin and splashed the refreshing water with a sponge to loosen and remove the dried blood off my face, skin, and hands. He sat in a chair across from me, facing the fire, gazing at me as I talked and washed.

"*I saw you at my birthday party. You were standing in the alley. You had on a long black coat despite it being very warm. You were scary to me then. I thought you were there to hurt me.*" I said, handing the sponge to him for him to help me. It was an obvious maneuver, but I couldn't resist teasing him.

No one else was around, and he already let me know that there is residual love for the Em inside me. I could see it in his eyes. I felt it in both kisses, although they were cloaked and distracting to me both times.

"*You couldn't remember that. You were only five. I have always been there, but I pride myself in my covert aloofness. You didn't know it, but I have been there, around corners, in shadows, even with binoculars fixed from far away. I have accosted danger without you knowing it was upon you.*" He said while refusing the sponge.

I couldn't understand why he now is resisting a moment with me, although it was an innocent one. It bothered me. I felt as if he was manipulating my feelings when he needed to and disregarding them at his convenient whim. I stood up and removed the silk pants that I borrowed. I stood there with nothing on, splashing water down the center of my back and shoulders. I was testing him, and he was failing. He cleared his throat and turned his head away in flustered tension. It felt odd knowing that it isn't me he lusts for. It's the being inside that he can't let go of. I wondered how long had he been attached to that being? He may have been in love with them all, Emily being the last. His discomfort is not in a sexuality distinction. It feels more like he is afraid of something. Something that I, too, should be afraid of.

"Nate, tell me why Navasha called Emily 'The Vessel.' What does that mean?

And if Emily is 'The Vessel' what am I?"

I said, wrapping myself in the comforter from the bed and sitting back at the fire, not far from Nate's feet.

"You are 'The Vessel', and time is not our friend at this moment. It is far too complicated for me to speak of in such a short time. To give you knowledge that is not complete would be unjust. You know what you need to know for now. Hopefully, Clymythious will unlock what you cannot. It is not for me to tamper. It is forbidden."

As the fire dance curled on the logs, my head suddenly was reeling in alarm. It feels like it is on a merry-go-round, and it's spinning faster and faster. The heat in the room multiplied and thickened in my labored breaths. A fever is coursing through my body, and my heart began pounding in my ears like thunder. Here it goes again, and I can't stop it. Energy is surging through me, and it is dimming in blackness. The best thing I could think to do was to get away from the fireplace. Stumbling to the bed, abandoning the comforter, Nate, and explanation, I could just reach it before the dizziness overwhelmed me, and I surrendered and lost consciousness. I dreamed of flying and being free in bulbous clouds. The world was normal, and I was normal in it, soaring with the breeze. It is not the first time a dream feels more real than reality. One world no less tangent than the other; I am no stranger.

"Em! Em? Wake up Em!" Was Nate's voice cutting through the clouds in my dream. His deep voice was anchoring me down in each stressed word. Awakening tangled in the draped canopy above the bed was startling, but having Nate there coaxing me to wake up crashed my ceilinged body to the mattress.

"Em, you have got to get control of your feelings! They could expose you, or even worse, expose us. What happened?" Nate said, stroking beads of sweat from my brow.

As my whereabouts came back, I scurried to the bed's large wooden carved bedpost farthest away from him, grabbing sheets to cover me. I am naked, confused, and humiliated. The past moments are flashing back in my head with every second with fear that trembled in ubiquitous reasons that I couldn't comprehend.

"I didn't do anything to you, Em. You were at the fireplace, and you said you weren't feeling well and stumbled to the bed, saying weird things out of your head. Tell me what is going on,

and maybe I can help you." Nate said, tugging on the sheets moving to me in the corner.

He rested his hand on my ankle in an effort to calm me down. It was obvious by the way I clutched the sheets around me I was in a panic. These blackouts are becoming more frequent, and the episodic dreams are becoming more lucent and revealing.

"All I can remember is feeling on fire. My body was flashing in heat and internal combustion, and all I could think about was escaping the fireplace. My skin was scorching in fever, and I felt lightheaded. That's the last conscious thought I remember. I dreamt of flying and the serenity in it. I awoke looking down at you from the canopy. The dreams are becoming real, and the real feels like a dream. I'm scared, Nate. All this is too much.

I don't know where I am.

I don't know you or the others. And I can feel something is coming. Something that's ominous and scary.

Can you make it stop?" I said in leaking tears that I was trying to control.

Nate crawled in the corner with me and wrapped his arms around me.

"Shhhh, what you are feeling is not untrue. Clymythious is coming, and you are able to feel it the closer he gets. Fear not. Your fear will propel you out of control, and you cannot control what you fear...yet." Nate's calming voice was soothing all the internal alerts that were rampaging sanity. He cradled me in the sheets and lifted me into his lap, quieting me in a clenched

rocking way. He hummed the song the others in the room next door were singing.

"'Twas las this time of wind and sail,

We cast no iron upon hills trails

To victory's blood and country's glen..."

I can't say if it was the song, or the scent or myrrh, or the comforting embrace of my bundled nerves that soothed me asleep. The last thing I saw was a reflection in a large mirror across the room. I might have been dreaming, but I saw Nate and I reflection. In it, large wings were outstretched from his broad shoulders and wrapped around me in his bosom. They were black with feather-quilts that arched from his shoulder blades stretched in musculature that was bulked in tension and flesh. Although they were there in the reflection, they were not visible to my naked eye. Sleep overwhelmed me, and I fly again.

The room's fire smouldered out, and its chill awakened me. I felt refreshed and invigorated.

Where was Nate?

The door is ajar, and I can hear the murmur of voices in conversation. I quietly dressed and crept to its opening in silence. Through the crack, I could see Simon and Benoit both sitting in conversation in a blind spot in the room the crack concealed. Before I could hear any of the conversation, they all stopped, and Simon and Benoit stood to their feet, staring at the door I was spying through.

"He is awake." An unfamiliar voice said, but Simon and Benoit didn't move. They stood as if something was about to happen. Just then, Navasha stepped into view from the side of the doorway.

"Come, love, we have been waiting for you." She said sarcastically, opening the door wide. The music in the distance stopped. Wherever the eerie music was coming from, it stopped almost on cue with my entrance to the room. In the corner was Nate, with a strange look on his face. Sitting alone at the table was a huge man dressed in black smoking a cigar. He was dark featured with long hair that was tied in a ponytail. No longer did the room smell like the fragrance of incense. Mingled in the putrid smell of a cigar was a distinct smell of an old museum. Old and rancid, like decaying sugar cane or rotting fruit in the sun.

"Come in and have a seat, Augustus. We meet again." Said the man with the cigar.

The reverence for him loomed over the others like a tide of silent fear. Only Navasha moved around in the room without being spoken to. She didn't sit at the table with him. She sat on the table's edge with her back to him and facing me in amusement and mockery. Simon stood with his arms folded. Benoit was standing with a wine glass in his hand, sipping it slowly and with calculation. It was easy to assume the man was speaking to me. I have been called nom de plume names since this all started.

"I am Clymythious, son of Tirus, descendent of the chosen. I am not your friend nor your enemy. So, you have met the others, and I will waste no more time or blood to make this

easier than it has to be. I will not ask you twice." He threateningly said.

I could see Nate was nodding his head toward the floor beside Clymythious where there was a beast snarling by his side with fangs that drooled saliva from its jaws, with eyes yellow like burning sapphires, hungry and ferocious. It was too large to be a dog or wolf, and its ears were pinned to its head, similar to a hyena but large enough to be a bear. The beast had no fur, and it had what looked to be appendages on each side of its front shoulder blades. The growls were guttural and resounded against the high-ceilinged room.

"Heel, Raja!" Clymythious screamed to the beast.

I must not have been moving fast enough, for Navasha grabbed the collar of the jacket I was wearing and threw me to the center of the room. She laughed as I put up a feeble defense against her. She had the strength of three men and the anger of a scornful woman. I could sense it from the first moment I met her. It was in her eyes, her gestures, and the lack of any patience for me, and I don't know why. She tossed me like a rag doll, and I landed near the large table that only Clymythious was allowed to sit at. Anger raged through me, and the thought of retaliating against her did cross my thoughts. As I lay on the floor, the rage turned to a glow that I have seen before. My fingertips were emitting incandescent blues and sparks of green seeping from its skin.

"You still have some fight in you, Augustus? You sicken me each time I see you." He said, spitting on me on the floor. "Simon, bring this abomination to me." I tire from this banter.

Simon walked over to me with a sword in hand. He kicked me with his foot and put his sword against my throat.

"You heard him, lest my sword will be your jury." He said as the cold blade pricked my chin. Control was gone. I didn't have to stand. I rose from the stone floor with only the thought of escaping humiliation. The emotions that triggered from within were fueled in each second.

"Don't Em!" Shouted Nate from the shadows. I heard him and didn't hear him. Something was unleashed inside me. I sensed danger, and something internal was turned on, and it was pissed.

"Stop this, Augustus! We both know the outcome. You are only alive because I was hoping this time you would join us willingly. Memories are flooding your every thought of the many times you have made the wrong choice. You might have thought that Nate was your comfort in time, but each time, his compassion fails you in agony. Think back."

Memories were flashing intermittently in a vivid awakening. I saw Em running through the mansion's gates into the woods that now is the park carrying an infant. She was being chased. At first, it looked as if Nate was chasing her, but as the memory unfolded, I could see that he was not chasing but following and fighting off her pursuers.

"Run Em!

Don't look back.

They want Izzy!

Save my son. Run!" He cried in a struggle.

With a child in her arms, she ran into the night's forest. Behind her was Nate in battle. She did not look behind, but the memory shows the battle lost. He fought bravely with sword drawn and slaughtering the hunters as they closed in on his fleeing family. With gigantic leaps and clanging metal, he intercepted them. As she reached the wooded tree line, the path narrowed, and the night air quieted in crickets and loons in the distance. The young mother and crying infant found refuge under a sycamore tree's branches.

"Quiet Isaiah. Hush boy. You be quiet now." Em cooed to the young infant.

In the distance, the battle raged with wails and cries as Nate was leading them in another direction to deceive them of his family's trail. They moved farther and farther away, and the sounds waned in the moonlight under the sycamore tree and moss.

The memory was painful and complete with the damp smells of the nearby brooks and creeks. Unseen heritage is as clear as I see the infants trusting face staring in his mother's eyes. It was that moment that moonlit recollection, which forced me back into reality. The agony yanked my heart and soul with a wretchedness that snapped me to the current.

I stood there with Simon's sword in my hand, and before me lies the beast bleeding, wounded, and whimpering with huge cuts and gashes in its body. In my haze, the anger has revenged in violence and bloodshed. Feet off the ground, I watched as Clymithious's minions and Nate took cover and flight. He himself stood alone in the room, courageous or off guard; he had not moved. My reflection in the pool below me is shocking and horrifying. There, in a pool of blood, was a man glaring in scorn and anger and hovering in the aftermath of battle in a bloody mirror on the floor. The sword was still dripping with the beast's blood into it. It is not me I see. If it is, I don't know him. He had more consumed hate than I could ever openly display or emote, especially in recompense violence. Above me was a fresco that I paid no attention to before. I can see it now because I am in my own energy, feet off the ground, and my head is feet from it. It is illuminated by the light that is cast from me and was painted on the beveled arched ceiling. It was a battalion of men behind a decorated soldier who held the very same sword I held so tightly in my welding hands. He, in the painting, was the victor, but his face was forlorn and sad in victory's wake. In various states around him on the battlefield were the rivals dead and wounded. Horses were riderless and gallant even in the war's end. Their eyes, too, were like his. The 17th-century fresco was still brilliant in its colors and brushstrokes. In the far corner, in the landscape of a battlefield, was the lake in the park. It was not gated as it is now. Could have been any lake or body of water to the onlooker in the ceiling, but not to me. The park has a personality of its own. A geographical fingerprint that gives it its identity and character. Much has changed in it since the oil fresco was painfully painted on these high plastered ceilings, but the artist painted the soul of it, capturing the things that never change. History, purpose, and the lives that pass through it are part of it, from the seedling trees in it to the aged large trunk trees that still to this day thrive in it like guardians of its story.

"You win, for now, Augustus Magnimus. To be driven thus is not a victory for you. Fortnight draws, and what you inherit in heraldic possession is not yours alone. I give you what will

hurt you more than you can inflict." Clymythious roared in retreat.

Oak-cleaving thunderbolts cracked through the walls and ripped through every office of my body. The thunderous sound trembled and shook as it coursed through me. I could only scream from its power and velocity.

What did he mean by *"giving me more than I can inflict?"* It was as if he had to relinquish something that he didn't want to part with, and he was sure I wouldn't want.

What could it be?

Chapter 3

Clymithious has gone and taken Raja, his beast, with him. Unlike the others, he is not afraid of the wrath. There is no music from afar. The exit they left in is not the entrance we came through from the stairs. In my de-escalation, I realized that I had to figure my own way out of the labyrinth. Exhausted and spent, it might be best to rest here and gather thoughts of what has happened, and all the things said and done. I was led here for a reason. Their intentions were foiled, but I still don't know what they were. Solitude seems loud with unanswered questions. Although I feel worn, I am recharged in the hidden quest within. Memories are clearing in my head. Perhaps, that's what Clymythious meant.

With everyone gone, I got a good look at the room. The stoned walls were adorned in embroidered drapery and paintings framed by gas lamps that were strategically placed. Two columns supported the Gothic arch that led to the domed ceiling. Marble and bronze sculptures were on ornate pedestals on the room's perimeter. The fireplace was large with a mantelpiece that was carved out of a solid piece of green granite with motifs of cherubs and Grecian women. The entire room was as old as each article in it, approximately dating back to a time long gone. The world has built on top of it with its modern architecture and culture, tombing it below.

What am I going to do now? To return to the rickety steps and climb back up would be as dangerous and intimidating as it was to descend down them. It is not helping that the influx of sporadic memories is clouding my thoughts and rationality.

Twenty minutes in and a couple of glasses of port later, new ideas emerged.

Maybe I could fly out of here using the stairway as the flight path, thus avoiding their fragile danger. It would mean I would have to practice controlling my new ability. So far, I have only been able to do it in havoc and defense. Somehow, I have to channel those bottled-up energies and manipulate them.

There are some facts that are right here at my disposal. A sword that Simon left with me that I think was mine to begin with. The synergy of time and the past somehow propels my abilities, like the paintings and the memories. And then there is the lost and confusing relationship with Nate. I know where the sword is. It lies next to the beast's blood on the floor where I dropped it. I can look up and see the fresco in the ceiling depicting a battle of significance. What is missing is Nate. He would have been the perfect vehicle to learn how to control it.

Nothing beats a failure, but a good try. With sword in hand, I closed my eyes and concentrated. The previous dreams have given me a clue of what I am searching for, but this will be the first time I have consciously tried. I can remember in the dreams a feeling of knitting in my insides, a will to combine mind and body together. I must focus on bringing all the energies to their height. Breathing, physical awareness, and extreme effort are how it occurs in the dream. From the tip of my hands to the tip of my toes must be aware. The handle of the sword felt heavy and odd in my hand, but I had to try. After a couple of minutes with nothing happening, I gave up in frustration, throwing the sword on the table and knocking all the goblets and tableware off of it.

"I wish you were here, Nate," I said out loud.

A voice from the shadows spoke in a calm voice. *"You are not concentrating right."* It said.

It was Nate! He is here, stepping out of the shadows. *"I am here."*

I was so excited that he came back, but what if he came back to finish me?

What if Clymythious ordered him to defeat me?

"Em you must focus all the pain with the joy in confidence and anger. You must believe the unbelievable. I came back to tell you more about what Clymythious wants from you but didn't get to.

What he has stolen from you many lives before and will steal again if we don't figure out how to prepare you for it. I also have some bad news to tell you. Above ground, in the world that we are beneath, you are a wanted man. The police think that you are a suspect in what happened to Mark. Your picture is all over the news. If you return to the topside, you will be apprehended, wrongfully accused, and persecuted for what they cannot explain. I could shelter you down here in the labyrinths and tunnels that traverse under the city, but the longer you stay missing, the more guilty you appear. There is one more thing. If you decide to return back, I cannot go with you. It is forbidden. I have the sanctuary of the night to move as I freely please, but the day exposes me to my cursed form that you don't know, and the world won't accept."

Nate's demeanor was sullen and mournful. He stepped out of the shadows and gently took the sword from my hands. He towered over me by more than three inches, and his intimate presence was full of power and mystery. I'm afraid to look into his eyes because of what I saw the last time I stared directly into them. He sensed my thwarted gaze and lifted my head into his gaze.

"I know this is confusing for you as it is for me. Look at me and let me share in what you see. You are Em, and in those scared brown eyes I see her. Don't cheat the only way I can be with her. I see that it is uncomfortable for you, and I know why. I can show you more in it than I can put in words. I have jeopardized all for you by coming back. You think that I am manipulating you and have no purpose that you can understand, but that is farthest from the truth. I laid with you when you slept, and I lost control of what I thought was right. You are still Em, although you don't believe it. I studied your naked body from head to toe. You are as beautiful as she. You sleep as she did, even in slumber you nestled beneath me. You smell as she did, of soft musk and delicate sweat. You even laugh and cry as she did. I came back for her/you. Look and let me show you." He said.

I took a deep breath and allowed my eyes to drink from his, wanting to see but not see. I started from his close-shaven, bristled chin and slowly gazed up toward them past his full moustache framed lips, to his pronounced nose, to his deep brown eyes tinged in green that were wanting, and irises bloomed in anticipation.

Night's air shivered over my shoulders as I was again under the sycamore tree, suckling young Isaiah quietly. My dress torn from thorns and bushes that I had trampled through in flight from danger. The sting of tiny scratches and welts ripped my arms and calves. It's late summer, and the moon is half full. I heard the chase die, and the threat of danger was subsiding in the faint, far of calls of Nate searching through the woods for me and young Isaiah. His shouts were getting closer and closer. I somehow know he will find me. Beneath this tree is a secret place where he and I, in early courtship, made passionate love years ago. He will find me here just off Edison's Edge, a rocky gorge that drops 100 feet into a gulley. Twisted back in forgotten paths, past where the motorcar roads end. Only light-trodden footpaths with vines of poison oak and primrose wind this far. A crackling of branches from the other direction in the mesh of footage and bushes alerts her that something else is searching for them in the brush.

"There's a special providence in the fall of a sparrow. If it be now, 'tis not to come."

From the wooded darkness emerged Clymythious, quoting Shakespeare in mocking humor. It was he that has led the chase after her. He clenched in one hand, honeysuckle blossoms, the other a sword.

"Let me see the child." He said, almost sentimentally.

Em stood up in fear of what Clymythious might do to Isaiah that would cause such a determined chase through Edison Park. She removed her teat from his mouth and recovered her exposed breast.

"Leave us be. We have not done anything wrong. Why do you hunt us like animals, and we have done nothing? I'm sure Mr. Lee knows nothing of this." She pleaded, backing her back to the trunk of the old tree.

"I only want to see the abomination that violates nature. Surely, you cannot deny a minor request. He is the first of something that cannot be." Clymythious said, lowering the sword on the ground beside him as a treaty. "The father will pay for his transgressions, and so will you in time. Before its death I'd lend my eyes to behold him last."

"No!" She screamed, waking the infant, who shrieked from the swaddling cloth he was wrapped in. His cry echoed through the saplings and timber, awakening fallow birds nesting. Their flight from the trees distracted the meeting and only fueled the child's cries. Like a charging bull, Nate crashed through the trees and shrubs, hearing the child's shrieks.

"Are you okay?

Is Isaiah okay?" He said, out of breath.

The cotton shirt and trousers he wore was soaked with sweat and splattered with blood. His skin glistened in the night's glow on his worried face. He clenched the two of them in a tight embrace as if he thought he would never see them again.

"The gods have fraught my actions with blood penalties. If I shan't see thine eyes once more, would certain end in torment." He said with his chin buried in her hair to mask the tears of joy and worry. "Sit down and rest. Isaiah will calm if you do, and so will I."

Emily hears what he is saying and can only look behind them where once Clymythious stood just seconds ago. As much as she felt secure in Nate's arm, she could still hear the words that Clymythious said.

"*We must leave this place. It is not safe. There was a man just here who said that he wanted to kill the baby and that he was an abomination. He is somewhere over there probably waiting to kill the three of us. For Isaiah's sake, please let's just go.*" Emily begged. She knew that Nate would not flee or chance not being able to protect her and the baby. He thrust her behind him and peered through the forest, putting his hand over Emily's mouth to silence her requests.

"*I know you are there Clymythious. Show yourself! If there is a confrontation, it is with me. Show your coward face!*" Nate shouted in the forest.

Silence moved slowly as they waited for a response or a sound, and it came with a slow clapping from the darkness. Clymythious's applause was just left of us. He stepped into the path and clapped louder as he approached, startling Isaiah again into shrieks.

"*So touching. So sweet. I almost cried with you, Nate.*

It was so....

so...

so heart-warming to witness the fall of a warrior in his lover's arms. Pity I have to kill you all. Just a pity." He villainously laughed. "*You were already supposed to be dead. You escaped the others somehow. It's amazing how love can strengthen a man, or should I say want to be man. No matter. I will extinguish this blight on humanity you and Augustus have conjured. The child dies first. Then her. And then the final death will be yours.*"

Voices that surrounded all around murmured at his comments. We were not alone. Through the dense trees, yellow glowing eyes blinked and stared through the branches, appearing not unlike lightning bugs courting. Their eyes were upon each other, positioning themselves from the ground to the upper branches, waiting for a command.

Nate stared into her eyes and told her to be brave. He opened the waddled infant cloth, pulling it from his tiny face to ensure that he was alright or to say goodbye. Both were heart-wrenching to watch, even as a vision. The infant had his face with eyes that pinwheeled in color, with his mother's mahogany complexion. Nappy curly hair covered his small head like lamb's wool. Feeling his father's touch calmed him, and he opened dark ocean-green eyes that sparkled in the night in a light of their own. As Em watched the bonding between the two, she watched both of their eyes twinkle light between each other, almost like an exchange of light. Isaiah is giggling and teething on his father's large finger, cooing, and playing, unaware of the imminent danger. She sobbed, watching a father's face smiling, enraptured in his son's.

"Prepare yourself." he said to Emily, and large wings spread and stretched in the air, causing the creatures in the brush to stir and scatter from the canopy of trees. He opened them full and turned his back to Clymythious and, in one wing flap, lifted his family straight in the air, catapulting with a mighty thrust upwards, cradling Emily, who was cradling Isaiah. From Emily's surprised eyes, I am looking down at a shrinking forest in a moonlit sky. With just that one thrust, he has propelled them hundreds of feet in the air, looking to the heavens in desperate pursuit of the sky, wrapping his arms

taround them like a bulleted cocoon. As the single thrust reaches as high as it goes, gravity forces their descent. For one moment in time, everything stood absolutely still over Baltimore. Nate opened his arched wings to catch the summer wind. He whispered over the wind in Em's ear,

"Know that I love you. Forgive me for not being able to protect you from those that cannot understand." He said to her in a ringed moon's sky that is flecked in stars. *"I will fight them off with all my being and die for you if I must. Raise him as mortal, for he is. Reveal to no one that you are his mother, the vessel to a connection of blood-forbidden folklore."*

Our descent was a glide down to an opening in a small meadow with wild tulips closed in the night. Nate's large black wings are not meant to fly but are meant to dominate the currents of air. In the silent plane to earth, Emily held tight to Isaiah and to Nate's embrace. She would not let go of either, not in flight, or in escape. As the horizon sank and tall pine tree tops bent and broke from the fall of three from the sky, and with just a foot above the ground, Nate let go and let Emily tumble gently in the soft meadows grass and kept his flight path as far away from them as he could at the meadow's edge.

"Nooooooo!" She screamed, realizing what his plan was.

"I won't leave without you!

Nate, please!" Her distanced shouts went unheard. He disappeared into the night's foliage. All she could faintly see was a faraway glow and Clymythious's voice rumbling to Nate in disdain.

"You dare hide Augustus's prodigy and face me in certain death?" Clymythious roared. "For this betrayal, you shall be cursed in night forever. By night you will appear however you please, but by day you shall forever have to cloak yourself in shadows. This treason will be your blight."

I snapped from Nate's hypnotic eyes back to reality. What he has shown me reveals memories that were locked away for a reason in a time long gone. I want to know so much more, but we need to get out of this lair of violence, and I think I know how.

"Nate, these visions are real, aren't they?" I asked, picking the sword off the floor.

He stepped back as if he wasn't sure the sword wasn't for him. I guess the anger of the vision spilled in my face. I could feel the resentment of him dropping Emily and Isaiah in a field and leaving them. For one second, I wanted him to be tortured by the thought that I might be that angry. Something said to strike the sword to the ground which made it and me burn and lift off the ground. Gravity melted around me, and I feel the same feelings that were felt so many years in my dreams. I can see my feet dangling beneath me.

"Stay focused Em, you are doing well. Will yourself still. Let go of all concepts you have about physics. You are energy, and the energy is you." He said as he watched me clumsily flailing my feet out of balance. "Now will yourself down. It's just as hard as getting up there. Focus on the ground and see yourself on it."

It wasn't that easy. Getting down was difficult. I was turning sideways, and almost upside down trying to get the control I needed to stay upright. As one foot touched the ground at a 45-degree slant, Nate rushed over like a coach, ready to catch me if I fell horizontally to the floor. He was laughing at my awkwardness.

"You are not the most graceful at this, but it's a start." He laughed.

As one foot solidly was on the ground, the rest of my body collapsed as if someone had cut the strings of a puppet. Nate caught me before I hit the stone floor. I'm glad he did. The sword threw my balance, and I could've hurt myself by falling on it.

"I always said that sword was too heavy for you, but young Frederick insisted on it being his weapon of choice. He learned how to weld it like an expert swordsman, and you will too, once you awaken fully." He said hefting me off the floor. *"For now, we walk the tunnels. I know a way out of here besides the stairs. Grab your sheath and let us hurry. I feel them coming back."*

He walked across the room and twisted one of the perched gargoyles on the fireplace mantelpiece that released a door behind it. Just as we were closing it behind us, we could hear the footsteps of them returning. We ran through narrow passageways sideways till we reached another door that opened into a tunnel.

The tunnel's stench was nauseating and pungent. The smells of brick and mortar, rust, mold, burnt wood and sewer combined to a sickening thickness. Nate's grip on my hand was painful and unrelenting in its lead. At many points, the underground maze was unlit, and my eyes never adjusted to the damp darkness through them. I blindly sped in the direction my arm had no choice in being led, holding the sword in the other. Our trampling footsteps splashed through puddles that I was glad I couldn't see. Nate never lost speed and seemed to gain more speed as we got farther through Baltimore's secret network. I summoned more strength from the fear of the following clan that I could hear echoing behind us.

"Pick up your pace Em, or they will catch us. Just a little farther, and then you can rest. We must get in the crosswinds of the tunnel!" Nate is dragging me in flight, forging each twist in blind haste. He has sacrificed so much to save me from a fate that seems to be inescapable. Eventually, street grates were overhead, and I could see better, but the traffic noises above were loud and deafening. In the light, I could see that both Nate and I were soaked and soiled from the granite walls and old sewage lines that transverse through old Baltimore underground. We came upon an old stairwell that was padlocked with eroded chains and grid steel fencing. With one kick, Nate crashed in the gate, yanking it from its hinges from the stone-blocked walls. Trash litters its bottom stairs, with rats jumping from disturbed nests. Each flight turned and heaved to the building above. After four or five flights, I was out of breath and had to stop. The lights of the building above were faint and glowing from what seemed like many more flights up.

We had been running for at least an hour through ancient lost urban caves that I couldn't help but feel I was trespassing through. Forgotten tunnels were built for gas, electricity, and utilities under a city that once burnt to the ground at the turn of the century. We passed signs that had stations and street names not used today, and some were no longer existing at all. Behind us, the trailing trackers' sounds have dwindled in silence. It is my own breath that fills the narrow stairway. Each breath echoes in it, magnifying against the old walls. When we reached a midway room, Nate pulled a skeleton key from his pocket and unlocked the steel-grated door. It grinded in the opening as he shouldered the metal door with ivy-carved relief ironwork. Dust sprinkled from its aching joints as it opened and vacuumed a breeze into it as if it were being revived after decades of dormancy. Nate first went in and moved a granite slab from a fortress-like window that was more of a slit in the infrastructure than a window. This midway room must have been for artillery once upon a time. Through the windowed slit, I could see where we were. We were not underground anymore. We are in a tower that overlooks an old railway shipyard and the historic neighborhood of Mount Vernon. Its view was panoramic and beautiful. My face was gulping fresh air, and its breathtaking landscape.

"Where are we?" I asked him.

For some reason, he is sitting on the dark side of the chamber in the shadows, composing himself. He needs to rest more than I. He fought hard in tonight's battles and exuded far more energy with me in tow. His rationality for gambling all on my safety is still a mystery.

We both recuperated in silence that was only broken by pigeons in the tower's stairwell. The sound of flapping wings recounted the visions Nate helped me see earlier. Curiosity and questions riddled my head. The perilous chain of events has layers of quandary, and I do not know where to begin.

"It should be safe to go out now. It's daylight, and we can inconspicuously travel unnoticed, except for these clothes." I laughed, using humor to break the silence. *"Besides, I am hungry."*

"We must wait for nightfall. I cannot venture into the light of day. It would not fare well to be seen in my natural form," he said.

Natural form? What form could he be speaking about? Thinking back about the times I have seen him does point out the fact that it is always at night. First was at dusk, then it was at night in Mark's apartment, and then in dark tunnels and secret chambered rooms. I stepped away from the window to let more light into the small room. I had to see him in the light to inspect what he was talking about.

"Don't look at me! You should never see me in the light of day Em. My curse is to never walk amongst the population in the sun. I cannot have your eyes condemn my appearance. I never want you to see the sun upon me."

It was for you Em, that I was spellbound to the dark. In the meadow Clymythious and I had our first battle over you. At least twice a century, he has found you, and the end never changes. When you were last, I refused to be a part of his ruthless and unconscionable plan. He cursed my love for you and my son in hellfire. It was the first rebellion I have ever given him, and his fury was not death, but life in the shadows. By day, I am an abomination, but by night, I am as you know me now." He uttered from the corner, hiding his face from the light.

What could be so grotesque that he hides from the world?

I have seen his reflection in the mirror, and he is beautiful in an angelic way. I remember those huge wings that enveloped me in comfort. I can still see him in my mind with heroic stature and regality, and he has seen all sides of me.

"I have seen you as you were in the visions. If it is the winged creature that rescued Emily, I know him well. I am confused about who or what you are. It can't be that bad." I said, approaching him and refusing to withdraw my remarks.

He raised his buried head out of his sheltered folded arms and gazed up at me. I was not prepared for what I saw, but I didn't flinch and crouched on the dusty wooden floors beside him. His face resembled the Nate I have gotten to know, with exaggerated distinction. He resembled an ape in the sunlit morph, much older and more ominous looking. Bone ridges ripped from his forehead to his chin, and every breath almost snorted when he exhaled. Even his eyes were different in that they had no whites in them and pierced through me in terror and apprehension. What hands I could see had talons curled from webbed fingers. His whole skin tone was a deep and darker brown. I wasn't sure if daylight revealed the Nate I knew or changed him into one I should be afraid of. Out of blind trust, I rested my hand on his knee.

"I am not afraid, and you don't have to hide from me. I do have one question and that is whether I should be."

Nate stirred a little and grunted. I was afraid, and he knew it. His nostrils flared, smelling the fear. Maybe he can sense my nervousness, and maybe he can't talk as well in the light. To reinforce my words, I sat down beside him as close as I could and rested my head on his shoulder, curling my arm underneath his. We both sat and watched the rays of light beam through the slit of a crack and through the day, it moved across the floor as the sun sped to dusk. Hunger has left my thoughts. Safety had left my concerns. Anxiety simmered down, and we sat motionless and quiet.

By sunset, I was fast asleep with my head in his lap. My eyes were still afraid of what they might discover if they looked up at Nate.

"Wake up. I think they found us!" He alarmingly said, shaking me awake. *"I can smell them getting closer. There's no time to prepare you for what comes."*

The sun is setting on the horizon, and I can hear the wings of the hunters flapping through the window's crack. The sound was first like crackling leaves in the distance, but it escalated to loud banging in seconds.

"Come out, Nathaniel, and bring the vessel with you. Time has come." It was Clymythious. "Bring Augustus to me, he ordered. With that, claws were ripping at the masonry, peeling stones off one by one. Out the opening, which was getting larger by the dismantle, was Clymythious flapping yards away while Navasha and Simon tore at the tower's walls. Nate was on full alert now, with me shoved behind him.

"It is now that you have to trust your instincts! He grabbed me and jumped through the now large opening. We hurled to the ground, with me screaming every foot. Wind gushed in my ears and my jacket that, now, is flapping like a collapsed parachute.

"Now Em! Now!" Nate hollered over the gale-like winds, and I could see the panic in his now normal eyes. I shut my eyes and tried to concentrate. I could feel the energy building, but I could also feel the ground approaching. With one jerk, Nate uncoiled his large wings that ripped through his shirt. The updraft snapped our bodies with wretched pain, so much that I lost my grip around Nate's waist, trying to hold on to the sword and dangled from the waistline of his trousers. The descent put us halfway down the large old watchtower. At my feet, closing in, was Navasha, then Simon. They rode the very same current that Nate was soaring to the ground in.

Shirtless and grasping my wrist, Nate struggled to hoist me to no avail. His aged, buttoned pants ripped, hurdling me to the awaiting ground covered in a brush that broke my fall. As soon as I rolled to my feet and stood, the sword glared, and I could feel the energy surging through me. Blinding light thwarted my hunters in caution. Nate was in the distance, half-nakedly fighting Clymythious and dodging his sword, swooshing within the air it cut through. His naked form looked godly and majestic. His developed muscular frame and wings were flexed in battle. His face was determined and grimaced in maneuvers. Unlike his daytime curse, his form was Herculean and beautiful. Good and evil in aerial battle. He was outnumbered and still holding defense, wearing nothing but a shirt and his leather shoulder utility strap that was weighted with daggers, a small sword, and assorted pouches. The time was now!

I raised the sword to the sky above me, and it jettisoned me to the sky with them, ending the oncoming slaughter and catching Nate gliding flight to the ground. Simon and Navasha landed not far from where we did and were only held at bay by the blinding light from the sword. I stood over Nate's naked body with his wings also covering his face from the light that dimmed on the soil. I could see Clymythious in the foreground yelling attack commands to them. Swordsmanship has never been a learned skill I had, but the sword in my hand led to a full sword battle, metal to metal, two against one, defending from two sides with Nate on the ground at my feet. I couldn't fend them off for long, and Simon was more expertise in his affront. One wrong move, and they would strike me or Nate.

A quick decision must be made. The battle is a sure loss heading in the direction it is going. The skies clouded, and a mysterious storm rolled with dark clouds rolling in the starlit sky. The heavens were disturbed, and it relates to me. In my panic, the storm exploded in streaked lightning, tearing the atmosphere, and charging the air with electricity. As Simon charged with the swiftness of a musketeer, a bolt of lightning stabbed through the clouds and struck me with an intensity that knocked me and Simon off our feet. In the distance Clymythious shouted,

"Damn you, Augustus Magnimus! The gods favor you again. Take your traitorous slave and retreat thus this end well for no one." Clymythious said in anger and defeat. *"Simon, Navasha, leave them be,"*

Sirens were approaching and the buzz of a helicopter was far off on the horizon. Their retreat is likely more for the escaped of the police that were approaching on call. All the destruction and open battle has them on alert and out running with guns drawn outside of the clearing on the neighboring streets. It would not be long before the trees and bushes would be besieged with armed policemen and bullhorns. Clymythious and his clan disappeared in the night, vanishing in the shadows. I helped Nate to his feet, and he stood up, using my shoulder as leverage to scurry to bushes to be out of eyesight of the approaching authorities. His smooth skin felt leathery and hot to the touch. He towered over me like a gothic statue, Romanesque, and a tribute to man in his natural glory with his huge wings collapsed and folded on his back and genitalia exposed. If I don't hide him from the creeping interrogation, we surely will be incarcerated.

"Nate, put them wings away! They won't understand a naked man with wings in the bushes. Take my shirt and tie it around your loins. I will run out there and give you more time to escape. The tunnels aren't far from here; as I distract them, make a run to them. Take my sword and hide it. They will shoot first and ask questions later if I take it with me. I wish there were another way. I have so much to learn and ask you." I said, removing my shirt and just wearing the long jacket. *"Good luck."*

I ran stealthily along the bushes' edge till I was hundreds of feet away, then I revealed myself to the police, who surrounded me and threw me to the ground in handcuffs.

"We got ourselves a freak here. Look at the way he is dressed. Call the Cap." One of the officers said over the blaring radios.

I laid there in the street until a familiar voice behind me told them to stand me up. *"So, I see the head wound has gotten better, Mr. Williams? The detective said. "Do you remember me? I am Detective Choo. You have a lot of unanswered questions to answer for. We can start with what has happened *here and go all the way back to the murder in Edison Heights. You wanna talk here or downtown?"* The detective was sarcastic in his tone.

I sat on a curb on the street for an hour while they canvased the area, looking for others and evidence. No one else was found or seen. Detective Choo surveyed the scene and returned to me with more questions. He had a whimsical way of asking incriminating, and at the same time, following them with whimsical answers that sound as absurd as the answers.

"You wouldn't know what happen to the old train station's tower, would you? If you knew how the walls were ripped 500 feet in the air, you would have told me. And of course, you have no idea how you got out of Edison Place on an elevator that two paramedics say a giant man got on with you? If you did you would have told me and showed me how that happens." Detective Choo rambled several of the baffling facts that he thought I would have answers to.

The interrogation went like that for a half hour, with the other officers laughing at his sarcastic humor. I was photographed, shackled at my feet, and searched thoroughly through every crack and crevice on my handcuffed body. The large officers were still upset about my escape from the building. Apparently, the news and the Internet have made me a trending topic. After they took me to the station to be processed and interrogated more, I could see a television in the bullpen with the sound low, but the imagery was clear. It's about 11 pm, and the news is on in a grated corner. The captions were horrifying and graphic with the details that captioned the images.

The Book of Emily

(Scenes from a bloody crime scene in Edison Park) Were captioned under horrid pictures of Mark's apartment in disarray and pools of blood on the floor and carpet. Smeared handprints were on the walls amongst red streaks of blood. And finally, the was a mugshot of me flashed on the screen. It was a picture from 15 years ago from a minor drug charge. I saw a guy that looked tired and malnourished, looking guilty, and convicted.

(Tyson Williams, fugitive and suspect in bloody murder)

There was silence in the bullpen as the other detainees turned and looked at me, connecting the picture to me. Its over-painted green cinder block walls with plexiglass and steel barred openings held us in transition to different holding and interrogation areas. Some have been here for hours, just waiting for the due process of the system. Mostly African Americans, it was mixed with whites, Hispanics, and a hodgepodge of others of undetermined races. There were men in here who were mentally ill and talked to themselves in anger and schizophrenia; like the man who was in the corner shouting obscenities to the walls and anyone who looked in his direction. By his clothes, he was homeless and possibly violent. Next to me was a tattooed thug who talked about every guy in the room, looking for a confrontation. He, too, was angry. It is not my first time in incarceration; I am just waiting my time out till Detective Choo and his investigators come back for more questions and whatever charges will stand. The guy next to me is in here for a domestic abuse charge from his girlfriend. His only complaint was that he wanted them to speed the process up so that he could get upstairs to the general population.

"That's you? Omg! You are a vicious dude man! You killed that guy, didn't you? They busted your ass and now you are

going down homie. They been looking for you for hours. I'm sitting next to a star! Even though you look like a Prince wanna be reject!" He shouts, erupting the whole bullpen in laughter. *"Ya'll gay niggas funny as shit! Just don't say nothing to me bitch and I won't have to knock your sweet ass out!"*

It dawned on me that it is being portrayed as a murder, and I am the suspect. It's hard to laugh at my neighbor's jokes when there is a subtle truth behind the homophobia. By all the facts, I am a murderer. They found me in a janitor's closet covered in blood-my own, but they didn't know that, and the clothes were burnt in the hidden stairwell. Even the lobby attendant at the front desk in Mark's building could incriminate me as the only person with Mark.

How do I explain the events?

Who is going to believe that there is a hidden room on Mark's floor?

How are they going to believe me when the paramedics say that I was in on the escape in the elevator?

The situation is looking bleak as I replay the way things went and what others see versus what I say. I can claim insanity. The whole two days are a nightmare of insanity. If I tell the truth, they will surely lock me up in a mental ward. If I don't say anything, I could be railroaded into 25 to life in prison.

"Yo, Prince! Sing us a song! Hoe about Purple Rain?" The guy next to me is joking. I don't see anything funny. Not anymore.

Chapter 4

I was taken to the interrogation room by two guards who put the leg shackles back on and led me down a long, fluorescent hallway. They have taken my clothes and given me an orange jumpsuit with the large letters BCCB on the back. Welcome to Baltimore City Central Booking.

I can only take small steps as the guards patiently escort me to the interrogation room. The speckled shellacked floor is slippery in spots from years of waxing. As we pass rooms on both sides, I can peek in and see some were offices and some were file rooms that have been renovated out of an old building's structure, hiding the Masonic time of its walls. We stop at a room that would fit in any crime show. Its furnishings are just a steel table and two chairs. The guards chained me to the table and left, stating that someone will be in shortly. With just one ceiling light on above me, I surveyed the room. It had all the usual things that you would expect. Two-sided mirror. Intercom box. Waste can in the corner.

Detective Choo came in just minutes after the guards left, throwing a large vanilla folder on the table beside his coffee. His mannerisms are sterile and fastidious as he composes himself before saying a word.

"Ah, the strange Mr. Williams. Can I get you some water?" He said, addressing me as if this was going to be an exceptionally long questioning. *"You have been very elusive, Mr. Williams. Just in case you don't remember, I am Detective Choo; I work in Homicide."*

I shuddered at the thought of being a suspect in a murder. I can't believe this is happening to me. As I sat there and watched the detective shuffle through papers, I am still debating in my head which course of action I'll take. It might be better to just listen and speak only when spoken to.

"Let's start at the beginning. You are Tyson Williams of 3232 Springfield Grove, born March 17th, 1968?" He asked without looking.

I nodded and remained quiet. Only his questions can denote what must be said and how. I looked at the small frame detective, never looking away from his occasional glance at me. His slanted Asian eyes were condemning and aloof.

"Let's jump straight to the first question. Were you in your Mark Harrison's apartment prior to the incident?" Now Det. Choo is looking me straight in the eye. His peevish appearance is only a deceptive ploy to snare me and anyone who was gullible enough to cast wits with him. My answer will be the first words I have directly said to him.

"Yes, I am a close friend, and I was there most of the evening. Please tell me what is going on.

Is he okay? I saw the blood everywhere and nobody is telling me what has happened."

I hadn't heard my own voice in hours, and it was shaken and not as calm as I would like it to sound.

Det. Choo scribbles the words down on a pad he has in the folder. He is left-handed and his awkward jotting is almost crippling looking. His summer tweed suit, slightly wrinkled and worn, is the wrong fit, and it is a little tight in his shoulders as he leans on the desk writing.

"I am not the one being questioned, Mr. Williams. Besides murder and destruction of public property, you have a lot of explaining to do. I must add that you have a right to an attorney if you choose."

The interrogation went on for hours with Det. Choo asking myriads of questions that I didn't have the answer to. I left out the details of what unbelievably happened to me, and only answered direct questions that had solid answers that I felt wouldn't incriminate me.

"You have someone waiting to speak to you. I would advise you to take this very seriously. As it looks, you are facing a murder charge; although we haven't found the body, but we will. You also are the only one found in the destruction of public and state property which could be, if convicted guilty 2-5 years. You are not telling the whole truth. Off the record, I think you murdered your friend in some kind of lover's quarrel. Your sexuality is not an offense, but murder is." He said gathering his files back into the folder.

That was the last straw for me. If he wants to see strange, I'll give him strange. My insides were churning due to disturbance; I could feel them surmounting. I jumped from the chair and shouted at Det. Choo. *"Mark was a dear friend and not that kind of friend. Someone has done something to him, and I must sit here and listen to insinuations and sexual assumptions? And for the record, he was a close friend to me and my deceased wife, and you insult me with the casual slurs of a romantic squabble gone wrong. I ain't got no more to say to you or anyone behind that mirror. Go to hell!"* I screamed with frustration. *"I want a lawyer!"*

The mild-mannered detective was unmoved by my explosive anger. He thinks he has figured it all out and, in his head, I am a man guilty of a horrid murder and hiding some kind of cult association that is behind it. A sort of sadistic sacrifice. Many of his questions hinted at it. I won't say another word without representation. I can't.

In Baltimore, to be different is an automatic prejudice. I know that I am going to be victimized in two worlds. One by the authorities that hate people or cultures that don't fit in the norm of what they have been trained in, both on the job and by their social upbringing. The other harsh reality is the other inmates. A loner in this system is prey. At this point, I can only deal with each situation as it arises. All will be harsh and unjust. None will be because of the dark truth. I am alone.

After he left, I had nothing to do but to stare at myself in the two-way mirror. The man I saw was the man that they saw, and I should be afraid. I see a small framed black man shackled to a desk and condemned of murder if some resolution and explanations don't surface. I try to imagine myself in the main prison population fighting for dignity in a world that bars have forgotten. No one has compassion or civility. I see who I am and there is nothing I can do about what they think I am. My past experiences in the penal system remind me that I am not just a guilty black man, but I am a weird homosexual in their eyes. An abomination of social dogma no matter how wrong a characterization it is. The truths will be unimportant in here. I might have seen the last of Baltimore on the outside. Hopeful ideas of having a family and children could be lost forever.

Maybe I am crazy. Maybe the events that have recently passed are just figments of an overactive imagination, or early insanity. It makes far more sense than convoluted events I remember. My memory loss could just be a reflection of a criminally insane guy who lashes out and violently kills someone he loved. A psychopath. Oddly, it makes more sense.

I was still in the middle of thrashing myself in question when someone entered the room. It wasn't a guard because he was dressed in a suit. I looked at his shoes to assess him and they were brown polished loafers. He is either the D.A. or he is a partner of Det. Choo, or maybe he is a psychiatrist that you sure could use about now. Bracing myself for more criticizing and assessment, I asked,

"Fuck you want. I said I am not answering any more questions until I speak to a lawyer. If you are not a Public Defender, leave me alone." I said in anger.

He stood about 5'11 and was about fifty years old. He had blond hair that was immaculate in its coif. He carried a leather briefcase and wore dark turtle-shelled eyeglasses.

"I am here to represent you. Mr. Williams. My name is Philonious DeCanton. I was hired to help you. You can call me Phil or Philonious." He walked to the table and opens his briefcase retrieving papers and his business card.

Philonious DeCanton

Attorney At Law

Lee, Anderson, & DeCanton Law Firm

"Uh, Phil, who hired you?" I asked.

Phil busily removed pads, pens, and copies of documents and aligned them on the table in front of him before he answered.

"I was hired by Mr. Herbert Lee. You don't know him, but he knows you. We can discuss this later when we have more privacy, but for now I need your signature on this and this." He said sliding papers in front of me.

The first was a consent to have him represent me. The second were the charges that were documented by the police to ensure that I knew what they were charging me with. The last one he wrote on a pad was just a symbol. I had seen this symbol recently. It was the one that was branded on Nate's arm. A circle with a diagonal line through it.

"Aw no! Aw hell no! I don't want any more to do with y'all!" I shouted throwing the papers to the floor.

Phil got up and picked them up, whispering in the lowest voice he could.

"This is your only way out of here."

This is unreal. It can't be happening. I have just rationed that I was delusional. I held my now throbbing head in my hands on the desk, but out of the corner of my eye, I could see Phil slowly picking each piece of paper up, intentionally slow, and methodical as to give me a moment to think about what he said. He stood up, adjusting his suit with the papers in hand and waited for my response. I had nothing to lose with at least some kind of representation and at least I could get some answers from him that I couldn't get from anyone else.

"Okay, Mr. DeCanton. You are hired."

"Good. You gonna be fine." He said, putting the papers away and closing his suitcase. *"Don't talk to anyone. Eyes are watching even when you think you are alone. I will contact you as things develop. If you need to reach me, call the number on the card, and ask for me. Someone will answer any questions you might have."* He said, standing up and extending his hand.

That is it? I have so much I need to talk about. So much I need to know, and he is leaving me with nothing but a card? The police are going to put me in the Detention Center soon and all contacts will be limited. I will be in there alone and defenseless with no answers, but in Mr. DeCanton's eyes says to trust him. I shook his hand, and it felt hot to the touch, like Nate's.

"Mr. Williams the intake process could take some time. The press has sensationalized the story which complicates how we do this. Sit tight and keep out of the news. No interviews. No communication with the press, and trust no one. And keep yourself calm in here. You still have much to learn and if you surge in here, you will be doomed." He warned and left as quickly as he came.

The next week was like hell. I was booked, transferred, and transferred again to various departments of correctional housing. The more harrowing transfer was from the J Block where I was put in with other inmates who were awaiting more serious convictions like mine. Murderers, arm theft robbers, and violent offenders were locked in 23 hours a day, two in a cell. We were only otherwise released for a daily shower and every other day's yard recreation. It didn't take long before I was recognized as the gay on TV who killed and hid his lover's body. Initially, they left me alone and I read the bible in a shared cell.

My cellmate was a guy named Ricky, who was being convicted of extortion. He has been locked up in here for five months and has made a home in his cell. Just a little bigger than I, his personality swallowed the six-by-nine-foot cell space. His bullying nature eventually took its course, and he slowly calculated how much his quiet cellmate could take. It ended badly with him telling the other brothers on the floor that he was going to have me removed from his cell once the news spread throughout the block about my bisexual nature. To him, it was an insult that he had to denounce. What started as a *"get along"* cell relationship turned quickly to a sour and aggressive belittlement. In the system, I was portrayed as a violent man, which was opposite to the man they got to know in days. By the second night, he had told the whole block how he was going to get me out one way or another. I spent my time devising weapons out of pencils and sliced electrical cords from a frayed outlet. My mind was on alert with all the maneuvers to protect myself in a confrontation. My advantage was to act unaware of what he is deviously planning.

The evening was a shower evening for our side of the block. They can be uncomfortable with twenty-five guys at a time in open showers. We are escorted into what could easily be viewed as a water chamber with twenty shower nozzles projecting out of the walls. Our clothes are left on the outside and the door is locked behind us.

What happens in there is unguarded. In there is where battles that brew behind the bars are free to express themselves. You would be surprised how a man changes when he is naked.

Most try to ignore the others and keep their space, doing their business and watching their back. I could see Ricky scheming with the like-minded about how to extort from the weak. I was on that list. It was obvious and they got a kick out of signaling that they were going to get me. Finding a corner to shower alone is a patient thing. Shy guys finish last. Quiet guys finish last. Life in the system has levels of masquerade and confusion.

Before I could get back to the block, two guards called me out of the procession back. They held the other returning inmates back and escorted me to get my belongings to be moved to another block. Somehow, the jail grapevine leaked all the way to the guards who took action to prevent an incident on the floor. An incident would mean a lockdown. A lockdown means no showers, no yard, and more work for them.

As I walked back through passing the other inmates, they hollered angry sentiments of dissatisfaction. For them, I was to be their form of entertainment in their lives that had no other. The comments were violent as if there was a personal vendetta each had to act on, but none had a reason. Yes, I knew some lurid street info about a few of them, but I never said a word about them or about what I knew they did for drugs and money. It might have been some of the reasoning they had for their plan. The only alliance I had in there was the Muslim brothers who will doctrine their philosophy to all.

Again, I am shackled and taken through the belly of old jail halls and over painted steel bars, through tunnels, gates, and fences. It is an eerie connection of grey bowels that send chills on the back of my neck. Stench masked in cheap industrial bleach singes your nostrils. The sounds of clanking metal and faraway screams are more than haunting. There were an interchange of passageways and even sections led above ground for a couple hundred feet. The air was refreshing and cool. The short excursion outside in a barbed wire tunnel was only to get to the next annex. No matter where they put me, the network of the jail would catch up to my new location. I might have escaped a stabbing execution, but I am nowhere near safe.

Where are the night nomads now?

My inner voice is repeating over and over,

Where are you Nate?

This is all because of them and a past that I am being held responsible for. Since I have been here, my nocturnal dreams and visions have been the only source of reasoning and rationality. In each of them a little more becomes clear. The first night dreams were a relief from the stark reality. In it, I was with Nate again a long time ago. We were flying over Edison Park, not fleeing, but soaring in the night sky with little Isaiah giggling in my cradled bosom. His large wings grappling the air with ease. His eyes fixed on mine as we bristled over the lush, glorious pine tree tops brushing over my tattered cotton dress. In the next moment we are rolling in the meadow making passionate love on a springtime day crushing lavender blossoms in love's newness. I can still feel Emily's small work-toiled hands clutched in Nate's wooly hair, hoisting her loins to his. It was enough to awaken me and return me to the dark, stale cell, aroused and smiling. It is these thoughts that I focus on as the forged steel shackles bruise my ankles with every step through the carved cement underworld.

We shrugged our way through the fenced labyrinth, ending at my new temporary stay. It had only one row of cells that lined twelve aligned. The guards unshackled me and released me in the boxed cell with my new cellmate, an older gentleman named Unc. He said they call him Uncle Luke, but "Unc" for short. He was a dark-skinned grey-haired man about 70 years old. His face was smooth and clean-shaven except for a goatee that was white as snow. He has dark deep brown ebony skin and almost blueish in its tone. Unlike my former roomie, he was glad to see me.

"We figured we put this one with you. He is quiet and doesn't start any trouble Ole man Luke. Watch your back. The wolves were at his heels in here. We will keep an eye on him just the same. This is Luke Garrison." The large stout guard said while closing the cell door.

"Nice to meet you, Ty. Them thugs ain't got no skates this far. I hope you don't mind sleeping in the bottom bunk. I am used to the top. Come in and make yourself comfortable and chat. I haven't seen one of you in a long time." Unc was pleasant and cordial to me as he wobbled around the cell explaining how he had everything set up. The cell was organized and neat and clean. In one corner were stacks of books that were taller than me. He watched me gloss over the titles and asked,

"You like to read? I have collected quite a lot of books in here over 15 years. Feel free to read any of them." Unc said.

On his bed, with the spine open to hold his place, was the bible with worn edges and bookmarks jammed throughout its chapters. He fumbled around the cell, moving books and his personal belongings, making space for me to use. As he feebly moved, he kept making small talk and soft, labored grunts.

"I got just two rules.

Don't fuck with nothing is not yours. and

Don't ask about nothing you don't want the answer to."

Unc had brown steel clouded eyes that mirrored my face in their glassy reflection, somehow feeling distant, although they cut directly. Once my old cellmate settled in, his undivided attention sat on the only chair in the cell- the metal toilet.

"So, you not talking?" He asked. *"Seems to me that someone in your predicament would be talking a whole lot. You like a candle that ain't lit- full of promise, but ain't worth nothing if ya don't put fire on it."* He laughed.

His laugh was a choked struggle one with hissing gasps of air in between each chuckle. He carries a neatly folded handkerchief in his pocket that he folded and returned every few minutes. Wisdom and time oozed from all he did.

"Yes, I do talk, but it's all been a blur lately. I think I need to keep things to myself in here. All that is happening to me is too hard to believe." I said dismissively. *"I would like to know how you knew my name and what did you mean by one of you?"*

Uncle Luke paused and shuffled through old books stuffed in corners and under the bed. He eventually got tired and said that we had plenty of time to answer my questions. Apparently, he would rather ask more about me than to help me figure out who I was and why things are the way they are.

"Son, tell me about you. Where are you from, boy? Who was your parents? And how long have you been seeing things?" His directness cut past my inquisitiveness. Whereas I wanted to

interrogate him, he was the one interrogating. I told him everything he asked to know, and he just occasionally said *"uh huh"* and *"no fooling"* with small intersjections as I recounted my lineage and past.

"My father was a medical tech in a research hospital in Baltimore. He was very smart and put himself through school where he met my mother. She was a teacher and was from Virginia. I have one sister, and I grew up here in Baltimore. I don't have a special story or some dark secret I need to hide." I didn't want to tell him about none of the weird stuff from childhood or of recent. It would make me look insane.

Uncle Luke walked over to me and stared into my face, first from the right, then from the left. "Uh-huh." He wobbled over to the calendar and began,

"Son, you can deny all you want, but looka here. This here calendar shows the moon's phases. By the way I see it, you got less than a week or so before they have to do something. I'm not your worry. Your ignorance is what you should be worrying about. You are what the book calls a seraphim or a rare form of one. In your eyes, is time veiled in a cloak. The sooner you uncloak it, the better chance you might have of surviving." He said circling the date a week from now.

He grabbed the open bible from the bed and flipped through its worn pages stopping in different places saying, *"Uh huh."*

My heart was racing hearing the first explanation that somehow makes sense. I have heard the term before. I am no stranger to the Word. Read this he said. He went to several books in the bible highlighting the multiple times it described

The Book of Emily

the sightings of one or their purpose. I found it hard to believe what he was insinuating. Both my parents were of man, and so is my sister. That first night I stayed up and read the bible, and fear was the most prominent emotion that found comfort in its sacred words. The scariest was the supernatural implications of it. There were stories of glorious ones and stories of evil ones. Some were described as ancient and servants of God, and some were exiles from Him. All were powerful, and all were older than man himself.

Old man Luke and I spent the next couple of days discussing the bible and what significance it had on all of man. I was raised to find comfort in its words. Somehow the words only opened more apprehension to what is happening. Luke's reasoning even leaped into the historical references in history that he firmly believed were interventions with God and his servants, from horrific tragedies in history to miracles and explanations that were from the fanatical to the irrational. I learned to respect his opinions. He always gave a two-way outlook to what was his point he was trying to make. Not once did he direct reference me until he asked what I was dreaming about each night. Like his stories that were embedded in parables and folklore, he sat listening to me tell him the dream visions that plagued me each night. Most fascinating to him was the appearance of Nate and Clymythious in them. It was on the first night that our daily morning story exchange began.

That night he woke me up from a nightmarish slumber, saying that I was screaming in my sleep. He said I was disturbing the whole floor, crying, and pleading. The dream was so vivid. He made me tell him about that first night.

"It's okay, son. You need to let it out, or it will consume you." He said, offering me a cup of water to calm my nocturnal sobbing.

He listened to the story of Edison Park, Nate, Emily, and Clymythious as I related them to the dreams. The one that night was so climatic and emotional that he wanted to hear every detail. It was hard to tell it, for it was shrouded in death and combat.

"Unc, this might be way too much for you to hear. I can't explain the dreams, and I don't want to give you the wrong impression about me. I'm just sort of messed up in what I'm feeling. I don't mind telling you about it, but it surrounds a lifestyle that I know you know nothing about." It seemed important to deny the dual sexuality of them to him. Although I didn't say it directly, he shook his head and told me that nothing I could say would be too much. We were going to be stuck here in the cell for some time. He would rather understand what's going on with me than to not know.

"The dream returned to the meadow in the night and in the distance was the ongoing battle between Nate and Clymythious in a far-off glow in the trees through Emily's eyes. The forest was luminescent from the battle of the two. In her heart, she wanted to run to the wooded edge to do anything she could to help Nate, but in her arms was tiny Isaiah. Her maternal instincts would not jeopardize his life, even for his father. Instead, Emily ran in the opposite direction toward Edison's Edge only to get interceded by Navasha and Simon. They came from the sky with red eyes and swords drawn. I can feel her racing heartbeat as she escaped through the trees down a path to the edge of the gorge hiding from her pursuers. She stood on the ledge hundreds of feet from the rocky canyon beneath her. Cornered and shaken, she had to make a choice to descend down its jagged edge, or to wait for Navasha and Simon to corner them.

"Sure, death awaits you, Ms Lee. Just give us the little one and you could leave here safe," Navasha said, closing in with her sword drawn.

Emily knew her choices. If they got a hold of Isaiah, they would kill him. She crouched down on the moss on the last threshold above the cliffs. From deep within her, she felt electric and tingly. Her whole body was being charged with energy. A haze of energy charged from within the more she panicked. Navasha's sword above her was in a violent swing, so Emily stepped from its edge and into the air, walking on it as if she were grounded with every tiny step over the misty bottom below. In her glow, she called for Nate over and over again, hoping he would again find her. Isaiah was crying and screaming over the cliffs. His tiny voice echoed against the walls sounding like a crow in the night. Emily was not totally out of reach from the sharp blade. Navasha's sword cut through her cutting through her dress and gashed through Emily's arm in a mortal blow before they could get far enough of the edge's reach. As she did, Simon sounded a horn behind her. Its loud, deep blast must have been a signal to Clymythious that they have killed the vessel. Poor Emily was still floating just a couple feet from the edge, wounded and bleeding from a wound under her left arm. She could hear the tree branches breaking underfoot as the battle party stopped and followed Simon's horn. Her blood dripped from underneath her bare arm to droplets splashing on the cavernous floor. Head down, and hair in her face, mid-air she resembled a statue of a saint, mournful yet still beautiful. As the energy oozed from her like blood, she was losing the fight to stay mid-air. Winds from Edison's Edge were gushing upward, splashing her own blood in specks over her and Isaiah. Her thick black, beautiful tresses of hair are now fluttering above her, parachuted in the wind. She is dropping from mid-air with slow grace and eventual death in the rocky gorge below her. This would be her grave if Nate couldn't help her.

Still trampling the trees and clashing metal swords in battle along the way is Nate and Clymythious. When they broke the tree line to the top of Edison's Edge, they both stop and survey the dire situation. In front of them were Simon and Navasha on the very edge looking down. I can see Nate running to the cliff's edge to see his love and family dangling in suspended descent. The shock of seeing Emily hovering in an upward draft splattered in blood was numbing to him. His diverted attention is unaware of Clymythious's advantaged approach until he hears the swish of air that only a large sword makes. This is difficult to make in a split second. He could turn his back on his family's peril and defend off Clymythious, or he could try to help his family who, without help is heading to Edison's Edge bottom.

Nathanael's choice was the only one for him. He leapt from the cliff's edge spreading his large wings, and like a champion, thrusting his self with all he had to reach his falling family. He had one foot left on the ground; muscular tendons outstretched in his large parasail wings. His choice cost him a defenseless injury. Clymythious's sword ripped through his shoulder, almost detaching his right wing between the shoulder blades. Nate's painful cry from it echoed through the woods and ridge. It was torturous and guttural. Emily looked up and saw his face twisted in pain and determined with his arm outstretched to grab her as he soared off the edge. The open gash on the mutilated wing causing him to get caught and tossed in the cliff's updraft.

"Em, hold on! I'm coming!" He screamed as he fought the tumultuous winds to reach her. He could see that the energy from her was fading. He could see in her face *"goodbye."* She lowered her head and sped faster to the ground clutching Isaiah with her last bit of strength.

"Noooo, Em! It is not this time that I shall lose again!" He said.

He knew what he had to do. He dropped the sword from the injured arm's hand and pinned his wings behind him, which made him spiral like a bullet straight to Emily. It was a feeble last attempt that got him closer. He reached them and the three were pummelling to the ground and high speed. It would only be seconds before they would be crushed on the rocky bottom.

"Let me go, Nate!" Emily cried. *"Take Izzy and save him."*

For Nate, this was not acceptable. He opened his wings which caused them to spin and jerk in chaotic currents. With only one strong enough to harness the wind, guidance was fruitless, especially with Emily and Isaiah in tow.

"You must let go my love or we all die. Please, baby, save our son!" She said, grabbing the infant's arm like a rag doll and lifted him over her head, and letting go of Nate's grasp.

"Oh God no! Why do you test and scorn all that I love? Please, how much must I endure?" Nate said, grabbing his son and getting control of their descent as he watched Emily fall

into darkness, arms still outreaching. Eyes full of pain and surrender. His plea was to God who he felt was punishing him. He held his son close his bosom to quiet his shrieking cries, covered in his mother's blood and wrapped in a swaddling cloth. It was those high-pitched shrieks that awoke me from the nightmarish dream.

"Your destiny lies in the truths that are in your dreams. You gotta see them as your past no matter how painful they are." Luke said taking the cup of water from my hand that was trembling. *"It's just three days till the full moon. Tomorrow, we start feeding your unconscious. We pray. We study. We talk. But tonight, get some rest."* He said, cutting off the cell light.

The following night the dream was more horrific than the last, but this time, I wasn't alone.

Chapter 5

The dampness of the cell aroused me out of my induced sleep. It was too similar to the dampness and coldness of the docks in Baltimore harbor. I don't know how I got to the cell, and I was face down on Uncle Luke's bunk. Its rumpled sheets smelled of ointment and aftershave. As I sat on the edge of the bunk, the recollection of my visit with him threw me into a panic. I remembered the wailing alarms and the chaotic-sounding medical equipment flashing and beeping in escalation. The smothering presence of hopelessness was heavy in memory, and the present distressed flood of confusion.

What more sorrow can I cast on others?

The sun had gone down, and I knew it was just a matter of time before either destiny or fate caught up with me. It's a full moon tonight, and according to Uncle Luke it was the end of the waning fortnight- a resolution or completion to an omen of time. Talking to myself used to feel crazy, but now is my best companion.

"What can I do to prepare myself?"

"What or who is coming for me?"

Or an even better question,

"Who am I?"

Sitting there in a self-absorbed pity party, it dawned on me what the last words Uncle Luke said. I began searching through the stacks of books for the one he told me to read- The Order of Man. I found it in the last stack of books in the cell's corner. Its cover was worn, and it had bookmarks throughout it. The illustrated faded cover read:

The Order of Man

(Hidden truths/Lost Heritage)

By Nazerah Kadesh

Uncle Luke read this book often. I thought it was just another conspiracy theory metaphysical dogma that he like to read alongside the Bible.

It wasn't a thick book to read, so as instructed, I began from the first page, the first chapter. I didn't get past the first page when I was astounded by leaved knowledge scribbled within it. In his own handwriting in the inside of the cover Uncle Luke wrote:

Property of,

Isaiah Luke Wellington

My heart pounded in the revelation of what this key info means. In the brief time that I have been here incarcerated with him, I haven't once heard his entire name. He had no visitors, and the guards affectionately called him Uncle Luke.

It also had an old document folded in it and by the way it was gently preserved within the first page convinced me that it was as old as the book, if not older. It had to be gingerly opened because it was delicate and crumbling as I unfolded its irrefutable secret. With ink, so faded that it was barely legible, I could see that it was his birth certificate. What it told was too hard to believe. The almost a century-old document stated that he was adopted and changed his name. His former name was

Isaiah Luke Lee, born in 1927! I dropped the old book and stared at the fragile piece of paper, absorbing what truths or lies it symbolized. Tears welled up in my eyes as the reality of the circumstances pivoted my emotions, but there in the lines following were undeniable credentials.

Parents:

Mother- Emily Lee Hughes (born 1907)

Father- Nathaniel Hughes (no record)

It was a little too much information to process in the quick now naked and bare associations, yet the loose ties are binding and connecting in shaking truths that beforehand were only hypothetical.

Izzy?

Images of a young Luke, fatherless, motherless, invaded my spinning head. Maybe Nate has been keeping an eye on him as he has been watching me and the other reincarnates before me. I'm convinced he watches souls through time, so why not his own bloodline? Other papers in the tattered old book were papers with each charge he acquired in the jail system. They read from circumstantial manslaughter to weapons charges that all were dismissed. It appears Luke has unexplainable resources, especially in confrontations like mine. The detailed accountings of five men slain by a sword that wasn't found, and more were stamped *"Criminally insane"* in various notes and attached psychological evaluations. No doubt he tried to explain what was happening to him, which led him to this wing of the jail for the dangerous and those that can't function in the general population. The irony of Luke and I was depressing and somber, not to mention the welling anger at Nate, who may have known all of this and said nothing.

"So, this is what is going to happen to me. Locked up and considered insane, I am a prisoner to vivid hallucinations I can't explain and outcomes that are not normal."

The seriousness of the revelations in the book drove me to uncontrollable anger. Uncontrolled surges boil in my veins. I tore up the small cell, tossing the nailed to cement bed to the floor with ease, ripping the metal sink from its bolts in the wall, and water was spouting across the room, clanging the cell bars with anything I could get. It wasn't a solution to anything, but I was desperately trying to let go of the confusion in, anger, and feelings of manipulation. I had nothing to lose. The neighboring cell inhabitants were hollering and making as much ruckus as I was. It only took a couple of minutes till the guards returned to calm down the lunatic frenzy of the unit. When they got to me in the cell, I watched all of Uncle Luke's books and notes drain underneath the bars in the river of sink water. I knelt in the center of the cell, wet, spent, and still absorbing the now exposed knowledge. Surprisingly, they weren't annoyed as I was expecting. Their tones were wrangled in a subtlety that felt odd, but nonetheless, I could only hear my own voice. I could only see Emily's face from my dreams and visions. I could only think about the little precious face of Izzy in her arms and then the last time I saw Uncle Luke with tubes and machines beeping and chirping in alarm.

"It's time to go Mr. Williams. We thought we might have to do this after the death of Uncle Luke. Calm down and put your hands against the wall where we could see them." Said the guard.

Uncle Luke died?

Isaiah is dead?

That was the last stirring point of the pent-up fury. It took three guards to wrestle and pin me down. With their knees in my back, I was face down on the floor amongst all the papers and books that were disarray on it in a marsh of papers. One book in particular, was still where I threw it. *"The Origin of Man"* was laying just within my reach. The only thing I wanted out of this cell was that. It was a gift from Uncle Luke that likely had more revelations in it to unravel. I probably won't see its secrets as gifts, but more like truths that tie, awaken, and explain the past and the gloomy-looking future.

I got one arm free and clutched it with everything I had, and something fell out of it. It was the pearl locket that Nate gave to Isaiah in the dream. My fingers grasped it, in a desperate struggle with the now multiplying guards. As soon as I picked it up, my whole body blazed in blue fire! I tossed the shocked guards out of the cell, against walls, and over railings with an easy fling. Although rage was the source, there was a calmness in me that flickered in blue cool, roaring flames. Guards were being called in from different units and they too were tossed as they attempted to subdue me. Roars and clanging sounds were deafening from the other cells as I made my way out of the unit with discarded guards in my wake. I looked down at my feet and I was no longer walking on the steel and cement tier. I was still walking in gesture, but my feet weren't on the ground. I hovered over the bodies of the defensive guards and through the hallway towards the gate out of the wing. Below me on the lower tiers helmeted, and body-armored officers that were armed and pointing, and waiting for the signal to take offense in the situation. It was no concern to me. The prevailing thought in my head was to get back to Uncle Luke and see him one last time.

"Ty, don't do this man. They will shoot you if you do things this way. Nobody is trying to harm you. Listen to me. Uncle Luke was a friend to all of us here; we know that you are upset. He wouldn't want you to make the mistakes he made years ago. Just calm down before you get more people hurt, and they have to take drastic maneuvers that nobody wins." Said the Superintendent of the unit. *"We were just coming to get you to talk to your lawyer who is here. Calm down and we can take you to him."*

No sooner than he said that Philonious walked cockily through them stepping over the ones that were injured and pushing past the ones that were posted up with guns and clubs waiting for the command.

"Walk with me, Ty." Is all he said.

I slowly lowered myself to his eye level and walked with him in silence. He was nobody that I wanted to trust. Rationality set in and I knew that he would be the systematic way of getting out of here, although I knew who he worked for, and it could be a trap to my death with the Immortali.

He led me through halls and around corners and I could hear the superintendent hollering *"halt"* with each step. Philonious never showed any reaction to them. He walked in his lawyer swag in front of me, unlocking doors with just a touch from his hand. Through a couple of units, the guards in pursuit would occasionally try to run up on me and all I had to do was toss them into the other ones behind him while I followed Philonious to the last door on the floor.

"Don't do this, Mr. Williams. We will fire!" The superintendent shouted using a bullhorn.

They gave us twenty feet and a lot of warnings before they threw tear gas canisters at our feet. It only made it confusing for them to follow. Philonious opened the last door that led to a stairwell. The stench from the gas was thick and camouflaging our quick exit. Once we got through the door to the stairwell Philonious twisted the steel door handle like a ball of putty into a knot that, from the other side, they would have to weld and dismantle to get open.

I stopped at the top of the stairwell refusing to go any further without explanations. I could be walking right into a trap. It is the last of the fortnight, and I don't know who or what is supposed to happen. I do know that it involves the Society of the Immortali and that is who Philonious works for.

"I go no further without you telling me what is going on." I said at the top of the stairs looking at Philonious down below me. His eyes were now yellow and shining like the eyes that were in the trees when Nate and Clymythious battled.

"Shut up. You talk too much!" He said.

I was still hazed in blue curling flames, but my senses were tingling and that made the flames spool around me in ferocity. I was focused in energy with anger and revenge. For all I know, he could have killed Uncle Luke and is planning on killing me. Well, not without a fight. It might as well be now!

"Fool! You are no match for me!" He said.

I heard clothes rip and metal clang as he emerged out of the darkness of the lower stairwell. It was Simon. He was laughing as he took slow steps up to me letting the sword clang on the railing as he took each step.

"You vessels are always so fucking naive. You contain the power to change humanity and make the world ours, and over and over you make the wrong choices and ask too many questions. You do know who I am, Augustus, or should I say Emily, or how about Ty? You sicken me with your naive arrogance. I was hoping that you would be different from your predecessors, but las, looks like you are like the others, and I must take your life like many of theirs if you don't cooperate. I can say that I am going to enjoy killing you though." Simon said laughingly.

A voice from the above stairwell answered before I could reply.

"Tis not the hour you seek your murderous plot, Simon. Nor will you force her full transform before its time. Hath no man loved and lost twice. You shall not harm this vessel!"

From above, echoing like flapping, swarmed bats soared Nate. He was in his cursed daylight form. Menacing and wings outstretched through the middle of the spiraling ironwork. Majestic in form. Naked and animal-like in his primal features. He swept down and snatched me from the platform with another following him. He cradled me in his arms as he continued the drop-down in between cement steps and iron railings. He wouldn't look directly at me for I was still ablaze.

"Bestill yourself Em. I need to course our way out of here and your energy is blinding me." He said in the plummet. *"Focus Ty!"* The voice from behind said.

The voice sounded familiar, but I was still in my rage and concentrating to not blind Nate took effort. I did as they said and buried my head in Nate's chest and let the falling cool wind and the smell of myrrh calm me to a light glow. I only lifted my head up to see Nate's grimaced face as we descended down several flight. He looked like the Nate I knew, and Emily loved underneath the gargoyle-like features.

"You gave yourself for my safety Em. We will be fine. Hold on, for we have reached the bottom."

I braced myself for a hard landing. At the speed we were falling, I expected could only be a jolting one. Over his shoulders, I could see his glorious dark wings in full outstretch to slow the descent to the bottom. His hooves feet landed in a solid stomp with his comrade landing next to us. It was such an abrupt stop; it knocked the air out of me. I could only stare into his eyes gasping for air as dust and debris followed in a tailwind rain. Nate's once outstretched wings wrapped around me in a protective cocoon as the disturbed debris bounced off his wing-shielded body. He whispered to me in the cocoon.

"Breathe Em, breathe! I have not lost you yet."

At the last of the falling debris, he opened his folded wings, and I gasped for air in recovery of the landing, still cradled in his now crouched lap. Seeing me breathe, he leaned over and softly kissed me on my forehead while he stood up to stand me on my feet.

"We ain't got time for that mushy stuff!" The voice said, walking into the stairwell light from above. My eyes couldn't believe what they were seeing! It was Uncle Luke! He had wings like Nate's, but he looked stronger than the last time I saw him. He stood erect and his old glassy eyes were renewed with vigor and youth. He had wings that gave him a sort of regality in appearance.

"Thought I was a goner, huh, Ty? I'm sorry I couldn't tell you too much about it. It didn't go as we planned, and it would have only confused you." He said, standing in the light looking half like his father at night and half the Luke I have gotten to know. *"We don't have time to talk. Simon and the others are up there strategizing their next move. We need to move fast."*

There was a steel door down here with us that I assumed we were going to break through to escape, but I was wrong. Nate pushed me back and removed the drain cover from the floor and dropped me in it, then Uncle Luke and himself jumped behind me.

"Now Em!" Nate ordered. *"Concentrate and let your light be ours."*

As much as I could focus on it, I failed to even spark. I knew what he was demanding, and I was trying hard, but nothing was happening. The frustration of not being able to weld control of the gifts, especially in times like these is infuriating. Nate walked over and kissed me. This time a full kiss on the lips. My thoughts were refocused on what is happening. I just got used to understanding that his love is not for me, but for his lost love Emily. Things must be dire for him to do this. The kiss was simple and quick, and it was followed by saying,

"Forgive me Em," and slapped my face with so much impact that it knocked me to the wet drainage floor. His large hand stung on my small face. Immediately the blue flames burst and curled around my body lighting the sewer tunnels in both directions.

"*Atta boy Ty!*" Uncle Luke cheered.

I was so angry about the surprise slap that the flames kept getting intense by the second. They went from a deep blue and brightened to an uncontrollable violet, spewing on the ceiling, and crawling down its sides. Nate and Uncle Luke were screaming for me to calm down and get a grip on my emotions. I heard them, but the sting of the slap was burning the side of my face.

"Em, please! *Think of controlling it to a candlelight. I am so sorry to have had to hit you. We are running short on time before they get down here. You are blinding me!*" Nate snapped.

It was Uncle Luke that consoled me back to a flickering blue flame. He knelt beside me, unbothered by the scorching bright light emanating from me.

"*How the hell you think she, ...he, ...them going to calm down by slapping the shit out of them?*

You lucky it wasn't my ass!

I would have fried us all down here! Let me handle this."

Uncle Nate was sounding like the man that I shared a cell with for a week- comforting, wise, and courageous. He put his hand through the now orange flames and grabbed my face forcing me to divert my attention.

"Did you find the book I told you to look for? And did you find the locket?" He asked and I only could blink a yes with eyes ablaze in fright and insecurity.

"Listen to me, Ty. You can use the locket to control your rage and power. You must become one with it. Nate can't understand what he thinks you should command after all that he has been through. Don't hold anger for him; it will only feed the uncontrollable fury." Uncle Luke took a chain from around his neck and put it in my hand saying to put the locket on it and wear it, promising that everything will be okay.

I did as he asked and immediately, crackling light seeped through the mortar crevices of the old under-city water system and surged through my body distorting who I was and who I am. More importantly who we are. By their faces I was it was evident. A warrior in glowing blue soft flames. For Nate, it was a relief from the blinding light and a welcoming vision of his lost love, for Uncle Luke it was a glimpse of a mother he hadn't seen in seventy years. For me, it was a rebirth. An awakening.

Nate looked away and, in the light, he transformed into the Nate of daylight, standing erect and naked as Adam. Those eyes were fixed on the apparition or the mutation of me/them before him. He was struggling for words and reaching for her is as if would never see her again.

"Hath my weary eyes so'er witnessed the beauty of a love so lost as to behold it once more." He said as he wrapped his arms around us.

His arms wrapped in an embrace that was nourishing as it was draining. My hand held tight to the locket to maintain the symbiotic connection. It was easy to allow him his moment after fighting to keep his pledge to her. The deep blue flames enveloped us both, and for moments we were pillars of fire in a fused reunion.

"You have to let me go Nate. You all are in danger. Clymythious is not far. I feel his darkness shadowing close. Run, Nate, and protect my son!" The irony of her words coming from Ty and her Union made Nate let go. They were the very same words she said to him a hundred years ago.

He let go listening to her warming. Frozen in a gaze, Uncle Luke sobbed as she turned her attention to him with her words to Nate. He had only seen her in Ty's shared dreams. To see her, his mother, standing before him has him too fumbling for words.

"Izzy, you have grown into a good man. Despite the discrimination against you, you never harmed anyone on purpose. Now is the time for you to take vengeance and fulfill your destiny. I have always watched over you your whole life. Although your battle and life struggle has been difficult, you should know your father and I never stopped watching over you from afar. What you did for Tyson was unselfish and courageous. The journey is only beginning. Go and know I am always with you." She said, and the flames turned a deep violet.

Nate and Uncle Luke looked at each other and then back at the new form before them. Not quite Ty or Emily, basking in full armor and shimmering in purple brilliance.

"We need to make haste and make it to the tunnels before midnight." Nate said leading the way through the narrow sewer in the purple ambiance. They made it to the tunnels, but behind them they could hear the trampling of feet in pursuit of them clanging and banging swords against the sewer walls.

"Die traitor! Die, Traitor! Die!" They tauntingly chanted from its depths.

The three of them hastily weaved through the underground abandoned passageways with Nate leading the way. Slowing only at deteriorated junctures stopping to take candid glimpses of the new Ty who still was fully suited in purple wraith-like hues and silent. Midnight was not far at hand. The few stops were for Uncle Luke to catch his breath till they heard the hunters getting closer.

For Ty, the tunnels looked all too familiar. These were the same maze of tunnels that he and Nate used to escape Clymythious. Its stale smells, old, wired lights, and disabled gas lamps were unmistakable.

"Augustus, you are making this far more difficult than your predecessors. Surrender now and I won't let Raja rip your flesh to shreds. Nathaniel and that half-blood cannot save you!" Clymythious' resonant voice shouted through the sub-level labyrinth.

It wasn't long after his threat before they could hear Raja's claws getting closer and closer digging the old, paved ground in hard pursuit and outpacing them. His heavy panting and growls magnified in the hollow cavernous tunnels. They knew they had to get above ground quickly. A confrontation in these tight quarters would not give them an advantage. Swords would be useless. As they approached the same steel-grated steps that led Nate and Ty to the tower.

Clymythious bellowed,

"I smell fear Augustus. Could it be that you know your journey nears end? Think about the cost you weigh forsaking honor and hiding in cowardice. Stand and I will let the others live. Attempt to flee and you all will die unmercifully." He said with a deep low cackle laugh that made Raja's monstrous snorting growls sound even more menacing.

Ty stopped at the stairwell's gate and insisted on Nate taking Uncle Luke to safety from under the old train station, pointing to the stairs without a word. It was easy to see that Clymythious's words evoked a confrontational choice in him. Purple was ebbing into blue fury.

"Don't do this Em. You may have defeated Raja before, but to fight here, alone, would be foolish. We only have two or three floors to go up and we can fight side by side." He pleaded, as royal purple flames began roaring into magenta.

"Nate please take Uncle Luke up there and I will follow. I promise this will not end here for me, but it could for him. Emily would have fought with everything she had to ensure his safety. The sacrifice has already been done. Hurry because Raja will be here in any second."

With that, the magenta burst into blinding scarlet brilliance, forcing Nate up the stairs in retreat from its nova intensity. In the sanctity of the abandoned station stairwell, Nate listened as Ty's curdling war cries met with ferocious growls. What took only seconds seemed an eternity for Nate and Uncle Luke as they scurried up into the abandoned station. The battle felt as if it would never end till Raja yelped in defeat as all the air within the station vacuumed into the stairwell sucking in debris and dust in an explosion and aftermath. Whatever happened was so intense that the heat through the stairwell was hot and equal to standing on the edge of a volcano's brim.

When the dust cleared, the two stood in the marbled carousel of the abandoned train station holding on to its supportive columns, both watching the stairwell in anticipation of the beast Raja or the triumphant Emily to emerge from the imploded chaos. No sound was heard, which for them was a relief and a torturous wait. Neither of the two men looked at each other. Nate approached the doorway in caution and dismay as he hollered down the now-distilled stairwell restrained by Uncle Luke.

"Emily...Ty?"

The sullen antiquated train station settled into its normal ghost, but now plus one. For Nate, there was no reason to fight anymore. Once again, he lost the vessel, he sought so hard to protect over and over again. At about 220lbs, Uncle Luke couldn't drag him from the tragic stairwell.

"C'mon big guy we can't stay here. Ty fought hard and he stayed behind so that we could get away. You will see your Em again if time is a circle. Nothing is in vain," he said.

The words permeated through Nate's mournful loss as he listened and collapsed on the old marble floor. From its balcony, a voice that he had been running from reverberates against the now boarded and grated turn of the century ironwork windows. As deteriorated and forgotten the old station is in its condition, it is holding up in its own tomb. The interior infrastructure is still intact with signage, ticket booths and murals painted on its walls, and beautiful stained-glass windows.

"Nathaniel, the fortnight is almost complete. I cannot kill you, but the half breed must die. Each century you fight against what must happen and now you have a prodigy that we must take as well. Why do you foolishly fight so hard?" Clymythious howled from the balcony. It was followed by the clanging of swords on ledges and marble rafters- a sign of warfare approaching with a gladiator audience perched waiting on the outcome in ceiling buttresses. There in the round windows encircling the domed glass ceiling, were Navasha, Simon, Benoit, and others. Their excitement is not only represented in the loud reverberated clanging, but in their nervous movement and mumbling.

Clymythious stepped from the shadows into the center light in calm bravado to begin a ritual that has occurred many times to futile attempts to stop it with the predecessor's vessels. Sure enough, in the skylight of the station was the moon rising to its zenith. He began the ritual with a ceremonial speech to the rafters:

"Once every century the Order of Immortali assembles for the "Slaughter of the Vessel" ritual. This year we have already sacrificed the vessel before the end of another fortnight and our comrade Nathaniel brings us his own flesh and blood for the sacrificial rite."

The clanging of the sword's clamor escalated with the sound folding on its own in the dome with cheers and applause.

Some of Clymythious's flanked minions were so excited that they jumped from the perches like freed gargoyles circling and gliding, waving swords when they were above Nate and Uncle Luke's head. The center station floor opened and what was once a ticket booth became a pit of fire that was stroked in cracking orange coal embers with a slab above it with four manacles.

Nate was outwitted. Not only did they get Ty, but now they want to sacrifice his only bloodline, and he led them right to him. In his rage his wings outstretched two feet over his head in defensive anger. Each time the soaring flank men got closer and closer to landing, he would snarl and brandish the sword at them. He didn't fear the battle so much as to face another loss.

"Can you use a sword?" He asked Uncle Luke.

"Never had to, but I can fight!" He boasted flexing his own fledgling wings.

"Good! You gonna need to." Nate said throwing Uncle Luke to the center with one toss. *"Counsel and friends, we have the vessels son. I have earned my right to remove the curse of night from me. Take his blood and mingle it in his legacy of his mother. Let my petitions be rewarded to bones, flesh, and gristle. I give you Isaiah Luscious Wellington!"* He shouted in pride and to the surprise of all the witnesses who roared in disbelief.

"Quiet my friends. You surely cannot believe that after all this chase and battle, that this renegade's alliance is true. He is a lone mongrel that twists the very fabric of each of us to his bidding. Lest not forget the battle in Edison's Edge when the traitor cost us the last vessel. Now he stands before us in manipulation to pitifully alter our judgements. Behold a traitor

that because of his treachery must hide in the shade of dark. Let us not be fooled!" Clymythious said from the balcony's edge.

The murmur in the room were indecisively divided in agreement with Clymythious, and in allegiance to Nate. Shouts and expletives crowded the air from the heated reactions.

"Traitor!"

"Hypocrite!"

"Nathaniel the vigilante!"

"Victory is Nathaniel!"

"Long reign The Order of Immortali!"

In the fever of the moment Nate brandish a dagger from his sword's sheath and plunged it into Uncle Luke's side, snarling in excruciation and convivial excitement leaving the dagger in his side and raising his sword toward the arena of Immortali. Uncle Luke's screams of pain and disbelief only excited the station onlookers.

"How could you Nate?

I thought...

I thought..." Was all he could say. The dagger in his side is oozing blood in a puddle beneath him. Afraid to remove it from his abdomen, Uncle Luke's hand squeezed around the wound tightly as it trickled between his fingers, spilling slowly through the corners of each finger's fold. He tried to squirm away from his angered father on all fours only to be dragged back to the center near the blazing pit.

"You cannot run Luke." Nate whispered as he dragged him by his leg leaving a smeared blood trail in Luke's soaked crimson wings back to center.

The place was so loud in applause and clanging of swords against the stone that they could not hear their conversation. "It is not your time Izzy. When the time is right you will know, and then, and just then, kill your mother's murderer."

Clymythious leaped from the balcony to officiate the sacrifice as the moon swallowed the skylight in an almost ocular stare.

"Well done, Nathaniel. You had us worried. Now we see the warrior that fought Caesar and rode next to Alexander. The warrior that slaughtered with the Barbarians, destroyed whole Aztec villages almost single-handedly, and drank wine and made merry as Atlantis sank. The last century we thought you softened fighting civil causes, turning the other cheek in dishonor, and working the fields like a human slave under oppression.

You are not one of them.

It is why I placed the curse on you, so that you may never be seen or treated as one of them. Welcome back.

Let the ceremony begin!

Time approaches." Clymythious said as he walked over to Nate, never looking down at Uncle Luke who was pinned under Nate's foot.

"What do you have to say my brother?"

It was now or never for Nate to distract everyone. He chose his words carefully.

"Through the age of time my soul has wretched in many losses and torment. My brothers, I have grown weary, and its tyranny must end. Tonight, it ceases with the last tie that binds me to disgusting weak mortal flesh and transgressions. No longer will I hinder the mission and oath that unite us together. We as the guardians of the prerogative, and pledge to uphold in true valor in creed that is as ancient as the tides of time. So, my brethren take not in accord of my actions but behold the allegiance and veneration to the finality of fortnight's end!" It was just what he needed, and he finished with his sword in the air and looked at Uncle Luke and nodded.

"It ends now!"

Uncle Luke sees Nate's plan and twists the dagger out of his side and Nate releases his foothold on him. Everything is going to plan. Clymythious is looking up to the amphitheater of militia and not seeing Uncle Luke's hand raise to plunge it in him from beneath. The wound Nate inflicted was strategically placed to avoid vital organs. He knew where to place it and do the less damage as he could. Just as Uncle Luke was fully leveraged the doors of the abandoned train station exploded open and lights and helicopters flooded the skylight cancelling the moon.

"Nobody move!" Shouted Detective Choo with a bullhorn. *"Drop the knives! Nobody has to get hurt here."*

Riot-armed police ran in from every entrance that was once boarded up spilling in like a river of uniforms with riot shields and helmets. The coordinated arrival had to be happening outside of the station for them to form offensive scrimmages in seconds. The station was lit only by torches that were held by hand in the ceiling. One by one, they were being extinguished and the space in the dome was busy with attacking flights from the pedestals like an angry swarm.

Detective Choo didn't plan for what he had walked into. There were a thousand voices from the dispersed officials- all were nervous and tense. What he saw in the aerial assault stunned his command. Before long, a lone gunshot from one of the officers fires into the air and anything that moved. It was followed by smoke bombs that rolled just feet from where Nate and Uncle Luke were standing. The gunfire now was aimlessly shooting. Through the smoke and gas, the only thing that anyone could see was strobes flashes from the muzzles. Amidst all the chaos Detective Choo is shouting orders to cease fire, but no one is listening. Soon they are shooting each other and along with the aerial attack of swords, a plan that could have run smoothly is now a bloody battlefield.

Detective Choo, nor the panicked participants noticed that Nate dragged his son off to the side. He has seen enough battles to know that in chaos the Immortali will not be the losers, not from mere bullets, but Uncle Luke could be mortally wounded, and he remembered his promise to Emily. She gave her life for her Izzy.

As the smoke began clearing amongst the noise of two-way radios and fluttering wings, Clymythious emerged from its mist. He was wounded in the shoulder by a gunshot and his eyes gleamed through the haze with intent to kill Uncle Luke.

"This doesn't end well for you Nathaniel or your bastard son. The vengeance is mine and my sword will have the blood of the Vessel upon its blade!"

In true valiant defense, Nate stood in front of his prodigy and what might be the final battle is beginning in a standoff. Nate has never defeated Clymythious in battles past, but he has more to lose with each loss. His fight in Edison's Edge cost him Emily. The flight in the tunnels and Ty's battle with Raja took another life from him. Before he takes on Clymythious he knows that Uncle Luke must use this moment to flee no matter what the outcome is.

That last look at his son was one of remorse. There was so much that over the years of watching over him from a distance, he didn't say. For seventy years, he remained a shadow in his life. Muted and silent. Words fail him once more. It seemed better to say nothing than to try to say it all and still have so much more that should be said. Like his father, Uncle Luke stood up and flexed his appendages in preparation for a fight even with his injury. Nate pushed him back in a gesture, saying to stay out of it.

"Now I have just about had enough of all y'all! First you shank me and now you think that I ain't going to stand toe to toe with you?

What kind of punk shit is that?

You might be my father by blood, but you damn sure didn't raise me, and I ain't no bitch! Just go ahead and do what you gotta, but I got your back.

You don't know how many others are out there too.

No disrespect Pops." Luke adamantly said ready to die in battle.

Clymythious and Nate circle each other a couple of times, snarling and accessing each other- Nate with nothing on but a leathered sheath and Clymythious in a long black duster with a ruffled silk shirt underneath. He removed the duster in the circle dance, talking and taunting Nate.

"You are a bigger fool than I thought you were. You actually think I am the bad guy in this and that you are some kind of savior to humanity? If you haven't learned anything over the centuries, you should know that you can't change time or bend its course. But let's assume that you can alter destiny and fate in a wager. Here are the terms, if you can defeat me, although you won't, I will not kill the half breed, and I will remove the day's curse from you and you, and your precious bastard can walk out of here and do whatever you do. But, if, and when I win this dual, I kill the Vessel, and I also reverse the curse, making you what you seem like you want- human. I will watch as your body wither and age to dust and the Order erases your name from their memories. Dried clay lost in a futile wind in waste." Clymythious is almost snickering as they circle closer touching swords. *"A tragic end to a warrior and a waste to your dying breed that will indeed die this evening."*

The two fenced with each other in gentlemanly fashion and technique for minutes before the first style evaporated and the battle became an effort to wound your opponent with less poise. The banter and rhetoric remained civil until Nate pre-empted and blocked a lunge that knocked Clymythious to the ground. He walked away from him with his back turned in swagger and bravado.

"Go Pops!" Shouted Luke from the sideline.

"I see you have picked up some new tricks in the past decades. Enjoy your last moments." He said trying to intimidate.

The smoke is clearing up and now because of the rhythmic sounds of sword attack and counterattacks that were quick and ringing with lightning speed responses in short spurts and bursts that resembled a dance as the two gracefully sparred and attacked each other. They looked theatric in the clearing of the smoke bombs with occasional spotlights from the helicopter beaconing from the skylight speering in with a high-beamed searchlight. As they danced, they stepped over bodies that were dead and wounded on the train stations floor from the gunfire. Many were shot by their own officers. The remaining interrupted members of the Order were high in the domed balcony and stained windows. Most had fled after the police broke the stations' condemned barricade. Only a few hid in the arches and supportive columns of the upper-level clerestory, perched in its huge arch windows watching the battle below them. On the ground, the police also watched with guns pointed at Nate and Clymythious, but not interrupting because sideline was Detective Choo who held his open hand above his head commanding a cease fire. The two swordsmen hurdled over benches and dodged around columns in a continuous fight, ignoring the onlookers.

The smoky station was cloaked in darkness and beams of concerting flashlights cutting through it. It wasn't clear to Detective Choo, or the other police whether they were watching a show's performance with fantastical characters or was it a gang battle that is masked in some sort of costumed armor.

Nonetheless, the sounds of metal and grunts held everyone's attention with the police using their pistoled flashlights on the assailants, prepared to shoot, but also witnessing the most incredible battle they had ever seen. They were so engrossed that when an attack was thwarted, or done with expert manipulation, they gasped and almost applauded.

The battle went on for twenty minutes or more with both warriors thrusting and wailing the swords in acrobatic finesse like gladiators.

"You got him Pops! Finish him!" Luke said from the sidelines that distracted Nate for a flash of a second. Hearing Izzy cheer him on was a distraction to a fault, and Clymythious butted sword hit him in the back of the head in a sidestep. He stood over Nate now with his sword at his throat savoring the moment.

"That's enough! Drop your weapons!" Shouted Choo from the sideline. Stepping in close to divert the heat of the moment hoping that he could steal Clymythious's victory blow.

"You don't want to do that, Clymythious. Look over there." Choo pointed to the doorway where they had Navasha in handcuffs. *"Not until now have I interfered with the Order of Immortali or its Orwellian nature. Baltimore City and several databases have long and extensive records on each one of you- whatever ya'll are. Indeed, you have friends in high places, but blatant violence and abandonment of your society's bylaws will jeopardize and compromise any allegiance they have for you and your own draconian punishment will do far more than I can. Do it, and I take you and others into public scrutiny and transparency."*

Where is your power,.Clymythious?" Detective Choo said in a low voice that only the two could hear and keeping a smiling face like a ventriloquist as he spoke. He looks small compared to the gladiators, but where he is short in stature, he is cocky in authority raveling and unraveling facts and outcomes like a chess player. As he approached them, he began clapping as if he was watching a live performance that had just concluded.

"Now we could do these two ways; all are subject to your actions. The way I think it should go with nobody getting hurt is for you two to take your bows and come with me to straighten things out in private, but if you use that sword in front of half of the Baltimore City Police and my hands will be tied and this goes public and viral. We have all three of you on surveillance footage from Edison Manor. The only one at the moment we need is Tyson to face charges of suspected murder and I think you gentlemen know where he is, and you are going to tell me. Logical reasoning indicates that he is just a pawn that is being maneuvered. An expendable piece in centuries of calculation."

The sharp-witted detective is now circling them while talking and still applauding. What might have appeared to be a plea for an encore was really a decisive ploy to postpone the finale. In a quick turn of events, the hunters have become the prey, and the prey is frozen in the hunter's fire.

"Bravo! Bravo!" Were the shouts from the gun-drawn officers thinking that it was just a spectacular show that they interrupted. Detective Choo turned to them too and egged them on for more fanfare for the performers.

Silence swallowed the room as Clymythious speared Nate in the abdomen with a double-handed grasp on his sword. The old train station for a couple of minutes was pin-drop quiet with the inhaled gasp from the officers, and Nate's desperate cry of disbelief and shock. Detective Choo still had his back to the horrific scene, but the faces of his officers and the sound of clanking triggers meant that he underestimated his cunning gladiator in an analysis that was intuitive and calculating but flawed in one variable. He didn't calculate Clymythious's monomaniac motives that were not in killing Nate, but in completing his task which was to kill Emily's spawn- Uncle Luke. Before Choo could turn to reassess the change of events, Clymythious had withdrawn the blade and had turned to Uncle Luke who now was rushing to his father's aid. In his haste to stop the battle, deductive reasoning had escaped his grasp for only a few seconds. Time slowed from a racing pace. He watched as Clymythious smirked in a glance at him. He knew that it was a game of moves and maneuvers, and he had checked the king, and he was soon to have a mate.

Choo saw the mistake in his manipulation as all the possibilities spun in his head and as Uncle Luke ran to what could be his death. Rationale was gone and with a nervous army behind him, Choo was in that slowed blurred moment strategizing the multiple outcomes that were about to unfold. He could hear the clicking of gun hammers prepared to fire on an assault that was a danger to all who watched, including their own detective who was in blade range of the sword. He saw Nate's eyes also plotting how to deter the onslaught of death by Clymythious who in finality, could once again be victorious in cutting down the periled lineage, despite the interruption of ceremony. His own injury to his shoulder from the chaos was

The Book of Emily

superficial in comparison to the next flurry of bullets that had him again in the line of fire.

"*Nooooooo!*" Uncle Luke screamed as he charged toward the sword. He didn't care about his own safety. He assumed that the blood battle was secure, only to watch Clymythious impale his father.

Clymythious's moment had finally arrived. He removed the sword from Nate's abdomen and listened to the rush of Uncle Luke's footsteps approaching from behind.

"*So, Nate witness again the vessel's blood spill. It is the same story that you foolishly think you can alter, and again, you will see time as your repetitious enemy.*" He said, raising the sword high above his head.

By the time Uncle Luke realized that he was rushing into a trap, he was already too close. He was at his father's side and beneath the sword that was cutting through the air to take his last breath and life from him. He could only shield with his wings in a desperate attempt to still protect his father in a sacrifice.

The stale air in the old station blew the station open from every window and exit smashing glass and debris in its aftermath. The gust of air sucked down the stairwell where Ty/Emily never came out of earlier. It was followed by blue streaks that carved through the dust causing all attention to be focused on the stairwell. Just as sudden as it started, the blast of wind stalled as the streams of light glowed brighter with more intensity. Deafening silence was hinged on anticipation of what might follow the strange surge of wind. The stairwell's pull exhaled with the gale-force winds, shrieking as it exploded in the opposite direction. Something was emerging out of the dust and light. Something eerie and powerful with almost thunderous footsteps. It was Ty, but not the Ty Nate and Uncle Luke knew. He was shimmering in the blue light- a hodgepodge of him and Emily. Not quite Emily and not quite Ty. A beautiful, suffused composite that was almost mythical in appearance. He didn't walk. He hovered, moving just a foot off the ground to the top of the stairs carrying something large, and dragging it behind him with its carcass thumping on each step he hovered over. What sounded like footsteps was its body dragging over each step.

"Nobody fire!" Shouted Detective Choo to his nervously alert men who were edgy and covered in dust and debris and ready to besiege the threatening anomaly.

Frenzied beams of flashlights were crisscrossing and cascading on the stairwell's entrance. Ty's phantom-like appearance detracted from the center station battle and almost murder with a presence that felt cold and vengeful in a beautiful essence that commanded an immediate re-evaluation of crisis. With an easy toss he threw the carcass of Raja's bloody defeated body to the feet of Clymythious.

Uncle Luke peered up from under his wings to see his excellmate hovering gracefully toward he and Nate. He thought to himself how proud he was of Ty for finding his symbiotic spiritual connection. In Ty's hand was a sword of flames that seared brighter than the blue aura that engulfed Ty. He held it out to his side as he got closer and closer to where they are. His eyes are fixed on Clymythious. Uncle Luke just whispered under his breath,

"Not here Ty. You strike here and you are damned to a life of hiding and misery like them."

It somehow seemed as if Ty heard him, and he stopped his approach and aimed his brandished sword at Clymythious. From its sharp edge tip came a brilliant blast of light that knocked Clymythious's raised sword from his hand.

Detective Choo seized his opportunity and interrupted the possible eventual slaughter. As it looks, he has lost control of the situation. He needed to calm things down and he wanted to bring Ty in for interrogation. This was his duty. All else would be hard to explain and document.

"Tyson, we have been looking for you. Put the weapon down and come with us. The last thing you want to do is have more blood on your hands. It would be a tragedy for you to be shot here for something we can sort out." The detective calmly said acting as if nothing was out of the ordinary.

Nate was still on the floor bleeding from the gash in his abdomen. He grabbed his son's hand to help him get up on his feet to say something, anything to prevent another death.

"Emily you must let Ty live." He said standing up and returning to the Nate of the night that Emily and Ty once knew. *"Retribution in flesh will not atone for or nourish revenge's thirst. What Ty is and what you are may be one, but the taste of vengeance cannot feed his completion. His destiny is not yours."*

Nate's pleading words did not fall on deaf ears, in fact, they agitated more out of them. The light burst in a supernova flash that blinded everyone, spewing from Ty/Emily with unbridled strength, liberating Ty from Emily's embodiment, imploding itself. Left in the returning darkness, writhed on the floor, and gasping for air was Ty. No sword or glow. No majestic spiritual persona. Just an exhausted man.

Detective Choo quietly ordered the squadron of men to detain and arrest him. He did not resist. The officers handcuffed him face down on the cold floor and let him lay there till the other pertinent confrontations were also addressed, but there was no one left in the station- only Ty. In the blinding flash, all others have escaped. They were gone from the rafters.

They were gone from the air and archways in the dome.

No bodies on the floor.

No Uncle Luke. No Nate.

No Clymythious

Just Ty weakened and displaced.

The surprised dispatched officers shined their flashlights and explored the dome's archaic infrastructure with them looking for anything to move, and nothing did. Just Ty looking demure and frail in comparison to the dazzling specter that flowed from the stairwell. The fantastical imagery was nothing like the crumbled man left in the center of attention. Where the apparition was radiant and asexual in its beauty with hair to its shoulders and in full armor, Ty was close cut and clothed in prison hand-me-downs. No longer a danger, he was fragile and lackluster.

The detective stood over him and scrutinizing the new creature below him. He knew Ty, but that doesn't explain the happenstance.

The station was still buzzing with paranoid activity still noisily canvassing the skies above the station and two-way radios blaring frantic communications. Detective Choo only spoke to his First Lieutenant, giving him instructions on the sideline while he contemplated what his next move was. The siege might appear to be over, but until he called an all-clear, nothing was over.

"Well, if it isn't the evasive Mr. Williams! It seems they have abandoned you. Why you are still alive is a conundrum. According to my research, nobody survives to tell a tale. This makes you not just a suspect to murder, but a witness." He said squatting in front of Ty.

He instructed his men to take him to Central Booking, the downtown headquarters for Baltimore City Police. Without any resistance Ty was placed in a squad car outside of the train station. By then, the press barraged them while he was being escorted.

"Where did you hide the body, Tyson?"

"Does this have anything to do with your disappearance from the jail?"

"Is it true this was some kind of satanic ritual?" The press shouted surrounding them as they left.

Millions watched all over the world as he was dragged out handcuffed with his head down looking guilty and captured. He made only one statement to them before he got in the squad car.

"I haven't done anything!" Is all he said staring into cameras.

Chapter 6

The ride to the station was frantic with helicopters hovering overhead like flies, and it was a sudden downpour of rain. The night sky softened as daylight crept in timidly with the morn fighting through the storm clouds. At 4 a.m., the Baltimore streets were ghostly, and people were sparse. Only the lights reflecting on the brownstone row houses signaled activity. The very streets that Ty was walking and running through hours before seemed alien now. The ride was short, and Detective Choo glanced occasionally to check on his passenger from the front seat who was despondent and quiet. As they reached the headquarters, the reporters were already there clamoring at the car window for candid shots and prying for answers from the accused who hid his face from them in embarrassment and shame.

They surround the car, and flashes blind him, making him angry. The doors of crushed inwards as he winced in fury screaming, *"Leave me alone!"* The sound of his voice shook the vehicle as the suspension bounced and rocked back and forth. The energy within him was intensified the more they knocked on the window. He began thrashing himself against the plexiglass that divided the car cutting himself against the rough edges as he lost control. Onlookers strained on the curb side pointing and trying to catch a glimpse of the murderer. It was Choo who realized that it wasn't the reporters who crushed the doors and almost overturned the squad car. He got on his radio and shouted to them to get the press and crowd from around them.

"Mr. Williams calm down. Nobody's going to harm you. We only want to get to the bottom of everything. I know you can hear me, and I know that you can get control of your anger." He said trying to ease Ty from escalating.

Other officers came to their assistance and removed him safely from the battered vehicle. As they rushed into a side entrance, the spectators cheered and roared in excitement. They didn't care if he was innocent or guilty. They wanted to see him locked up. The atmosphere was charged with violence and a riled-up crowd. In it were spectators that had other reasons than being nosey. Eyes that weren't excited or driven by judgment.

Ty sat in Detective Choo's office which was cluttered with files and empty coffee-stained cups. His desk had a framed picture of his family- two girls and a boy and his beautiful wife. His walls were decorated with assorted certifications and awards with a picture of him with the major in the center. He scribbled down notes before saying a word to Ty, and when he did, it wasn't a direct comment to him.

"It's the irrational drive to evil that can be detected in the most humane of men." He said with fastidious care.

Ty sat slumped and still handcuffed I the wooden chair. Only the jingling of irritated metal made sounds as he shifted to keep adjusting them. His small wrist can easily turn out of them, but for now he is just trying to make them comfortable.

"Let's start from the beginning." Det. Choo said looking up directly at Ty. *"You are Tyson Williams?"* He stopped to wait for an answer.

"No" he replied.

"If you are not Tyson Williams, who are you?" The amused detective said waiting to hear what possible explanation he could hear.

"My name is Augustus Magnimous!" He said with the first confident answer he has said since his incarceration.

For Ty, it has been a long journey of growth and confusion. Just hearing himself identify himself as Augustus was a revelation for him, and puzzlement for the detective. Somewhere in the past evening he has emerged as many, but is in consternation of who he is, resorting to honesty although it is incredulous.

"I am Tyson too, and Emily, and so many more that calling me Augustus fits from origin Detective Choo. Everything I tell you will be a melange of all." Augustus said in forthright candor.

"The last couple of weeks have been revealing in what has come to pass. If it is answers to questions that have no meaning in the world you live in, then I would suggest not asking them. I can answer what I know from how I know." He said leaning on the desk and devoting all his attention to the questioning detective.

Choo was scribbling down notes at a rapid pace, flipping pages and grabbing assorted papers from out his desk drawers. It was obvious he didn't believe any of what Tyson/Augustus said.

"So, am I talking to just one of you now?" Choo asked.

"In a way, you are speaking with all. I am all of them and they are me. Look at me Detective. Have I not changed since I saw you in Edison Manor?" He questioned.

The leery detective put his pencil down and stared at Augustus and he was right. His hair was just a little longer and his face was softer with an odd presence on it that was beyond explanation. His eyes had depth and mystery within them. He looked at the jail mugshot in his file before him, and then back to him, and he could easily see that the man in front of him was recognizable, but very different. He was far from the mugshot, and far from the man he met in Edison Manor. As much as he wanted to deduce that Ty was suffering from delusions, he could see that something traumatic had happened to him to converge all of the personalities that he says he is into one person. Ty was still there- a humble demur guy. Emily was there with a fairness in beauty with an air of defiance. Augustus was there in sternness and staunch bourgeois attitude speaking for all.

"All I need to know is what happened in the apartment in Edison Manor. Do you know? Whomever you are?" The detective said with a short temper.

"If you are referring to the alleged murder, I do not have all the answers. What I do know is Ty was triggered on that night. He is the vessel, and that attack was meant for him or rather us. It was the Immortali that interceded and stopped it by kidnapping me from the apartment. He wouldn't come with us. I heard his screams as something tore him apart. I haven't seen him since. I'm telling you that I know nothing about it." He said putting his head between his shackled hands on the table in frustration.

"Mr. Williams you are going to have to come up with a better defense than that. Let's say that I believed your story and I knew something about this secret society that you claim rescued you from the fate that Mark received.

Has it crossed your mind that the beast that you or whatever you want to call the apparition of the combination of you might have been what attacked Mark? Has it ever dawned on you that this secret society has strings and connections that are in every facet of government and political affiliations?

You can't be the only person that has had an altercation with them?"

All the detective's questions and hypotheses ran through Augustus's mind. He has never thought of the points he made. He sat in silence as all the twists of facts realign in his mind. It could be that he has been a pawn in a scheme that is woven together by powers that have been maneuvering at each turn. As it stands, only he has seen them. Only he has seen the past in relation to the present in visions and dreams. He only has a story based on what they have told him. Detective Choo has awakened a rethought, a second guess. The truth is so ambiguous now.

The detective continued with the flood of information and reality checks that stung in accusations.

"In fact, Mr. Williams, we never found a body, although there was an obvious struggle and a lot of blood in the apartment." He paused to see Ty's reaction.

"We found nothing.

There is no Mark.

There is no record of him ever existing. The apartment was leased to an E. Hughes, and we suspect that is also you.

The blood we found in the apartment is all yours. The surveillance footage in the lobby shows only you are entering and returning. DNA never lies."

Ty was in shock and total disbelief at what he was hearing. In recall, he spins the memories of the last two weeks back like an old movie and it is not hard to question his own logic and sanity.

"This is not happening! You saw the scene in the train station. You saw Nate and Clymythious. They locked me up with Luke who is my son! You gotta believe me. If I tell you anymore, you really going to think I'm crazy! Something happened to me that no words or rational explanations can explain. Look at me Detective. Really look at me. The last I saw you; I didn't look like this. I didn't feel like this." Ty said while pulling his now curly tresses that waved back on his head streaked in gray.

Years have evaporated from his now softened face and skin. His hands were smaller sleek and gentle. There was an obvious change in him that he pleaded with Detective Choo to notice, hoping it would give some validity to all that he was saying. If he had something to confess, it would be that the only thing he was sure about was the change within himself. Where once he was comfortable in his skin, he now isn't. The question of why he was the way he was wasn't important anymore and it made lucid sense. Ty was gone. Emily was at rest in his mind and out of all that he has been through, Augustus has returned.

Choo said no confirmations to any of the strange happenings he witnessed. It all was too fantastical to report.

What he did know is that he had a flurry of press and inquiries about the guy in front of him. He just wanted to have answers that would be easy to report to his supervisors and fellow detectives and officers. No one would believe the story if he told it as he saw it happened. It infuriated him that Ty had no explainable alibi or defense, and his escape and recapture made him, and the other officers look like fools.

"You fucking freak! Why don't you just take a plea for insanity and get this over with. A judicious course of action would be the result, and it might help you and get you in a good mental institution. Otherwise, you have no friends. If I release you, the press will eat you up, and if they didn't, the Imortali would persecute you until you yielded whatever cult or spiritual agenda they have. It's not my concern. I should just let you go and go home to my wife and kids. Clearly, you are demented schizophrenic and a danger to yourself than others.

Augustus sat in the wooden chair and replayed all the past two weeks in his head. The pressure of it all was only relieved by escaping in his own mind. He closed his eyes, and in his head, he was in a lavender field on a summer's day in Edison's Edge Park. He was Emily, but this time there was no fear or dread. She was tranquil and serene amongst the flowering purple petals that bathed in the sun. The memories of rolling in them in the night with their dew petals speckled on the lovers' bodies in passion were fresh. Although she was alone in the field, Nate was racing in her thoughts as well as Ty's. All the painful memories were washed away in the stillness of the field. The sun felt warm on her ebony skin and flower aromas carried in the summers breeze. She was contemptuous. She wasn't smiling, but the inner turmoil of the past visions of her were not there. We closed our eyes, and the haunting words filled the memory in Detective Choo's office.

"Seek the path of dead and forgotten and travel to Edison's edge. There you find what others trodden and bid love's eternal pledge." Augustus said out loud for in his mind he was not there.

Detective Choo stared at the perplexing words and state of Augustus. His eyes were despondent to him, and he snapped his fingers in his face as if trying to wake someone out of a hypnotic trance.

"Mr. Williams, I need you to stay with me. You are talking gibberish. You can act crazy if you like, but that will only force me to call in a professional and you will not be leaving anytime soon if I do that."

Augustus did focus on the detective, but it wasn't his small voice that he heard. The words that came from his suspect were now in the voice of Emily. She locked into the detective's slanted eyes and spoke,

"It ain't me you are fooling. I's sees through you sir. Ain't that boy's fault for nuffin. It was him that fought and kilt the beast. It was him that ne'er hurt nobody. You and them that want to hurt em will pay for all the hurt you's done to my family for over a hundred years. You's think you are innocent from the guilt of chasing me to my death at Edison's Edge?

You are not! If you's harm the boy, the fate of my family will become the fate of yours. Vengeance will be ours." She said.

The Book of Emily

Choo didn't like hearing a threat to himself or his family. He jumped out of the chair and pointed his small finger in the apparition's face, knocking over the chair he was sitting in.

"Are you threatening me?" He belted in anger.

Emily never stopped staring through him with eyes like a python preparing to strike. Choo could feel the energy welling up inside of her and he didn't want to show it, but he was fearful.

"Let me tell you something you fucking freak. I ought to release you right now to the press and reporters that are waiting to chew you up and spit you out. If they don't do it, then the Immortali will when they catch up to you. As a matter of fact,..." He said while he was stacking all his notes together to leave until a knock was at the door. He continued rambling while he answered the door that was behind Augustus.

"You are on your own, and as soon as I get the property assessment and the trespassing charges in the system, I will be looking for you too Mr. Williams."

Emily heard murmured conversations at the door, and it swung open. The person who came in stood directly behind him, still whispering with the detective.

"Ty let's go! They can't hold you here any longer." Emily knew the familiar voice. *"You remember me, Ty? I am your lawyer Philonius De Canton."*

As he stepped in front of the table and threw release papers in front of him, Philonius knew he wasn't addressing the Ty he knew.

"Emily?" He said while nervously reaching to lift his head so that he could stare directly at the new being he saw before him. He tucked Emily's wavy hair behind his ear. A desperate move to calm the situation down. He knows that what could happen would not be good for anyone in the room.

"We got to go Ty." He whispered. *"I have some people that want to see you. Don't let this situation get out of hand. I have filed all the papers for your release, and we can leave. If you want to see Luke, then you need to cooperate."* Philonious was convincing until she saw the tattoo of the Immortali on his withdrawing hand. Chairs and tables vibrated like an earthquake was underneath the building. She leaped out of the chair and grabbed Philonious by the throat, throwing him against the wall like a rag doll. Philonious outweighed her by at least 30 lbs, but the fury that charges out of Emily was no match.

"For centuries you have been slaying my ancestors in a murderous plot to control the future of man, and now you think that I will walk willingly to death?" She said standing over the shaken lawyer. *"Ain't goin like that no more. Tell Clymythious that I am coming for him. Harm my son and I will kill all involved. Do you hear me?*

No weapon will protect you!"

Rushing through the door were frantic officers that heard the disturbance in the small room. What they witnessed was hard to believe. One small man that has broken the restraints, and a scared detective is holding on the wall in fear on the other side of the room.

"Get them out of here! They are free to go!" He said refining his composure in front of the officers.

Philonious crawled off the floor and straightened his tie and suit jacket while gathering his papers and briefcase. Choo signaled to the officers to let him go. Already the situation was out of control. He wanted the entire confrontation over. He cannot write any of it in a report. It would sound far-fetched and delusional.

"I got what I need. Both of you get the hell out of here!" He ordered.

Philonious turned back to Emily before he opened the door to say one thing. The room stiffened in pause as he turned to say it.

"This is not over. You will be hearing from us.

He cracked the door and reporters, and cameraman jammed their path out of the room screaming questions with bright lights and cameras. Their comments were boisterous and aggressive.

"Are they indicting him?"

"Is it true that he hid the body?"

"Is it true he escaped from jail?"

"Rumors are saying that he is a she. Can you elaborate on that?"

Philonious ignored them, pushing through them with them trailing behind him bullying him for a comment. From inside the detective's office the busy sounds fade as they chase after the sacrosanct lawyer. The silence in the room was thick. Choo with his incredulous blank expression, and Ty awakening more and more as if out of a slumbered stasis. A light knock at the door signaled Detective Choo that the hall was clear. It was finally the end of what might be the most unbelievable night that challenged both the men's ideologies. It was the revelation of the duality of himself that has been questioned in both. The detective's spin on the facts could be real, and that would mean that Augustus is either emerging into conscious clarity or delving deeper into an abyss of uncertainties. There was so much said, and so much that needed to be said. The alleged murder, the escape from the police in Edison Manor, the battle at in the tower, Choo unusually is lost for the concluding words to say to Ty. His shaken confidence has cracked the professional and aloof exterior and dismantled his cocky demeanor.

"Detective I can see how it appears that this all could be a deranged accounting of a madman. There are no rational explanations I can use to make a rational defense. What I do know is that two weeks ago I was a man that was divided in internal confusion. What looked like probable insanity with visions that made no sense and the awakening of senses that without this journey, were cancelling out all of the normal consciousness I was desperately trying to clench to. I was losing my memory. I was opening old ones that weren't mine and as long as my mind fought for its own ration and dominion, I would be insane until I let them converge. As the adventure and things unfolded and revealed more, I felt a metamorphosis that I couldn't deny. With the death of Tyson from within, birthed more power than I knew to do with. I accept this change. I look at it as a cocoon that has peeled away, leaving a winged new creature that is very young, yet very old and powerful. I am Ty, Emily, Augustus, and many more awakened into one. Knowing this has given me the sight to see that everything has a reason and course of life. Mine is to be blessed with eyes that remember the past with sights on tomorrow. Death is not an enemy, but a gateway to the next flight of wings yet spread."

It was almost dawn when I walked free from the detention center into a new night more atoned and purposeful in the fortnight's aftermath. The dark sky was nailed in a moon that I never noticed before. Not quite full anymore, she shined like a pendant amongst a velvet violet backdrop, making the surrounding stars look like crumpled edges of a once smiling full moon. She no longer represents time passing. Even the air was sweet in its dew-like breath. The coming morning coated everything in its mist and my face felt every minuscule droplet. Still was the sound as Baltimore slept. I had nowhere to go and no one to escort me there. No hammering press, no prying police officers, no friends, or family. Just the night.

The serenity of the slumbering city was peaceful and lonely in its inactivity and abandoned bustle. I strolled slowly from the stasis, aimlessly walking anywhere that would lead me out of the commercial district that was soulless and dead to the peninsula of neighborhoods crowded on its edges. The desolate streets of downtown left my thoughts alone, and echoing in the barren cement and steel empty businesses. Escape into the neighborhoods at least offered a distraction, although Baltimore's night activities are dangerous and far from entertaining.

I felt comfort in the stacked row houses with the identical marble steps and iron railings mirroring themselves in alignment and symmetry. Now, more voices than my own were owning the night. Besides the ones that seeped through cracked windows and dark porches, one I heard was familiar. It called me by the name it knew me as...Emily.

In the shadows of an old elm stood Nate. He wore dark clothing that camouflaged him in the shadow of streetlights. Despite it being a warm night, he wore a long duster with only a black tee shirt and dark fatigues. His large and statuesque silhouette, even without light, dominated his space.

Before I heard him say anything I felt him.

Not in physical touch but feeling him as a presence. What I couldn't distinguish was whether he was a foe or a friend. He stood at the front of the corner house before an overpass, but I felt him block before. My senses have been heightened since the end of the fortnight. All the inherited senses from each part of my past now have a solid converged voice for all. It was they who recognized Nate. They, we, felt all the emotions of hundreds of years of allegiance and connection. I wanted to run to him, but I stopped just on the edge of the shadow in the yellow streetlight to feel what I was supposed to do or say to him. I had so many questions and explosive feelings and I wasn't sure how to handle them. He hadn't seen me since the old train station. He could reject the new being I have become. He may even be working with Clymythious, has already killed Luke, and is here to finish the lineage. My fear was not of death but of uncertainty.

"Come closer and let me see you." He said from the shadows.

"This night has been foretold many times, but I see with my eyes that no longer is tragedy marred in a masquerade of confusion. Full cycle you have emerged the victor to the seed of time. You have become the vessel, and much is in your future if you choose it."

That didn't sound like my executioner. Tension ebbed away with his words. Whereas they are words of victory, they are underlined in a tone of eminent conflict.

"You are ready to shed the confines of mortal limits. There is a new unexplored destiny before you Em. I have never left you and if you honor me to continue to walk with you through the ides of time, I will never leave you. I will bravely wield my iron aside yours in battle. Hast, it is not my choice. It is a sacrificial pledge made by me centuries ago. I ask to walk in the light and not in the shadows." Nate stepped out of the elm's streetlight shadow and waited for my reply. In my newness, I could see him as if for the first time with these eyes. Memories flooded like snapshots spindling images and emotions like strobes in my head. I couldn't move. I was paralyzed by my own neural awakening. Air was hard to swallow, and my heart felt as if it was going to burst from my rib cage. It was not just the flashes of memories of him, but the reflections of myself in them through his eyes. Each was different, but he was the same. All were now me.

Nate watched from just outside of the shadow, as if he could see that I was distressed in a collision of thoughts.

"Em, you can't do this here. Come with me and I will help you through all the answers you have to questions you have not yet thought of."

I know why he said it too. As I looked down at my trembling hands, I could see that I was seething in a bright royal blue that lit the sidewalk around me. There was no more fear and apprehension anymore. I could feel the air thinning and folding about me.

Nate finally walked over to me and grabbed my arm, whispering trusting words to cut through the cloud of amazement. In his eyes, was a focused passion that was familiar to so many memories that I walked with him to the overpass's edge that was stories above the blackened pit below us.

"*Let's go.*" He said as he pushed me to the edge.

The cold damp updraft from below swept up and sent chills through me.

Is he asking me to jump to my death to complete this transition?

Should I just walk on his blind trust and step into the steep darkness?

He felt me stiffen in doubt at the edge of the embankment. If he wanted to, he could push me from it with ease, but he wanted me to do it, although he could sense my resistance. He smelled of old myrrh and lavender amidst his own smell that coaxed me to just do it and trust him.

"*Em, this is not a request. Luke is out there exposed like us, waiting. If you can't do it for yourself, do it for him, and if that isn't enough...do it for me.*" He said while loosening his grip on my arm and leaping off the edge.

I screamed in terror as he disappeared into the cloaked darkness.

"*Nate!*"

From misty cool depths I heard him say,

"*Now Em!*"

All I could hear was my own doubting voice repeating over and over,

"You're going to die!"

Misty upsurges of wind brushed my face and thundered in my ears. I was not afraid. It would only be a couple of seconds now till something definite would be inevitable. The seconds seemed to crawl slowly with my racing anticipation of sharp-pointed rocks, or a shallow creek bed that they would find my fractured body in the light of day. Or maybe there were old, splintered rail tracks that bounced my writhed body into some brush like forgotten roadkill, or worse a lonely splash in a murky damned reservoir to wash up weeks later and puzzle everyone as to who I was. In that moment of surrender came tranquility I wasn't expecting. Thunder waned and gale winds were replaced with rushing water in a far distance that felt reassuring in its splashing tumble the dark.

Stepping off the ledge did not send me down and flailing for my life to death. My resistance to falling had me mid-air, hovering in a now dark violet haze that ringed in the damp mist. Not like flight, but certainly not like falling. Standing on an invisible ground with my eyes shut tight like a blind lightning bug.

The sound of huge wings whistling in the wind was just out of view. I knew it had to be Nate. He swooped from above and cradled me in his soaring descent in a perpendicular glide.

"Go Dad!" came a grounded cheer from below.

"Someone awaits you. It is not only I that hopes for you." Nate said.

The earth below us was speedily rushing under us and branches snared and broke beneath us as we greeted her. The closer we came to the ground the clearer the mysterious surroundings removed the mask of night. The water I heard was the sound of a rather large damn stream with overspill rolling off its walls. I looked over Nate's shoulders to see the overpass now far off in the distance. It looked small compared to the engulfing forest. An occasional car would ride across it, and it would ache in sounds as it crossed over it. With only a couple of feet left till we reached a canopy of land next to the gurgling stream; Nate tightened his grip around my ribcage and under my cradled legs. His feet hit the moist moss with a calculated thud, only taking a few small steps from the vertical velocity.

"Wow, now that was an aerial show! You guys looked like a ballet in the sky." The new Luke said while emerging from the bushes. *"Ty, or Emily, or Augustus or whatever you are, if it weren't for that bright ass light, I wouldn't have believed. One thing is for sure, you could be seen from miles away."*

I ran over to him and hugged him tightly. Just the thought of all the times I thought he was dead made me want to hug him tighter. As my eyes adjusted, I could see he still had his new wings that were extended, and he had a reborn youth. I could see the face of the infant from Edison Edge resemblances. Through it all, he only had a handkerchief tied around his leg where his father deceptively stabbed him.

"Uh, Ty, you can let me go now. You know that I don't go like that even though you are my mother." He laughed. He started out down a path through the trees, talking to himself and chuckling.

Nate stood in the cast of moonlight, motionless and slightly bewildered. Whatever thoughts that were crowding in his head, were forming a conclusion.

"Izzy is a good boy. You should be proud of him. What you did for him long ago is no different than the sacrifice he has done for you. It was him that turned and told the jail guards about the danger you were in in there. It was him that convinced Philonious that he was on their side to ensure your escape. He knew who you were and couldn't tell you. Without his orchestration, I couldn't have found you, though you were never totally lost. I have no promises of safe tomorrows or rekindled lost time. All I can say is that I have never left you. Through centuries of time in any form you were in, and I will fight to always protect you and our son Em. The hardest part is done. You blossomed into the Vessel. You are all one and it will be your greatest power in what happens. My oath is to be here, regardless if it is by your side or in the distance. I have waited for you Augustus, Frederick, Emily, Tyson, Savannah, Elizabeth, Sven, Josiah, Cadan, Rose, or Neb..."

I interrupted him and grabbed his arm leading him to the path after Luke.

"Em just suits me fine."

Chapter 7

The threesome scurried along the gurgling night stream guided by the full moon's light. Above, the monolithic overpass occasionally would hiss with the tires of stray cars that careened over its back in complaint. Crystal-bubbling water smelled of moss and drainage from the runoff of a dormant city asleep.

"Keep up Em! We need to meet the county line by dawn; besides, it smells like rain approaching." Nate warmly said while crushing twigs and dry branches, making a path for Ty to follow.

He could not look directly at me. His eyes whispered in words that were soundless. Their longing was to be with Emily, which was just short of what I could ever be. After a while, I would allow him to steal the moments and pretend not to notice his study. In them, I was equal to Emily, and only in those moments did his heartthrob come alive again. Sometimes, I would forget that he was in that special place of memories and catch him, only to have him be clumsily embarrassed at my witness.

Yards ahead, Uncle Luke's rapid steps were almost running. Old age was not his foe any longer, and he sprinted like a free man no longer bound. Nate's pace was seemingly in avoidance, disguised in the fleeing of the unseen pursuing enemy. Far into the dark, the gigantic overpass shrank in the distance of the clandestine travelers. Slowly, the branches pinged in snaps of water droplets from the dark skies. The further they escaped, the louder the droplets began to sound like cheering applause at a lynching. Cold water saturated the

Renaissance clothing I was wearing, and I shivered uncontrollably, wrapping my arms around me as the weighty clothes got heavier and heavier. The shelter of a huge maple tree forced me to take refuge and hang back. Having not slept in days and the chill of the damp raining night is overtaking my courage and resilience. Maybe I can wait this out and catch up to them later, was my thought as I bundled under the tree, teeth chattering, and lost in a whole lot of second thoughts.

As the rushing puddles of water surged around the tree's base, I hadn't noticed that the once small stream was swelling close to my only shelter. What once was bubbling and clear was now roaring and muddy. In the distance, I could hear Nate calling back. He didn't notice that I was not close behind. Soon, both he and Uncle Luke's voices were distraught and yelling to locate where I was behind them. I tried to respond to them, but my weakened cries were drowned in the now river-like steam. I would have to find safety soon. My feet were covered up to the ankles with the rising water. My vision was blurred by the gusting winds, and only in flashes of lightning did I see them searching frantically near me.

"There he is! Over there by the water's edge. Luke, give me a hand. The water is close to sweeping him away. Hold on Em!"

The two closed in saying encouraging things to keep me calm, but their faces were faces of worry. I had no idea that I was very close to being washed away in a swift-rising current. My body wouldn't have been found for weeks downstream if they hadn't doubled back.

I felt Nate's large hand grab my shirt and climb away from the treacherous edge in an iron grip that trembled in its own clench. Where I should feel relieved and rescued, I felt stupid, and weak as Nate muttered ambiguous banter as he hoisted me by my arm up an embankment. There wasn't a road, light, or anything that would resemble civilization for miles. We had been traveling for a couple hours and the cloak of night is not only hiding us but disorientating me.

I think Nate is angry. He is dragging me to a clearing ahead and when the flash of occasional lightning strobes, I can see his stature and focused facial expression. He looks prepared like a fisherman in the unfriendly weather, whereas I look like a soggy, burdensome fool who could have died. Luke was directing at the top of the clearing as we reached it; his questions weren't to me but to Nate.

"*Is he alright? He is not hurt, is he?*

Poor little fella. We should have put him in front of us. He might be the Vessel, but he is still mostly feebly human."

Nate stopped and released me as we reached Uncle Luke. He was breathing heavily, perhaps from the haul or, more likely, from the close, harrowing call with me and the water. He sat uphill behind me as Uncle Luke attended to me, checking for injuries.

"*He's shivering and freezing! Ty, look at me. Are you hurt anywhere?*"

I didn't answer but shook my head no while lifting up in marsh edge grass that felt fluffy and lumpy in its tuft to see Nate. Wet clothes are clinging to my small frame and my words stutter as I try to convey my well-being.

"I I I'm okkkkkkkay. JJJJust a little ccccold" I fight to say hoping that Nate would see that I am stronger than I really am. It didn't work.

Rain fell as hard as any storm could, and my composure was slowly regaining, but exposure to all the elements came at a cost. In this storm, after the past couple of days and the fight on fortnight, has left me too fragile to travel. Both men had looks of concern on their faces.

Nate grimaced at Uncle Luke, who moved out of the way and came to my side. His dark eyes said uncertainty and anguish.

"*Em, my darling, in you lies the future of a line of vessels of past and of future. He looked at Uncle Luke as if in a confirmation.* "Fight for not only yourself, but for so many more. Odds favor extinction, but you are my one chance to change all that fate has destined. You must forge through this."

Nate stood up, towering over me. He looked at the crying sky and then to the ground at his feet, where I lay drenched and depleted.

"*Hold it, Nate! You're gonna hit him again! If so, I gotta stop you. That last smack in the tunnel was a wallop. We gonna have a fight if you do.*" Uncle Luke is standing toe to toe with his father, prepared to fight in the middle of the cloud-burst-soaked clearing. When Nate took his duster off, Uncle Luke began dancing and raising his guard like a fighter.

"*Nooooo, I'm fine, guys. Don't fight.*"

Nate stood holding his coat in hand as if he thought about the battle between them. With his coat off, he looked more muscular than Uncle Luke. They were similar in height but not in pound for pound. Nate was far larger, and the battle would have been short. Instead, he kneeled down, put the coat over me, and sat beside me, staring at the now foolish-looking Uncle Luke like an angry father. Luke calmed down and sat a little further in the clearing to keep a distance from the pre-empted confrontation. He sulked uphill behind us as rain battered off him. The confrontation might have been avoided, but he kept a watchful eye, still not trusting the outcome.

"Rest Em, the change has exhausted you. I shouldn't have pushed you so hard. I cannot let consumption take you again away from me." His eyes said so much love that I relaxed as the now cool rain pecked on his duster over me. Sleep overcame me.

I awoke to hear the two talking and making plans. The early sun was beginning to creep on the low orange horizon. The rain had subsided, and I felt refreshed. Nate didn't feel me awake as I curled my head out of his lap. As long as I didn't flinch or move his hand off my shoulder, he would be unaware that I could hear their conversations.

"Pop, what we going to do? When the sun rises, we will be fully exposed. We are on somebody's land and might not be welcome."

"True, Luke, but as with the scorned sun comes also the curse of daylight. I will become what I am, and all will see, and we could face certain prejudice. We are not far from the city's edge. Where I was hoping we could reach is an old, abandoned rail station. There, we could rest and plan for our nocturnal escape. Just feet from here are the old tracks covered in weeds and brush. Go ahead of us and make sure we are not walking into a trap."

"What about Ty? Look at him! Something is different in him as the approaching morning comes. Does he know about his burden, like yours, that will change with the sun?"

What Uncle Luke was referring to was a change that Ty hadn't noticed while awakening. Overhearing them talk forced his curiosity to reveal his consciousness. As he looked up into Nate's face, he saw him blush with delight as he stared down at him. Stiffened by the sleep in the clearing, Ty sat up and understood what Uncle Luke meant. His form had changed. His hair was once again longer, and his familiar masculine form had diminished to a softer, more feminine one. He had seen this before when he was upset and raging in blue flames, but never in a natural state.

"What is going on, Nate?"

"Why do I feel different?"

The two men said nothing. There were no words to say that could explain what they saw. Each saw something so prolific that words choked in their throats, although they struggled to not look astonished. In Uncle Luke's eyes was almost humor and delight as he stared at Ty. His gaze went from smiling at me to watching Nate's response to my question. Nate's gaze was far different. His eyes watered in happiness, smiling within themselves. I had to see what they saw. My hands could be lying as I felt the soft curl of lengthy, soft, wooly tresses. Everything is definitely different. I had to know. Down the grassy embankment was the now bubbling stream. I jumped up and ran to its edge to look into its now calm reflection and see what they see.

The water's edge lied. I don't know who is staring back at me in it. This can't be happening. In the rippling stream, I saw Emily staring back at me. She is not quite the Emily in the visions, but she definitely is present. Cheekbones defined and high, full lips, and eyes that were mine, is what I saw. It is as if looking at myself- but not. As I checked the rest of me, some things were new and some were no longer, and I felt robbed.

I screamed as loud as I could in disbelief.

"Oh God, what's happening to me!" banging the reflection to not see it anymore with my fist, splashing the bank's side water in a desperate attempt to rid the mirror.

Nate and Uncle Luke left me alone as I eventually lost the battle with the mirror and was weeping at the water's edge, now wet from attempting to shatter the deceptive mirror with my splashing hands. When they came to console me and explain what they thought, I again saw them look at me as if I were someone they knew, but I didn't. Awkward glances over my now feminine being stung in unprepared circumstances. The wet clothes clung to the new form, curving, and clinging to my breast and hips. I have never been shy, but this form feels stripped from dignity on the water's edge and Nate could sense it. He ran to the edge and wrapped his coat around me.

"Irony has a sense of humor. By night, I return to the Nate, you know and by day, you return to my Emily. Life laughs at our discomforts. Come, we must keep moving."

In his grasp, the punishing morning sun slowly was transforming him into a creature of the daylight. He held me close in an effort to adjust for more hold on to the waning night embodiment. I felt his body swell and his breathing against my breast increased as his large wings emerged in the now orange sunrise.

"C'mon, you two!" Uncle Like interjected from the clearing, *"We ain't got no time for a reunion this morning! This is not how we die!"*

His grasp let me go and he has totally converted to the creator of light, bursting out of the shirt and pants he had left on. Again, he was standing there glorious and naked except for his weapon harness on his shoulder. Hearing his son plea for safety, he asked no questions, turned to lift me up on his shoulder and began to run at a pace I could have never kept. Each step of his hooves imprinted the earth with huge thuds that had strides that would have been three of mine.

"Now we talking!" Uncle Luke said, running beside him with the same agility and pace in jubilation.

We ran from the water's clearing into adjacent woods using the canopy of trees as our only cloak. Their objective and course, which I heard when they thought I was asleep, was the old, abandoned rail station. At the turn of the century, Baltimore's industrialized period had advanced to a new line of railroads that service commerce and docks. All other antiquated local stations and tracks were long forgotten, overgrown, and hidden in areas that once nourished the local farmland community. Judging by the sun, it was about 10 am, and we have been traveling for at least two or more hours following twisted, rusted tracks, forgotten areas, and phantom thoroughfare.

"There it is over there! I can see it between those two hills. Let's hurry, we are almost there!" Nate yelled as he ran far ahead of us.

The longer we traveled, the more my now delicate frame ached in pain from the jostling as his massive arms and shoulders held me tightly through the steep, treacherous hills, rocky gorges, and craggy cliffs that he jumped off and soared in gentle winds to hoofed landings.

"Please, Nate, let me walk the rest of the way. We haven't seen Clymythious for hours. I need to stretch and adjust myself."

I lifted my shirt up to show the slight bruise from bouncing on his shoulders so. My smooth brown skin was bruised in blue discoloration and hot to the touch. He blushed as he looked at the injury.

"We need to get you somewhere to rest so I can take care of that bruise. I forgot that I was carrying Emily and not Ty. I could have been gentler and more considerate to whom I was carrying. Sit for a minute and compose yourself. We only have a couple of miles left. Can you see that small building on the left in the distance? It's not that far and we can walk the rest."

In the mid of the day, the sun was at its highest with its warming rays that melted the chill of the Fall night away. It felt inviting on my skin, and I laid in the moss and fern that bedded out feet. Nate's warm duster now was hot and sweaty from the shoulder saddled carry. I dropped it off my shoulders and let it fall to the ground in a huge stretch. Eyes closed, face in the sun swallowing each ray, I felt invigorated by a cool breeze that crossed through the changing leaves of the forest.

"Perhaps you need some water Em, I mean Ty. You need to stay hydrated. We know not what comes in the future."

Now is not the time to worry for me. A personal inventory felt good as my hands inspected my transformed womanly figure. The clothes I was wearing were now tightly fit and the seams were tortured in their bind. Nate's eyes followed my hands as I slowly went over firm breasts and hips. Neither were large, but much more than what I was accustomed to as Ty. As Ty, I was never shy or prudish, but in Em's form, it felt natural to clutch the opening in the strained shirt to hold its edges together. More interesting was my exploration of my groin and lower extremities. It perplexed me that a piece of me was missing. I felt no loss, but I still ran my hand over the area to ease my manly concerns about its disappearance. I stopped when Nate's breathing interrupted as it got louder and louder. His nostrils flared in uncontrollable grunts while gazing at my new form and personal inspection, choking on air as it must have quickened in his mind. Oddly enough, I found pleasure in his bridled discomfort. Here is this massive simile of a man cast in the light of a daylight curse, naked in his form unabashed, and before him is the love that he has surrendered everything for. His eyes danced in excitement, with his whole body in tow in excitement, too. I never flinched or mocked him in his entertainment, though he gave in to his reluctance and ran off to find water for me. Before he returned, I had removed the ill-fitting clothes bound the shirt in a knot in a makeshift brassiere and wore his trench coat tied around the waist by its belt as a temporary dressing gown. In that brief moment, I could take a personal moment to find that everything was anatomically correct...for a woman. I hadn't noticed that on the hill far above me, secretly drinking the unobstructed view, was Nate. He approached as I tied my now longer curly hair with the frazzled threads of the pants I could no longer fit. He gave me a flask full of water and found the words that choked him minutes before.

"It's always been you Em, always."

Chapter 8

"Are y'all coming, or what? I was damn near at the station before I noticed you guys was way back here." Uncle Luke said, running back to Nate and me.

"Damn Ty! What the fuck did I miss? Wow!"

"Please, Uncle Luke, don't make this more difficult and uncomfortable than it is. I had to get out of those wet clothes." I said, opening the split of the duster to keep my footing through the brush.

"You don't look uncomfortable to me! And stop calling me Uncle. Luke is cool. I'm glad I backtracked. Y'all standing wide open, staring at each other, looking like Beauty and the Beast or something. Woo-wee, you sure clean up good!"

Nate said nothing and forged in front, pushing Luke aside with ease, and disgruntled hostility. He didn't find his humor amusing. With a gait three times ours, he soon was a distance away from us, thwarted by only the trees that dwarfed him in comparison; Luke and I struggled to keep him in our sight line, and soon gave up keeping up with him. We could see the station not far off. Its once-exposed tracks still deterred the weeds and forage from overtaking its place history; although they only surfaced in sparse spots like driftwood in a sea, they carved and wound owning the right to once had been.

Luke was quiet in the remaining journey. He had something to say and was waiting for the opportune moment to say it. In the sunlight, he looked more like Nate than I had noticed before. Strong chiseled face and jawline, eyebrows that twisted with every sentence like an explanation mark, dark smooth skin set with almond-shaped eyes, all features that, as an older man in jail, was hard to see.

"I'm proud of you, Ty. You handled all this shit, and you might have changed more things than you think."

Luke's words sounded like the Luke who gave me all the fortitude and wisdom to shield me from my own naive thoughts. Without his guidance, rage would have been my vehicle. We haven't spoken about all the things that he shared in small doses in the threatening fortnight. It was his protection and guidance that, at the time, seemed worthless and riddled like the truth. There was no one answer, and he fed me many in the fleeting period of time in the cell.

"You found the locket, but you had me worried. If I would have told you what was going on, or easy answers, you wouldn't have believed me. I have to admit, this is nowhere near what I could have possibly imagined."

Two strangers trailed behind one another, following forgotten paths in the face of a reality that there was more in their destiny than they foresaw. Eventually, they reached the old train station and safety. It would be months later till danger raised its ominous head in a county of Baltimore, being careful to blend in, Ty as Emily in the curse of day and Nate in the freedom of night. In time, the three made themselves comfortable in the advancing Fall that fell over the county of Montgomery in subtle hues and short days and long night's promises. A small cottage sat alone, surrounded by wild violets, asters, and deserted sunflower fields bowed in summer's wake, harvested by wild feral crows whose song declared the fields as theirs. Their rescuer was a descendant of the Lee family, Victoria Lee, whom Nate knew would harbor them from harm's way. It was her protection and compassion fueled by an old family tie that, over time, has not tethered. We arrived at night and Nate, in his night form, did all the talking for us, introducing us as two friends he was traveling with. There was a strange bond between he and Victoria. She made us comfortable with basic provisions and stepped outside of the small cottage to talk with Nate as if things they had to say between them were not for all to hear. As Ty, I had just a little twinge of concern. The way they looked at each other was tensioned in more than respect. She was a beautiful woman with long red hair that, by candlelight, glowed orange against it. To be a woman well over thirty, her fading summer tan gave her white skin the allure of health and beauty. She questioned nothing while in front of us but darting occasional glances at Nate while accommodating us with clothing and bed lodgings. It's as if she knew we were coming.

"Ty, is it? I have put a couple things that should be able to fit you on your bed. I hope tomorrow we can get a better fit for you."

There was a mix of comfortability and trust in her pale green eyes. On the bed were jeans and shirts in one pile, while in another, clothes that only Emily would want to wear- a couple of worn flowered cotton dresses and personal undergarments. She gave Luke shoes and overalls so that he could blend in with the community in the area. He and I were grateful for them, but I was more than curious how she knew about the day and night curse. For me, I am not sure which is the curse, and which isn't.

Nate, by night, was the same heroic Nate that I bumped into at Edison's Edge back in what feels like a long ago. He had already changed into jeans that struggled to contain his massive legs and hips and a flannel shirt to cover his daylight form and serve as an oversized shirt at night. Although I gave his duster back to him when we arrived, he never wore it while we were there. He saw it as something not belonging to him, or maybe he just didn't want to be close to the Em that he longs for and won't surrender to; either way, it now symbolized a pain and a joy we both would rather ignore. By day, I tried to stay in the garden, take a walk, or do any way I could to lessen the impact of him dealing with Emily. This also gave a chance for closeness to Victoria, who knew both Nate the beast and Nate the warrior man without prejudice. It didn't take long before she asked the backstory of he and I's connection. By day, she became a great friend as we gardened and did all the chores around the cabin while Nate worked in the barn, which became his own space he retreated to in the day, and Luke worked in the neighboring town as a carpenter as a jack-of-all-trades. Perhaps she was just as curious as I was to know the connection between them.

"Looks like we are going to have a severe winter this year. The early frost is a sign that it is going to be a rough one." Victoria said we were harvesting the greens and potatoes that were the last soldiers in the garden. *"You are welcome to stay at my place till spring. The guys will get through it better than you. Not saying that you wouldn't."*

I knew where the discussion was going, but I chose to not take a chance on speaking about the guys or my disposition, although she knows me as nocturnal Ty and the haunting Emily of the day. Victoria and Nate have some invested past together, and I figured that if I didn't inquire about it, then neither would she mine.

"Thanks, Vickie, but I will be fine here with the guys. We are kind of a family."

"A family as you and Nate together? I'm sorry if I am being nosey, Emily, but I see the way he looks at you. I just thought it was none of my business. It's obvious that he loves you day or night. How can you act so nonchalant about it?"

Her comments didn't go unnoticed by my senses. Her transparent concern was more about being more than curious or concerned. The earth dug deep in the hole in the garden that I forced with more transferred vigor, pretending not to be bothered by her remarks. There is a certain prying that a person does that is undeniably searching for answers in disguised compassion. In truth, I had no answers for her. Nate, Luke, and I are more than any family than I have ever known.

"Never thought much to it, Vick. He's a little weird like that, always staring and avoiding me. Besides, it's you who he looks at like that. So, what's up between you two. How do you know him? Give me some dirt, girl!"

The levity gave us an escape from the uncomfortable discussion we were having. I was so glad to have this unavoidable topic with her as Emily and not as Ty. I don't know why, but she had a distinctive way of how she behaved, as if the one was two. I am different in behavior in day than night; she felt closer to Emily because we spent the most time together. At night, she returned to her own home not far through the meadow closer to town. There were a few nights she stayed after dark at the cabin. At first, I thought it might have been me with which she was uncomfortable. In the still of the evening, with everybody in the moderate cabin, she became the only woman in a cabin full of men. After a couple of weeks and the onslaught of winter, I could feel that I was not the culprit. In the cold of a Maryland winter, Nate's hardened exterior warmed as the threat of danger lessened over time.

The sun was losing its daily battle with gravity and the frosty bite of a Fall evening signaled that we only had an hour or two before the change- not just the change between day to night, but a change from within. Victoria knew that it was a difficult hour for me. I have become comfortable with the conversion to Emily over the months, but it is always something I try to do alone, for it is never easy. I never wanted to be anything but a Black man, but each twilight comes to the sorrow of losing Emily to night and each day an expulsion of the strong Emily. Ironically, a sort of death for Ty and a birth for Emily. She is becoming more and more a part of my spirit, possessing far more than gender. The first time it happened by the water's edge felt relieving, while now that outlook is not only confusing and difficult, but it comes and goes with a price. There still remained the most obvious changes, but each day and night, behold less external acceptance and a deepening in the internal. Nate, Luke, Victoria, and I treat those moments as they are- without judgment.

Our normal departure would be us going separate paths in different directions, but this time, she stayed behind and watched me traverse the byways of the forest alone. Something was peculiar about her behavior today. She seemed not herself and was prying for information. The further I was away from her, the better I felt and allowed the transition to begin. It was easy to surrender to it rather than fight against it. When she was far off on the horizon, I stopped to change clothes to ones that were more suitable to Ty as the change moved fast. That's when I noticed that Victoria was standing feet away, quietly spying.

"So, what is so interesting, Victoria that you need a private visage to complete?"

She walked through a briar patch unbothered by the sharp thistles that was tearing at the bottom of her skirt. She moved as if she was hunting, with slow, deliberate steps and never leaving her eyes from mine as I tried to finish changing into pants.

"Ha, ha, ha! You're not much to look at as a mortal man. No wonder Nate finds you repulsive. I'm just saying, Dearie, you are a scrawny little man. I see you still wear that locket around your neck as some kind of protection charm or something." she said vehemently while she approached with the thickets almost appearing to slither at her feet.

"You know that's your mother when she was a little older than you. You look like her. Those dark pooled eyes, that tiny oval face with high cheekbones and full lips are a spitting image of her."

"Vickie, mind your business. I won't be your entertainment tonight. You have said enough today already."

Every sense in my body was electrified with the intense feelings of danger. Her grace through the thicket was haunting and cornering. In a flash, she came from feet behind me to in front of me out of the thickets.

"Before you run to Nate, let me tell you about your mother, Ty. There's a lot you don't know."

With her just a breath away from me, I could smell the pungent fragrance of night in her being. Her pale white skin burned, ignited by her in the orange twilight. Her coy, personal invasion into my personal space was alluring and deliberate. Her hands brushed my hair back and she gently kissed the corner of my lips while her eyes hungrily coursed over my Emily's dissipating form.

"She was as beautiful and enchanting as you, and we were as close as you and I. It is as if she is right here as I look at you. You don't mind, but I miss her so much. If she were here, she would let me comb her soft and curly wooly hair. It's always pinned up and neat. You should let it fall free. It becomes you," she said as she pulled a hairpin loose and the heavy tresses fell in relieved stress on my shoulders. Her closeness to me, with the vexing sweet tones and soft brushes with her fingers through my tangled hair, had my heart racing.

"And why not?" Her moist lips cooed as she manipulated herself, making advances I did not refuse. I had been with women before, but not as a woman. I found my breathing pacing hers and my heart racing to keep up with the unknown. She saw my timid but flustered temperament and moved closer, smelling my hair as if it were scented with an elixir that intoxicated her. She moved behind me and let her lips trace over my shoulder blades while I locked my hands together between my legs. The feeling was new for me, and I liked it. Cooing behind me, she freed one hand to clutch my wrenching hands between my now moist groin and like a hypnotic snake she

slithers the other under my arm and danced her fingertip over my excited breast nipple.

"Let go, and go with it, my pet! Be a woman and this is what women can do between us."

Suddenly, the overwhelming sensations shuddered through me in multiple waves, and I let out a soft moan that embarrassed me. In the state of Emily, Victoria has subdued me using my state as a woman playing with naivety to manipulate. If it weren't for the darkening sky, the direction her and I might have ventured into the unknown pleasures I am sure I am not ready for. My insides were on fire while beads of sweat fought to extinguish them and cool them off. It was her soft hand caressing my breast under the cotton dress that violated the emerging emotions of Ty in the dying sunset.

"Sweet Emily, you know nothing of being a woman and I can take you on a blissful ride in discovery. Kiss me and taste me as I you. You know you want to. Your mother and I were close as this," she said as she slid her hand from my heaving breast to the locket Luke gave me. The one with the portrait of Emily in it and gave the control of rage.

She continued to coo sweet things about what only a woman could give me, but slyly, she had her mind set on getting the necklace from around my neck. I looked up and saw not the same Vickie who each day conversed, played, and did chores with me like a friend. What I saw was an evil hag with fiendish grins and age. What once was beauty and trust, was now just a serpent with divided motives and ugliness. I pushed away from her, baffled, and confused, as I saw the Vickie, I thought I knew was not there. She had revealed herself as a toothless old hag that was masquerading as the fair and beautiful Victoria. Gone was the fire-red hair, taunt skin, and youth. As I ran, I could hear her last words trailing off.

"You dare to mock me and run, child? Alone, you are a child, a hopeless fledgling among those who want things from you that you yourself cannot possess! Run chile, run, for soon you will be Ty for the last time!"

The decrepit hag didn't bother to chase me back through the forest to the cabin. She cursed some words that were indistinguishable, or in another ancient language, and the pit of my stomach wretched as she yelled them.

"Goodbye, Ty! You were a good man!" She laughed and cackled in the distance.

The last sun's rays disappeared along with Emily's form. I stopped in the forest to readjust my now too-big clothes and catch my breath. Control returned to me as Ty. I was born a man and as a man, I am confident, but all this weird stuff is off-putting. My thoughts are now in rage. Rage as if someone had molested my sister, mother, or child. I summoned up the courage to return back and find Victoria and, in anger, address her inappropriate transactions. I wasn't sure of what I would do, but the need to stand up for Emily was strong and it wanted revenge. For hours, I searched for her through the night forest till the chill was converting to the cold of winter. As my taste for revenge wore off, I headed back to the cabin through the bare-leafed trees and clear skies of the night till I heard travelers below me on a path chasing each other. It was Nate and Victoria. The two were so engrossed in their chase that they didn't see me on the rise above them. It was very dark underneath the trees and tall brush, but I knew the voices.

"So, what is it that is so damned important that I chase you out here to see Vickie? This is no time for your foolery."

Victoria, who was just ahead of him, stepped from behind a spruce tree, completely naked. Her fair white skin gleamed, and the streaked light that filtered through the forest canopy conformed in sensuous shadows; her red hair was illuminated like fire as she poised herself against the aged tree's base, fondling her own body in self-pleasure.

"Does this look like foolery to you, Nathaniel? Don't think I haven't been watching you stare at me with beast eyes and wild imagination."

I watched as she writhed and allowed her body to slither to the ground. Even from a distance, I could see that her every movement was a calculated act of seduction and something more than a physical lure. Nate reluctantly watched, hypnotized by a soft song she was humming. Even from the hilltop, I could see that there was more in play than womanly devices. Nate held his ground for moments until the compulsion to join the dance overwhelmed him as he moved closer and closer.

"Don't tempt me, sorceress. It is not your fair heart that I long for, but if I submit, will you promise no harm to Emily. She knows not your contempt."

"Nathaniel, how long has it been since you have been with a woman? What happens between you and I stays between us. What I offer you comes with no bond. Surely, you don't think that you will find your hunger quenched in that confused

seraphim of a man? There was a time where she had dominion over your heart, but that time has waned and crumbled like ancient bones in a forgotten graveyard- dust! Feed your lust on me and forget the bedded memories you honor. Come to me."

It took all my strength and reservation not to interrupt in anger and jealousy. He was being manipulated like a pawn, sacrificed to a vicious queen. First, he approached her and pressed her body between him and the tree, drinking her every exhale in his panted breath while she unbuttoned his shirt. When her lips kissed his, I knew he was captured. He placed both his large hands above her head as she untied the burlap shorts that fell to his feet. Still resisting except the kiss, the temptress used his outstretched arms and hoisted her hips in one back arching move on to his pelvis. I could hear him groan from the sudden rush of pleasure as she did it. Like an animal, he responded with deeper and deeper thrust while still holding his hands above her on the tree. His fight was lost, but he did not surrender completely.

I too was enveloped in their moment till I saw her eyes gazing up the hill at me. It was as if she wanted me to see her victory. Her fire eyes flicked with their win over his now sweaty shoulder to me in the exhibition. She could see me. She plotted the entire scene and manipulated my friendship to get to this point. She could sense my anger and was smiling with her arms around his neck in a clenched fist. I could not take anymore and settled behind the bush I was peering through. I could not leave nor watch. She whelped and moaned so that all the forest could hear their copulation, especially me. Whatever enchantment she had on him was also on me. Their rhythmic breaths became mine. I tried to bury my ears between my legs not to hear, but an ill wind chilled up my spine, merging their scene in a subtle commentary. It was the deep, calm voice of Clymythious.

"Look at them, Augustus. Look at how he makes love to her, like he never will to you whether you are Emily or not. Gaze into his total envelopment into her flesh. Does it not find you jealous of her possession? How quaint and primordial it is in the cast of night. I can feel your heart racing in longing. Pity it shall never be you- has never been. To him, you are a poor abomination, a facsimile, ephemeral imposter. It is I that has returned to you time and time again in the seas of time, yet you know me not in its hunt. Smell the passion of memories past that you refuse to acknowledge. It was you that many times in each form, be it man or woman, that I have loved like that. You have never known the feeling of rejection before."

The voice rode in the whispered wind, breathing on the back of my neck, taunting in mockery of my secret admiration from afar of the lovers. From its reared reckoning, I heard the memories of rejection and a scorned declaration from the enemy. I shuttered from each one as I peered into their ecstasy as they moaned and contorted to completion, quieting the forest in crowned excitement and, in Nate's final thrust, scattered the disturbed nesting sparrows from a spruce's limbs. The two fell limp on the moist canopy in exhaustion while I was wrestling with an amused ghost whisper that tortured things I would not admit or turn to put a face to. I knew the voice, but I didn't turn to it. I let it unravel in chills on my spine.

"Soon, I will defeat your reluctant heart or pierce it with my sword in damnation and loss. Augustus, see your future in our past or die in it. All the love and desire you have for that

pitiful creature of dishonor who is not worthy of your love, visit it upon me!"

The chilling words fled with them giggling and frolicking into the forest, and the bravery to turn around found nothing but intruding shadows with no soul in stillness. Bemused, Ty remained posted, overlooking the hiding place, questioning the complexed barrage of emotions in the face of possible danger from behind.

How can Clymythious be so close as to speak softly in his ear in a whispered current? The remainder of the night Ty spent pondering on the natural passion of the two lovers heaving and seething and whether he would tell Nate and Luke about what his eyes stole in secret. Clymythious came to him riding the wind and vapored away just as fast He sat on a slope of dew-soaked asters on the hill overlooking the cabin. In a couple of hours, Nate returned from walking Victoria home, creeping lightly and never went in the cabin; instead, he went to the barn, and I held fast my distance till I saw his light go out. Tomorrow I can make a better judgment, but as for this eve, I am without conclusive answers, but one. It takes only a small wind to change the hunter to the prey, and the wayward wind still prickled in Clymythious' taunting. Confusing emotions plagued my thoughts. If I had courage, or any remaining certainty of who I was, I might have found a rationale that could be a means for plying the evasive answers within myself regardless of their ugly truths. The moonlight on the hill and countryside felt solemn in recompense. Not jealousy, or envy, or tempered anger; it could neither smile nor cry; like me, it was on its duty.

Lost in his own thoughts and pity, Ty descended off the soft petal hill, only hearing the replay of songs in ecstasy moans and crickets courting in the naked night. The cabin's pillar of smoldering smoke spewing out of its chimney grew closer and closer as he approached it. This was not home, although the love within it was comfortable in its rustic bosom and sanctity. Each step merged in misty tears welled in his empty eyes of guilt as he sat alone on the old wooden cabin's porch, emphatic with fear and effort, keeping each trembled moment stealth. While the warmth and safety are just through its front door and logged walls where Luke slumbered, Ty couldn't take his gaze off the rustic terrain, accepting Clymythious' words and presence as a score he didn't want to hear, brooding in their reflection and very sound.

"An abomination " is what he whispered.

Somewhere out there were succinct answers to questions that groomed pain in lost explanation as the flanked moon sank to the Earth in death of night's courtship. With it comes the curse of day and the confusion of love and rejection. With it comes a new day and an old transcendence that was new to only him and just as old.

Within the hour, the sun will creak through the veil of night, compounding the night before, pleading in a struggle to find peace in its light. He knows that he will become her, and she has no answers to easily tell, but this night dispels Ty's confidence in his soul's options. Thoughts of composing his emotions distracted his awareness of the surroundings. He did not hear Nate's approach.

"I can hear your thoughts and although they are familiar, they cry differently this dawn Em," he said, sitting next to him.

Ty resisted looking at him, although he startled him. Over the months, Nate has had few words for Ty. By night, Luke is the only one who acknowledges him in conversation. The refugees share the small cabin in uncomfortable tension and recluse, speaking little about the dire situation or the evolving future.

"What is it that I can do to quell what plagues your mind and heart, Em? I know that this journey was not of your choosing. I, too, have voices that crowd my head. Forgive me if, in their avoidance, I have no answers to ease you. You see, undoubtedly, you are my true source of being and also my weakness."

In the fading darkness, his words were searching for an answer, too. As Ty looked up into his dark eyes, as in each time he looked into them, they excite in response. It is hard to hold their glimpse, but not tonight. Maybe he could sense the traitorous thoughts of rejection and unfounded humiliation. His eyes were full from bathing in Victoria's spell and lust; nonetheless, they fed on Ty's resentment.

Nate's silence after staring into Ty's solemn and confused eyes stumbled into wordless emptiness. He needed Ty be a warrior, even if it meant to fight him as well. What he saw was defeat in his eyes- a demoralized man. Not knowing how to address Ty has been the issue from the first time he bumped into him at Edison Edge Manor. Then, he allowed his curiosity to shed his preconditions in rescue, calming him with a kiss in the middle of the street in broad daylight. Now, he lacks the bravado he took then. Nate's thoughts privately interrogate themselves in want to encourage and nurture, but in the solitude of the retreating night, cannot feed the confusing emotions to Ty or Emily of day. *"Can it be that only in peril will I ever discard the barriers? I must be a fool to think that in this guy, there is some hope of kindling a love so deep as to revive itself with each generation."*

Not this time, not with this vessel. Unlike the vessels before him, Ty possesses the ability to connect all his past and the battle that lies ahead, the most important one for the world. Nate's pacing back in forth in front of the cabin in thought eventually led to him repeating his actions he did when he met Ty. Large arms lifted him off the cabin's steps, pulled him into him with little resistance and kissed him softly. He had forgotten the kinetic energy that no matter what form, felt like surging energy between them. Ty held him tight and wept while Nate made his best feeble attempts to share what he felt in the embrace.

"Why are you playing with me, Nate? I know the danger that you are protecting me from, and I am not afraid. You don't have to pretend. I can't let your past emotions govern mine."

In his arms, Nate could feel the heat of emotions surge within Ty and held him as tight as he could till he found the words to convey what he had betrayed his alliances to protect and keep. In his arms, he felt the transcendence in Ty as well as within him and with it, the beast ebbed in, and Ty reluctantly submitted to Emily in the break of dawn. He knew he had to release his massive grip on her fragile form and every second was priceless he held onto. It was Luke's thud of his knapsack on the porch that interrupted the moment.

"Aw, Mom, Dad, ewwwwww!" His humor is always sarcastic and perfectly timed.

"I hate to interrupt you two, but I have to head to town, and I am late already. What the hell did I miss? You guys have been avoiding each other for weeks and now you both have been out all night. Don't take this wrong Pop but do her...him or whatever already and get over it. It's getting crowded dealing with the four of you!"

Luke brushed past them both, laughing hysterically and disappeared down the path to town. His chuckles were only thinned by the early rise of morning sparrows' song as he got farther away leaving the two embarrassed and exposed in their day forms. Nate only snarled as he realized what has Ty so emotionally distant.

"Say it isn't so Em! You followed me last night, didn't you? It explains much. I will not explain my actions and you don't have to either. What you witnessed has no excuse except one of lust and desperate folly by Victoria. I fell to her ploy willingly. I owe you nothing. Can you say the same?

With what will we have if not complete honesty?"

His words cut like condemnation and hurt. He returned to the barn without waiting for a reply slamming the large door in anger. There was nothing Ty could say that would reverse his candid eavesdrop. Not only was he at a disadvantage, but the curse of day takes a minute for him to adapt to. It's why he fights so hard to allow it in private. The temporary death of his manhood each morning is sad in each returning one. Already, he is planning for Victoria's visit. Revenge will be unleashed for her deception and in it she will feel Emily's wrath. That much, he is sure.

CHAPTER 9

It wasn't long before Victoria was in the yard drinking from the well. How ironic!

Through the dry, rotting Venetian shutters of the deteriorating cabin, Emily peered at her unaware prey. In her head, violent, inexplicable urges seethed inside of her, calculating methods of revenge- thirsty and new.

"C'mon Em! I know you are not asleep." Victoria said, sounding refreshed and playful.

Delightful and soft, Emily answered her enemy's deceptive call, acting as if nothing was different, although everything was. What she heard was a war cry, and like a soldier, she prepared herself for battle. Revenge was a new taste, and it was bitter. She only wanted to give her enough of a noose to hang her in her guise and let her choking neck gurgle in surprise and anguish, and so, she presented herself as meek as any other cloudy morning, with innocence lost.

"Wow, Emily you look different this morning. I love your hair out and on your shoulders. What's the occasion? Is it for me, darling?"

"Yes, Vicky, it is for you alone, girl. What do you think? I pulled Nate's old leather trench out. I think it compliments my figure. It makes me feel so much like a woman. You know that feeling, don't you...darling?"

Winds scurried from the west, which meant a storm was coming. Darkening skies telegraphed that it was not long before it would be overhead. Emily stood on the porch letting the occasional gust blow the slit in the long duster open, exposing long, silky dark mahogany legs and bare feet as she leaned coyly on the porch's wooden support. Victoria's reaction was ill-adjusted by her almost arrogant, sensual demeanor. She watched on the well wall while Emily allowed the storm to almost radiate within her as she faced it, allowing it to wash sensuously over her in its disturbance.

"I was hoping we could forge for wild strawberries today, but it looks like we might have to wait till the storm passes. You are not afraid of a little water, are ya? You and I could just stay indoors?"

Victoria's ivory hand brushed the soft, woolly curls from Emily's nape of her neck. The chills Emily felt in every touch, she masked in aloof stillness, never turning out of the eastward wind. A forced smile is all that she wore, stone and emotionless to keep her snare open and inviting. Victoria has many times gestured how she and Emily could be more than friends, and Emily allowed the lure of it to be bait.

"You know Em, I can show you how to feel more like a woman...if you let me. There are pleasures that I think you know nothing about, and I think you want them, don't you?"

"Don't call me Em Vicky, but maybe I would like to feel more like a woman. And you think you are the woman that can do that?" She paused and let the words incite. *"Let me think about it."*

Victoria's soft fingers were now ever so lightly traveling down from her shoulders, slowly trespassing on her breast while speaking with heated breath in her ear.

"There are pleasures waiting for you if you wish. I can make you comfortable in them. I can show you how to explore what desires I think you secretively have. Your ancestors had them. I could tell you stories of love and passion that you and I could rival."

Finally, Emily saw her plan unfolding. She wanted to quiet the violent thoughts that had her heart pounding and racing in anticipation enough to continue the lure and get what she needed before she confronted her. It was more difficult than she imagined it would be. In preparation, she made sure that the trap would be irresistible, and it was working. Scents of patchouli, musk, and lavender invaded Victoria's senses from her skin. Even her hair was freshly washed in homemade scents of citrus, peppermint, and natural oils that drew her victim closer, unaware that she was not the hunter but the prey.

"You know nothing of my ancestors or what you think I have experienced. Perhaps you should be heading back home; the storm is going to be a short one, but nonetheless, charged in nature's anger." Emily said coyly, gazing into Victoria's fire-flecked eyes-only inches from her pouting lips.

Totally aware of what she was doing and in control of her allurement, Emily closed her eyes while Victoria's hands wandered over her body, leading to the eventual kiss that was gentle, sweet, and repulsive at the same time. What she was not prepared for was the intensity of her body conforming to sensual pleasures. Sensations that were perpetrating at first, but the more she danced to her prey's advances, the more she became aware of her own pleasures as Emily that were untapped,, and violently rushing in, mirroring the storm that broke overhead with thunderous lightening and ominous energy rolled in dark clouds.

"So, what will it be sweet Emily?

Shall we go and pick the last of over-ripened strawberries on the hill outside of town, or shall we take refuge and wait through the storm while I show you what you can only imagine?"

The first strike of lightning cracked through the fuming curling clouds and struck a tree near to them and set it on fire. This was no normal storm. It seems to manifest in Emily's disturbed, confused emotions, impersonating her anger and passion, both in destruction and danger. It was time!

With one push, Emily pushed Victoria off the porch and into the yard as the storm pelted them both in splattering raindrops. She landed in the water, soaked soil marbling her in the mud in juxtaposition to her pale skin. Winds amped up in the outburst of mounting anger while the relief of unexpected redemption changed the game for the two. She stood her ground on the nineteen-century cabin porch, awaiting Victoria's retaliation, holding her breath in tumultuous adrenaline. In the filth and mud, Victoria's expression was one of disbelief and surprise. She defiantly stood up in the wash of the hillside, fist clenched with her evil nature no longer camouflaged in flirtatious play, but now was gaunt and deceptive.

"Chile, how dare you raise combat with someone who meant you know harm. I was hoping that it wouldn't come to this, but you draw first blood. I summon all the powers of the Earth and universe to unleash that which you have no idea to battle. You bitch of time, whore of Babylon, false deity, and

mistress of dethroned gods. Feel my wrath as death surely has been courting you. The hour has come for you to meet your end. I see your true soul, although you lost it long ago. Pity that such a beautiful reincarnation of regal lineage will end here and now!"

Words continued and competed with nature's call as if Emily was her daughter and she was defending her temper. Victoria continued in Latin and other forgotten languages in incantations and curses while Emily composedly stepped off the shelter of the porch to duel her. Another jagged crack of lightning peeled the dark mass of clouds, brandishing a large sword for battle from their dark ceiling.

"It is not I that will suffer this day," she said as the sword fell to the ground at her bare feet.

Dead leaves of the hibernating forest blustered in whipping winds as she knelt to grasp it. She knew what to do with it. It is the same sword that conquered the savage pet of Clymythious, and in it was power that tapped into all the vessels in inheritance. Immediately in her touch, the sword began the virtuous transformation into the warrior of intense incomprehensible violence and ancient summoning. In hues of blue, she struck Victoria, just missing her except for a small slash on her thigh. Before she could finish her, a voice interceded,

"Stop Em!"

From the barn, Nate must have heard the ruckus. He ran up to Emily but did not dare touch her. Her blinding light, for him, made her unapproachable.

"Please Em, save your energy for those who oppose you. Her blood will not settle your jealousy. If you kill withoutconscious, you will not survive the battle you were born to fight. All that bestows you and your ancestors has been getting more and more powerful in preparation for the final battle. Check your damned emotions Em, for you have no discord with Vickie. Stop it now!

Stop it now goddamnit!"

Never has Ty heard Nate's roar. It was guttural and commanding, swelling up in him with wings outstretched and nostrils flared. Ty, in his daylight curse in all of Emily's power and rage, was obedient to Nate; after all, he was the reason and the accomplice in his feelings of betrayal.

His words quelled the raging storm and with its stalling surge, returned Emily to this world, thus saving Victoria's life and the spilling of unnecessary blood. In his eyes, Emily saw that she had one purpose, and it was not to turn Nate against her. He has been here to protect her. She fell to the ground in exhausted light and her knees sank into the same humbling mud that she penalized Victoria in. Self-pity was like quicksand in her lost vigor, like the ebbing storm. Nate's tucked wings revealed a distraught, vindictive, soggy, and mud-covered Victoria who rose to her feet and continued her incantations and chants; whatever they were summoning, they were summoning on Emily.

"Dark forces hear my plea,

By lovers' scorn and hearts that bleed,

Be my jury, evil throes,

Cast him into lunation's woes,

Dianna's curse shall come and go,

and she shall see seeds not sowed,

Curse the night like the day,

Bind her to her true loves way

But give her not what she seeks,

Until she gives up what she cannot keep."

Victoria turned and limped into the forest, cackling and cursing, waving the brush open with one flick of her hand. Nate never moved from towering over Emily. His initial maneuver was to protect Victoria from Emily's wrath, but he has heard many witches' curses and spells over the centuries, and he remained in his spot with a dual purpose, now protecting Emily from Victoria. He will not allow anything to harm his Em. If he wouldn't allow her to spill Victoria's blood, then he also would not allow Victoria to gain composure and hurt her.

"Em, are you okay?" he said, squatting down to her in the mud.

"Leave me the fuck alone Nate!"

He did just that too for a minute. He stood his ground but watched her scramble and slip and fall in the mud. Unlike Victoria, her dark skin left just the whites her eyes visible through the mud.

"Em, let me help you."

"No! Why don't you help your white girlfriend who think it's funny!"

She fell a couple of times, making her way back to the cabin. With each couple of feet, Nate wallowed behind her, sinking his large feet in it from his weight. Finally, when the last fall winced tears from her, he picked her up, cradling her in his massive arms as she fought, kicked, and wept out loud. It was futile, but she just didn't want help- not help from him. She cried over and over again to be put down, scratching and flinging, flailing fists in his grasp that were no more effective than a crying infant. As he stooped in the cabin door, kicking it open with his feet, she quieted to a whimper and sat in the wicker chair he sat her down in, despondent and averting his eyes. She was wet head to toe, but the mud on her face mapped tributaries where tears washed away the mud.

"C'mon baby, it's not that bad. I am not mad at you, if that is what you think, and that old witch Victoria has seen far worse battles. Calm down and let's get you warm and cleaned up."

She did not move nor look at him as he rekindled a fire in the old stone fireplace and dragged an old tub to the hearth to ensure that she was warm. Memories of a hearth like this one, aluminum and cold that he and Emily had on the Lee plantation over a hundred years ago, leaped through his head in deja vu. He wept with his back to her, stabbing the crackling embers of aromatic hickory wood as it roared to a blaze. The sounds of little voices of the children and of Emily busy back then were both joyous to remember as it was painful trying to forget. His focus was on the catatonic vessel bundled up in her own arms in the chair behind him.

The Book of Emily

Emily sunk in the warm, sudsy water, still not in the same room as Nate, eyes distant but unbelievably beautiful and unabashed in her naked ebony beauty. His words, like the water, washed over her in empathy.

"I used to bath you after you had Isaiah back in another time. Do you remember? Your hair was as beautiful then as it is now. Soft and curly. Not like mine, rough as a wild goat in the winter," he said taking her hand and putting on his beard.

"You were a spitfire then, as you are now. Just as cantankerous and sometimes downright mean, but that does not make you wrong. It's what makes you, my Em."

Down the path yards away, Luke was returning from his day working in town. He was singing, drunk, happy and being hoisted over someone who helped him home.

"I want you to meet the guys. They are my family. You gotta come in and meet them," he said as he got to the porch.

Nate hurried Emily out of the tub. She was just coming around and smiling a little as he told her of the memories of a simpler time. Besides, he didn't want to have to explain to Luke or a stranger the predicament of him bathing her, not that he cared about the way it would look, but he didn't want her to shy back into silence and resentment. He got her quickly out of the tub and got night clothes together for her as he heard him singing from far away.

"Nate, Ty, I want y'all to meet somebody," he said, stumbling up the steps on the porch.

"Oh, there you are you old dog! I want you to meet the sweetest lady in the whoooole world, Annie. She works in town at the general store. Annie, Nate...Nate, Annie."

The pine door was held to Nate's back as he stood outside the cabin to intercede Luke barging in, and Annie sat him in the only chair on it. He plumped down in it, still singing the same song over and over. From the pungent overpowering downwind from him, he smelled of whisky and tobacco, both he occasionally indulged in when he gets paid. This is the first time he has brought someone back to the cabin, though.

"I'm really sorry to meet you this way Mr. Nate, but he insisted on coming home tonight. Please to meet you."

"No need to apologize. He works hard and he gets like this occasionally. We really appreciate you making sure he got home and call me Nate."

"I want you to meet Ty too, Annie," he said pushing around Nate to go into the cabin. His foot kicked the door open, but Nate held him at the door's frame, blocking him. Both men paused in an uncomfortable vision of Emily still sitting on the edge of the bed, wrapped in the towel. It couldn't have been just a few short minutes while Nate was on the porch, and the two stumbled in the gaze to adjust to Emily still half wet and half naked on the goose-down bed.

"What the fuck!"

"What the hell are doing here?"

"And why she naked in here?"

There was no reason to answer Luke in front of Annie and he had no explanation. He needed a moment to talk to Luke alone to tell him something.

"Excuse me, Ms Annie. I need to talk to him for a second," he said while wrestling him into the yard, leaving the door wide open.

"Get the hell off of me Nate. Let me go! Fuck happened to Ty, nigga?"

The two whispered in the darkness of the yard, with Luke's occasional outburst escaping discretion.

"Luke, it has been a long night man. I can only tell you it is confusing. I will tell you all about it in the morning when you sober up some but do me a favor and stay in the barn tonight."

Luke argued and fussed, but finally went to the barn, taking his bottle with him and returned to singing. Both men forgot about Annie. Nate thought that she had left and went back to town till she said something as he returned back to the cabin.

"I mind my business most of the time, but it looks like you need some assistance. I know that look on her face. It's the look of trauma. If you don't mind, I can help. I help all the women in town and sometimes you got to let another woman deal with another woman. Just give me a couple of private minutes with her and I will help her get it together and you can come back in."

Her tone was one of compassion and sincerity, and it made Nate trust her, although they just met. Annie could see the love and concern in his alert eyes. She could see that he was doing his best to deal with both in a crisis and he was reluctant to let her do it.

"Is she your wife, and Is she always like this?"

"No, she is not, but we have been through a lot out here and today was a difficult day. I can tend to her myself. She doesn't know you. I don't think she even knows me now. Took me a while to get her this far, so before you think I did something to her, I need to clear up that I didn't. I have never seen her depressed like this. I'm doing the best I can to bring her out of it."

"And you seemed to have done well. She is bathed and looks calm. I know that you don't know me, but I think I can help. I know that look in a man's eyes when he loves someone and would never hurt her."

With that, she gently pushed him off the creaky porch and asked him to get some fresh water while she went into the cabin. Her directness and nurturing demeanor took over his mistrust as he watched her slowly shut the door inside the cabin. He could hear her soothing voice speaking to Emily, *"Hey there, Ms Emily. I'm Annie, Luke's friend. Let me help you get dressed."*

He took his time to get the water out of the well. It has been the first moment he has had to replay the day and the outcome of events. When he returned, he entered the cabin, unsure of what he would find. The solitude of thoughts to himself guiltily has given him misjudgement and regret.

"How could I let my urges get the best of me and be with Victoria? This is all my fault, and now Victoria's spell has *locked Ty in Emily's form and made a mockery of a love he has fought for centuries. I could have done more to protect her, but instead I took all the wanting and desires and misplaced them. I am centuries old, and Ty is like a child in comparison. I should have saw through the witch's plot, but I let my mortal desires lead me. This is a setback for sure."*

Even though he had just undressed and bathed her, when he walked back in, he held his eyes down and waited for the ladies to notice his entrance.

"Hey Nate, I am so sorry about earlier."

Emily's soft words filled his tortured thoughts, and he turned and saw the Emily he knew well. Her face had its glow back and her hair was pulled back into a bun in the back with her night clothes on. Like the first day he met her a century ago after being sold into slavery on the Lee plantation, she seemed to be beautiful in her resilience. He found no words to reply, and Annie interjected the delayed response.

"She is going to be fine Mr. Nate. I'll be heading back to town, but I would like to come back and check on her tomorrow if it is okay with you?"

Nate looked at Emily before he answered. I haven't had a discussion with her about what happened and what could possibly happen. In her shock condition, she hasn't noticed that the sun has gone down and she, who is everything to me, has not returned to God's original plan form because of whatever Victoria has done. It's a telltale of how she really is feeling. She may be looking like everything is normal, but she should be curious, angry, and afraid, with layers of depth in each. I hid the sword under the porch, removed the broken branches that the storm struck down, and swept the dried mud off the steps so as not to remind her of the scrimmage with Victoria.

"We will have to see. Her delicate condition requires rest. I thank you for what you have done for us, by I think I can handle it from here."

"I understand. Would be a problem if I stayed with Luke in the barn until dawn? I'm used to his snoring and frankly I don't want to travel back alone."

It was a good idea, so she and Nate went to the barn to make sure there was everything she needed. Luke wouldn't know where anything is. He rarely goes in there since I have been using it for shelter during the day.

"May I be honest Nate?"

"Luke and I have been dating for a couple of weeks and he talks about you, Ty, and Emily. I know I might be prying, but did Ty do something to Emily? It seems like everyone is avoiding talking about him."

Nate never thought about how it must appear to Annie that Ty is the only person missing, as if he might have done something to her and that's why he wouldn't be here now. And now to tell a lie...

"Ty is away on business and closing loose ends that have to be done. I'm sure he would have loved to meet you."

On the outskirts of town miles away, a tickled Victoria admires herself in an antique mirror gilded in gold and snickering as she is pleased with today's outcome. Her modern two-story house sits alone on the block. Unlike the hideaway

The Book of Emily

cabin of the travelers, its rehabilitated home is no comparison. The town of Elliott is in a small valley with rural farmland surrounding it on all sides over and through the beginnings of the Appalachian Mountains. She waits. The spell she cast was not one of revenge but one of trickery. Nate will return to find her, and he will make a sacrifice for his dear Emily. And when he does, she will seduce him and, this time, possess his soul with a more powerful witch's spell than lust. With just a few drops of his seed, she has made a potion that is powerful enough to enthral an immortal. He cannot come till days end because of Clymythious' day curse, but she knows that all that he has traded alliance for is not all that he bartered for, and she waits with a banquet of succulent food, drinks and elixirs, her body perfumed and adorned in jewels and silk. For now, the town sleeps unaware of the tempest in their midst and one eve, he will come searching for answers, but this offering will bring the reluctant love to my side.

"Spill this blood in lovers bind,

With its last breath and silenced cry,

Cast a fate time denies,

Blind him to his virgin bride.

Bring him forth or let her die,

Curse him in his passionless pride!"

The knife blade sliced through a young calf's artery. It lay motionless and dripped its blood on her lap, soaking Asian silk in crimson pools. She moaned and whispered as she smeared it within her loins and then all over herself. The power she awaits can only come from her wicked plot. With Nate, she can atone for all that she desires. Hell has no fury, and fury has many masks.

The chirping of morning woke Nate up from one of the best sleeps he has had in decades. In his arms was Emily, her face as peaceful as he had ever seen it. Beneath the quilted bed coverings, their exhausted bodies were interlocked in deep slumber, both naked and at rest in each other like a hairy goat cuddling a fragile doe. The night replayed in his head, revealing how weak his resistance was when he returned from the barn after taking Annie there. He didn't plan to sleep in her bed, but the orange glow reflecting on her squatting at the fireplace, stroking the fire, was enchanting and invoking. He'd like to think the chill of the cabin kept her awake till he returned, but it couldn't be farther from the truth.

"So, what has happened to me, Nate? Why am I still this way?" She asked, keeping her attention on the dancing, snapping flames.

"I am not sure Em, but I will figure it out when I find Victoria and she will feel my displease. As much as it pains me each day to see you as your ancestor, my heart welcomes it- even in its denial. I love...loved you Em and let time be that love's only enemy. No words will embody how I have loved you over the centuries and stood fast in shadows admiring you from afar."

She turned and stood up, searching my eyes for answers that got lost in words that were selfish in their meanings. Benefits of the short periods of being Emily were outweighed somehow, and her eyes glazed over me with a new hunger. Each step she took closer invaded my secret.

"*I think I will stay on the porch tonight. Luke and Annie are in the barn. I was just making sure you were okay. I'll just get more wood for the fire to get you through the night,*" he said just to ease his discomfort of invading memories that wouldn't quiet.

We talked for hours together like friends that haven't seen each other in years. The more we talked, the more both of us became uncomfortable in that recognition of it. Emily kept busy using the distraction of making flapjacks with raspberries. I had forgotten that we hadn't eaten all day. Words quieted under food's guise, and we occasionally looked up to see the other's nervousness in short glances. Each swallow of sweet flapjacks was delicious and more difficult as choked words in food gave way to unsaid words that were getting louder as we ate.

"*Don't sleep outside. We have slept together in this cabin all Fall. I have gotten use to not being alone. What is different now Nate?*

Stay.

You can sleep in Luke's bed over there. We both need to get a good rest. Besides, who knows, by morning I might be a mouse," she laughed.

I couldn't fight her, and if I did, I would lose. I never thought I would ever feel the grace of Emily like this again and I inwardly knew I didn't want the night to end. As I got up from the oak table to go to the other side of the room, she grabbed my arm and kissed me with sweet raspberry kisses good night. After she turned and went to the other side of the room, I watched her walk away, licking the flavor off my lips. The sudden kiss caught me off-guard, and it stroked more want than

I was prepared for. She first untied the bun out of her hair, and it fell on her bare shoulders, then she did the unexpected. She let the nightgown fall to the floor while she ran her fingers through the curly, wooly tresses before she got in the bed. Her beautiful ebony silhouette drowned my eyes in desire. In the striped moonlight shutter's shadows, her name escaped out of my thoughts out loud. It just spilled out from within in an exhale and I surrendered.

"Emily!"

In the glow of early morning, in the wake of the nocturnal reunion, I softly talked to her while she slept beside me, still fragrant as raspberries and it was the chance to say what I felt- even if she was asleep.

"More than thousands of years I waited for you Emily, and I would wait a thousand more bound to mortal existence that is eternal. This night I re-pledge my love for you. Though the words betray the first time I said them, they are the same. I have always loved you. I loved you as Em. I even loved you as Ty and so many more that mirror you through the forgotten eons. I know not what the presage dawn promises, but I know my heart never broke one."

She stirred as I kissed her on the forehead and sighed in her sleep, still with a small smile at rest. I knew that the morning brought the beast, and although she knows him, with him comes a clumsiness that may contaminate the night's end. The violation would have been twice compounded in rekindled love soured- or at least that is what I thought. The transformation has begun. My hands first thickened in leathery skin much larger than any man's, large enough to snap a mortal neck in ease with power and strength. These moments ago, mortal frame is swelling and contorting by the second with Nova's rise. My body is multiplying in mass sentient exoskeleton that stalled in her magnificence without so much as a battle. If I lie here any longer, she will awaken to a full repulsive mutation trapped by the sun and my ransomed heart. In the curse of day form, the goose-down mattress weighs down in crushed stuffed feathers and she fell more into the gravity of my weight, unbothered by it and wraps her silky naked body around mine. Arousing me and seducing the beast. The feral pheromones increased with my sense, and I could smell her awakening body through flared nostrils that relished each feminine whiff. Where this was going, I refused to go in this state. As I jumped up and grabbed the sheets to avert temptation after a beautiful night with her, she woke up from the sudden movement, but before I could explain, Luke burst through the door.

"Goddamn, Pop! Looks like I got here just in time. I'm really sorry, guys," he said, fixed on Em's exposed naked body on the bed and my embarrassed excitement wrapped in the sheets and quilt. *"I need to get some clean clothes and go to work."*

When he realized that he was staring, he turned his back and kept talking while he fetched his belongings, glossing over the obvious.

"Uh...Nate, you need to cover that up and put some clothes on. Annie is out front. It's bad enough to have to explain you without the...the...theatrics!" He said, gesturing his comments on Nate's covered excitement.

"So, you took my advice and slept with Ty last night? Or does my memory serve me right, I thought I saw Emily here last night? I'm not judging either way, Pop, but somebody tell me what the hell is going on! It's none of my business what went on, but I want to know who went on- sort a speak. Maybe shit will ease the fuck up around here now!"

Luke's abrupt entrance was timely enough to calm Nate's beastly nature down and he dropped the sheet to find his shorts and dress appropriately while briefly explaining what had happened the day before with Victoria. The beast is anything but shy in his form, but this has never happened. Never has the man and the beast both wanted to share the same passion, disregarding their disadvantages.

Emily watched as he dressed, never letting her gaze signal the interest and thought. His large wings were tucked tightly flat to his muscular back. His skin tone was dark and almost black in the morning light that crept through the cabin's shutters. Although he was completely in day curse form, she has been with these two guys for months and nothing is embarrassing to her. After the journey this far, it is nothing to what she has seen.

"Come on, Luke!" Annie shouted from outside. *"I have to open the store this morning."*

"Go, Luke, before she comes in here and stop being an ass. We will see you this evening and don't get drunk tonight. We have to make different plans, and I want you to stay here with Em while I visit Victoria and figure what she has done."

Luke hurriedly got his things and left, stopping only to say goodbye to Emily, who was on the bed. Always wanting the last line, he stopped at the door, waiting for Nate to hide off to the side and with a typical Luke sarcasm and smirk, said, *"Morning, Miss!"* he laughed as he ran through the yard to catch up with Annie.

Chapter 10

The early winter morning was like any other Maryland one- cold and biting. In the time worn cabin constructed of aged cedar, the walls seethed in crevices that lost to the seeped morning chill. Nate and Emily kept the fireplace blazing to warm the temporary nest with very little words shared between them in the aftermath of the night since Luke left. Nate always feels insecure in the exposed day, especially around Ty as Emily. Through his insecurities he won't leave her today. His bestial nature felt it best to protect her from its hideous abnormally. He sat in the corner reading and periodically looked up when she did chores outside hoping she wouldn't find any residual evidence of what happened.

"Why you keep staring at me that way whenever I leave?" She finally found the courage to ask.

For weeks now she has been in the transient form of Emily by day, and it no longer feels like an unexpected visitor- more like an old friend coexisting in a paradoxical dilemma. On the outside she might look beautiful and adaptive in her ethereal femininity, but her mind is still Ty and singular in existence. Time away from the city in their isolation has given introspection to reflect on the journey and she/he left all the peculiarities of the experience as blatant truths that for the moment, masked themselves in denial.

He was surprised by the sudden question and adverts his eyes out the window of the cabin where he watched her every move. If she were to leave his sight while out there, he likely would have panicked and stepped out of the shelter of the cabin.

Each time she returned there was a relief in his eyes and a relax in his furrowed brow. To her, he was being stubborn and ornery, as she tormented him deliberately by just being, or not being Emily. After a couple of hours being alone together in the confined refuge, unease had become tension.

"I am just concerned. Enemies are many. If it were my choice, you would not leave my inspecting eyes. You would never be at the whims of evil and malice. It's nothing more than me protecting the vessel. A duty."

Emily walked over to him with him fidgeting as she approached closer. There was a confidence in her that made each step confrontational and suspect to manipulation. Sweat on her forehead beaded like pearls of glass, rolling down her oval face and down her chin dripping into her cleavage from her chores, and she saw a moment to grasp with the beast in his uncomfortably. She wanted conversation and she felt she had, more than ever, the right to demand it.

"Don't Em," he snorted.

"What happened between us is not a device you can wield at my disadvantage. I can only apologize for crossing the line with you last night in urges that cannot be.

What happens when Ty returns?

What happens when you again grow old, and I have to let you go in deaths plan like the many times I mourned over the centuries?

I need to change the omen that is. I need to break the death of a flower. To let its thorn scourge anyone who attempts to end its cycle. Not just for me. Not just for you. But this time for all and end this tragic repetition and senseless death despite the irony of it all."

"So last night, I was a mistake? All this time you have been watching and leering for an opportunity and you took it, and it was beautiful, but today you apologize for it? Fuck you!" She screamed in justified hurt.

Like a reflex, she slapped him as hard she could. Her small hands didn't budge his large, big head, so she slapped him again, but this time in tears.

"You used me to fill your need to connect with yours and my past and don't even have the respect to acknowledge it. I don't know what kind of woman Emily was, but I can tell you, I'm not that kind of guy!"

Nate heard her anger in the words and the light-handed slap. In them, he remembered that Emily is Ty and the two may look gender specific, but the rage of Ty was emerging in emotions. Emily started hurling anything she could get her hands on, plates, vases, glassware, tools, and even fruit. He ducked as things crashed against him and around him.

"Yo, I ain't never been that kinda guy, and I'm damn sure, I ain't that kind of...whatever. You didn't say all that when you were one last night! That's it I am out. I'd rather take my chance out there than be with you. And I'm taking you damn coat too!"

Over time, in the form of Emily, Ty has deliberately focused to not let his masculine demeanor overshadow hers. It wasn't thought about in a calculative way, it was just natural to not confuse them in the constant change over the weeks, and as he did, Emily got more stronger in it. As she speaks in anger, its fuel adds to combine the duality of the two in a stronger voice, and word choices that weren't as soft and feminine.

"B...b... but Em. I didn't mean it like that!"

"Calm down!" Nate stuttered realizing that he had pissed her off.

Anger replaced the remnant glow that befell the cozy cabin with broken clutter and thrown items in tantrum. She feverishly stuffed all the clothes she had that would fit both her and Ty if returned- and it would be welcomed. Thoughts of what she would do if he would only come back now mutters out of her mouth as she packs.

"I didn't sign up for this. You, all the way through this have had the upper hand. The minute I drop my guards, you make me feel like I'm a mistake? How dare you! Just don't say nothing to me. I am leaving!"

"B...b..but Em!"

Dusk was settling in as she barrelled out of the cabin with clothes slap dashed into a knapsack and wearing only a hoodie and Nate's duster with pants that fit tightly over her hips. Not knowing where she was going, or how she would make it out there alone saddened her and she collapsed on the porch railing, still sobbing in fury. The orange and purple hued sky was embracing the end of day. Night creatures were awakening in songs by crickets, cicadas, and courting toads that echoed in the surrounding trees that to her felt uninviting. There was no turning back at this point. She stepped off the porch as if it would be the last time she would ever do it.

"God what am I supposed to do?" She thought to herself, foraging apprehensively into the darkness, only once turning back to see Nate step onto the porch as himself at night. Tall unshaven with clothes that now fit loosely on him. He called out to her from the doorway. His deep voice sounded husky and shaken. He couldn't see her at the shadowed edge of the clearing. It chilled her to think of being with him the night before in so much passion, and love. Now she is estranged to the cloak of night in flight from the very thing she surrendered to- imperatives afraid with nowhere to go.

It was miles way before she stopped hearing Nate's searching cries amongst the evergreen thicket of trees and brush strangled in winter dead Spanish moss. Aimlessly traveling and thinking of all the things in the night that are far worse than her imagination planned. There were thoughts of giant deer, rapid possums, sneaky foxes, and even monsters of the imagination. To make it worse, it began to snow. At first the flurries were subtle and dusted the bed of leaves and snapped branches. As the temperature dropped the inclement weather worsened with the snow blanketing everything in gelid white. Her own footprints crisscrossing over themselves meant that not only was she lost, but she was circling. Without shelter she would freeze in the frozen bosom of the woods alone, and no longer angry, and regretful. Perhaps if she avoided her own imprinted steps would lead her back to the cabin or at least to town.

What seemed like hours of trees and woody uplands that all looked the same flanked on all sides, finally, in the faint far off distant twinkling through the evergreen willowwacks was the lights of the town. Burdened tread turned to a lifesaving trot to them, running as if it were a race against time to get there.

Emily had never been to the town before. Its outskirts were fenced around it in fields and livestock pastures with welcoming lights on in windows she found comforting. She made her way into the town main street that was part cobblestone repaired in asphalt. Strangers stared at her curiously whispering to each other in their hushed conversations along its sides. She must have looked a sight with snow layered in her hair and the pulled together ensemble that said *"passing through or running from"* clearly- wet duster tied tightly and ice crusted boots.

Instinct led her to a small tavern called The Mill Inn with a weather-beaten sign with a faded Mill sign swinging on a chain in the storm's winds. Music ebbed from inside mingled with laughter and jovial conversations, and the hungry aroma of food. Although she was freezing, Emily took a minute to compose herself, shaking snow and water out of her hair and tying it up as neatly as she could. Way out here in the rural suburbs a Black woman must be careful- prejudice and discrimination might seem antiquated in the urban areas, but here it could be just as racist and arrogant as fifty years ago.

"Deep breaths and go straight to the bar," she thought to herself in preparedness of whatever the warmth of the Inn would bring.

"Emily darling! Come over here!" A strange and loud voice shouted from the other end of the bar.

Sitting at the mahogany shellacked bar was Annie- face swallowed in a big smile that eased the rest of the onlookers that were interrogating her entrance with their eyes.

"My God, you look like you been through hell," she said while pulling the wet coat off her and wiping her wet face.

"Girl you are freezing! Let's sit over there by the fire. How did you get here and where is Nate?"

"I'm a grown mmm...woman and I don't need no man to do anything for me. He is not my man or nothing. I just needed some air out of that stuffy cabin."

She and I talked about the weather, the small mill town of Elliott, and of course men, her favorite subject, and why they are not worth shit. Not once did she mention the state, I was in on our first meeting. As we sat there, her attention kept diverting to the other side of the room- distracted. Annie seemed to know everyone there, but something had her attention.

"Do you know them over there? They haven't taken their eyes off you since you came in. I don't know them, but I have seen them in here before."

At the table she was speaking of was four people with disdaining grimaced expressions and they saw me see them. My heart sank to my stomach as I realized who they were, Clymythious being the center figure in the foursome. His face was the only one that didn't look disapproving, yet his were the only ones I avoided. His composure was of confidence and patient for my recognition. Like me, they were just odd in comparison to the casual townsfolk, foreign with dark clothing and unfriendly posture. Each time Emily looked in their direction his eyes were fixed on her.

"I have met them before, Annie. Let's just say we are acquainted with each other."

"Well Emily, I don't like them and obviously they don't like you. I think we should leave. I have a plan. Go to the restroom and crawl through the window and I will meet you out back. I will take you to my place not far from here. Something ain't right with them," she coyly said while getting up to distract them.

"Drinks on the house!"

The room exploded in caroused celebration and activity at the bar, but the four never moved until Annie went over to them and blocked their direct view of Emily.

"You guys must be new in town. Free drinks on the house! I am celebrating my birthday," she said lying while swaying back and forth intercepting their beeline view across the room.

"You hath need to occupy your own concerns witch. This doesn't involve you. Now step out of the way!" Navasha said leaning into the table as to keep her tone hushed among the gay patrons of the Inn and exposing her sword harnessed on her side as she did it.

"Damn! Just trying to be friendly to visitors to our fair town. Have it your way, but you are missing the best home brewed ale in all of Baltimore County!"

"Oh...and I got your witch bitch!"

The two women were locked in an eminent confrontation. Navasha, cool, lovely, and oppositional in pale skin beauty, and Annie's buxom, full-figured stature disclosing a knife clipped on the side of her jeans. Clymythious grinned in the possible battle between them. He sat with arm over the back of the chair and watched Annie, captivated, and bemused. With one wave of his index finger, he dismissed her, and Simon and Benoit pushed her aside only to find that Emily is gone from where they saw her last. The three companions of Clymythious scrambled to their feet and spread out and canvassed the room. Clymythious, cool and collected, just calmly stood up and adjusted himself and walked behind Annie.

"You think you are clever miss.,"

"The name is Annie, and I have no idea what you are talking about. Maybe you are just not to friendly folk...Mr?

"Clymythious just Clymythious."

Annie's plan could possibly backfire if they exhaust their search and venture outside. Through the merriment and activity, she camouflaged with them, using a side exit to sneak out without notice. As planned, Emily waited in hiding out in the wooded back area under the boughs of fir trees. Her small footprints pressed in fresh snow, trailed behind her. Annie knew that if she tracked her so easily, then Clymythious, Navasha, Simon, and Benoit would too. Worst weather for being chased on foot through snow, the pace was slow, and even if they went off path, footprints were like breadcrumbs directly to them.

"Why are we zig zagging through the woods recrossing our path. I thought you said you lived close?"

"I live very close, but just not in this direction. I am looking for a way to cover our tracks. Those guys seem like they have no love for you. I need to buy us some time. At this point, we are in this together. The main one, Chlamydia I wouldn't want to meet in a dark alley. He is the Black person tall, bald one, with *a goatee, and those piercing eyes?"* She prodded. *"Before we go any further, you need to tell me what all this is about."*

"His name is Clymythious not Chlamydia!"

"Oh, I see. You two got history. So, I was right. I could feel a danger about him, but he looked at you warmly. No need to be so evasive with me darling. There is something that's peculiar about you and it all. I can't put my finger on it, but..."

Annie was interrupted by her cell phone ringing in her pocket. In the still of the night, its antique ring echoed in the forest. It was Luke.

"Where are you?"

Luke has a personality that is normally quite calm, but the panic in his voice said that he was not normal. Over the weeks he and Annie have shared much together, and he always is collected.

"I might have to go out of town, and I would like to see you before I leave. You and your sexy ass self! But wait, there is so much I want to tell you and talk about and there just doesn't seem like enough time."

Annie continued her conversation with Luke at the foot of a bridge. Its unlit arched bowed over a stream that probably flowed into the Patapsco River, and then to the ocean. Like rain in the distance, it hissed in a small waterfall. The mist carried in the air- moist and damp the way unfiltered water smells alive and connected to Emily. The more she reached its apex the louder the elements became. She could hardly pay attention to Luke on the other end of the phone watching the world that almost summoned around her. The charge in the atmosphere swelled under her presence. She could swear she could see energy interchanged between them, saddened and brilliant with her face upwardly absorbing it in a subtle suffering.

"Luke let me cut to the chase. I am with Emily and some guy, and his acquaintances came into the Mill acting strange and a little hostile. We lost them and got away without them noticing. I'm taking her to my place to avoid whatever they had planned. Been weaving through Old Man Crawford's to throw them off."

"Goddamnit! Why the hell would fucking Ty go in town and where the hell is Nate? Dis the shit that fucks me up bout them two!"

Annie heard him loud and clear and said nothing to explain what she doesn't know anything about; besides, it was too cold to hold a conversation on the run. Being on the bridge had its advantage by seeing both sides, and the disadvantage of being exposed. Emily sat on the railing of the bridge transfixed on the ringed silver moon peering through wispy clouds. There was no doubt that she had heard the phone conversation. Her arms bundled Nate's large coat with her arms folded. Danger was likely along the soldiered tree line searching for them, but in the cooler upward surge of winds gusting over the vertex of the bridge, tranquility in the night dampening in white.

The rest of the traveling was only difficult in the sparse conversation the two had before finally through beaten thoroughfare arriving at Annie's house. Its southern architecture was a welcome sight with its wrapping porch and gabled roof. On it, was Luke pacing. He got there before they did. His expression was in relief and subdued anger.

"Fuck! What took y'all so damned long? I been here at least a half."

Annie and Emily stomped up the large house wooden steps brushing by Luke and ignoring his comment.

"Hold up! Why y'all mad at me? I didn't do shit!" He said following them in cursing under his breath.

Annie made Emily comfortable in her beautiful, pined den while she went upstairs to take off the now wet clothes. Luke followed her barraging her with questions, but Annie was busy on the phone.

"Hello Phillip, meet us at the crossing at High Cross. We should be there within the hour. Flash the lights and I will know it's you. The signal out there might be too weak to call me. We will be there by 2am. I really appreciate you coming through," she said while jamming clothes and personal items in a large bag.

"Oh, another thing, I'm going to need some cash. Being what you can and when we get safely, I will give it back."

Luke was seething in restrained angered curiosity sitting on the bed listening to the phone conversation. When she finished, he continued with more questions beginning with the obvious.

"You called Phillip to help? I can't believe you called that nigga!

Where are taking Emily?

If you tell me nothing, you ain't going nowhere. I swear to God somebody going to tell me what's going!"

He was inches from her face holding her arm tightly. He had refused to be ignored, and there were no more jokes with him. Downstairs Emily could sense the tension.

"Let go my arm Luke before I break it. Now let me say this, do you know who needs to start talking...? You!"

He could feel the blood coursing through constrained appendages, bulging the seams of his shirt, his incarnate being becoming. With shallow breaths, he tried to control it, to remain in what he appeared to be to Annie. It has been weeks of deliberate control that he has tried to blend in. How will he explain to her the transition- before or after? Could he? These are all the options he weighed in his head before answering her.

"Okay, okay. There is a lot that I haven't talked about that we need to if you are planning to leave. It just gets complicated every time I try to tackle it."

"Try!"

Briefly, he and Annie talked about everything he could in a short time. He reluctantly began from the beginning and only paused when it became hard for her to digest. Annie never said anything about the almost revealed wings that calmed down in his brief explanations of how things have escalated to where they are. Each time she tried to interject; Luke shook his head gesturing her not to until he was finished.

"Everything isn't what it appears. We are not as we appear. There is a battle between man and the gods of a forgotten time who want to change its outcome. That person downstairs is the first to have the power, linage and others that want to ensure the path behind them. So here is the kicker, Emily is an escaped

cellmate of mine that technically, in another life was my mother and is cursed by a witch who put a spell on her. Emily is Ty, who is what they call a vessel that every couple of generations inherits the power and duty to defend off the Order of Mortali. She is the first to live past ascension and that is why Nate, and I protect him in hopes that no more blood will be spilt. The group that is after her are the assassins that have over the centuries murdered all prior vessels before they could wield power. Nate is sort of her self-appointed guardian. At one time, a century ago he fell in love with her, but she was slain by the guys you met earlier, but not before having a son- me! I have both DNAs in me, but I am not a vessel like her. So there, I have told you what I could do in a short time. I left a lot out to make it easier to understand."

"So, Emily is a guy named Ty? You got to be kidding me. That docile sweet girl looks nothing like a guy, but it explains a lot. Can she change back and forth from a man to a woman?"

"No. That evil Victoria cast a spell leaving her as Emily. That's how when you saw her after they battled over Nate. There was really no battle. More like a slaughter. Emily, when upset, is very powerful. It would have been a short fight."

Annie had heard enough. The story just was too far-fetched to take it all in. Her unchanged plan was to help another sister in crisis despite the incredible story he shared. With all the bags packed, she headed back downstairs to pick up a few more things and leave to meet Phillip.

"I need to know where y'all are going. If I'm not going, then I need to tell big guy something. He is probably out there right now searching for us!"

The two ladies drew blanks in search of what to say, Emily with empty expression, and Annie with the same.

"I don't want to see him!" Emily quickly rebutted looking out the window.

"Can you go with us?"

He scratched his head and said,

"Try to leave without me!"

Its 3am and the three fugitives waited on the side of the rode for Phillip to arrive and flash his lights. On time as he said, he packed everything up in his truck and they headed off and out of Baltimore County. They needed to get as far away from the area as they could.

Phillip talked the entire time watching Emily in the rearview mirror.

"You alright back there?"

She sat in the back with Annie and Luke sat upfront. His fixed gaze in the mirror on her felt scrutinizing, and whenever she looked up into it, his marble blue eyes were there searching. The questions fought for replies till she finally gave in to them while the others slept.

"So, I guess we are like a family on the run, huh?" he said using humor to engage.

"You know we got you. We are going to be so far from them that they won't be able to catch you."

It was odd that he instinctively or presumptuously knew what was going. Emily didn't want to have to say more than she had to, but miles of asphalt and time revealed he knew a lot, and she didn't know how. Annie couldn't have said too much in the phone conversation and yet his inferences said far more, those eyes framed in a rugged white face, and five o'clock shadowed dark beard had a confidence in them that rivaled cockiness.

"So 'Emily', how long have you known?"

"How long have I known what?"

Phillip pulled over to the side of a small road and asked again, but this time turning completely around to say it."

"Are we going to keep playing games about this? I know you know what I am talking about. There are no accidents or luck in any of this. As soon as we can settle that point of view, we can at least have a better conversation and maybe, we can learn something about each other."

As he spoke, his arm that was over the rest of the driver's seat resting his slender hands hers that were on her knees clenched trying to look relaxed and evasive. She didn't know what he was talking about, and it could be so many things.

"Okay, you don't have to. It's going to come out anyway in time. Your face glows with it. When you are ready to talk about it, you will."

We traveled for hours north on back highways with endless fields and pastures dull in hibernation, stopping through Delaware for food and rest, and then traveled on to Pennsylvania, and then to New Jersey with its miles of farmland and patch quilt agriculture sown together in rural majesty and fenced wooden borders where we took lodgings in a bed and breakfast. It was a quaint Early American two story called the

Ocean Mist complete with shuddered windows and expansive land behind it with sentinel electric towers as far as the eye could see on the hills and plateaus of Hillsborough, overwhelmed by a sky that curved on top of it close to the shore, flat while backdropped by the wooded hills of Pennsylvania shaded in blue mist far away. We stayed there for three weeks, and everything was still and quiet till one evening the comfortability of diverged honesty cracked through on an early March evening. Luke was at his normal, holding most of the table talk with insights into history intertwined with biblical references. On this night he delved into the book of Revelations mixed with his own convictions in metaphysics and philosophies that he rambled on about when Phillip saw his opportunity.

"Emily, what do you believe? You being the Vessel and all."

At the table were the Grenwalds, Harriet and Gerald, Luke, Annie, Emily, and Phillip who silenced the entire dinner party with his arrogantly bold question. Silverware ceased clinking, and the room's surroundings suddenly became more interesting than looking at one another except for Phillip's and the Grenwald's centered attention on the humiliated Emily.

"Leave the poor dear alone Phillip. I won't tolerate it at my dinner table. Now everybody eat and leave such inappropriate talk for another time," Harriet said banging her fist on the table.

"Eat!"

The table resumed its eating in reserved quiet, but now the anxiety was directed at Phillip. Emily slowly ate with her head down, never looking at anyone at the table. Soon she couldn't take anymore and jumped up and ran from the table still saying nothing. Still not answering what Phillip asked. How could she? She had no answers. God was what she had faith in, and the past months have tested it. When she left the dinner table, Annie's anger regained and unleashed on Phillip.

"Why did you do that? It was uncalled for, and you know just as much as anyone. You are a mean selfish asshole! Mr. & Mrs Grenwald I apologize for ruining your gracious dinner. It's been a long journey for all of us. Excuse me while I check on her."

"No dear, finish eating. I will check on her in a couple of minutes. Give her time."

The rest of the evening held little in talk. The men went on the porch while Annie and Harriet cleaned up.

"You don't have to explain anything to me and Gerry. We mind our business. Be kind to one another. You should listen to an old lady. Time is precious and it's obvious that each one of you are destined for something with each other. I don't think you would have traveled so far if you didn't have a purpose. Gerry and I have been in this old house for 45 years and we have seen it all. Before we bought this house we lived in New York. I met him when I was twenty-one and working there. He was a carpenter, and I would see him in the neighborhood in Queens. He courted me like a gentleman, flowers, candy, and dances in Brooklyn. We haven't been apart since we got married and bought this house. Sweetest man I know. A quiet giant.

You dry and I will take Emily some hot tea and check on her."

The Book of Emily

Harriet left the kitchen with a cup of herbal tea for Emily. Outside she could hear Gerald and Luke chattering and smoking while Phillip was in the den watching the news. As she crept up the creaky old wooden steps lined with old photographs and memories, she smiled at each one, courteously looking at each one. The three-bedroom house, furnished in 20th century decor and wallpapered on every wall, was home to her and Gerald, and a refuge to many in the past. At the end of the hall is where Annie and Emily shared a room. She knocked softly on the door and walked in.

"I brought you some tea dear. You don't feel well, do you?

Drink this herbal tea and I promise you will feel a little better."

Emily who was lying on the bed in the dark sat up and turned on the side table lamp. She didn't know how Harriet knew she didn't feel well, but a hot cup of tea perhaps would do the trick. Harriet slid a desk chair across the room and sat at the edge of the bed wearing a gentle smile as if she wasn't leaving until she drank it.

"If you need someone to talk to, I'm hear dear. Looks like you use all the friends you have, and you have some really good ones downstairs that care about you no matter how it might appear."

"No, it's not that Mrs. Grenwald. It's the missing home part that is probably getting to me. We have been here for a couple weeks and before that somewhere else for a couple of months. I just think I'm homesick for Baltimore."

"You sure it's Baltimore, or someone in Baltimore?"

Harriett's facial expression, although she put it in a sentence, said that she didn't believe it was homesickness. She wore her hair pinned up in an elaborate bun that made her look like a young sweet grandmother. Even the cotton flowered dress conveyed a simplicity, demur and powerful demeanor that would be difficult to lie too.

"Honey, how long have you known?"

Emily's weak stomach sank back into queasiness, and she ran to the bathroom. This hasn't been a good evening for all this inquisitive investigating. While she wretched in the bathroom Harriet came in and dabbed a damp wash cloth on her forehead over the commode.

"It all began what seems like long ago, but it started about a couple a years ago with weird dreams of flying and unexplained memory loss. It got worse and worse until...until. Well anyway, people I didn't know started showing up in shadows, and then in the light, and it all began with some kind of weird prophecy or omen. Pick your choice what to call it. Now I'm on the run and I'm supposed to change something for the future. I can't figure it out and now they have been preparing me for a battle that I don't want."

Harriett listened and helped her back to the bed and passing her more tea from her old ceramic teapot. It helped Emily with the nausea and telling how she got here seemed relieving.

"Honey, that's interesting, but that is not what I was asking you about.

You do know sweetie, don't you?

You would have to be born yesterday not to know!"

The Book of Emily

She picked up her tray and left out the room telling her to get some rest and we could talk about it in the morning. Somehow, Emily wasn't looking for morning and didn't plan on seeing it with them scrutinizing her. She packed the little things she owned, and borrowed and packed them in her knapsack wearing the darkest clothes she could find. There was an overwhelming feeling that something was coming and whatever it was, it would be menacing irritated in her head. In the distance, out the small panes window of her bedroom, a far-off storm electrified the night horizon with cracks in the sky of lightening. Nate is out there somewhere searching, and Emily could feel him getting closer as well as Clymythious. Running for her was the best immediate choice. In that way nobody will have to fend for Emily. She waited till the house was quiet and everyone was asleep and crept down the creepy steps to sneak out the front door. The plan was to get as far as she could from her friends and fend for herself. Humiliation and helplessness are compounding enough without prying eyes.

One last door to freedom and escape. The old screen screamed its rusty hinges as she eased it open. The slower it opened the more it sounded like a cat being tortured. A voice startled her on the porch. It was Mr. Grenwald sitting in a porch swing smoking a pipe. His rotund outline was grandfatherly and the spiced smell of his special blend of his tobacco filled the misty might air.

"I'm not the only one that can't sleep, huh? Storm coming and it looks like it's going to be a good one. Have a seat," he cheerfully said. *"Looks like you a bit scared and by the looks of things, you are planning on going on a trip."*

Her mind was not processing what she was doing or where she was going so, she sat next to him as he rocked the swing slowly with the heels of his feet and back forth like a ship on swelling waves before the storm. Normally, she finds his pipe pleasing to the senses, but combined with the waves of the swing, she ran to the edge of the porch and again vomited over its wooden overpainted railing.

"Harriett told me that you weren't feeling well. What's a gal like you going out there alone? You don't look like you are up to traveling. Tell ya what, you wait here a second and if you still want to leave in the middle of the night, I will take you to the bus station. Deal?"

Gerald achingly got up and left her to her thoughts on the porch alone. The surrounding area looks desolate and barren with fog crawling on the dark fields. She could hear the distant highway traffic whizzing noisily back and forth to the north, which is where she was heading for, but south were candles in old light poles that flickered and were blotched in darkness except for a figure standing down the road from the house.

"Oh, he has been there for the past couple of nights. Never comes close. He just stands there in the shadows." Gerald sad returning to check on her.

"Harriett and I don't say much about other's affairs, but could that fella be there for you?"

Emily waived off the cup of tea he was trying to hand her and walked off the porch into the darkness. She knew that it was Nate. She could feel it. The figure stepped back in the shadows in an attempt to camouflage on the roadside, and the closer she got the faster her quickened steps got.

In the distance, back behind her on the porch lit with one yellow light was Gerald.

"You ought not go too far from the house Missy."

"I'll be fine Mr. Grenwald. Don't worry, I know him."

After all she has been through, fear has no place. Where once she believed she was the architect of her life, she now believes that all that is in front of her cannot be avoided. If it is uncertainty that made her decisions and choice without her input, then she can walk into darkness in brave conviction.

"I know you are there. I should have known that you would be here." She said to the shivering in the wind brush.

The sound of the brush rubbing and bristling against the sound of open space and occasional distant highway reminded her of Baltimore where no road is too far from the same sounds. Through the quieting caws of the night crows in the trees his voice spoke over them not feet from her. His timber and deep voice made her heart speed in excitement.

"You are with child, and you still run from me?" is all he said.

She knew that it was what Mrs. Grenwald was inferring to, but it was too impossible to believe. Her hand rubbed on her still flat stomach in denial and contemplation. Women might be natural to childbirth, but Emily is not whole women, or at least not most of her life.

"No! It can't be. I mean I hope not. I should say I didn't plan this."

He stepped from the shield of cloak and darkness. His dark silhouette, large and patient in each closing step. Emily's urges to run to him she stifled, unsure of what he had to say next.

"With every fiber of my being, whether day or night I have thought of nothing but you. I have traded my comrades and ignored the dogma of my kind in my change of heart and selfish emotions hidden in condemned ideology."

He always spoke so eloquently when he has time to think about it, and he has had plenty over the weeks. Emily was frozen in his words and his closing approach. Like anything large or enormous, the closer he got, the larger he appeared. She felt small and naked.

"What I have done, I have done, but what it has done to you perhaps God might have mercy on my trapped soul and resolute my error. For every captive moment with you threatens one without you, and for that I allowed it to punish the very thing I adore."

Just a few feet away, she could see that he is unkept, yet ruggedly beautiful standing upright and open as if awaiting something to embrace, but Emily held fast in shallow breaths that spiraled steam in deliberate exhales. He wore a wool pea coat and knit cap, appearing like a fisherman returning with an empty bounty. A full six or more inches taller than her, he consumed her in space, stopping just a breath away from her and towering down on her with his locked eyes.

"I lied.

I told you that I owe you nothing.

But I do. What lies in the future is everything for many reasons and I cannot know all of them. I owe you to try if you let me. Please Em..." she stopped him with her hand over his mouth and then fell into the empty arms and hugged him.

He continued talking but Emily heard it from the inside of his chest deep like a caged lion in pain, roaring in deep rumble. He was delicate with his words that overran in passion and regret but ended in a question.

"Would you prefer that I leave?"

"No, Nate don't leave," she said still pressing against him and avoiding his struggling eyes and furrowed brow.

From the house, Mr. Grenwald has awoken his wife who is coming down the dark road with a flashlight and her husband in tow.

"Hurry up Gerry! She could be hurt or lost!"

"Are you okay Emily?" She said almost trotting to them. *"You shouldn't be in this damp night air. We'll take her from here. Thanks for finding her. Where did you come from? Never mind, never let it be said that Harriett Grenwald don't have no manners. Come in and warm up. I can't get you something to eat or at least a cup of coffee,"* she said prying Emily from underneath his arm behind him.

"What's your name son?" Mr. Grenwald asked as the ladies hurried ahead of them back to the house.

"Nathaniel is the name sir."

"Gerald Grenwald Jr. Is my name. Friends call me Gerry."

The two pairs settled into the quiet home, ladies in the kitchen and the guys in the den, each having their own conversations.

"That's him ain't it Emily? Again, it's none of my business, but I like to know what is going on in my own home."

Mrs Grenwald was in the handmade cabinets and cupboards getting together coffee and cookies for the men in the other room, talking almost to herself.

"Seem like a good man. I pick up on those things from people, you know? Are you running from him?" I don't play that domestic abuse or whatever they call it- especially someone in your condition."

She rambled on and on about what women should take and what they shouldn't quoting Madea and The Color Purple movies as if they were facts. Emily's attention had drifted to the miscellaneous bric-ca-brac lined on shelves, in the window, and on the counter. The room itself was a memento of her life- from her fading flowered wallpaper to the tea kettle on the stove with hand painted pansies on it and a cracked handle, this room in the house was hers.

"Till you do right by me everything you even think about will fail!" She quoted from the movie.

"So, are you making plans for that little boy?"

"I'm not pregnant! I'm just tired from traveling and might be coming down with something, that's all.

"Sweetie, I think I know what I am talking about. Had a dream about you. Saw you with a powerful son and he is going to change the world. My dreams most of the time are right on the mark."

"You don't understand, I can't be."

"By the look of the gentleman in there I would say that you know how this happened. No man looks at a woman like that unless he been with her. You know how you got like this right?"

In the other room the men were sitting around with the television blaring avoiding conversation. Mr Grenwald and Nate were ignoring the interaction between them. It was Mr Grenwald father-like inquisitiveness that spoke first.

"You been out there for a couple nights. She must mean a lot to ya. If I were you, I would just tell her how I felt and apologize for whatever you did. What did you do anyhow?"

"Mind your business old man. I haven't done anything. She ran off."

"A woman just don't run off for nothing son," he said while lighting his pipe.

"You too old a young man too not know that. Did you apologize yet...for whatever you did?"

"I'm not going to tell you again to mind your business."

"Excuse me, uh Nate, is it? I'm just an old man that don't know nothing."

"No, you don't."

Mrs Grenwald interrupted bringing in a tray with coffee and cookies on it.

"Don't get that man all riled up Gerry. They have their things that they have to work out.

Have some cookies sweetie."

No one heard Phillip creep down the steps from the upstairs, and he stood at the bottom of the steps listening before entering. He and Nate knew each other, but he didn't want to be a third party in the conversation till invited. Instead, he went into the kitchen where he found Emily alone.

"*You called Nate?*" He flippantly said.

For what all he knew, they were escaping from him and his friends. He kept his voice low so that the others wouldn't know that he came down.

"*I didn't call him, and I don't know how he found me, but I'm glad he is here.*"

Mrs Grenwald returned to the kitchen and was startled that he came down without her seeing. The tension was a little uncomfortable and she could sense it.

"*Well, soon the whole house will be up, and I bet everyone could use food and coffee. Phillip go in there with the guys. Gerry bout interrogated that poor man to death. Emily, you stay with me, and we can scramble up something. Get out of womenfolk way now Phillip.*"

Mrs Grenwald has an uncanny intuitiveness and brandishes it with a casualty with no reserve. Though Phillip didn't want to go, it was better than going against her. He stopped at the swinging kitchen door to turn back and look at Emily. It wasn't just a couple of hours ago that he embarrassed her in front of everyone at the dinner table. If Mrs Grenwald hadn't come back so fast, he would have apologized for it.

Nate and Mr Grenwald were quietly sipping coffee watching sports news when Phillip came in with them. Nate reared up like a pit bull preparing for a fight.

"Hold it gents, hold it! Let's keep this civil. Don't be breaking stuff up in here!"

The guys ignored him and kicked the coffee table from in between them. Nate's huge black wings ripped through slits in the side of his flannel shirt whisking ceramic figurines off shelves behind him. Mr Grenwald' face was stunned as he watched his home crash around him. Phillip's eyes had no whites in them. Where he was just seconds ago, white with red hair, he now was the color of death, a pastry undead color with sharp teeth and a budded horn in the center of his forehead.

"What the hell!" Gerald exclaimed.

The two wrestled and careened over the delicate home throwing each other in punches and grunts. Drywall dented in like tissue as they body slammed each other into it. Phillip outweighed Nate, but not his anger. The ladies ran from the kitchen in time to witness the final blow as Nate retrieved a sword from his knapsack and cut off Phillips head like a sharp knife through butter. It rolled across the floor thudding at the feet of the women, Mrs Grenwald was screaming in terror beating the decapitated bloody head with a straw broom. Her screams woke the rest of the house up and they ran downstairs to see that Nate has taken a life.

"Is that Phillip?" Luke hollered standing over the grotesque decapitated cadaver in the center of the den floor.

"His name isn't Phillip or is Nashik. He is one of the...others," Nate said hiding the blood sword behind his back.

"He was leading y'all to Clymythious and Odeous. Who bought him here?"

The entire room turned to look at Annie who was in as much surprise and shock as anyone. She aimed her attention and reply to Emily who was stalwart and unemotional still standing at the kitchen threshold.

"Emily, I don't know what's going on, but I didn't know nothing about this." She turned to Luke next. *"Honey, I know you believe me!"*

He had no reply. There was a dead creature on the floor and two distressed witnesses that were in shock that he thought more important. He and Nate quickly grabbed the body and dragged it outside, Luke was grumbling under his breath with each heave to the yard.

"Pop, put them away before we have to explain more than we need to." He was speaking of his large muscular, leather like wings. *"It took you long enough to get the message I sent to you. I didn't know this kat Phillip well, but I knew that they wasn't going anywhere without me. At every town I sent messages back telling you where we were."*

Nate and Luke tossed the body in a ravine behind the house. The stern look he gave Luke was similar to anger. Retraction of the wings were not possible if he couldn't calm their defensive mature. Unlike the beast of the night, he can control them. As they returned to the house, Luke felt small in their shadow. Alongside the road in front of the house, crows the size of vultures were crowding the trees and air with beating flapping feathers in mock applause. Their cackling calls sound panicked and announcing.

"Don't be mad at me. I did what any one of us would do and that is to protect Ty. This wouldn't have happened if she wasn't in town alone. Thanks to Annie, she avoided Clymythious, Navasha, Simon, and Benoit, so if anyone is to blame it is you."

The two talked and walked slowly to the house planning the next plan action for all involved, that included the Grenwalds.

"I don't blame you, Luke. It is more her or his, or whichever way you want to see it, use your own prerogative. We have one mission we need to be ready for. While you and Emily were running north like fugitive slaves, I confronted Victoria about her dark curse. I waited for the cloak of dark to challenge her and forcibly coerce her to remove it from Ty.

When Em left, I could only assume that she was going after Vicky, and I went in that accord. I have dealt with witches before, and they can be a worthy opponent which in her case was true. She took a beating and fought with all the dark forces and power she had until I cornered her at Hallowed crossing not far from her house. It was a fierce battle that I underestimated, and she fought with bravery. It was with my foot on her neck that she told truths in defeat. She said,

'The lovers curse and lovers fall

Hex the heart that won't recall

Twist love fate and silence cries

Give her more she can't deny

From the lust and faint remiss

Curse her in what she can't dismiss

Sunset rule and nature calls

And she shall be trapped in one and in all'

   I made her tell me what it meant in plain English, and she said it wasn't a curse but more like an urged foretelling of what was to come. The hag laughed about the accusation and that her spell should only have lasted a couple of days. Anything after that was because of the nature of the cursed."

   "You are saying that Ty is Emily now because unconsciously he wants to remain her?"

   "We know what we are but know not what we may be- to quote a friend of mine. And now in the state she is in, more is at risk than her awareness. You must not tell her what I have told you, *"He* said stopping on the porch before opening the door and pulling his wings tight under his vest to go in.

   "Hey, I ain't saying nothing, but what risk you talking about?

   Stop talking in riddles!"

Chapter 11

After the near complete demolition of the Grenwald's home, Luke, Emily, Annie, and Nate thought it best to move on. If Nate could find her, so could they. The goodbyes to Harriett and Gerald were difficult for Emily and Luke, and easy for Annie and Nate. Over the weeks they have almost become like a family. Harriett never told about what she knew about Emily. Only when they were completely alone did she mention it in concern and wisdom. What she did openly talk about was Nate's appearance and the loss of precious things that were destroyed in the battle with Phillip. She spoke about Emily as if she knew that he knew that he needed to protect her with innuendos that he didn't like or acknowledge. Late that night they departed the temporary lodgings and new family.

"Take this honey," she said giving her a parcel tightly wrapped in twine and a closed hand with money rolls into a handkerchief.

"My number is in there too. Call me if you ever need anything. You hear?"

"She will be fine with me," Nate interjected grabbing Emily's knapsack and the parcel out of the door to catch up with the others who were waiting on the road outside.

The sun was quickly peeking in the horizon and his rush was to avoid explaining any more than he had too.

"You better take care of them! I'll get Gerry to take the car and get rid of it in the opposite direction."

He sucked his teeth and shook Gerald's hands on his way out.

"That little fella is a special child, and I think you know it. Why don't y'all stay here for a while. It's not good that you are traveling. Don't know what you are running from, but I do know that you won't be running that fast in a couple of weeks," she said while resting her hand gently on her stomach *and if it is anything like what we have seen while you were here, I don't want to know."*

The next couple of nights journey was a combination of bus stations, rides with strangers and a couple of overnight stays in cheap motels along the back roads heading north. Emily only told Nate about the hundreds of dollars Mrs Grenwald gave her and she kept it a secret only giving Nate enough to secure expenses. They finally settled for a couple of months in an apartment that was cozy enough to hold four and allowed privacy. To the outside world they appeared to be a pair of vacationing couples that remained to themselves except for the crow's song that each night serenaded at twilight no matter where they were.

The nights were Emily's favorite because they functioned as one family with a daily dinner and occasional movie or visit to the nearby town off the ocean outside of New York. Small forgotten towns filled with descendants of the Amish community still riding horse buggies and vending their wares in small shops from roadside stands and shops. They felt safe among them, although they didn't fit in. The townsfolk would sometimes ask were Emily and Nate married and for the sake of comfort, they would allow it. Now showing, the assumption was an easy one. Afraid of being identified, she finally found the courage to get prenatal care from the midwives in the community without any other condition but one, and that was her health. No ID, no judgement, and definitely privacy. Luke and Annie grew suspect, and what looked like a little extra weight could be dismissed as they lived inclusive to themselves.

Midwives estimated that she was almost three months along. The questions about women health and what she does or expect upset her every time. She is mentally still Ty inside and the pregnancy was too much to wrap his head around. Her face glowed in the radiance, her once tiny waist now was pudgy and expanding. She often would catch Nate and Luke staring at her breast as they too were enlarging over the weeks. One thing is for sure, she would be no contender in battle. By day, Nate hated her to leave his side while he was in his cursed beast form. He preferred to practice with her on her tactical skills for he would never hurt her. The ritual spar was in preparation for a time that is eventual, with child or not. Nate was never at ease with it, but if it were a choice of her finding something else to do or teaching her defensive and offensive maneuvers that included boxing, swordplay, knife play, and even moves that were tactical in easy death with the most calculated agility. She learned all of them with confidence as if she was not learning it for the first time but reviewing some inner abilities that were dormant inside until disturbed. Most of the time Nate would allow her to attack him without holding back. It was the only way she could learn, and besides, in the day she was almost harmless against his mammoth size, but nonetheless, she fought like a man in ferocity, like life and death depended on it and releasing pent up emotions using Nate as the target.

"You hit like a girl Em. Concentrate. You won't have a second chance in battle. Look at you! You are weak and nonthreatening. Show me the warrior that defeated Raja the beast. Haven't you been through enough pain and anger to use it. No one cares about you or that little bastard freak of nature you carry. Maybe we should just give up and hope that their mercy and sympathy for the poor little boy... maybe Clymythious will make you one of his bitches and just be kind to you. Maybe...."

Emily had heard enough of his taunting and baiting. She spun around hit his temple with a kick hard enough to knock him down flat on his back landing in a one-legged extended squat from the rebound of his rock-hard head.

"Lucky blow! Now that is what I am talking about!"

She landed just feet away from the sword with one hand resting on its hilt and the other holding her slightly protruding belly, simmering in a blue hue. If arousal is what he intended, then he got the full thrust of it. He smirked while looking up at her from the floor.

"You know you can't beat me without unleashing your unbridled sentient embodiment. Hope that it will save you when you are in battle. I will defeat you otherwise. Calm down and fight me without it...boy!"

Emily got to her feet and focused on every word he said using the same anger to calm down. She wanted this fight, and it could get out of control if she doesn't. Blue walls returned to cloudy daylight reflected from the window.

"How dare you say that to me man! Fuck you and that yak you spitting at me. Fall back man...that's all I'm saying. Fall back! Fuck you gonna be part of all this and make me the bad guy. You ain't say none of that shit that night," she sobbingly said while dropping the sword on the floor behind her.

Both were amazed at the angered words that flowed out of her mouth. They both had forgotten that Ty is still very much present. Out of respect, Emily has kept him quiet for everyone else. The pressure of all that has happened cracked like a damn flooding! Drowning the valleys of that upheld walls in protection. One after another the venomous words charged the room. Nate stood up face to face to her in a stare down with his huge, clawed hands in a tight fist.

"If you gonna hit me then do it! I can take it. Don't hold back. I ain't scared."

But she was. One blow could hurt her and maybe hurt what's growing being inside her. She made a mental note to never speak as Ty again. His pride, anger, and hurt to the unfairness of the situation is forever mood changing like a pendulum for weeks now. She closed her eyes and braced herself for the blow. Whatever fate has planned for her, she is tired of fighting its losing battle. Nate never flinched or backed down, contemplating whether he would. Beast eyes studied each pore and feature on the breathtaking Emily. He couldn't find Ty in her, though he heard his words clearly. What he saw was someone he knew well who has been beaten and surrendering to the painful victory stubbornly holding firm in contending stance.

"I cannot."

Nate reeled from the sting of an open hand slap from Emily small hands. It snapped him into the present. His mind had wondered as he swallowed in her beauty while she had her eyes closed and jaw clenched. It reminded him of a fight long ago with her in another lifetime. They too had an argument then, in the small cabin on the Lee plantation on the edge of Edison's Manor on a hot summer's eve fighting on whether to run and be free up north. Emily could not understand why her husband wanted to escape from the complacent life of a slave with empathetic slave owners. It wasn't an easy life, but it was the only one she knew. She never took anything without an explanation- at least not from him. It was a time when negroes spent their lives not openly questioning or challenging authority. He made the mistake of not asking her but telling her his plan with no explanation. He couldn't tell her about Clymythious and the centuries of him being there and making it his purpose to watch over the Vessels before and not sound as if she was only another one that he loved on the way, nor did he want to tell his part in their demise with the Immortali. Clymythious had told him his plan to either snare her heart or cut it out and he couldn't let it happen again. He betrayed his brethren for her mortal love and had no time to explain, and for that he chose to surrender that argument and stayed. Eventuality owned his mourning till this day in his regret in that choice. Now a century later, here she stands in front of him, unreal and just as poignant. Again, he has to make that decision.

"Please Em leave with me now. Tell the others that we have to part ways. There is a lot about the future that is too much a ripple of the past. I have so much I need to tell you and prepare you for. Trust me, but first let us move from here. What is for us

should not endanger others and vice versus. So much you don't know or understand."

Emily face flushed in anger was stunned about what he was proposing. Eyes wide with jet black lashes damp in sweat and drying tears froze on his. Thoughts about the visions of Nate and his Emily secured all that he was saying, but she did not want to trust him. Since she met him as Ty in the beginning, as a protector and defender, he has selfishly relished in old memories that he punished her for, and when she gave into him it felt as though she could never live up to the idea as a reflection of her ancestor. It was as if God is forcing them both to atone for it by crushing them together at every turn. All was fine when Emily was a ghost of a time gone, but now the ghost is her and she the ghost.

"Okay Nate. I will do what you think is best, but no more secrets and tell me everything. I can tell you are holding back something you not telling me."

The two said their goodbyes to Luke and Annie without explanation- Luke being the one that didn't want them to separate and lost his temper.

"Go the fuck on then! Now that big guy got here, fuck me, right?"

Underneath that fury, masked in anger and disappointment was a man that has given so much to someone who now seems unappreciative and has discarded him and all that he has done. It took Emily's side bar words to calm him.

"Uncle Luke I didn't want this to go like this. I owe you so much and just let Nate have his way for now. Go back to the

cabin and when and if things make sense or even if they never do, I promise I will contact you. I couldn't have gotten this far without your old ass," Emily said while hugging him goodbye. It reminded her of the same goodbye her vision had of Emily letting go of the small infant from her bosom over the cliffs. In a paradoxical way, history and the past has re-emerge over and over again.

Luke stopped fighting and gave her his cell phone and nodded at Nate as they went into the night.

CHAPTER 12

Winter unleashed a terrible storm that week and they moved slowly up the coast, stopping at out-the-way motels and bed and breakfasts posing as a weary three traveling home. The blanket of snow whitewashed the back roads in a tranquil beauty with tufts of snow weighted on everything with ice cycles dripping from bare branches and cat tails that bow to winter's breath.

"Are you sure about this, Nate?" Emily asked in between one motel to the next one.

"I'm sure if you are."

"What does that mean?"

"Em I didn't tell you about what I found out when you left. I tried to beat it out of Vickie, and she told me some things I didn't know. I have been wrestling with telling you what she said."

Nate kept walking ahead of her waiting for her to ask more. In a couple of feet, the crunching sound of two was only one. She had stopped walking and stood back a couple of feet, not moving until she thought she could take what he had not said. In the snow, she looked like a broken stump, frozen and unpromising.

"Tell me, Nate!" She yelled to him.

"I will tell you when we are safe from the elements," he said, grabbing her mittened hand and pulling her along. He carries most of their belongings on his back on one shoulder,

and he gently toted her with the other hand, muttering while he made his way through a bleached road that only had their footprints behind them. With the storm gone, the night stars peered down on them, twinkling on a clear winter's night.

"We don't have time to go into this. We have at least seven hours before the sun, and we have to find shelter soon."

She didn't reply anymore on the trip. Eventually, he let her hand go as they approached a small town. Welcome to Ocean Crest, the sign just on its edge said. A comfortable bed and breakfast attached to a gift shop with a separate entrance was just the perfect place to stop and wait out the weather. Since Nate hasn't told Emily what he and Victoria talked about, she has been quiet. The days that passed slowly normally consist of them remaining in the backroom Bed & Breakfast for weeks. It snowed more and the television was the only entertainment in the one bedroom. Tensioned broke when she asked,

"Give me your hand," she put his hand on her stomach which was about sixteen weeks and not easy to hide now.

Although they sleep together and are locked in each other's company, intimacy has not existed. His large hand lightly laid on her stomach and he felt the baby kick. He jumped from the surprise of it and snatched his hand back. Through everything they have been through, it hasn't sunk in that this phenomenon is actually happening.

"He knows you," she said while rubbing her hand on her stomach to calm the baby down. "He has been kicking for about a week now. You seem not to show any concern about it, and I didn't want to say anything. This is weird for me. Just a year ago, I was a man with no family and now I have a baby or

something coming that is very much alive. I don't want you to feel obligated. But when I say I have a family, I am not just talking about the baby. I am talking about you and Luke too. I'd like to think that if the baby survives all this then maybe we can raise it normally. Do you think it's going to be alright?"

It was nine in the evening and Nate was in his normal form, dressed in flannel and jeans with big boots on that clunked on the second-floor room. He was pacing at the window, staring at it in its beautiful winter darkness. He never answered.

"It's March and if the Midwives are right, the baby will be here in July, but the way he is kicking and moving, I think he won't wait that long."

Nate finally decided to answer,

"How do you know it's a 'he'?"

"I don't know. When we were back with the Amish, they said that the baby had all the signs of a boy, so I just believed them. I don't care whether it's a girl or a boy. I just want it to be healthy."

"Em, well, now is a good time as any to tell you what Victoria said. It might be kind of difficult to hear."

"Omg! She said something is wrong with the baby?"

"No, she doesn't know about him. She said that the curse she put on you was only a spell for a day or so. She said that your remaining as Em is your choice after it wore off. There is part of you that wants to be and remain Emily. I believe her. I have not shared my heart openly and for this I apologize. These months with Emily I have treasured as a blessing. I never

thought I would get a chance to love her again and here you are. I think a part of me refuses to accept it because of the fear of losing you again, and now like deja vu, I am once again seeing more to you that is like your great great grandmother whom I loved more than life itself. I look at your glowing face and see her. I see her in your smile. I see her in your anger and joy. I see her in the way you talk to the baby as you sleep next to me, and the fear only grows with my sight. Somewhere out there are people that wish you harm and with everything I am I want to protect you, Luke, and the baby. My family."

His words were heavy and filled with bundled emotion. Emily stood and walked to the window as he spoke and listened to all that he was saying. In her head, portions replayed over and over.

"Do I want to be a woman and therefore I am? All this time I thought that I was cursed into being her and the truth is it was my choice?"

Emily stood in the full-length mirror and let her eyes judge. She saw the woman she has seen for months now. She was a little curvier than before. She has seen a lot of women and to her, she wasn't equal to them or felt she deserved to be a hybrid of one. She didn't have hips like women do, or large breasts, or any of what she considered black women to have. The reflection to her was a feminine version of Ty minus parts and accentuated ones filled in. The dull summer dress she wore indoors protruded out and emphasized that she was well into her first trimester. Where she, if born a woman, would feel mentally prepared, she is not. She blamed herself for not being careful when she laid with Nate. She fed on his hunger, and he wanted to fill the emptiness. This all could have been prevented if she had accepted it and not played on a lonely man.

"Maybe I should get rid of it. You don't want this, and I definitely didn't sign on for it; besides, what kind of parent will I be?" Suppose it's a monster of some sort? Suppose that this is just another cruel joke that God is having, or a punishment."

Nate stopped her from wallowing in the unknown. He walked behind her in the mirror, wrapping his hands around her bulging belly.

"Em, don't ever let me hear you talk like that! Lest you forget that this is who you wanted to be, and I was fortunate to have again. This what your God planned. You have been on journey all your life, and this too is part of it- a summation to the lives before. Have you taken a minute to think that maybe this little one is the one to change the world? Who are you to judge it?"

Emily felt comforted by his words. Even as Ty, she was reluctant to the possessive love that he cradled close to his heart. She did want to be Emily. She wanted to be that great love that she saw in her eyes, and in the mirror, she saw that. She felt safe in his arms and the guilt and shame waned away. He reinforced what she knew from the beginning...he loved her eternally.

Nate picked her up and carried her like a child to the bed and gently put her on it. He knew she had to be tired and hungry. He sat on the edge of the frayed quilted comforter that had tiny lavender stpring blossoms holding her hand.

"What would you like to eat my heart? You must rest and nourish yourself."

Emily slid up to the wooden backboard, looking intensely in his wrinkled brow eyes. Her small hand brushed his wooly beard and stopped just short of his ear.

"Don't you ever stop talking like that. At first, I thought it was odd and a little arrogant and dated, but it is what makes you, you. I love to hear you talk. You should do it more often. Wrap up from the snow and take my phone. Oh, and could you pick me up some pickles and French vanilla ice cream?"

Nate made his way through the small town of Edgeville and found a small storefront gas station that was still open despite the weather. He thought to himself how odd her request was for pickles and ice cream. She was Em alright. Back on the plantation, Emily would ask for odd things to eat when she was pregnant, too. Once, he had her look all through early Baltimore for cheese and grape marmalade. He knew he ought not return without it and spent all night looking for it till he found it. This time was more successful. The friendly clerk had what she wanted, and he bought himself a cigarillo as his own reward.

Edgeville was quiet doing the dormant snowstorm. It's building's roofs, cobbled sidewalks, and streets were untrodden and layered in undisturbed snow that swirled in the mild gusts. The cigarillo aroma and flavor blended in the calm of the moment. He stood on the storefront porch and took it all in. And then it hit him.

"I'm going to be a father again!"

The gelid elements and the quiet allowed his mind to trace back what had happened and what spawned out of it was a surprising pride that he, again, will be a father. The sides of his mouth curled into a smile as each tote on the cigar swelled in a father's joy while no one was looking. They were followed by the truth of the situation which snapped him back to his normal reserved self. It's time to get back to Em. He would feel better if he was there instead of here, drifting like the wispy snow in pride and realization.

With bags in hand and cigarillo in the corner of his mouth, he headed back through town to Emily. Stillness still roared in crispy cold, but where there should be one set of tracks, he counted four. They were footprints of at least three people that turned into an alley a block back from where he came from. Alarms were tingling, sensing danger. He unbuttoned his coat to make his sword and sidearm accessible. Thoughts of confronting who was following him were interrupted by the phone in his pocket playing a loud ringtone of some obscure gospel song that, in the muffled snow covers the town, was loud enough to cause an avalanche. He fumbled through his pockets to find it.

"Hello, Em?"

"No, this ain't no damn Em! Where is she and why do you have my phone, I gave her?" The voice said, screaming through the speaker. Somehow, he hit the speaker on it.

"Luke? Is that you? I can't talk now. Em is safe, but I'm not sure I am, and if you keep yelling, I'm going to hang up."

"Wait, wait, Nate! Don't hang up," Luke more quietly said.

"You guys need to get low. Annie and I have had to lose them guys more than once. I think they want Em. Where are you guys? We should be together. We haven't seen them for a couple of days, and they might have gotten a lead to y'all."

"We are in a small town named Edgeville north of Jersey in a small Bed and Breakfast on Main Street. Someone is following me while I went to the store. If I don't call you back, go and help her get out of here."

It's 3 o'clock and the sun is starting to sink on the horizon, reflecting hues of orange and purple as it froze the small town in the approaching night. On one hand, he wants to head in another direction, nowhere near Emily; on the other, he will be a prisoner of the night soon and not easy to hide. Instincts said to confront them as he hunted the footed trail in the alley. Apparently, the footprints went around the back of the building and back to the front. If he had gone the other direction when he left the store, they would have probably been waiting to trap him.

The sun is now melting behind the horizon and Nate feels the change begin. In anger, the beast emerges from within faster, transforming him into his night curse. With large beast hands and bulging wings that now course with blood, stretching them two feet in the air, escape will be easy. Nate the beast climbs up the side of the building and jumped from rooftop to rooftop, watching the ground below for the hunting party. The short snowstorm has covered most of the tracks, but he wanted to be sure that they weren't heading to Emily. Clymythious led the four of them, struggling to track the almost covered tracks.

"Find him; he can't be far." He ordered Navasha, who instructed Benoit and Simon to go in different directions.

"Nate, I know you are out there! You are trapped and I can sense you. Let's stop these silly games and talk. It's not too late for you. Surrender them to me and I will release the curse, and everything will be like it was. I have spoken to Odious, and we miss our brother. He told me himself that he wants you back in the Society. You belong with us!"

Like a displaced gargoyle on a parapet over Clymythious's head, Nate is listening and weighing the choices he has. None were choices of surrendering Emily. His head was crowded in the beast mode. Thoughts and emotions become primordial.

"I could kill them all and Em will be safe, but I will be forever in his flux and curse. If I do nothing it will be only a matter of time before the others find her. I choose to die here in honor," he thought to himself.

Nate jumped from the shadows in the sky with his black leather wings full extended and sword in hand, riding the current in attack from above Clymythious landing on him, slamming the hilt of the sword in a flurry of rage. He held him down with one hand and pelted him until Clymythious kicked him off of him, wiping blood from the corner of his eye and laughing as he stood up, wiping the snow off him.

"Now there's the warrior that I have fought side by side over the centuries. Hiding in shadows is a cowardly characteristic that doesn't suit you. We can battle to your death if fate insists, but consider my offer first, my brother. There is no glory in betrayal. As Immortali, we stand together to judge time and evolution in a crusade of honor. You may have

forsaken the very gods that created you and, in their scorn, you will perish with the mortals you protect. A fool's death is never a valiant one. This is what the third and last time you raised iron against me. Odious might favor your allegiance, but I can no longer hold content for dishonor."

With that, he removed his camouflage jacket and, on command, summoned his battle mode. Much like Nate's, large wings protruded from his ebony form. He drew his sword from its sheath with the tip touching the ground while he charged through the blood-speckled snow toward his opponent. With feet between them, each leaped in the air, clashing sword against sword, metal on metal, in an aerial wrestle. Clymythious' agility overwhelmed the clash, and his elbow connected to Nate's jaw knocking him from the air into the wall of the adjacent building. Where Clymythious landed on his feet, Nate lie on his back on a trail of slid snow into the building. Mortar dented from the force of him hitting against it so hard. It took his breath away for a couple of seconds, and Clymythious was again charging with his sword in front of him to impale a direct pierce to end the battle. As in slow motion, Nate saw his attack and moved just inches from its death blow, causing it to lodge itself in the brick-and-mortar tight.

Every man fears his own death, and it is that fear that spurs an innate fury for survival when it is more than oneself at cost. Nate's choices have been clear since Emily died over Edison Edge cliff. For him, it was not time to die.

"Clymythious, what you want, I cannot give. You want to murder and slay for gods I no longer worship or honor. If it were simple as doing the bidding as a duty, then it would be so, but blood in innocence is not honorable nor courageous."

Nate kicked Clymythious off the wall and the lodged sword. The two stood eye to eye and the stances were clear. Both men, in a moment, peeled back the taste for combat long enough to not think of themselves and see the men that have been friends and enemies, for the difference is little.

"I cannot let you walk from here old friend. Soon Navasha, Simon, and Benoit will be returning, and I cannot subdue them. Just give them to us and be spared the wrath of the Immortali."

"Again, I cannot give you what I don't have. They have gone their own paths weeks ago. I travel alone in search of her that I love. I think I can find her and if you promise to take her to the Counsel and let them be the judge, I will assist without prejudice," Nate said, dropping his sword out of his hand.

It was this gesture and retracted arched wings that symbolized reconciliation between indifferences.

"Fair enough, Nathaniel. Our agendas may be not of one accord, but it is enough for now."

Nate's plan was to lead them as far away from Emily as he could and hope that Luke would find her. If he couldn't protect her by her side, he could sacrifice himself by leading them away from her and the unborn child. It was no greater than the original sacrifice Emily did. His heart ached as the realization tortured his thoughts as he leads them further north. True to his word in irony, Clymythious removed the night curse and now more than ever, he wanted to be with her.

Luke and Annie did find her in Edgeville. They harbored her back in Maryland safe from peril. Nobody would think that they would return to so obvious a place. Spring left and summer came. The baby's birth was on any day now, but what would have been joy, shadowed the occasion. Emily had no idea what happened to Nate. She could only assume that he died in defense of her in Edgeville. Her swollen belly now cresting to the final days. Luke and Annie took care of her, working and sharing around-the-clock care. Neither of them questioned what or how the birth was going to be. It was decided that no matter what, the child would come first.

"I think that it's going to be a boy. He kicks and moves around like one. Seen enough mothers of sons to know one when I see one. Look at you! You should be glad that he is almost here, but you wobble around here as if the end of the world is coming. He will probably look like his father; God rest his soul. Have you thought about what you will name him?" Annie asked one night when Emily couldn't sleep.

Nights were difficult for Emily. She would sit at the window of the trailer they had rented and inconsolably staring into the night sky. Both Luke and Annie did all that they could to ease her mourning for Nate, but it would never last more than a couple hours before she lulled herself back into depression.

"Honey, it's not good for the baby to be so sad all the time. You are going to have to let go of the loss of Nate. He would want you too. Why don't you talk to me about him sweetie? It might help."

Although the pain of desertion and uncertainty was only getting harder to forget, Emily opened up that night and talked about the child's father.

"The first time I remember I saw him I was a child at my ninth birthday party. He stood in the alley where my backyard

party was being held. He said nothing, but I could feel him, although he frightened me. I saw him in the shadows all the time and if I tried to get closer, he would disappear until he came to the rescue in Edison's Edge. I can remember his full lips on mine, and I swooned in confusion. Here is this towering Black man who came out of nowhere. Not just any Black guy, but the one that I have been wanting to meet since I was a little boy. Girl, he was all that too. He smelled of unfamiliar scents that calmed me. Just as quickly as he appeared, he vanished. I still remember those piercing eyes that seemed to dig into me. He was a man of few words, but when he spoke, it was like poetry."

Emily never took her eyes off the night sky as she spoke of him as she rubbed the restless child inside her that was kicking every night. She would sing the song that she remembered hearing in the underground hideaway that Clymythious and Nate took her to. Only hearing the tune once, she somehow remembered the song.

"Hold it! What you mean 'when you were a little boy'? You are talking about that weird stuff that Luke won't discuss. You mean like in another life? Cause honey you all woman. Girl you crazy. What do you know about being a little boy?"

"Weird indeed Annie. You see, I died a century ago."

Annie was enthralled in the story; she told of a connection to past lives and sat in a chair by the window as if listening to a storyteller tell a fable. Emily told all that she could remember. It was a catharsis for her. Still locked in the serenity of night, she only paused when Annie had a question to help her understand.

"So, wait a minute. The woman in the oil painting was you carrying my Luke? That would make him much older than he is, and honey, ain't nothing old about him! Maybe the infant in the picture was you now and it could be telling you something. You said you saw her move when no one else did. If she took the baby into the woods, than it might not be a look into the past, but a glimpse into the future. Think about it. You said the picture was on a plantation and the woman had other children that were playing in front of it. You said she took the baby she was carrying into the forest and returned to the painting without it. I mean, your story is hard to believe, but it all keeps coming back to you. It all sounds crazy, but in a paradoxical way, it answers a lot about the missing parts." She said, coaxing her interest.

Out the window were the crows gathering in the yard and on the trailer. Tonight, they seemed irritated and overly excited. They fought with each other, flapping their wings and screaming caws from blackened trees instead of leaves; they filled every branch. The more they continued the exploration into the past, the more agitated they became until one smashed into the window and died on its ledge. Annie grabbed Emily from her window seat and shut the small curtains.

"I need to call Luke. Something is stirring tonight, and I don't think we should be alone."

Just then another one smashed against another window. The birds were deliberately smashing into the windows and circling over the trailer, swarming and more and more were arriving. Annie helped Emily to the bed and turned up the radio to drown their cries.

Genesis 3:16 To the woman, he said, *"I will make your pains in childbearing very severe; with painful labor, you will give birth to children. Your desire will be for your husband, and he will rule over you."*

Out of all the stations they could get in the outskirts trailer park, she could only get a sermon. Annie thought, hopefully, it would calm Emily down while she called Luke to come home. From the other room, she didn't hear crows who were still swarming around the trailer, but the fevered pastor continued his sermon. His topic, mostly on Genesis, eerily foretold what was happening...or that is how Annie saw it.

"Genesis 6:1-7 *When human beings began to increase in number on the earth and daughters were born to them, the sons of God saw that the daughters of humans were beautiful, and they married any of them they chose. Then the Lord said, "My Spirit will not contend with humans forever, for they are mortal; their days will be a hundred and twenty years." The Nephilim were on the earth in those days—and also afterward—when the sons of God went to the daughters of humans and had children by them. They were the heroes of old men of renown. The Lord saw how great the wickedness of the human race had become on the earth and that every inclination of the thoughts of the human heart was only evil all the time. The Lord regretted that he had made human beings on the earth, and his heart was deeply troubled. So, the Lord said, "I will wipe from the face of the earth the human race I have created—and with them the animals, the birds and the creatures that move along the ground—for I regret that I have made them."*

A knock at the door chased the crows, scurrying into the skies. Annie knew that Luke was on the way home, but he couldn't be here that fast. The knocker rapped on the repeatedly, getting more forceful with each knock. She answered, thinking that it was a neighbor concerned about the swarming crows or maybe Luke got a ride home. Nonetheless, she opened it without hesitation and there, in nothing but a grey hooded sweatshirt and jeans, stood a white man about fifty years old with deep Mediterranean toned skin whisking his shoulder length hair out of his face. He had gentle blue eyes that calmed but were objective in their stare.

"Is it possible I could use your phone. I live not far from here and the phones are down. I see that this may not be a good time, but I will be brief," he said while pausing to let her assess him. *"My name is Elijah. Do not worry. You, the mother, and the child will be fine."*

She let him in, and he touched the threshold as he came in and the crows became quiet. Still ranting scripture in sermon, the radio continued,

*"**Mark 13:27-29** And he will send his angels and gather his elect from the four winds, from the ends of the earth to the ends of the heavens. "Now learn this lesson from the fig tree: As soon as its twigs get tender and its leaves come out, you know that summer is near. Even so, when you see these things happening, you know that it is near, right at the door."*

Annie heard Emily let out a cry from the back of the trailer. She had left her in the bedroom and the cry was a familiar one. Something must be wrong, or her labor has started.

"It has begun," Elijah said. "Go and tend her. I will keep the dark from the light."

Annie didn't know exactly what he meant, but he said it with commanding authority that she left him to run to Emily.

"The baby is coming, Annie! I don't think I can do this. The pain is too much. Take me to a hospital."

Emily was screaming so loud, clawing at the sheets and Annie tried her best to restrain her. "Let me see what's going on and if it looks like we need to go to the hospital, I will drive this fucking trailer myself to the hospital," she said while wiping her forehead with a damp cloth. One of them has to remain calm and she eased her to trust her and lay back and hopefully, nature will run its natural course.

"*Hallelujah, hallelujah!*" The radio screamed.

"Omg! Emily, I can see his head! I better get you to the hospital. I have delivered calves, horses, puppies, and a couple of kittens, but they knew what to do. I am going to ask Elijah if he drove. Maybe he can take us to the hospital."

Annie ran back to the front of the trailer, where Elijah was sitting calmly. As Annie ran out panicking, and sweating profusely and stuttering, he stood and said that it wasn't enough time.

"The child will be here within the hour. You can handle this. It's the reason why you are here. Go in there and calm her, for she is very afraid. You are prepared and this day was foretold."

"Who the fuck are you? I'm telling you that I don't think I can do this! Boil some water or something!"

Elijah put his hand on her head, and she quieted and knew that she could do it. Something was soothing about his confidence and demeanor. He had the bluest eyes she had ever stared into.

"Okay, get me some towels out of that closet over there and give me a basin from under the sink with hot water. Make yourself useful!"

"Quiet woman! My job is to defend the dark ones that sense the child's arrival. They will come cloaked in shadows, waiting for the moment to siege this place. Heed nothing, they say or do. Never leave her side or look into their eyes. They appear hideous and smell of the smoke of hell. To look into their eyes would mean sure death to you, Emily, and the baby," he said while packing his knapsack with odd weapons that were ancient and sharp.

Elijah brushed everything off the cluttered table to the floor and laid each weapon and device, checking them as he proceeded. There were daggers and bows, marbled handled sickles, and a revolver with a long nuzzle, and things that Annie could not recognize and didn't want to know. Most were still covered in dried blood and dirt. She could hear him muttering a foreign to her prayer that sounded like Latin or some old form of it. The entire time, he ignored the incessant thuds of crows hurdling their bodies against the trailer in increasing thuds.

"Do as I tell you and tend to her. This has no concern of yours. Somethings you don't want to witness if you don't have

The Book of Emily

to. The devil's servant approaches close and that means the boy will have his first breath in the death of the crows."

Annie checked on Emily, who heaved in anguished breaths as the labor pains intensified and as they did, she simmered in an ambient violent hue rambling in the same gibberish language that Elijah was praying in the front of the trailer. Through a small slither of crack in the vinyl partitioned door she could see Elijah, unaware that she was watching, but the Elijah she saw was not the man in weathered clothing she left in the room. He was dressed in hooded linen white as snow with a gold belt tied around his waist with Hebrew symbols embroidered with a sword sheathed on his side. He had wings that arched from his back, resembling that of a dragon and when he turned to peer back at the room, his eyes blazed in fire. He spoke to her as if he could see her in the candle-lit room, but his voice now thundered though his lips seemed not to move upon them.

"You have been warned and what your eyes befall shall burn within you with no answers. From this point, do not trust them, for the deceptive one will try everything to get to the child. Behold him from afar," the sword pointing into the darkness where yellow eyes approaching peered through vine branches in the concealment of darkness.

Tingly cold shivered in his words, and Annie ran back to Emily in terror of what she had just seen and heard. Her eyes still scorched in the image of Elijah in his true form.

"Could he be right?"

"Will I search the rest of my life for explanations to things I cannot explain or understand?"

"What could be out there that would want to harm a child?"

By now, Emily is muttering in indecipherable rambling in raging purple. Her hair and face are drenched in sweat and Annie is now afraid of what could happen next. All she could think about is surrendering herself in prayer. She is way out of her league. Out the side window of the back room of the trailer where they hid, she could see Elijah step to darkness edge with sword in hand and encircled by chaotic crows, but the ominous eyes were not there in the wooded hedge. She was breathing so hard in fear that the open-sashed trailer window lost its opulence in her rapid breath in a mist she had to keep wiping with her sleeve.

"Get away from the window!" Emily screamed in a hallucinating state.

By the time Annie turned back to the window, she was staring directly into the face of a fang yellow-eyed beast that let out a curdling scream to match its grotesque, blood-drenched face. Dead crow feathers drying in their own blood in its teeth. With eyes too numerous to count, they were fixed in Annie's that were locked in them as if paralyzed by their fixed stare.

"Get away from the window, Annie!"

What she saw were the eyes converge into the eyes of Luke, pleading for her to let him in. Only Annie saw him.

"Luke, Luke, help us!"

"Let me in, girl and I can help. You know I love you and want to make sure you and she are safe," he said, clawing at the window.

She stood pegged against the window. She could hear Emily's pleas to get away from the it and she could not move. She was entranced by the morphed creature that was willing her to do his bid and let him in.

"Baby, you have to help me! He is going to kill you and the child! Don't you know me?"

Emily was screaming in the corner with her legs spread apart and her broken water streaming down her leg and, cursing the creature and beaming brighter than she was earlier. The light repelled the creature, who was keeping his gaze on Annie and whimpering.

"Stand from the window, Annie," Elijah yelled as he, in flight, flew through the night sky with crows trailing behind him. His wings were beating in powerful thrusts with each foot, he got closer.

"Nie eve shall relieve the destiny of man. Spawn of Lucifer, Legion of the damned and exhumed, you should feel the reckoning of God!"

The words filled the air with thunder, but they were coming from behind Annie. She turned and saw Emily hovering in the corner with her pupil-less eyes batting in each of the spoken words. They were not hers, but they were Elijah's.

"He that has been foretold since God created the Garden is close. From what should not be shall birthed him and the seal of Tartarus shall never be broken! Odious be gone!"

Luke/ the beast was called by name by Elijah and his appearance returned to the fanged monster that Annie could see. The trance was broken and with its break, the beast rammed his clawed hand through the window and clutched Annie's neck with his sharp talons, severing veins close to her arteries. She gasped for air as they dug deeper and deeper into her neck. Gale winds pummeled from him, tossing debris and dirt in a cyclone around the trailer with the crows descending and pecking on Odious, ripping flesh and some of his eyes from their many sockets, but he never let his grip from her throat.

"Odeus, Deceiver of men, feel the sword of fire!" Elijah said as his sword burst into amber and orange flames that rolled around the blade with a pillar of fire at its tip."

Things were happening at a rapid pace, with Emily screaming in delivery, Annie gasping in a deathly strangle, and the loud screeching of the crows as they swallowed eyes whole, each in their own individual agony. Her lions were being torn from the labor of childbirth. She had never felt pain like the pain of tearing flesh as the baby descended in her new womb and no one could help her or relieve its increasing torture. Her mind drifted into what she thought was hallucinatory delusions, hearing Elijah's words fall from her mouth. It wandered in the past memories. At first, they were just memories of the others of her past that mutated into ugly recollections of their deaths. She relived Amelia's sliced throat, and she could taste the blood and surprise as it flowed down her gown at the top of the stairs, and Frederick's strangulation by Nate's large hands, looking at his bloodshot eyes that surrendered in violent jealousy and shame. She felt the sharp rocks smash her bones at the bottom of Edison's Edge cliffs and seeing and hearing young Izzy's shrieking cries as his father fought the turbulent winds mid-air after sacrificing herself so that Nate could save him. She saw so many deaths of herself that only exaggerated the pain.

Elijah's sword pierced through Odious in a flanked attack from behind, projecting blood splattering against the windowpane with a sound of bone and cartilage crunching. It ran through him and the wall of the trailer like melted butter, stopping just inches from Annie, forcing him to release her limb body to the floor. Elijah's wound wasn't a fatal one, but it pinned him to the hilt of its blade, setting him on fire.

"It's coming! It's coming!" Emily said, hyperventilating on the floor that agitated Odious into an angered rage and tore his pinned reptile-like body into to a gaping hole in the side of the trailer, all the while squeezing his mangled body through the jagged opening, hissing and flicking a slimy tongue in front of him like a snake after a mouse- smelling the air with each flick in search of his prey. He crept over Annie's half-conscious body; she was not the prey. He flung his tongue across the old linoleum floor in blind search and blistering fire that had singed his scaled skin, smelling like sulpher, and burnt flesh. Outside, Elijah closed in, shining with blinding light and now crackling sword that dripped fire from its tip in fiery droplets in its path.

There was one last scream that silenced and halted all that was unfolding. It was Emily's last push and the wails of powerful new lungs that cried with each new breath. In the corner, amiss bodily fluids, and afterbirth, still attached to a dangling umbilical cord, covered in triumphant sweat and tears, was the new family, The newborn cries awakened Annie. She stood to her feet and grabbed a bat in an attempt to deter the now-moving, faster Odious, who also could hear the child. She smashed the large tongue and crawling appendages with everything she had while stalling to get Emily and the child from danger, her raspy voice sounding like gravel on gravel.

"Get up, Emily! This thing is still coming for you. I know you are tired and exhausted, but you must find the strength to get the baby out of here!"

Just then, Odious spoke to Emily, disguising his voice as Nate's. He is a master of deception and trickery. Emily has raised to her feet while coddling her infant in one arm. She held the old trailer's wood-panelled walls to get to the door to the adjacent room, but Odious's voice made her stop and listen.

"Emily! Emily! It's me, baby! Hand me my son so that he may know me. You know I love you and would never harm him."

Emily turned to see that Odious looked like Nate on the floor with his hands outstretched in a desperate plea. She looked down at the baby's face and screamed. His face now was covered with eyes and his face, which was just moments ago sweet and demure, was now growling in a soft hiss.

"Nooooool! This can't be. What happened to my baby? Nate, what have you done to our son! Oh God, no!"

"Let me hold him, Emily. Everything is alright. Bring him here," *he* said, still slithering across the floor, but Emily didn't see that. *"I'm hurt, honey; come closer to me."*

Winds funneled through the gape in the trailer preceding Elijah, who, while holding the crows at bay, sucked Odious out of the cabin, his claws ripping up the old floor in resistance. He held onto the splintered opening, still reaching for the child with the other hand, although partially disembodied. Emily crossed the room and stomped his hand that was holding onto the hole.

"Go back to hell, Nate, or beast, or whomever you are!"

She kept the baby wrapped in a bed sheet. She was afraid to look at him. His cries were distraught and terrified, as infants do when they sense their mother distraught. It took Annie's assistance to dislodge Odious's grip on the window that was still sucking everything out of the trailer except the two women. They cursed him as they delivered each blow to him. The wind carried him to the feet of Elijah and ceased. He stood with his archangel wings fully outstretched, and the moonlight could not compete with his radiance, the sword held above his head still ablaze and conducting cracking lightning from the sky. He looked down at Odious as if waiting for a command before making a decision about what the next punishment would be.

"I am God's decree, as told to all the fallen, you shall eternally be cast from the kingdom and never see it again until you and your brethren are thrown in the lake of fire, so be it now that you return to the prison of Tartarus until that day which falls upon us in haste. Days are numbered for all creatures and yours are as sure as the Lake of Fire is the end for you and the fallen two hundred!"

Elijah, in violent strokes, began hacking at Odious in a fiery onslaught that dismembered Odious body in pieces. The tortured screams were curdling. Whack by whack, until Elijah's dazzling white rob was so splattered in blood more than a butcher. It was more of a butchering than a death sentence. He kept chanting indecipherable prayers through it all. A hand, then an elbow, a leg, a torso, and lastly, the head that was still pleading for him to stop. The ladies watched in horror at Elijah's vicious wrath. Emily ran from the hole in the trailer because she couldn't watch the vindictive bludgeon, while Annie held her hands over her ears for the cries and grunts as each piece not only was severed but diced into small pieces that the crows fought for in quick gulping bites. This went on for at least an hour and they found themselves jumping at each chop as Odious screamed in pain.

It stopped abruptly and everything got quiet and still- even the crows. Winds calmed and the skies revealed a red full moon. After such a laborious ordeal, Annie tended to Emily who still would not look at the child who now slept wrapped in the bedsheets.

"Emily, you have to let me cut the cord. You did well, honey. Let me help you. Give me the child and let's finish making sure the both of you are alright."

"Take him! He is an abomination that has brought nothing but trouble since he was conceived. I don't want to look into his deformed face. Cut me free from that...that...thing!"

"What are talking about? I'm sure he is not a creature, and you will learn to love him. All newborns are insightful at first. Let me see."

Emily handed the sleeping infant to her, still bundled in sheets. To be not born a woman, her instincts still cling to her child, although she was exasperated and frightened by what she saw earlier. Annie talked smoothly and calmly as she cleaned both mother and child and cut the cord between them as Emily, with a blank expression, didn't say another word while she did it.

"There! You two are fixed up the best I could do under the circumstances. You need to feed him, Emily. This is where you

two bond. He has Nate's eyes and is dark as you...the little thing."

As Elijah said, an hour later and a whole lot of pushing and crying, the baby was born. He had all fingers and toes and was dark like his father. He cried loudly with a pair of lungs that signaled that he would be okay. Annie ran to the front room, hollering and rejoicing his arrival, only to find Luke coming in.

"It's a healthy boy! It's a healthy boy! I did it! I did it!"

Luke looked puzzled over all the excitement. When she called him, all she said was the crows were attacking and for him to get here quick and now to walk into her overwhelming excitement is a lot to catch up to.

"Where is Elijah?"

Luke grabbed her by the shoulders to calm her down and get her attention, but she kept rambling. *"The crows, and the windows, then Elijah, and I want to run, but he told me I could do it, so I did. He said that is why I am here and then I did it. I did it, Luke!"*

"Hold it, slow down. First let me see Emily and that will give you a moment to get yourself together. You not making any sense," Luke said while going to the back bedroom.

The room was dimly lit by candles that flickered light on the now smiling face of Emily and gave the room an ambient illumination. For months now, she hasn't smiled like that. In her arms, wrapped in an old blanket, was a chocolate baby that suckled on her right breast. His fine, straight hair and fat cheeks reminded him of a cherub. He went for the light switch, but Emily stopped him.

"Not yet; he is sensitive to light like his father. Give him a minute to adjust. Annie, could you bring the candle closer so he can see him?"

Before his eyes, he saw a miracle. A little new to the world being. Luke saw his father's resemblance in the way he frowned as the candle got closer, as if any second he was going to cry. Luke's breaths were short in his presence.

"Hey little fella? You had us worried, little man. Can I touch him, Emily?"

"Even better. You can hold him. He is named after you- Isaiah Nathaniel," she said, passing the squirming bundle to his nervous hands.

Luke's large, un-manicured hands from doing hard labor shook as he cradled him as if he was afraid he might hurt him. As soon as he held him close, the two glowed as if there was a kinetic bond they shared. After all, in a way, he is Luke's brother.

"Oh shit! Take him; something is happening. I didn't do anything. I swear. I'm so sorry."

Annie took the boy from Luke and immediately, the dim glow ceased. She put him back with Luke and it returned.

"Well, I'll be damned! Blow that candle out. If I didn't see it with my own eyes, I wouldn't have believed it!"

Annie's astonished face was priceless. For someone who has thought she has seen it all, every day with Luke and Emily reveals more than her imagination could have ever imagined.

"Lawd, does anything happen normal for you guys?"

Chapter 13

As Emily slept with the brown miracle in her arms, Annie and Luke exhaled and stood amidst the destroyed front of the trailer. Its rustic fixtures and cracked windows from the crow's attack looked like a tornado had coursed through it. Shattered blood, smeared glass, debris, and dead birds were scattered on the floor and old appliances. The cleanup would be extensive, and they knew that this was no environment for a newborn. Annie led the cleanup, instructing Luke to do the exterior and she, the interior. She avoided conversation and prolonged eye contact with him to no avail as he was waiting for what she was going to say. He arrived after the turmoil and chaos, and she hadn't explained it all to him. Eventually, he plopped in a worn, small love seat and followed her with his eyes until she got tired of averting him.

"I guess you want to know the details of all this." She said with her hands on her hips, surveying the trailer. "If it weren't for Elijah showing up, I don't know what would have happened. It was like he knew before we knew what was happening. He showed up knocking on the door right after the crows started acting all *"Hitchcocky".*

"What the hell does "Hitchcocky" *mean?"* He said with his voice raised an octave higher than the norm.

"Who are you yelling at? You know exactly what I am saying. Damn crows been following her since I came around. Now you want to sit there and act new about it? Nigga please!"

The trailer shrunk in their frustration as the heated agreement closed the tin-tempered walls, but Annie continued explaining how the stranger showed up and his just-as-eerie disappearance. Luke's anxiousness settled down as she accounted the events as she remembered them.

"Just before Elijah showed up, Emily told me some stuff about her, and you, and of course the mysterious Nate. Why didn't you feel like you could tell me about all this? You and I should have no secrets. I have left my hometown, my job, and family and friends on the faith that it was the right thing to do, and I know it was, but you need to be on the up and up with me. Start from the beginning and don't leave nothing out."

He began from what he remembered clouded in deliberate amnesia- foster parents and when he knew he wasn't like the other kids. Like Emily, he didn't know how to control or divide his emotions from the surging sentient awareness that was awakening as he got older. It led him to solitary isolation from his foster parents out of resentment and the wrong crowd. It also bought a lifestyle of drugs, fights, and spiritual detachment that ultimately sent him repeatedly to jail, and finally prison, where he met Ty and put all the pieces together.

The two talked for hours about Luke's life and connections to Nate and Emily. Long overdue, the conversation gave depth to what they must do and prepare for. It also brought them together.

"Do you think we are part of a celestial plan that has already been blueprinted and architected by something more powerful than us? From what you have told me, we are part of some prophetic plan that is heading for a final end. Shouldn't we be prepared, and how is Emily going to fight with an infant? I have a plan. I don't know if she will be okay with it. Elijah said

I was here for this and maybe I am. I could take the baby and disappear until this is over. I think you should stay with her. Do you think she will go for it. I think that is what Elijah meant."

"I don't know, Annie. Ty, I mean Emily might feel separated from the kid. Let's wait a couple of days or weeks and feel it out. I like the idea baby; things will only get more dangerous, and something is hallowed about him. I know Nate knows about him, but I don't think that Clymythious and them know anything."

With the cabin restored back to its clean antiquated confined space, and the mother and child are now out of bed and doing fine, the family of four started collecting their things to move to a better place for baby Izzy. There was an edginess that suffocated them in anxiety. It was time to go. Both Emily and Luke could feel eminent danger on the horizon. What Luke didn't tell anyone is that he had been sneaking away texting Emily's phone and touching base with Nate. The first text communication came from Nate. It read,

"Luke, this is Nate, I have thrown them off your tracks for weeks and they are no longer falling for my ploy. They are backtracking back to Maryland. Be careful. I don't know how long I can mislead. Could you somehow give Emily this message?" The next text read more urgent, and it was short and cryptic.

"Edison."

The last message made it pertinent that he shows the girls. Before it arrived, Luke wanted to keep the peace and security that they all felt for months as little Isaiah grew. They all thought about the somewhat far away presence of danger, but hid it behind the smiling face of Isaiah, who no matter how hard they tried, looked like a spitting image of his father.

"*It's time for us to move, ladies. Isaiah is strong enough to travel. Hell, the way he is crawling around this trailer, he could almost walk with us!*"

The ladies listened and passed the phone around, reading Nate's text. Only Annie seemed disgruntled and upset. Emily's face cast a sullen, withdrawn expression as the reality of moving and Nate's warning set in. She sat still and let the others gather and pack the loose items that weren't worth traveling with. Annie and Nate barked plans as they did it.

"*We need to prepare for the road and be prepared with just the essentials. For the life of me, I can't see how they would find us, but he wouldn't have warned us if they weren't close. Gotta love big guy. He held them off for months,*" Luke said as he went out to pack things in an old car he used to get back and forth.

As the trailer got farther and farther away as they wound down the side dirt road away from what has been home for months, all but Isaiah felt as if they were leaving home. It was late November, and the fall leaves blustered behind them in a swirling dirt cloud. What was hard was the abandonment of the home they were a family in and the return to the chaos of a future tiding a final war. First stop was a gas station where they could grab food, water, and gas outside of Elliott. Annie advised that Emily and young Isaiah stay back in the car while they handled it. They could be traveling for hours and if they didn't have to stop, they hadn't planned on it.

"Emily, we are going to be fine. Take that worried look off your face. I have an idea I want to talk to you about," she said, lowering her voice as if the fall wind would steal and carry her conversation. "I could, if you were worried, take the baby to my family house while you deal with this confrontation everybody is afraid to talk about. You know I love him like he is my own and after this is over, you could come and get him and know he was safe. It's just an idea. I think you could focus on the task at hand if you didn't have to worry about him. I think that is the reason why I am here in some weird way."

Tiny Isaiah coo'd in his mother's arms, smiling at Annie. Emily's mind raced to make a decision she didn't want to make. Like a Madonna, she sat in the back seat of the old ford truck listening. Motherhood is so far from what she planned in life, but along with the circumstance and paradox of it all, she has accepted it- it's unnatural by every philosophy and imagination for her, yet here Isaiah is and she, who was born he, is now them. Justification lies only in emotions that have bred in her from as far as she can remember.

"Annie, I appreciate what you are offering, and it makes sense to protect him foremost, but I don't think I will ever let him go. I might not ever get the chance to be a mother to him again. Suppose if things revert to the way they were for me? How do I explain to a child what I cannot understand myself? What would even be worse is I didn't survive the dark future. Before him, everything was dark, and now my joy rises and sets with him. He is a miracle and a reason for me to live for tomorrow."

"Girl he is your reason to live for tomorrow and tomorrow is almost written for you, and you know it. I didn't want to tell *you, but Elijah said I had a purpose for being here. He said that nothing was an accident and that I will know what to do. My heart says this is part of what he meant. I am supposed to be right here to help you, Isaiah, and Luke through passage of crisis. Lord knows I don't know exactly what he meant, but I can see that this would be the right thing to do,"* she willfully admitted.

When Luke returned with the supplies and filled the tank, he asked the ladies what the plan was.

"I know that look ladies. Just tell me what you gals want to do, and we are doing it. I might be an old fool, but I know when women are strategizing, and I know which battle I can't win. So, where are we going?"

Annie looked from Luke to Emily and waited for her response. Surprisingly, she chose to take her suggestion.

"We are going to let Annie take Isaiah to safety with her family. Nate and Clymythious are tracking us down and they might not know anything about Izzy. Let Annie take the truck and you and I will secure another means and wait for our hunters to come to us. It's time," fell reluctantly from her lips as she passed the swaddled baby into Annie's arms, kissing his forehead with a soft peck that was like goodbye. His tiny mahogany fingers grasped her hair in delight, totally unaware that this could be the last time he saw his mother. *"Promise me, Annie that you will let him know his father. Tell him how he came to be and how his father sacrificed for him."* She said tying her hair back after Izzy pulled it out from its edges. She continued, but this time, she spoke directly to Izzy as if he understood what she was saying.

"Little miracle man, there is so much that I want to tell you and so much you should know." Her words were soft as any mother can to a child. *"You fight this ugly world, and you hold your head high like the special child you are. Know that your existence is one of love and God, and that in you lies the secret of the universe. Not an exception, but a rule that you embody with each breath you take. Know that and walk in pride through all the prejudices and barriers that will only make you a great man and though you might be the last of hopelessness and the first of beginnings, you have a purpose."*

It was as heartbreaking as anything Annie ever has seen. No parent would ever resolve anything by separation if it weren't for sacrificial love. Emily adjusted herself and turned to Luke, whose face was shocked and unprepared for the sudden plan. Over the weeks, he has seen things that could only be predestined and this likely wasn't any different. The woman who turned to him was defiant and much stronger than he has ever seen her in months. There was no argument, nothing he could say, or any re-evaluation of the events that would alter her choice. The decision was made, and it was more concrete as it was emotional. She was tired of running and what he could feel in sadness was only stifled in her anger, which raged in a subtle aggressiveness that she harnessed in her pain. He didn't feel sympathy for her. He felt sympathy for her hunters. The time has come, and she has more than herself, Nate, or him to combat with.

"Aw hell, it's showtime huh?" Luke said while dividing the food supplies. *"Annie, you take care of that boy, and I will catch up with you. Think I will feel better too if you are safe as well. Ain't nothing to worry over. I love you baby."*

That old truck gunned away in the wake of day in the approaching night, clanking in its repaired gears and loud exhaust. Emily watched it till it was a speck of dust in the far distance before she moved. The further the truck went away, the more her hue turned from faint to brilliant and the clouds curled overhead in connection to her surmounting fury. She raised her right arm to the bubbling sky and lightning struck her and the sword split the heavens and fell to her beckoning clutch, followed by a cloudburst of rain. Luke stood beside her, watching the skies obey her command. He let his large wings expand beside her and shield the rain that soaked them both. No time for subtleties anymore.

"You ready, Luke?"

"Been ready. I was born ready!"

Chapter 14

On the eve of night, the two traveled down the dark roads, only navigating by the stars above after the storm quelled Emily's outward blaze. Her mind was caught in its own anxieties of a mother who felt the sudden loneliness and feelings of abandonment. Still burning in hue, carrying a sword by her side, every step was challenging her future, and each step promised a resolution that could only end one way in her mind- finality and a reunion she was certain how to face. Luke paced beside her, chattering the whole time in a one-way conversation, keeping himself involved with the now distant and eerie Emily.

"So, do we have a plan?" He asked, not expecting a reply.

"I hope Annie and nephew are okay. I'm still not sure if it was a great idea. She doesn't know what could be on her heels. Suppose they go after them? What do you think Nate will do? He could very well be setting a trap for us. He didn't even ask about the baby," Luke angrily spat. *"Damn it, talk to me, Ty!"*

She turned and gazed right through him. His slip of names exposed his building apprehension, and it was easy to see that she heard nothing of what he said, although her eyes answered what he was directly talking about in their smoldering, icy, unresponsive depth. Her plan, that she kept silent was to intercept Clymythious and part as they were getting closer using the element of surprise to bring the battle to a head. For her, replying to Luke's questions was useless in changing the events that were. As they kept moving and talking, Luke's badgering escalated her anger. Soon she was not walking but hovering inches from the ground, focused, and defiant, in illuminated blue hues darker than the night sky, brightening the way. Unlike the other times where she lacked control, she now embraced it in retribution.

"Can you not be so obvious? We are going to be seen from miles away...oh, I get the point. Let me shut up," he said after realizing that might have been her point.

After about ten or twelve miles, on roads, paths, and brush, she stopped and hovered in dead air vibration that made her brighter and brighter. Now, the sword is raised to her side as if in anticipation of something awry. Something that wasn't welcomed.

"Someone is with us. They have been following us for miles now. There, just behind that tree line, they watch," she said, pointing the sword in that direction.

"Show yourself, or I will come show you. You cannot hide!"

As she said, the tree line rustled and amongst the bush and bramble emerged Elijah, who had been on their trail for miles. Neither Luke nor Emily have ever met him, so for them, he was a potential enemy- a stranger. He walked from the brush directly to them, unafraid of Emily's now curled-in-blue flames sword.

"I am not your enemy. You know of me and what you feel is not threatening. I have come in aid as I did the night your son was born. My presence is not solely to silence the crows, but to raise armor in protection against dark forces and powers that want what they cannot have."

Elijah approached cautiously to them. His scruffy clothing, which consisted of dingy whites and tan layers of clothing, hid his tall form. Though he approached quickly in with urgency, his tone never wavered.

"Because you seek truth in apocalyptic chaos, I will fight beside you and defeat the ones that oppose you, but I must warn you- this will not be an easy battle and it's scars run deeper than the flesh."

Emily can now see his chiseled, worn face as the shadows fade. Unshaven, but not dirty, his leathered skin seemed in an odd way prophetic. He had eyes that burned in blue coolness and sedated discern. His skin was dark as the deep tones Indigenous around the equator. Although his words forecast an uncertainty, he, himself, held all emotions in assured calm.

Luke, with his appendages, outstretched between them, did not trust so easy. Like his father, in his anger, he had no compassion for subtleties.

"Hold up, man, before you get more than you want! You don't just go walking up on a nigga in the dark like that. We don't know you like that, and you sure don't want to catch a beat down." Luke held his ground in preparation for an offensive attack despite Elijah's words.

"I trust him, Luke," Emily said stepping around Luke and lowering the sword to her side.

"How you going to trust a white guy that has been trailing us? He could be up to some sneaky shit. I don't care what he said."

Elijah kept walking closer and closer, ignoring Luke's skepticism, and keeping his eyes locked in Emily's.

"You are not afraid, are you? He is right not to trust anyone. The line between the light and the dark is not seen with the eyes and wears many masks of deception, but you, Augustus have seen both and know the difference. The day of finals are approaching. Many times, I have ushered you through the difficulties of its arrival. You are your ancestors and their prodigies in one. Like you they awakened and surrendered. It has long been written in forbidden folklore that your coming is what begins the end."

"Aw here we go with the Augustus shit. Okay, okay...so you know some shit. You ain't slick with it. So, I guess you got a better plan than we got. Might as well let us hear it. I think the plan that Emily has is crazy. Who goes to the enemy knowing that they are outnumbered?" Luke interjected.

The darkness and chill enclosed around the three as Emily's now dimming hue is barely a glow anymore. The dark road now squashed and weighted in stellar skies that suspended over them, supported by far mountains and tree lines velvets their journey. Luke scourged ahead, muttering, and talking to himself while Emily and Elijah talked behind him like stragglers.

"You know you are the first of a long lineage of Vessels to command your past selves and embody them. He that you love powers you. Nathaniel has gone from enemy with Immortali to protector, and now he has sacrificed himself to protect you. Like you, no Seraphim before him has changed their fate. It very well might cost him his immortality."

"Elijah, are you telling me that he gave up his life for me?" Emily said, stopping mid-road.

"His deeds will seal his death for he loves you more than his duty, and your love for him is what transformed you to suit him. You were not cursed by another as you think. It was your choice. It has always been your choice. The witch might have induced it, but you embraced it and your child. You have the power to return to your birthright if you so choose. You were not born of the flesh a woman- only in the reigning spirit. Know this and own your own destiny whether it be in victory or defeat."

Elijah's words fell on Emily in as if they, too, loomed heavy like the moonless sky, heavy and cumbersome. They meant that she wanted to be Emily more than she wanted to be Ty for Nate's love. Nate held onto the love he lost over a jagged bottom canyon in Edison's Edge, and although the love he lost was a direct transient descendant, her love for him burned in Ty. Emily has a son now born from that rekindle and the ponderous thoughts crowd her thoughts as Elijah elaborated more and more.

"Behold yourself as you are, be it woman or man; flesh is temporal. Both are warriors and both Nathaniel loves. Be warned, my friend. It is that same love that can distract you from your mission and cloud your judgment and decisions. Only you have to make the choice of which serves you best. What I say are not facts or future in stone, but nonetheless, they are truths that only God knows."

She had no more to say about it after he put it in his perspective. The emotion vestiges run her choice and fate. In the old world of division and separatism, she lived as Ty. Emily was much easier to handle in ideology as a curse or something that was not in his control. It was a subjection that made him a victim with no choice, but what Elijah has said means that inside of her was an unconscious being who chose and rose from that choice. She dropped the sword and fell to her knees. It was too much to take after everything she has been through. All the chase and confusion has overwhelmed her in doubt and uncertainty. Elijah stood over her and gave her a moment to digest what he has revealed to her.

Ahead, Luke pacing waiting for them to catch up. His shadowed gestures, though too far to hear, was clearly impatience and full of anxiety. She hadn't thought about how this is all affecting him. He has not known his father, and never had a chance to know his mother, yet he won't leave her side whether she embodies her or not. This very well could be a horrific battle for him, too. He, too, might witness the death of his father and the destruction of all that he has, over the months, found a family in. As she sat on the ground in defeat and personal judgment, she wept. Didn't take long before Luke was running back to them in panic.

"Fuck did you do, man? Emily, are you okay?"

Before she could answer, Luke had Elijah collared by his coat against a tree, tussling with his winged appendages flapping and cutting the wind with each of its beats. She had not seen Luke's rage in his youthful form. Elijah resisted little and Luke tossed him into the top branches with one thrust.

"Nooooooo! Stop Luke, stop!" She cried from the ground as Luke was in pursuit after him in the skies. The two fought a battle with large wings beating the air like an aerial cock fight. Luke's initial blows now were defensive ones. It was obvious that Elijah didn't want to hurt Luke; nor would he allow him to

hurt him in anger and confusion. Elijah's strength and agility was far in control than Luke's. Final blow was a blow from Elijah as he had one hand around Luke's neck and one large fist above his head that wound through the air with such force that thrusted Luke's chest and sent him careening through the branches, beaten and out of breath.

"Again, I say I am not your enemy. Recompose yourself and think. If harm to any one of you was the objective, then you both would be dead. Luke, you did very well in the fledgling battle, and I can teach you more to help you become a formidable warrior, but for now keep your focus on what has yet to come. Real enemies are not far in front of us. We might have two, maybe three days until we are face to face. In this time, I am here to prepare you, not only with sharpening your fight skills, but to fortify your consciousness and explain the past that you know little of and what you might be giving your life for."

The last blow hurled Luke feet away. He emerged with thickets and leaves on him, and he calmed down while helping Emily up to her feet.

"So why are you sitting there balling Emily? I thought that he had done something to hurt you when I saw you on the ground in front of him. Fuck is going on?"

Neither Elijah nor Emily volunteered an answer. Emily was still not quite sure what she was feeling. There was no warrior present in her. It had been thwarted by Elijah's painful words.

"Look, I don't know what just happened, but somebody is going to get this shit together!" He said, picking the sword up and shoving it at her sternly. *"Yo Ty man, you better come out of it. We done come too far for you to let whatever homie has done*

or said to you. Don't let whatever he said make you forget who you are and what you know we gotta do. Think about Isiah. Think about Nate. Hell, think about my ass!"

She stopped him with her hand out, signaling him to say no more. Her clenched fist ignited the steel blade again in rolling blue flames. Whenever Luke has called her *"Ty,"* she knew that he was serious about whatever he was talking about. It was enough to bring her around despite feeling sorry for herself.

"Now that's what I'm talking about!" Luke cheered, following behind her with Elijah.

The next few days were filled with combat sword and weaponry training and long talks about a time when the world they thought they knew was different. Elijah's spars were difficult, and compared to the daily stories, were the worst part of it. Emily adapted well, but Luke complained through because Elijah added more weapons to train with for him. For the two, it was as if they were in a military Boot Camp for the *"Gifted."* It included sword and shield defense, and offense moves, aerial battles, and martial arts that resembled two birds fighting in the air. The object in this one was to dominate the air and to ground your opponent. Luke excelled in it like his father does and Emily has an innate flair for the sword play. Her steel blue hand-carved handle weighed at least 50 lbs, but in her hand, she maneuvered it as if were straw. She learned how to summon it to her side no matter how far it was from her. It was during this training that some of her vigor and aggressive personality returned.

Each night, after the long workouts and battle strategies, Elijah would talk of a time not recorded. He spoke of an ancient time when the world had dimensions and worlds within themselves. Emily and Luke found his accountings to be a revelation of truth and looked forward to them whenever he offered them. Times when beasts, gods, and other creatures reigned over the Earth and universe until God tired of their arrogant ways and destroyed most of the ones that believed they could rule. Few remained to this day, and they have hidden themselves amongst God's chosen.

"Let no man govern over your soul and ancient treason shall spill blood no more. Augustus, you feel lost, and you feel betrayed, but the test is to repeat man's mistake as well as his victory. Judge by your heart and decisions will bear the fruit of eons of suffering. To disobey it would be a sure damnation of the last of your kind," Elijah said one chilly early night resting by a campfire and eating wild fruits and nuts.

"'I have never saw a choice, Elijah. You speak as if I had or have one. I don't think I never have wanted one, although all my life the paths have felt familiar, it has never felt like a choice," Emily solemnly confessed. *"I don't think I would have the pain of being different and alone, black and persecuted, man or woman. I have thought about everything you have been talking about and it only makes me more confused the more I know."*

"Y'all too deep for me. I'd go crazy if I tried to rationalize this stuff! It just is Ty! You got a son when once upon a time you had balls like any other man but look at you now. Just as real as any woman I have ever known. Explain that one Elijah," he said getting up from a fallen tree he was sitting on. *"Let me say this, I know God and I know that ain't nothing going down unless he wants it to go down, so if you got something that is*

The Book of Emily

going to change the future or get them niggas off of our back, you need to share it now," huffing off into the night.

The sounds of faraway loons held the left conversation between Elijah and Emily. Only the occasional crackle of moisture in kindling caused them to look at each other. Overhead, the night sky full lit with pinholes of light spun in its constellations. Elijah fell asleep as the embers of the fire dimmed. She could not sleep, though she closed her eyes and thought of tiny Izzy's face and the way he looked into her eyes in study. It kept her collected to hold the memories of him close. The way he smelled, his squealing giggle, the way he felt, and the babbling baby talk he did, soothed the irrational thoughts. Even the distant crows sounded like his cries when he can't have his way. The smoldering smell of burning oak smoke reminded her of the old trailer and wood-burning furnace also stilled her anxiety. Soon, sleep crept in. She dreamed of a time she does not remember in a room like any other that she has ever been in, with high fresco ceilings with elaborated molding in gilded in gold with walls adorned with beautiful art and animal head trophies. A candlelit chandelier labored to brighten the extravagant room. Large windows framed in crushed velvet blue drapes and its marbles floors. Not one of the paintings smiled or appeared to be happy. Most, were regally poised in chairs or horses frozen in active motion. The entire dream was in a renaissance period with servants that occasionally would cross through its long halls dressed in satin and velvet. She was in the library of a large mansion. Nothing like she as ever seen before. She awoke lying in a chez chair that was softer than the ground she fell asleep on. Its soft petals of Ivy and floral patterns match the aristocratic elegance of the room.

She was dressed in a beautiful yellow satin and lace gown with an irritating Petticoat under it, with ruffles and tight bodice. On the other side of the room hung a huge antique mirror that slanted down from the hearth. The woman she saw reflected back to her was indeed herself, but more beautiful and fairer. Her hair was tightly coiffed in pin curls and pins and all she could say to herself was, *"This can't be real."* She stood up to compose herself and saw her reflection. She was radiant with coifed black tresses pinned in mini mother-of-pearl pins. From the tight yellow satin slippers, she wore loops of pearls she wore around her tiny neck; she was a vision of enchantment and beauty.

In the corridor, beyond two white large doors, she could hear voices in debate and conversation. One voice sounded familiar. The only way she could be sure is to get close to the large doors opening and listen. This dream was so unbelievable that she summoned the courage to walk through the large doors and interrupt the conversation between the two men. Both men paused mid-sentence as she entered. Each man nodded as to greet her, but one held out his hand, gesturing for her to take his. It was Clymythious! She was locked in her own footsteps in shock at seeing him in what was a dream, and now would classify as a nightmare.

"Come, my darling! You look pale. Come sit with the Earl Hamilton and I. We promise not to bore you with our man talk of hunting and business. Your beauty, as always, is breathtaking and will be a welcomed distraction."

The reality of the dream was too real to be considered a dream to Emily. She could feel the binding dress cut her breath down to short pants in suppressed labor. The look in his eyes was not of malcontent, but almost in complete adornment. He waited for her to walk to him as if he expected nothing less, with his hand still extended in patience. With a confident smile, he stood regal and handsome with his embroidered gold jacket with paisley leaves stretching over silken shoulders. He and the Earl, who stood as she entered the room, dressed in silk, velvet and lace with powdered wigs, were not the ones out of place. As she got closer, his large statuesque presence towered more than six inches over her, and she reluctantly gave him her hand and he gently kissed it and led her to sit by his side.

"It is with great honor to introduce Lady Amelia of Winchester, my lovely fiancée, although she won't concede to it. One day, she will and rule over Dorchester Manor," he said while firmly holding her trembling hand.

The Earl chuckled under his breath and stood up to get a closer look at Amelia. Pale, and much older than Clymythious, she dared not gaze at his inspection. His snorting breathing that ravaged her with his outward please made the chill of the extravagant large room bitterly cold.

"Mmmm...what a beauty of a Nubian bride Sir Clymythious. Do tell how you found such a delightful treasure."

Amelia felt like a slave on an auction block as Hamilton lifted her chin to gaze into her eyes. His cold, chubby fingers, un-manicured nails, and snarling breath seem to find pleasure in hoisting her. Well into his late fifties, he required no recuperation.

"If I were you, sir, I would make her my bed wench and skip the formalities. She is a feral creature that looks like she will bite!"

The two heartily laughed at their domination of the situation only interrupted by a servant waiting in the doorway to announce a guest.

"You have a guest, sir. A Captain Nathaniel Gustant," he interjected and cautiously left the room.

"Are you expecting guest Clymythious? This evening is getting more and more interesting. Shall I give you some privacy? I would love to get to know the Lady in your absence."

"Dear Earl, you old fox, I wouldn't leave you with my horse, let alone my sweet Amelia! I trust you can hold your honor. Amelia, run fast, my guest dear has his eye on you," he laughed, leaving the room.

No sooner than he left the room, Hamilton besieged on Amelia. His ghoulish pale skin and foul breath lost all friendliness and grace as he tried to coerce her into his advances, flickering his tongue after each word.

"Aw, my dear, we have a moment. Clymythious is a fool, but I am not. His heart makes him your pawn, although he eventually will do what needs to be done. I can make this more pleasurable for both of us. In my youth, I was known as quite the lady's man. A sweet young brown morsel like you should be happy to have me interested. Be nice to me and I can ensure that you will feel no pain in what must happen," he said while pulling pins from her hair and tugging at her gown.

She slapped his wrinkled face and caught him by surprise as she tried to escape his grasp on her dress that tore pearled buttons to the floor as the satin ripped.

"Sir, you have me confused. I am not that kind of a woman. I wouldn't allow you to touch me if you were the last man on Earth, you disgusting impetuous excuse of a man!" Amelia said, thinking she could have the last word and escape his clutch, but she could only run as fast as she could in the torn gown without tripping on it.

She ran through the large halls as fast as she could, holding the petticoat and silk gathered in one hand and the now loose bodice pressed to her bosom. The dream has become a nightmare, and she has no idea of which way to run. All she knew is that the Earl had evil plans that sickened her as she trolled the dark, torchlit halls that were lined with grimaced face paintings whose eyes seemed to follow as she scurried past them. Ahead, she could see a marbled stairway that could lead to her escape from Hamilton or maybe the nightmare itself. Behind her, beside her, and echoing, she could hear the sound of wings and laughter, taunting her and mocking her attempt to flee. At end of the long corridor stood a dark form hunched over with large bat-like wings and still laughing.

"I am going to enjoy your flesh like nothing you can imagine. Your heart might not be mine, but it will taste just the same!" It was the Earl.

The ominous flying creature closed in on Amelia with just a couple of beats of its wings. She only stopped to turn once, only to see its ghoulish snarling face as he grabbed her by her throat over the banister at the top of the stairwell. Consciousness was fading as she struggled to breathe as he squeezed her air from her.

"*Pity we haven't gotten the chance to get acquainted, but maybe the next descendent will be wiser than you,*" he smirked as he whiffed her perfumed hair, relishing her even in murder.

"*Unhand her, Earl!*" yelled Clymythious, who heard the struggle downstairs and couldn't believe what he and Capt. Gustant was seeing at the top of the spiraling staircase.

"*Fool! You dare to give me a command? I can snap her delicate neck and end these charades. She is the Vessel, and her choice has been made. With the power vested in me by the Order of the Mortali and the freedom of the exiled 200, I sacrifice yet another Vessel from its inexorable fate,*" Hamilton screamed as he committed to what he thought was the final act.

As the two gentlemen lunged up the steps to rescue the now gurgling Amelia, who started to radiate in a blue hue and diminishing resistance in Hamilton's strangle, she heard a cry that caused the blue hue to scorch in brilliance, forcing him to release her at the top of the winding steps. It was a cry from the Captain Gustant. A familiar one but it had no relevance in the dream.

"*Em....!*"

He bolted up the stairs, never taking his eyes of her, sword drawn in hand and only making it to the first landing of them.

"*It's too late, my dear. You are no threat to me and submission is inevitable.*"

She tumbled down the steps like a rag doll, hitting her head on the last step before Clymythious and the captain could reach her unconscious body- no longer blue, but just as radiant. She was only asleep. Gustant held her writhed body in his kneeling lap.

"Wake up, Em, wake up!"

HAPTER 15

"Wake Em, wake up!"

Emily could hear the voice as if it were down the maze of halls. Drowsiness made it unclear where the voice was coming from, but it kept repeating itself over and over again. As she opened her tear-soaked eyes, she made out a face to match the distraught voice. It was Luke and she was lying where the dream had begun- by the smoldering campfire as dawn crept through the tired night.

"You were having one hell of a dream. Who is Earl? You were screaming his name so loud that I thought you were in trouble," he said, as he leaned her upright. *"Don't just sit there, Elijah! Put some wood on the fire. She is trembling. You ain't no damn help, man!"*

Elijah didn't move to assist but did give her a bottle of water from his knapsack. His calmness was as if he knew what she had just experienced, and there was no reason to get excited.

"Your sleep visions tell a story your mind can't suppress anymore. For each Vessel, it is different. Tell us about what you saw. Don't let it fade back in ambiguity. There are keys and answers in them that can only help your future."

Reliving the dream isn't what she wanted to do, and certainly, she didn't understand much of it. It was as real as her sitting right now with Luke and Elijah. She is awake now, but the burdensome emotions linger.

"I really don't want to talk about it. The dream was with Clymythious, and it must've been centuries ago. I don't know

how to explain it. In the dream, I was me, but I wasn't. It's all so confusing," she said, trying not to look directly at either one of the gentlemen that were locked in her every word.

"You must continue and try hard to remember everything from what was said to how you felt. Account for all senses- theirs and yours."

"Okay, well I think it began in an old castle or manor and Clymythious and some old guy named Earl of Hamilton dressed like something out of a Three Musketeers movie. You know, with the powdered wigs and stockings on. I remember that he called it Dorchester or something. They were calling me Amelia...Lady Amelia! This place was huge, drafty and cold with servants and everything."

Elijah interrupted and interjected, trying to help her make sense of it all as she told it.

"Dorchester was a plantation in Virginia in the late 1700s that was considered one of the largest of the period. The families go back to the early colonies in North America. Its wealth was from the slave trade and cotton but go on. You are doing fine." Elijah said, urging her to keep going as the last songs of the night crickets got louder and louder around the campsite.

"He made me feel like one. One that he had picked out to wed and possess like property. Apparently, she, I, was intended to marry him against my will. He and the Earl were scrutinizing me like they were looking over a car or piece of jewelry. At first, they were polite with it, but when Clymythious left the room, the Earl attacked me with no intentions of stopping to he had his way. He ripped at the dress with hands that were like claws and

he didn't care if Clymythious knew what he had done. I fought him off and ran through the manor, where he caught me and tried to strangle me over a marbled railing. He turned into some kind of grotesque monster with wings and breath that was foul like the dead. For an old man, the creature he turned into was far more agile and far more aggressive than the feeble, drooling old man. Before I blacked out, I heard Nate, who was there with Clymythious, scream my name. The funny thing is he didn't call me Amelia. He called me Em."* She paused, letting the interpretation of the words out loud sink in their meaning. *"For God's sake, make them stop! Make them stop!"* Emily cries out, referring to the screaming calls of the insects that were now almost deafening, like a continuous pitched buzz.

"What you are experiencing is part of your past that is in your head. There are truths in them because you are part of a long dynasty of Vessels. Each one is somehow chained to the other in one fate. I cannot stop what cries from within. Only you can atone for them. It is what this final part of the journey is: the end of a beginning, not a beginning of an end. The world feels your unrest and unless you find the complacency with all, all creatures will mourn with you," Elijah said in cold comfort.

"If I continue, will they stop?"

"That I do not know, but the tranquility I am sure of. You are not my first Vessel accompany. Not all are the same, but they are one. Finish telling us about the dream and set yourself free from the past."

The sun creaked over the morning horizon and the crows overwhelmed the morning songs along with the crickets as Emily held her hands over her ears, trying to silence them. Their waxing cries, along with the haunting recollection of the dream, were tormenting her.

"I remember laying at the foot of Nate, who was in his military dress trying to look aloof. I didn't want to look at him. I thought he would see the sins of the flesh that Clymythious forced on me. I felt dirty, and I thought if I didn't stare directly at him, I could hide his comrade's trespass. It was awful. I tried to go to that place in my head where I went each time, he raped me. I still can smell that smell of soap and wretched cologne mixed in sweat as he did it over and over again. I wanted to escape to that place on that floor as he held me, but he forced my gaze into his eyes and he saw, and he knew.

'Clymythious, you son of a bitch, what have you done to her?' Nate yelled.

'I think I like this one. She has fire. And what a beauty. I didn't do anything she didn't like. Ain't that right, honey? Besides, if you didn't show up, I would have had her willing to commit to us. Not like the other ones, I could have saved this one, and with that, he kicked Nate from behind hard enough for him to drop me to the floor. He withdrew Nate's sword, which was a part of his uniform at his side and slid its blade across my throat. Last thing I heard was someone whimpering and Clymythious saying it was a pity to lose this one as the light was fading and the voices muffled away."

As Emily finished the recall of the dream, she let her hands go from her ears and the birds and insects quieted. The sun had taken the night sky and chased away the stars.

Anxious days turned to fortuitous nights that were filled with insight and bond. The three learned each other's hopes and perspectives. Enlightenment threaded them in a tight-woven friendship of trust. As Elijah told them of things long forgotten by modern society, they learned about their own past. The history lessons were both woven in what they have heard before in scriptures and old nomenclature, and in secrets that have been entrusted to few.

"There was a time when angels roamed the earth equal to mortal man in God's eyes, but there came a time when the Lord saw them corrupt and arrogant in their own existence. He spoke of creatures as if they were commonplace on the Earth until...

"When human beings began to increase in number on the earth and daughters were born to them, the sons of God saw that the daughters of humans were beautiful, and they married any of them they chose. Then the Lord said, "My Spirit will not contend with humans forever, for they are mortal; their days will be a hundred and twenty years." The Nephilim were on the earth in those days and afterward when the sons of God went to the daughters of humans and had children by them. They were the heroes of old, men of renown. The Lord saw how great the wickedness of the human race had become on the earth, and that every inclination of the thoughts of the human heart was only evil all the time. The Lord regretted that he had made human beings on the earth, and his heart was deeply troubled. So, the Lord said, "I will wipe from the face of the earth the human race I have created and with them the animals, the birds and the creatures that move along the ground for I regret that I have made them," he fluently recited passages from the Bible, but he likely had read them from the scrolls themselves or maybe perhaps lived through them.

"200 survived and were cast to Tartarus were they meant to be eternally imprisoned. A handful escaped the wrath of God. No one knows why the few that weren't cast were exempt. Not all deserved to be free while many are not. You must be cautious for those reasons. They have many forms and over time have merged with man. It's a well-kept secret to those who cannot see, but you, Emily and about one in every generation (he said turning and looking at Luke) return with a destiny that many of the "Fallen" fear and want to use to free the imprisoned 200."

"Mother fucker don't look at me!" Luke shouted getting upset. "You mean to tell me that all my life I have been fighting because I was different only to find now that I am some kind of enigma that is hunted?"

Emily shushed Luke for his language and almost blasphemy. He, of all people, knew more than her. When she was locked up with him as Ty, he coached her in the study of spiritual literature. Despite Luke's temperament and anger, Elijah only paused to let both the two absorb what he has said.

"That is enough for tonight but remember all that I am telling you. It can only save you in its acknowledgement," he said on the night before what must happen.

"Kiss my ass, man! Where were you when they were whipping my ass cause of this shit! Where were you when I did a twenty-year bit for murdering one those bastards! Where were you when my mother died over Edison's Edge cliffs to save my life? I had to go to the same mother fuckers that are hunting us to get out of prison and make a deal to convince Ty to trust them. Where were you, huh?"

Emily had never seen Luke so irate and that angry. She tugged him away from confronting Elijah and physically fighting. By the sounds of it, he has been harboring all those emotions, and hearing the ancient history stories sent him off. She got him as far as the tree line around the opening where they were camping before she replayed what he had said in her head and let him go. He went soaring through the air in full arched outstretched wings for Elijah, who has prepared himself for battle as well in transforming into a white-robed winged warrior with size and blinding white magnificence. The two met mid-air and tussled like mating birds in the air while Emily remained at the tree line edge perplexed in all that was said and revealed. Solemnly frozen where Luke left her, she has never felt more alone. No one is telling her the complete truth and it felt like betrayal in every way. She watched them fight in the air, grunting and throwing each other into trees and brush with stone emotions. As acrobatic as the battle was, with two warriors looked clumsy as they fought, releasing their frustrations with no regard to what she thought or felt.

"*Stop!*" Emily yelled and the two released each other and fell to the ground on their feet.

"*I got more of that if you want some more mother fucker!*" Luke said, holding his fists like a fighter with his wings erect and thrusting and feet pacing.

"*I let you live, Luke; you would be no good to anyone wounded or dead, but before you think about it again, let me say that I have always been there for you. I made sure you were safe in passage through your life, even when your father sent you away to England to protect you. When you were shuffled from one foster home to another, I was there with you. I was there when you became of age and resourced your gifts; I am here now when it is crucial that you know who your enemies are and what it all has led to. Use that anger to defend what is rightfully yours- not me. Push forward to a hopeful future."*

"Fuck you!" Luke barked and walked back to Emily.

"Hey Ty, I mean Emily, I am so sorry you had to hear that like this, but I couldn't think of any other way to get you out of there. Way I saw it was that we were trapped and to give them what they needed to get out there was the only way. All they asked me to do is to get you to cooperate with them- and you did. I haven't left your side since we got out," he pleaded, looking at the uncertainty that she was looking at him with.

The anger of betrayal and disillusion made her leary of both. Luke made an attempt to hug her, and she pushed him away. Her mind raced with thoughts of a hidden conspiracy between them. A plot to, in the end, hand Clymythious the one thing they assured her wasn't going to happen.

"Look we alright, don't touch me though! You might be telling the truth, or you could be, again, looking out for your own ass. Either way, you are a fraud I don't want to trust you or him. Just get away from me!"

Luke wouldn't accept the hurt rejection from her. He can see and feel that she has every reason not to trust him. He tried to hug her again and she immediately turned blue and slammed him feet away with one toss. He got to his feet and raise his appendages, too. He couldn't let her think whatever she was thinking.

"Aw c'mon Emily, you got to be joking! I did what I did to help you. If you wanna feed into it more than it is, then you ain't thinking. What would I have to gain from turning you over to them without a plan? Hit me again, and I'm going to forget that you a lady!" Luke burst into laughter, and she had to laugh as well.

"It's not funny, Luke!"

"Then why are you laughing, huh?"

This time, when he hugged her, she hugged him back. All the things that they have gone through this far outweigh the minuscule points that he just shared. The jailbreak, the escape and refuge together, and most importantly, never passing judgment on her.

"Naw, it's cool, you dumb old coot."

"I know it's cool! Hit me again like that and imma show you how old a nigga is!"

While the two are laughing in the moment and Emily is brushing twigs and leaves off him, Elijah interrupts. For him, this isn't a laughing matter. His solemn disposition swept reality back and its dire focus. Still, the brief moment of levity energized the two enough to address the re-assessment of the dream, although it was as if reliving it again.

"Emily, you only see what you wanna see. The dreams are not a torment of unconscious, but an awakening. I can help both of you peel away the concealed if you'd like. There is far more to it than what you remember. Take each other's hand and close your eyes and concentrate."

What more could they have to lose. Elijah knows more than the two combined, so they did as he asked, and almost instantly, they were in the dream where Emily left off. Her dead, limp body in Capt. Gustant's lap, blood running from her gashed head and corner of her mouth with the yellow satin gown still ripped and dyed in blood. Luke's astonished face and mouth hanging open from seeing the entire scene as if it were in real time.

"Well, I'll be goddamn!"

Luke snatched his hand from Emily's in disbelief and the dream faded. Elijah coached them both about maintaining the link and other rules to adhere to in the connection.

He said,

"Never break the link.

Remember that you are an outsider and never attempt to change the outcome.

Allow yourself to feel everything, even what is painful to witness.

Time is different while connected. What seems like a long time may only be minutes in the real world.

And most importantly, stay together."

Luke was resistant to returning. He had more questions that he wanted answers to before returning, while Emily said nothing and waited for his adjustment. She had been experiencing dreams and nightmares like these all her life.

"Wait, wait, let me get this straight. That looked like Nate in there, but the dead girl with busted head only kind of looked like you Emily," he said while pacing and trying to get his nerve to return back to the weird link that was more than he anticipated.

"Fuck it! Let's do this, but I ain't promising nothing."

Back to the dream, he and Emily stood over Capt. Gustant as he fought to hide the loss of Amelia. Clymythious' clenched hand tightly held the captain's sword, prepared to strike again if he objected to the outcome. Satisfaction with macabre bravado seemed to give Clymythious pleasure as he watched the life spill out of Amelia.

"Surely you knew what this was coming to. Must I remind you of who our allegiance is to? The next one you can have," Clymythious said as he relished the moment as if to feed on claiming a Vessel's life.

"Dispose her worthless carcass and be done with it. While it is true that once again we have failed in fervent goals, there will come another and we will have victory," he said, dropping the steel ornamented blade to Gustant's side.

As Captain Gustant gently laid her body to the floor out of his lap, he stood and faced Clymythious. His anger was obvious in his labored breathing and furrowed brow. The slow moments of silence echoed and distorted the captain's closing steps on Clymythious. The two were locked in a rival stare as the distance between them was shrinking, as Gustant seemed challenged and disturbed.

"*Careful, my friend. You hadst not presume to make me an enemy over a mere slave girl. Why this one? Don't let your lust and appetite guide your demise,*" Clymythious laughed in his own amusement. "*Come, let's drink to better times, women, and anything we want! You never could do the kill part of a lady that well but let me help you jog your memory. What was the last vessel's name that you yourself took his last breath?*"

The mention of the deed that haunted him and perhaps softened his ease of sacrifice slowed his steps to a recalculating halt. Nathaniel remembers the name, for he did take his life with his bare hands. The name ached from his threat in strain and torturous regret.

"*His name was Frederick, and do not mention his name again. You have made your point well, sir.*"

"*Aw yes, young Frederick. Not only did you snap his neck in jealousy, but he too you loved in some love/hate fashion. I remember that very well my friend. It didn't hinder you to end his life. It is because you couldn't love him. You were jealous because I did, you are ardent, judgmental, petulant fool. You really think your brethren didn't see the lust you shared with him. That very same nerve and bravado drove him right into my arms with no prejudice to his temporary persuasion. He was just a mere Vessel that was subject to the same preconceptions and flaws each one does, but that didn't stop you, did it? The way you are looking at me now is the same contemptuous eyes I had for you on that night. He was beautiful in his own way. I seldom have the taste for men, but he was indeed a delicious and worthy of my attention one.*

I think you have forgotten what we pledge to uphold, my friend and let your emotions cloud your purpose. That warm night in Virginia when you had had enough is still fresh in my mind as the look on your face when you snatched him from my bed in my drunken stupor. It wasn't till much later when the others told me how they riled you up with their teasing and mockery of you and your forbidden antiquated morals. They told me how they ridiculed you in your own pitiful sorrow while I made love to him in the same house, and how the only deception was yours. It was young Frederick that also pines for you, even in my arms. You should have been there for him after you blatantly ostracized him to the condemnation of a 16th century religious dogma. Whereas I offered him protection and immortality, you on the other hand could see any other way than to let the sanctimonious hatred of his pure nature be the excuse to strangle him in it. They had to peel your hands from his throat in your anger of your own helplessness," Clymythious said in flippant rebuttal to Nathaniel thwarted challenge.

It was a time before the grandeur of British rule and Dickensian imitation of negroes. A time when the ideology of equality was available to all. Settlements of indentured servants and freed men could buy into the early American dreams of the new promise land, despite their origin. Nathaniel had his own land and property- an accomplishment for any man in those days of a new frontier and freedom from British rule, unlike the surrounding ones owned by other negroes who suffered the unjust of privation. The proud free man owned hundreds of acres of farmland and uncultivated acreage where he raised animals and hired cheap labor to feed his flourishing farmstead. It hid the secrets of the Mortali, harboring its members and discriminated prey such as Vessels and other sentients under the cover of expansive property and isolation. Then, under the camouflage of rural life, Nathaniel bartered and functioned as an agricultural businessman who, unlike other negates of the period, ranked in his rustic possessions. He was considered affluent and even used it to secure slave's safe passage by owning many. Frederick was one of them. Born in slavery, Frederick was sheltered as a slave. His mother died during childbirth and Nathaniel bought him as a sickly young boy of thirteen. Deep brown skin and those wide eyes that had seen more than a young boy should have experienced, he thrived on the Lee plantation with no known family and a gentleness to equal his small size and demeanor. The years were kind to him and by nineteen he had long forgotten the horrible tragedy and severe past he had gone through. The other slaves thought him to be peculiar, soft, useless, and excommunicated him as not one of them which forced Nathaniel to keep him close as a personal servant. It didn't take long before whispers and slave quarter rumors about his arrogant proclivity for his master. He stood just under six feet, ethereal in comparison to the others, almost resolute in convictions. His duties included all that pertained to his master and did so with unrivaled respect and devotion. It wasn't till the other members of the Order visited did anyone object directly to Nathaniel about their unusual closeness. Nathaniel kept him close and well taken cared for. From his appearance, he too would be thought to be a free man, but the other men of the Order quickly reminded him that he was a slave, and so did the other slaves. They taunted, beat, and disrespected him for his allegiance and bond with Nathaniel who denied anything they inferred.

It was there on an early summer night in mid-June that things took a turn for the worst and the very thing he prided himself for became hurtful and oppositional. Clymythious visited unannounced late that night. He would often come through for just a few hours with slaves in tow to rest. This evening, he came alone. He found Nathaniel and Frederick asleep in the master bedroom. Frederick curled snugly against his master's back. He had suspected that the two had an odd bond, but he witnessed the unusual behavior with his surprise visit in late night hours.

"What is this? Am I interrupting something," he said while standing at the bed's edge holding a lantern over them.

Nathaniel jumped from bed out of a dead sleep and kicked Frederick from his side to the floor. In his embarrassment he overacted and chastised his servant for crawling in his bed.

"Damnit Freddie, I said you could sleep here if the slave quarters were crowded. Get out of here! I will deal with you later. Do you hear me?"

Clymythious said nothing as he watched Nathaniel squirm to cover up what he knows is more than a slave relationship. The talk amongst the Order and the obvious bond the two had was only a secret to Nathaniel in his own self persecuting shame.

"You know I have been a little suspicious that you never have a winch with you when I came. I know why now. Hell, everyone knows why! Stop beating that boy to prove a point. I too have appreciated a young boy here and there. Send him to fetch me some food and stop the charades," he said, plopping on the large feather stuffed bed.

"Lies, all lies! He is my favorite, but his insolence is intolerable. I just got tired of the other slaves beating him and cursing him. He is just a bed warmer in the meantime. No more significant than a dog!" Nathaniel said after he tired of beating him.

On the floor whimpering, Frederick gathered his nightshirt off the end of the bed with shock and scurried out walking backwards. In all the humility and disgrace, he still held his respect and slave etiquette, although his expression was of hurt and shame.

"You heard him! Fetch him some food you wretched bastard before I chain you in the barn and be quick about it!"

With just the two men left in the room, Clymythious laughing and Nathaniel trying to change the topic with wine, it took a longer than comfortable moment to regain conversation. It wasn't unheard of sleeping with slaves, but much more uncommon to sleep with just one. It didn't return till Clymythious explained his visit.

"I'm not here on business. I came to warn you of the uprising up north against the abolitionist. Free men are being stripped of their rights. I have been sent here to convince you to sell your land and to retrieve the Vessel before ascension. You can't convince me that you didn't know that boy's linage. It's perfect that you have his allegiance to you. We can take him to the alter and finally free the 200 with his willing transference. Thousands of years we have been waiting and failing with each one refusing."

Nathaniel had no plans of sacrificing Frederick. He had no plans of admitting that he felt more than a friendship him, but he knew he had to deny that he had any emotional bond for him.

"He is not ready; at least like you are implying. I have not allowed him to sleep in here because of the tension he causes with the others. I haven't done what you think. It's immoral. It's ridiculous and disgusting," Nathaniel dismissing the obvious.

"There is no time for us to wage discussion on delicate morality and your self-denial. I am tired. When the boy comes back send him to the guest room with my food. We can continue how to encourage him tomorrow. I am weary. Good night."

As requested, Nathaniel sent the food to his visitor as soon as he returned. Frederick wanted to talk, but talk would mean commitment, and he already knew that he was over his head after hearing what Clymythious was saying, and others was assuming.

"Take the food to him and sleep somewhere else. I don't want to talk about it. I have taken care of you and perhaps far more, but it ends tonight. If I hear any more about it from anyone, I will sell you at first opportunity. Now go!"

Frederick couldn't move hearing Nathaniel speak to him that way. It compared little to the beating just took from him. He has taken many all his life, but none has stung as the one he just got. The tray in his hands shook and clattered in his hands. His mind wish that he would just beat him than to dismiss him like this. For sure, he loved him and although he has never said it, many nights they shared as if it needn't not be ever said.

There was no choice in leaving the very same room that he has been sleeping in, and with, the only submitted love he has known, but he left and did as he was told. Clymythious was waiting when he knocked at the door.

"*Come in son. What took you so long? I am starving!*"

The room smelled of horses and sweat. He must have been traveling for days by the smell of it. Clymythious pointed to the small desk in the corner and Frederick placed the still trembling tray on it and bowed as he retreated to the door.

"*I'm not an oath or as callous as your master, nor am I going to treat you the same way. Keep my company while I finish washing up and eat. You do speak, don't you?*"

"Yes, sir I do."

"*Do you love him?*"

Frederick dared not talk to him about the very thing that has disrupted just minutes ago. He saw the embarrassment in Nathaniel' eyes when it was implied that there was more between them. Denial he was used to from the locals, but Clymythious' question was more of a statement.

"*He has taken good care of me sir. He treats me as if I am a free man. He has taught me to read and write and all the graces of a gentleman. So, in that way, I guess I do love him,*" Frederick said while never looking up at Clymythious.

The curious guest wiped shaving cream on his face and gestured for him to come over and shave him. He looked tired, but nonetheless smiled and spoke to him in soothing tones.

"You could do well with me if you cooperate. I would never deny you as he has. A gentleman like yourself could go far with someone who appreciates his nature. Times are changing and all that you have gotten accustomed to will soon be gone and as you see, Nathaniel will never give you what you desire."

He had nothing to return to and he could see in those eyes that hungrily stared at him with each careful stroke of the blade, that he would only make his life miserable if he didn't comply- both for him and for his master. Besides, he promised real freedom.

It was the end of the night in the crack of dark morning when Frederick awoke to a knock at the guest room door. He had fallen asleep after securing his favored freedom wrestled in the snoring Clymythious' grip. He earned his freedom at a cost he yet has to pay. Groggy, half asleep and feeling innocuous, although a sense of guilt weighed on him as he opened the brass handled doorknob hoping that Nathaniel would be there apologizing and begging for him to return to the way things were, but that is not what happened.

Standing there frozen in each other's unforgiving presence, neither said anything. Nathaniel grimaced as he peered over Frederick's boney shirtless shoulders and saw Clymythious in deep slumber naked on the large bed. Frederick's gaze stared at the floor when he saw the disgust and disappointment.

"I said serve him food, nothing else! Are you trying to make me sell you by making a mockery of me? Git your ass out of here," he said snatching Frederick by his woolly nappy hair and dragging him through the threshold where he threw him to the ground.

"*Git up and put some clothes on! How could you? I saw the way he was like looking at you while at the same time insulting me in my own house and then you sleep with him?*"

By now, Nathaniel is face to face with him spitting mist on him with every venomous accusation. Frederick wanted to defend himself with explanations, but to do so could be taken as insolence.

"*You sorry excuse for a man! How many others have you been with?*"

Again, he grabbed Frederick by the back of his head, clutching the roots in between his fingers still inches from face. His eyes mapped over Frederick's oily face, from his high cheek bones to his wide nose and full lips that already have been split in one corner. His large, frightened eyes that bravely stared back and didn't resist till Nathaniel bashed his large fists over his left eye. Frederick finally has had enough. Still gripped by Nathaniel's other hand and a tiny drizzle of blood that trickled from a cut over his eye, he glimmered in the slightest blue. In the confusion, of mixed emotions as Frederick the slave, he might have taken it as punishment, but in his first ascension, festering anger, he was anything but complacent.

"*Aw shit! It's on now Emily!*" Luke said on the sidelines as he and Emily witnessed the scene from the dreamy link.

"*Be quiet Luke! Can't you see the importance of this all. Never thought that anyone has had those experiences, but me, I mean us.*"

As Frederick's reaction fueled itself in uncontrolled fury, Nathaniel knew that he had pushed him to that point and regretted ever doing it to someone that he selfishly wanted to keep to himself. The ascension into Frederick's untapped power couldn't be pulled back. The eventuality of it all registered too late.

"I'm a free man Nathaniel. You cannot possess me to your will anymore. Clymythious has promised me that he would grant me that. As much as I love you, I can't miss this opportunity, and I have done what I would do again for it. It was you that discarded and shunned me away. Now let me return to him and let me be free. The cost is no less than you gave me," he said as he got brighter and brighter.

Nathaniel knew that Frederick was right and let go his hair only to place his hands around his throat. He was damned if he allowed him to live and he couldn't see Clymythious possess what he felt he could keep and hide.

"You are choking me, Nathaniel!"

With each tightening grip, the light dimmed, and Frederick was lifted off the floor and fought futilely clasping at the large hands that saw no alternative than to extinguish his life than to see it manipulated and contaminated by another.

"You don't understand. What I do, I do this to make this easier than letting them sacrifice you. You leave me no choice," he said as the last of life was choked from him.

He wept.

The dream faded away like a bad memory leaving the three: Emily, Luke, and Elijah back at the wooded campsite and all were numb from what they not only just witnessed but felt. For such a brutal recall they shared, the emptiness that all were overwhelmed in, only foreshadowed what was to come. Elijah cut through the intense after-feelings snapping them into conclusive reality.

"What is meant for you to see, you must internalize it. Though time is already written, no less the journey a choice. Choose well your paths for it too has been foretold."

"Then I have chosen, or rather it has been chosen for me. If my predestination is set, then I won't let another Vessel die for it again, in sacrifice or in murder. I have a son that one day might be the life I save. Clymythious and the others are close, and I am ready," Emily said placing the Sword of Destiny into a sheath at her side.

For the next couple hours, they shared nothing more than insecure glances as they each could feel the gap closing as they got closer and closer. By dusk, the guy's insisted to settle down before night, but they continued at Emily's insistence, using her inner blue hue to paint the trees in illumination. Elijah guided them to what he called *"The Sacred Ruin"* which was just on the edge of Maryland using the old paths of the Appalachian trails to reach it. The rushing sounds of water, the chill in the air, and its heavy scent meant they were, in night's blindness nearing the place Elijah was directing them to.

A starless night hid what they could only hear as thunderous running water. In the far distance, the lights of Baltimore nestled under a glowing sky. Sounds of roads and byways were welcomed familiar sounds that calmed the fear of water coursing before them.

"I know where we are," Emily said as the tree lines shrank in the horizon to a huge lake that had no visible shores.

"You might well," Elijah answered. *"The paths we have been following have been a refuge to many during the revolution. Some call it 'Freedom Trail' some call it 'The Underground Railroad. Many of your ancestors were guided by these secret trails. We have traveled far, and like the tributaries that flow to the ocean, we are near its last wind. It is here that we will intercept your rivals. They too are convening to this place. It's time for us to rest and I must insist on it."*

"About damn time!" Luke shouted dropping his knapsack. *"My ass is tired!"*

Elijah sat down and bowed his head in a seemingly private silent prayer while Emily stared at the endless shore with goliath black silhouettes on its other side sown together by bridges and rail trusses binding a large monster to the water. She could feel the history Elijah spoke of as if she had memories of being at this very same place before, watching the same unchanged geographical panorama.

"Join us, Emily. There is one more thing you need to see," Elijah whispered in his deep meditative calmness.

"Aw hell! Why we gotta keep visiting this old shit man? I ain't feelin' seeing those trifling flashbacks. Ty, I mean Emily ain't quite got over the last one."

"We must understand the past in order to prepare for the future. Although it might be painful, it has its secrets within its pain," Elijah said with his eyes still shit and hand open for the two to link together.

"We don't need any more pain man! You could be making this up with all your spooky mumbo-jumbo junk! We need to be

resting. Ain't nobody got time for your seance Dionne Warwick shit!"

"Please Luke, it might be weird, but I need to know all I can know. Just one last time let's indulge him. Besides, I want to know what Nate has to do with all this," Emily pleaded while sitting down and holding Elijah's still hand.

Luke didn't budge from his spot not far from them talking to himself and struggling to take off boots that must have been hurting his swollen feet.

"Now you all concerned about the part Pop play in it? See that's the problem right there! Bad enough that you are stuck in this Emily shit and got a son we haven't seen in weeks, but you are worrying about the same guy that is helping those that want to harm you. If you love the guy, then you love the guy, but don't be no fool!"

Emily knew Luke's stubbornness was staunch. She sat for a moment and tried to think about what she could say to make him join hands and unleash the last memory that was locked. In her frustration and the night chill off the Harper Ferry's water she was sniffling. The breeze rode over the water and was bitter with its north blown gusts. Luke heard her sniffle and assumed differently.

"Aw, don't do all that tears stuff. Damn, that's below the belt! You win," he said, sitting beside her and grabbing her hand.

Instantly, they were transported to the belly of an old ship, tossing and pitching. Were they stood were chains of women and children afraid and crying. The smell of decay and death was overwhelming and pungent. Different from the last one, Elijah was with them, and he pointed to a small young girl about 15 yrs. old who obviously was the center of this visit. Her ankles and wrists were bruised from chains. She sat to herself young breast naked and exposed. There wasn't much to her. She was very thin and underdeveloped as a woman, with the same almond shaped eyes that Amelia, Frederick, and Emily had.

"It's important that you see some of the linage of the Vessels before. Half of the women that are here in this vision didn't survive the voyage from their homeland. Even as we watch, she is sick from the exposure of germs and diseases that are foreign to her," he said.

The vision faded into the landing of a schooner in Virginia in the late 1800s and a sickly cargo of slaves on its docks being auctioned off. Crowds of merchants, traders, and colonial farmers were shouting and bidding on the surviving remainder of Africans who have been ripped from their home country. First on the auctioning block was none other than Emily. The auctioneer didn't expect to get anything for a sickly malnourished young girl, but amidst the gathering crowd stood Nathaniel, standing behind the Earl of Hamilton, but the two appeared different from the last vision. Nathaniel was not in military attire and the Earl dressed as another affluent colonist.

"That one!" Nathaniel whispered in the Earl's ear. *"I would know her anywhere."*

With patience and strategic bidding, the Earl bought the shaken slave girl against his better judgment. Shackled together were far stronger women that he had his eye on.

"You better be right, Nathaniel. She appears far too weak to be the one. If I purchase her, it will be your responsibility. I think you are wrong this time. Look at those tiny hips and tits. She is dreadfully pitiful."

The auctioneer could not get anyone to bid on her. He grabbed her to feet by her hair and paraded her before the uninterested audience. To him and to the others, she wasn't worth anything. She would be a poor farmer or cropper. She looked like she couldn't sire any children or take care of any. An impatient bidder heckled her, yelling,

"I'll give you my sick old dog for her! At least you would get the better bargain!"

To be such a horror for the captives, they all laughed and dismissed her as entertainment. Nathaniel elbowed the Earl in his rib cage, and he tipped his hat at the auctioneer, signalling he had a bid.

"Finally, we have a bid! What would you like to bid for this gal sir?

"I'll give you two shillings if you move to the next one," he said, encouraging more laughter and humiliation.

"Sold!"

Luke, Emily, and Elijah watched how affectionate and delicate Nathaniel was over the next couple of months, nurturing her health back and teaching the young Emily to speak English and all the social etiquette of the new world. The other slaves told him that she was from a small village near Senegal, and they knew little about her. She said her name was

Dalilli as she got stronger but had difficulty pronouncing the *"th"* in Nathaniel.

"Just call me Nate and I will call you Emily. They kind of frown on keeping your African name; besides, it kind of suits you."

In time, the bond between Nate and Emily grew strong. He protected her in his obsession with her while keeping her hidden from the Earl until one day he asked who she was. It wasn't uncommon for the Earl to take advantage of the women and men he fancied. Although she feared him, Emily felt protected by Nate. Nate not only nursed her back to health and clothed her in the best dresses he could find her, but he also excused her from any of the chores and labor. In his current disguise as the head of the slaves. Life for Emily improved each day till one day while sitting outside of Nate's quarters, the Earl came looking for him.

"You must be the secret that is occupying Nathaniel's time. Wait, you look familiar. What is your name, child?" The Earl said while eyeing her in obvious lust and fascination.

"My name is Emily sir."

"Aw, I remember you! What taste in women does Nathaniel have. Nonetheless, fetch me drink of water, and make it quick."

Emily carefully stepped off the wooden porch and did as she was told, keeping her eyes on the ground and never gazing directly at him. As she passed, the Earl took his walking stick and, lifted her dress up and slapped her rear, letting his attention to her be known. His grunt and laughter humiliated her to an uncomfortable extent as he followed her to the well.

"I do love deep chocolate and you my dear are the deepest," he said while trying to maul her with his ivory hands. His aggression held no reservation, and she fought him off.

"Stop, sir, it is not my inclination to do immoral deeds for favor."

"Inclination huh? I see Nathaniel has been teaching you. I don't care about your inclinations. I own you and you do what I tell you or I will sell you from this plantation. You are no more important than those trees, that pond over there, or the wild fowl that flies over it."

The Earl grabbed her arm, pulling her close and trying to kiss her and at the same time, pulling her cotton dress up from the bottom, groping and roaming his hands from her silky thighs and invading her with his fingers. She cried out for Nathaniel, who she knew would not let this happen. And from the fields Nathaniel ran to the well, but the Earl did not stop his forceful ravaging. Nathaniel charged in and pulled her from his grasp.

"Boy, don't play with me, but if you insist, we can both have her. Now give her back. I want to taste some of that dark chocolate," he said, wrestling her from behind Nathaniel.

"Diagonious, you misinterpret what I am saying. She is not just another slave girl. She will be my wife, and I cannot let you have your way with her. Go find another that you can choose for your carnal exploits. Let this not be our friendship's undoing for this would surely come between us."

"Isn't that the runt slave girl that you made me buy? In all accounts, she is mine, as is everything on this estate, and I

thank you for nursing her to health, but I got it from here," Diagonious laughs while still sneering at Emily, who is behind Nathaniel. *"Everything on this land is my property. Now, not unless you are stealing from me, is there going to be anything between us. I have an idea. She is about worth $500 dollars. If you bring me the money than she is yours."*

Nathaniel thought about how to solve the dilemma. On one hand, he is right in ownership, but on the other the rebellion against slavery is now all the political topics in the South, and he and Diagonious were getting the land ready for sale because the abolitionist had changed the climate with their radical resurgence. The Society of the Immortali used the slavery to mask themselves everywhere in the new colonies. It never was their doctrine or principles. Nathaniel and Diagonious fought in heated arguments about it. Diagonious did more than blend into the culture. He adapted it in his pompous arrogance and avarice.

"My dear sir, you had the last one, or was it the one before that, either way you'll end up strangling the life out of her. Let me have my way before her eventual fate and then she will be all yours Nathaniel."

Nathaniel resented him bringing up the death of Frederick in front of Emily, but he walked away back to his quarters, leaving her defenseless at the well with Diagonious. Where once she held her head up in defiance, she now lowered it to the ground and started unhooking her bodice that was laced with silk strings.

"That's more like honey. This won't be as unbearable as you think."

Before she could get the last lace loose enough to step out of its hoops and ruffles, Nathaniel returned and threw a velvet purse at Diagonious's feet.

"This is a little more than the two pence you paid for her. Take it and leave now! In his other hand was a sword held tightly at his side. His eyes said he would like nothing better than to use it on Diagonious. His words were hard and stern as he spoke. His brow was frozen in a frown that his temples supported with arched eyebrows.

"Aw shit! Pop mad as hell!" Luke said while standing as if he was watching television.

"Shut up, Luke!" Emily said as she, too, was wrapped up in the tension of the vision, feeling all that her alter ego was feeling.

The six were all quiet and waiting for what was going to happen next- three witnesses and three participants. Elijah's gaze was fixed on the Emily of the present. He already knew the outcome; it was his insistence that they see it, too.

"All visions are pertinent to you both, but this one reveals the prophetic turnabout that nears the end. The last sacrifice," Elijah said.

"You feel that strongly about her that you would risk your life for her. I could easily have you hanged and still have the bitch. This is not a win for you and today I'm feeling generous," Diagonious said, picking up the satchel of coins and walking away. *"If you ever steal from me again, it will have a different ending. You know you have some explaining to do, but that is for another time. Congratulations."*

Diagonious walked off in his regal swagger as if the intensity of the situation unbothered him, not once looking back out of his pompous indignation. Nathaniel attempted to go after him. Perhaps because he had the last word, or because his last comment about explaining made him feel like a servant and not like a comrade. He kept his back to the disheveled Emily while she, in fluster and embarrassment, tried to re-cloth her half-naked body.

"Go inside and clean yourself up," he shouted without turning around.

"But I did nothing! Why are you angry at me? Both of you think that I am some piece of property that you can do wish as you like. I expected from the Earl, but you, I expected more from," she cried as she ran to his quarters. Inside he could her cursing in her natural language and tossing things.

For Nathaniel, it wasn't the plan he had for asking Emily to wed him. He had planned a much different proposal that was as romantic as he could do it, but now it will all sound like a diversion to own her like the property she mentioned. Time has its experience, and Nathaniel knows that cultures and ethics change. Over the centuries he has witnessed domination and rule come and go from the beginning with the early Order of the Immortali in primitive humanity to modern culture. Enslavement has always been a condition that repeats itself in each society, but for Emily, he wanted better, and he would have fought to give her better, and she reigned in it. Her beauty seems to blossom in the finery of opulence, and he loved her more than he had ever mentioned to her. Besides being the Vessel, he has fallen for another mortal who has made his heart a slave.

As a member of the Order, it is not condoned to wed or get informally attached to them. They are allowed to intersect, but not to intertwine if not necessary, for it can turn the outcome. It was the murder of young Frederick from his own hands or the helpless death of Amelia, but this time, he hadn't planned on losing. He would allow nothing to harm Emily, even if it meant that he would be excommunicated from the Immortali. As he followed Emily into the meager quarters, he retrieved an old cedar box from under his bed. In it was a beautiful locket that he kept from the early 16th century. It was made of mother of pearl and gold with a detailed cameo of a woman in its center. Its story was long ago, but now is the time he thought would be the best time to give to someone else. Someone he felt deserved it.

"It is not that I am mad or deserve to be," he said while grabbing her hand at her side as she pretended not to be interested in talking with him. *"From the first time my eyes saw you Dallili, you have possessed me. It is only out of that enchantment and love that I protect and secretly worship you. I cannot allow him, or anyone harm you. My ill timing could have been much better, but no other time obligates my devoted love for you than now."*

Like a noble gentleman, he knelt behind her, gibbering his freed emotions while condemning himself in each word for not doing it sooner, as if time was running short. What if he hadn't had heard her cry? What if Diagonious refused to let his claws off her and repeated the tale of death and sacrifice?

"Emily, it would be my highest honor if you would marry me. The world is at your feet, and I can only hope to give you

what you have fought so hard for and deserve," he said, still holding her delicate hand and staring at the old pines floor.

She snatched her hand from his and moved further away from him in furious disdain and scornful countenance. Indeed, she was angry, but she didn't want to make it easy for him, although each word couldn't have been more inviting.

"How could you ask me to marry you when you already own me. Take what you want. Do what you want. There is no need disguising it for appearances and selfish pride. You and the Earl Diagonis made it quite clear that I was a possession that both of you felt privy to." Emily sobbed. *"Is it immoral favors that is the debate here? You think that you have a right since you nursed me back to health and taught me English and British etiquette and now, because of a rooster in the hen house, you want to brand me as yours? I don't think so, and you can force me to lie with you. He can force me to lie with him, but no one can force me to love."*

This was an unexpected reply for Nathaniel. Over the months, their obvious affection for each other had run its course in its early bond. While he kept his heart at a distance, it had already broken from its prisoned control, and his past transgressions weighed on the eventuality of his decision. Within Emily was all the Vessels combined. They, too, were emancipated in his surrender.

"It is you who own me, Em. I have kept secret the love you inherited, for I, till this day, have denied them their entitlement. You can never replace a love. You think that you can, but they are only lost and repeatedly you can find them. Each time I find you. I recognize you, and you promise the very thing I mourn. I

love you Em! It is this love that I beg your heart. I have been a fool for many things, and I ask not for selfish reasoning of amorous eternal commitment. No man can love you more than I have and will. Let me hold that love with all my soul in yours. You will never be a possession to me for you are gift no matter what your decision is. I think you know and have always known that I languish in reluctance, for there is more than I can tell you at this moment. Refuse me and I will still be yours, I am the true possession."

    Emily did give into Nathaniel's heartfelt proposition, and they married under Maryland law outside of the Edison Edge community in the tenant quarters on the Crimea Estate that had been abandoned as agriculture moved on the outskirts of Baltimore of what was a Russian immigrant summer home- the Orianda house, but other than his love for her, Nathaniel never told her the history of the connection between them. The Estate was once a lavish palatial mansion isolated in the hills of Leaking Park, complete with a horse stable, Carriage house, Chapel, Gatehouse, Caretaker house, and the Springhouse where Nathaniel and Emily stayed. With all the grandeur and European design, it was more than enough to keep her content and happy as any other woman and he never again thought of her as a possession. She bore him three children, two girls and a boy. As the times moved on and racism and social dogmas heated under the threat of Civil War and freedom, Emily wanted to leave from the oppressive threats of Southern doctrine and attitudes to run north where she could ensure the future of her children and family. It was in the crisis of America that Nathaniel knew that things were out of his control.

As a tobacco farmer, horseman, and hired hand, along with the secured backing of the Immortal, Nathaniel and Emily remained in the old Baltimore land parcelled by the Lee family that would one day would be the expansive municipal Edison Edge Park and community. As the climate of civil war escalated in the mid-1800s, tension eroded their tranquillity of isolation along the streams of the Jones Falls that flowed into the harbor of Baltimore that now was being occupied by the troops from both sides. Diagonious only visited in the summer months, and he stayed in its mansion on the estate, never approaching Emily again, but just the same, looming in contempt. He and Nathaniel held their interactions private and only at night after Emily and the children retired.

"Nathaniel, you are actually trying to live as one of them, knowing that what must be done must be done?" Diagonious said over brandy on the veranda of the second-floor mansion.

The cool breeze of the acreage of forest fragrant in wild honeysuckle and hyacinths bated in night dew dueled the cicada and mating calls of frogs that held night conversations echoing in its hills. Nathaniel hesitated to reply. Neither did he want or have an answer to either of the statements, but Diagonious knew the correct answer- the only answer.

"Can man change fate? Have the hands of time ever been wound by him? You ask me a question that has no absolute ending or prophetic constructs. If I, we could control the outcomes of life and deeds, than we would no longer be living, but merely writing out bids at whims. The answer you ask is not one to pry from me, but one you personally must answer. Whereas you deem yourself the thread, I have come to the realization that I am not. I am merely a tailor, if you pardon the

metaphor, Diagonious," Nathaniel spoke while leaning over the terrace staring into the mist of night.

"Nathaniel, how long have we been friends? We have fought arm and arm in wars and battle, and it looks like another one is not far away. This is not a riddle that I am asking. It is the obvious declaration to the manifest we have for centuries in august earnest upheld. Surely, you are not thoughtlessly dishonoring the canons of the Immortali for your lustful conventions of a slave girl?"

"Enough of your ancient reasonings that have gotten us nowhere! Through time we have exterminated Vessel after Vessel to no avail. The 200 have remained imprisoned and we are its ill-equipped portrayers, debacle after debacle. I do not see myself as a foolish man and this time I follow a different path to seek the answers and resolution that consistently eludes us. Leave here and let my choice be my own whether you or the Immortali condone it or not."

Diagonious glowered in dissatisfaction. His minatory scowl reduced in discountenance and Nathaniel's zealous rebuttal. The rest of the evening was short in further dialogue, smoothed only by brandy and Diagonious' defused foil. Upon Nathaniel's retirement for the night, Diagonious had one last word to end the evening.

"In the morning, I leave Crimea. Let's hope that we will not meet again under these circumstances. I was ordered to either return with the Vessel, or kill her, and to prepare you for your orders regarding the breaching war. From what I observed and must report, she has not awakened and that sir, is to your advantage, for if she were we would have a more disagreeable

conversation, but heed my warning my friend, there will be others that will not be so lenient. If you love her and your family she must ascend. Our brothers are still wrongfully imprisoned in Tartarus and with their freedom we shall rule the Earth and beyond. Traitorousness and betrayal do not fare well with the brothers. Your selfish love will in the end hurt them. She is part of system the brotherhood still upholds. Prepare yourself for enlisting in the Confederate!

Nathaniel left him and the words permeated his head as he returned to the tenant's house where Emily and his daughters slept. He dimmed the lantern light as he sat in the front room, contemplating how he could protect them all in angst. He must've been noisy for Emily woke and came to his side. She could sense the inner turmoil.

"Nate, what is wrong?"

"Go back to sleep Em. I didn't want to wake you. That damned Diagonious gets the best of me every time he visits. It's nothing."

"You are lying to me Nathaniel! Tell me what is going on?" Emily insisted, kneeling in front of him.

"You are right. I have never lied to you, but I haven't given the whole truth neither." He stopped as he does when he is gathering his thoughts.

"Never mind honey, this might as well be the conversation I have been trying to find a way to have with you. I think it is time for us to leave this place. Talk of revolution and difficult times are ahead and we have children that we need to worry about. I don't want them to feel the hatred and racism that I had to feel.

I want them to have a better life and maybe if we go north, we can spare them. I know you have some attachments to this place and to those others that come here from time too but think about your daughters and your newborn son."

Just then, then young Isiah awakened and was crying in the bedroom. In the stillness of night, his angered cries amplified in the small cottage.

"I will be back. I don't want him to wake his sisters" she said, kissing on the forehead as she got up from kneeling in front of him.

Fear has a smell and Nathaniel wreaked of it. It was a cool summer night, but he was sweating. Emily trusted him and she knew that he would only worry about things he couldn't control. The minute Diagonious showed up to visit, she had the feeling that something was awry. It wasn't so much as how he himself behaved; he was his normal arrogant and rude self, but it was how Nathaniel changed. He was very short in his conversations with her in front of him. His eyes held command behind the subtle words he said to her, and he never went far from the house. He let his chores of tending the horses and livestock, which he found peace in, go unattended. Even the children could feel the tension in their father, but what could she do? He barked gentle innuendos and dismissive gestures that meant not to question him.

After she quieted the baby back to sleep, she came back to him, and he was pacing in front of the window as if something ominous was out there in the darkness. Something that shook him like she has never seen him shaken before. At first, she thought it was the brandy that she could smell on him, but it was more than a slight stupor in his demeanor. He turned to her when she re-entered the room. He spoke as if he had made choices that she had none in.

"Em, tomorrow you should get the children ready to visit your friends for a while. There is trouble on the horizon, and I need to know they are safe. Don't question me about it tonight. Just do as I am asking you. We cannot leave yet, and you need to trust me. I have so much to tell you that I have been keeping secret from you. So much that is so important, but I was hoping that years wouldn't catch up and hold me to this day."

"Nathaniel, my husband and love, I knew that there was something you weren't telling me before I married you, and you are scaring me. I will send the girls off, but young Isaiah is too young. If he is in danger, then I need him to be with me. Are you sending us all away? What has changed from this morning to now that you think we can't face together? Maybe we should all go. This place is starting to feel unwelcoming. It's just odd stuff lately, but there are things happening I can't explain. I am having weird dreams that make no sense. Things I have no idea what they mean."

Nathaniel's heart sank in his chest. He knew what she meant, but he was starting to believe that he was wrong about her being the Vessel. Everything she said meant that she would no longer be the Em that he married. Soon, the transformation would ebb the sweet black mother of his children into a warrior; she would have no choice in it, and neither would he.

"In the morning, after I get Diagonious horses and carriage together, we should talk. Things from here get complicated and I need to prepare you for it. Let the girls ride

The Book of Emily

with Diagonious in safety. Prepare them now," Nathaniel said, gathering his horse saddling gloves and gear and walking out into the creak of dawn.

He convinced the caretaker to ride with Diagonious to ensure that the children were met by their friends further north in the county. It was difficult to think of them traveling without their mother or father, but it was the best choice out of the two he had to face. Diagonious' threat was about Emily not the girls. The more time he had to prepare her, the better. It will be the first Vessel to make it through the ascension alive and he was willing to risk his life to help her and save his family. If that meant opposing the Immortali to do it, then he would fight in his newfound honor and love and in violence if he had to.

By sunrise he tied the carriage to the bronze lions in front Crimea and relit the lanterns as the clouds masked morning in shadowy overcast. Diaganious opened the mansion's front doors, pointing at his bags as if Nathaniel was a servant. He had his riding tweeds on, and although the tension between them was malevolent and snide, he was more defensive than offensive to Nathaniel. The caretaker came from the side of the mansion with kids in tow and packed them. While he secured the baggage and sat the kids.

CHAPTER 16

The shores waterline shushed the night along its rocky union. Emily's thoughts were transfixed in ambivalent concern about all that has been revealed to her. The distance twinkling of towers and bridges posed an ominous competition with the night stars in juxtaposition. She neither paid attention to how far away they were from the campsite, nor what it all meant. The more her thoughts immersed themselves in gloom, the more the skies became crowded with eerie clouds disfiguring stars gleam. She only knew the direction she came from and sat on a beached log to rest hoping clarity would wash over like the water on to the shore. Her mind raced with inner turmoil in discussion with itself.

"You have been a fool man. Everything you were is gone. All that you are now is betrayal to your heart. Where love is ruling, you are a slave and master of none of it. Nathaniel has not shared the whole truth with you. In your growth, you have summoned up strengths and metamorphisms that defy logic and possibilities too deep to understand. You are disgusting and an imposter, and to top it off, you have a son. You are trapped and your demise that most certainly is certain. Others think that you possess the powers to change the future when you can't figure out today."

The next voice she heard came from behind her. It was a familiar one.

"I feel your spirit weakening Em. I am here."

Standing behind her was Nathaniel. He must have come out the forest edge to find her as he promised. He looked rustic and larger than she remembered, but gentle in his words of comfort. Emily wanted to run to him in refuge but doubt still loomed in her thoughts. He could be here to end it all- his ethos unclear.

"Em, it is time. They are searching for you, and I have come to escort you to what must happen."

As she stood turned his face lit up with joy that melted away all the doubt. That look was one of relief and surprise. He smelled of the forest and the familiar smell musk and masculinity that invited her being with his piercing eyes that drank from hers.

"You look different my love. Sort of wiser and more beautiful than my memory justifies. We must go. Your friends will not understand, but surely you do. We must return to Crimea. I have accomplices that await us to help prepare you for the Immortali. As I found you, they will too. If we stay here, we endanger Luke. It is time," he said while outstretching his large black wings and arms to her and she was not afraid.

With one thrust, Nathaniel took to the sky using the currents to ride inland with Emily in a secure embrace. She watched the campfire of Luke and Elijah diminish into a fleck of light as they rose high into the stratosphere. They will worry about her, but as Nathaniel said, with her traveling with them could endanger them all.

"Hold fast Em, we must make time to arrive before Clymythious, Natasha, Simon, and Benoit get there. It won't be long before they notice that I have departed from them."

Once Nate beat his wings as high as he could get, they could see the Baltimore City lights on the horizon and descended downward. Baltimore has a night horizon that is like none other. It twinkles in colorful dots of light that end in the expansive darkness of the distant tributary of the ocean. More frightening than the ascend, Emily could not look at the fast-approaching ground and buried her head into his chest. His heartbeat was strong, but his breathing was shallow and effortless. In that moment, in the dark of night, she felt safe and assured.

"We are going to land in the corn meadow outside of Orianda it might be a little rough, but I won't drop you. It has been awhile since I carried anyone in flight. It was long ago that I carried you and Luke over Edison's Edge cliffs."

They were met by four of his friends as he said. Two men and two women. They hurried her to the cottage they once lived in a century ago in a time of a previous vessel. Abandoned and unkept, the cottage looked nothing like it did then, covered in overgrown ivy and vines. Already prepared, the ladies huddled around her and stripped her bare of the traveling clothes she arrived in. As they washed her in bath water, they used every moment to give instructions as to what the fuss was about.

"You sure must be important to Nathaniel cause he and the others have gone through great extents to get you here and ready for the Immortali Ball tonight. You don't look like much to me, but I mind my business. You might look a little uncouth now, but when we's finish with ya, you should clean up real fine," said Ms Clayton, the older of the two.

The two women scrubbed, pampered, and primped her for more than a couple of hours talking and coaxing her about the ball the entire time.

"I think I will choose that gown!" She said pointing to the assortment of dresses they had to choose from.

She chose the more simplistic of them. It was reminiscent to the one Amelia had on in the vision, and it compelled her to it; made of satin and form fitting with a bloused train that looked like it would float behind her. The others were frilly and overburdened in lace, ribbons with bright colors and Victorian elegance, but not for her. Before they could debate with her about her choice, Nate came in the cabin shaven and clean, dwarfing the two women in comparison, and silencing them in his presence.

"Leave us," he said politely, but they didn't move.

"Get out!" This time he said it more forcibly and they scattered gathering the other gowns as they tried to gather their things hurriedly.

"You didn't have to bark at them that way. They were only doing what you asked them to do."

"I have no time for politeness Em. In a couple of hours, we walk into the midst of danger masked in social etiquette and grandeur. I think your courage and beauty will keep them at bay for the ball, but I have to make sure that you and I have an important talk before it."

"Stop right there Nate. I know that this is what everything is leading to. I know that they want to use me to free the 200 imprisoned and I cannot do it. I can handle myself like the predecessors before me and what happens, happens. So don't lecture me about how I could die at their hands. Peril has been my legacy sir, and you can skip the warning. I need to finish

getting ready. What could be more important?" Emily said while studying the gown.

"I just wanted to ask if you remembered how to waltz? I know your predecessor did, but I wanted to ask if you knew how since you have retained many of the characteristics of her. I would never question your eminent valor."

The room's demeanor changed in a sudden second and the women discretely left to give the thickened air space. He wanted to know if he could dance with her, and she, in her suspecting brash defensive reply, chastised him. It has been a long time between them, and he was trying his best to be the man that loved her more than anything -again.

"I think I can remember enough of it to get by. You taught her, and I remember. Let me show you," she said stepping close to him with a curtsy and fragility that cracked through his hardened exterior as they danced. He held her waist and hand with a stubborn tremble. No music was played, but they danced in each other's rhythm. Him in her beauty and grace, and her in his statuesque and handsome ardent staunch. More memories than the dance came back to them as they moved closer and closer into each other familiar. As they maneuvered around the small cottage, the rhythm felt almost sexual with him leading her around stepping stools, chairs, and an ironing board in graceful glides. His heated breath on her poised neck inhaling her as they spun together drove them both to an embarrassed stop. For the first time in a very long time, they laughed together. He stared at the small vein throbbing and pulsing on the side of her neck, and she heard his warrior heart racing in the intoxicating excitement of the moment.

"I know you think me a fool, but for centuries I have constrained this forbidden love to no avail. I did things that are unforgivable, and cowardice in my denial and avoidance thinking. It would be terminal if I acknowledged it. Whenever I did, I lost, nonetheless. I love you Emily/Ty/Amelia/Frederick or whichever form God allows me to hold you. Tonight, we cheat fate's end and the victimization of your linage. I fight beside you no matter what the outcome. I have been selfish not believing in what my heart and the layers of time consistently convey."

Though the dance had stopped, he moved closer into her, focusing his eyes and wanting lips on hers. His mouth was dry as the heartfelt words fell from it, and the moistness of hers was the only thing it thirst for, and hers too, were longing for fulfilment.

"No matter how this goes tonight, I promise to never leave you and to love you however you are. The witch's spell only lasted a couple days, and she said that if you remain in the state you are in, it is because you are only there for the love of me, and in that, I can now profess that my love is no longer conditional, or subject to whatever state it is in. Stay with me Em. It is your soul that has enchanted me into surrender," he said as he leaned in for a gentle kiss to quench beautiful words Emily has been waiting to hear.

At the touch of their lips, both of them reeled in an orgasmic collision as they embraced each other, and their minds exploded in years of completion.

Like fireworks in their union, time in the kiss reflected hundreds of kisses over centuries. Both were exhausted, as if in that moment a thousand kisses suffocated them in joy, updating time in a stopped breath. If it was not for the door slamming open and interrupting them, it would have been a welcome death in a blissful kiss.

Rushing in cackling and swinging straw brooms and handkerchiefs, were the ladies returning. They attacked Nate, hitting him with the brooms and shooing him with matron authority. At the doorway, two men waited while they laughed at the barraged two lovers. Like the ladies, one was more mature than the other, and both found it amusing watching Ms Clayton and her assistant Mary chase Nate around the small cabin like angry dogs herding a sheep.

"*Run, Nate, Run!*" Angus, the elder of the two yelled in his laughter.

"*She swings a mean broom!*"

Each time when Nate would submit and do as they asked, he would get to the door with the men and make a dash to get another kiss before he left, and the women would go into a frenzy hitting and chasing him all over again until Nate's exhaustion, in joined laughter, tired and the men dragged him out to get him ready too. In the corner on the bed laughing hysterically with her hands outstretched with puckered lips as if she too couldn't separate from Nate, was Emily. The humor of the lighthearted moment with the ladies in between them, masked the immediacy of the impending eve.

A whole Fall day elapsed and Ms Clayton and Mary worked feverishly on Emily. Everything from her hair intricately twined off her shoulders in French folds and twists, to the color of her nails. When the men returned a couple hours later, Ms Clayton and Angus, in concert together, held the two from seeing each other till it was time to head up the winding path to Crimea that was transformed into its former regal mansion. Over the trees you could see the brilliant lights casting an amber glow over the surrounding forest. Music ebbed through the trees dancing along the leaves in sweet quartet compositions that quieted the sounds a night in slumber, and the always circling crows that follow Emily wherever she goes.

"*Goddamn! Is she ready. She must think she is Cinderella and she's not going till the clock strikes twelve,*" Angus hollered outside.

Angus and his son, Junior, were having a good time. They had Nate prepared and ready, but Ms Clayton wanted it to go just so. He might be having fun mocking their progress, but it was all part of a plan to make this occasion something more than somber.

"*You men shut up out there! If I come out there and smell anything like hooch on y'all, you won't be laughing then,*" replied Ms Clayton out the shuttered window. "*Ok, she is ready. I think we did good by her, and you gents hold your tongues in front of a lady.*"

"*That's your cue, boy. Go on there and get cho woman. Look at cha! You look like you is ready for burying!*" Angus and Junior said, passing a jug between them as Nate knocked on the cottage door. "*Oh, and another thing....*"

Nate stopped and turned to him before he knocked thinking it was something serious that Angus wanted to tell him.

"*Don't rip your stockings!*"

Nate was dressed in a gold lame, silk and velvet jacket that elaborately stopped at his hips bellowing in a flair with gold trimmed panels mastered in seamless tailoring. The shoulders were intricately embroidered with leaves of white silk ivy brocade covering a fine starched white linen shirt that laced out of its front, cradling his neck in stiff pleated ruffles that framed his thick manicured beard which braced his chiseled bone structure from temple to temple. His thick legs began where the jacket ended contouring his thighs and calves in course pale white nylon with gold studded shoes that made his feet look flat and extra-large. A soldier to heart, he wore a decorative scabbard gilded in gold, holding his saber to his left side polished to a gleaming shine. His dignity was ever-present in his posture.

Angus and his son continued to laugh and tease him. They rarely see a black man dressed in formal attire. Although they were familiar with helping white men as dressers, they laughed satirical mockery. They are what the Immortali call "stewards" and come from a long line of family that work and serve them. Uneducated and skilled with their hands, they are the unseen commodity that hinges the Society together across North America. Their lives never question the motives or structure of whom they work for. Many of them have known their employers since birth, in an unusual way, they are their family too.

The cabin door cracked open, and all eyes were transfixed on Emily as she steps on to the porch, radiant and breath-taking. Even the crows quieted and settled in the fir trees. Her hair was pinned up in a coif of intertwining French curls with scattered amber jeweled hairpins that shimmered from her head resembling burst of light from lightening bugs about her. Nate had told Ms Clayton to alter the dress to fit her, but the vision before him was just as stunning as anything he has ever envisioned.

She wore one piece of jewellery. It was the locket that she got from Luke in jail, and it was appropriate. The shimmering yellow satin and gemstone gown was strapless and cradled her ebony shoulders. Its bodice was crusted in crushed stones that sparkles in every move. The gown flowed with each step as she stepped on to the porch. It had a train of tiny gemstones over the thinnest silk with a petticoat under it.

With her satin gloved hand, she stretched it out in a curtsy to Nate and bowed her head. She was captivating, and he nervously fidgeted with his saber as he graciously bowed and helped her up. Noise from the women in the cabin were of sniffles and soft awes. Their faces pressed against the old dusty windowpanes as they watched.

"You are beautiful as a queen my love, but you are missing one important part. You must summon the sword. You have done it before. Raise your hands to the sky and summon it with your mind. Call it."

The night clouds swirled in sudden wind that disturbed the quieted birds.

"Try harder Em! Think about everything you have been through. Think about Luke, Elijah, and Izzy. Think about the centuries of Vessels before you that have gotten to this point and died!"

The more Nat forced her emotions, the more the clouds above swirled open with rolling thunder and the sword emerged and plunged from its cracked skies, piercing the ground at her feet, and the crows hushed in the phenomena.

"In a secret compartment in that dress is a place to hide it. Ms Clayton and I made sure you could access it easily. You will know when to use it."

She looked odd with the sword in her hand, still looking demure and regal. The moments of fantasy and beauty has dissipated. The realities of the night returned with its guarantee of a cataclysmic outcome.

"Let's go M'Lady," Nate said, taking her hand after she secured the sword.

The two traveled the winded ivy-covered path up to the house. Each step made the trees reverberate as the crows followed batting their wings on the branches and leaves. The lights, music, and chatter within Crimea was jovial, but to both of them, it was anything but that. As the mansion got closer, Emily's heart raced in anxiousness. Nate saw it in her face as each step seemed to frighten her, with eyes wide and nervous.

"You look lovely, my dear. How should I introduce you? It would do me great honor to introduce you as my wife. At one time you were."

He stopped just as the path led to the front of the mansion and kneeled on one knee as if he were proposing and grabbed her hand. For Emily, it wasn't a good time for it. Such a special moment shouldn't happen on the eve of her ascension or blood. Nate looked surprised at her dismay. She snatched her hand from his and pulled a small handkerchief from her bosom and dabbed her welling tears.

"What is this Nate? How could you ask this on this night of all nights? There is so much we need to talk about, and I refuse to answer at this moment. I could very well die this evening. And what about you? Why would you want to?"

He stood blocking the path in front of her holding his breath and stunned by her refusal. Emily knows that he is gathering his thoughts and brooding them over in his head. The struggle for words seemed to infuriate him. Without another wasted thought or stumbled words, he moved closer to her and, grabbed her and pressed his lips to hers. She resisted a little, but the exchange of a kiss has ended many arguments between lovers. The kiss wasn't an aggressive one. It merely said all the things he couldn't find the words to say. She smelled of delicate floral lavender and an unusual blend of other fragrances that only stroked the flames of what his heart was feeling. After it, he held her and pressed her tightly bound corset body to his to whisper in her ear.

"I have surrendered, my love. If it is your wish to torment me, then let it be so and I deserve each lash of pain you bestow me, but I ask...if we both know the repercussions and possibilities of the prevailing eve, why shan't this moment be as if the last opportunity for me to say what it has taken centuries to say?" He said, lifting her chin so that he could look into her eyes that seemed like dark wells of want- wide and clear as this star night.

"You are my soulmate no matter what happens. Time's allusive hand wedges no distance in the way I feel. I cannot go

another moment without you believing that. Let us go in here unbridled in this love and propriety, and together we can face anything. Know that I am yours. Know that I have always been. Take this ring that belong to the Emily of your past and wear it with the dignity and love that she had for it. It's you Emily. It's always been you."

Nate placed the tiny blue sapphire ring on her finger as he did decades ago. Immediately, it lit in brilliant glow and the beating trees quieted again like an audience in suspense. He knew it was the right thing, but he also knew of Clymythious' love for her could, on this eve, oppose everything to win her heart as he has with each Vessel.

As they got to the large mahogany and brass-trimmed double front doors to Crimea, two footmen opened its large, crested panels and sounds of laughter and music flooded from them. Nate looked at her, and his eyes were transfixed as everyone else's were when she crossed the marbled threshold - head held high in majestic, stunning beauty.

She paced herself to be on the same footing as Nate, who firmly held her satin gloved hand in escort, as if the sapphire led the way as a statement of possession, he wanted all to see it. Nate paced himself, too. Emily's long, beautiful dress trailed behind her, and each move she made, looked gracious with poise and a fixed smile that hid her nervousness and apprehension. They had to walk through a long corridor adorned with gold candelabras, gilded mirrors, large oil paintings, sculptures, and overwhelming fragrant flowers in aligned ornamental vases. At the end of the hall, two doormen waited for guests to enter and exit. They, too, were in renaissance uniforms, as were the outside two, wigs and white gloves and deep burgundy jackets adorned with brass buttons and tights. Emily stopped at the last wall mirror to check herself before she enters through the doors.

"I'm scared, Nate," she said while checking the numerous jeweled pins that held her tresses in curls and French twists in intricate weaves of black pressed hair that shined as if polished in veneer. The woman she saw in the mirror was a new vision for her to see in gilded panache. With cheeks that were lightly blushed and just enough make-up to bring out her high cheek bones and full sultry mulberry-colored negroid lips- she radiates.

"Let's go, my love. You look enchanting and will be the most beautiful woman in the room," he said, towering beside her.

He knew what she was thinking and used his intimate presence with her as a distraction that would hopefully encourage her.

"I wish Luke could see you. He'd probably say something like 'Daaaaaaaamn!'" Nate said, doing his best to imitate Luke's melodramatic humor to make her smile, and it worked.

"He would probably say something just like that. I hate that we left him and Elijah without saying anything. They are probably worried sick about me. And what about Izzy?"

This is the first time that she has mentioned her child to his father, and she paused in its echo to await his response. He seemed uncomfortable at the thought of processing it. He stared in the reflection of her in the mirror, saying nothing, but choosing the words in his mind as he always does before, he spoke.

"I cannot wait to see my son. I know that you have him in safety, but you speak nothing of him, and I want to know so much about him. He is a miracle and a prodigy like no other Vessel before you. Now is not the time, but when this is over, I want to know everything about him, Em," he paused. *"Does he look like you?"*

"No, he is the spitting image of his father." She said, staring at his reflection in the mirror. *"I am ready,"* Emily said, turning to Nate, changing the subject, and fixing his collar.

As they approached the doors to the ballroom, Emily's corset seemed to be strangling her, trying to contain her rapidly beating heart. The sword under her dress's cold blade kept the whole purpose for attending this elite aristocratic affair focused. As the doormen opened the doors, the cacophony of music and gaiety assaulted her anxiety. The excessive opulence of it all consumed her. Clymythious was the first to acknowledge her beyond a head nod as the room's attention diverted to them. Emily held Nate's hand tightly until he let it go to greet the guest that he was acquainted with. Before long, he hadn't noticed that she was left to fend for herself as the guest in formality greeted him. She fanned herself to be occupied as the women around her eyed her from head to toe. She didn't know if it was because she was with Nate or was it because there were few persons of color attending the ball who weren't staff. It was the opportune moment for Clymythious to intervene between the curious peering eyes and in chivalrous rescue, ease spectacle by them.

"Good evening my parhelion goddess, I wasn't expecting you here, but we both would know that would be a lie. You look ravishing, my dear. You absolutely are the most beautiful creature here," he said, kissing her hand and staring into her bosom at the old necklace. *"It has been sometime that I have the honor of your captivating beauty, how is it you still maintain my undivided attention?"*

His eyes blatantly devoured her in his dialogue, saying far more than the coaxed dialogue. Dressed in fine emerald silk with brocade ivy with excessive padding, he looked quite dapper, although in her eyes, he appeared as a predator who was manipulating the other guest, even from a distance, with a devious plan. Other men gathered in small clusters around the room, admiring her Nubian beauty. Few dared to introduce themselves other than Navasha, Benoit, and Simon, who allowed a moment between them before encircling her.

"You clean up well darling," said Navasha.

"Delightful" said Simon, passing her a glass of champagne.

"Lei che non dovrebbe essere" Benoit tauntingly sneered.

Emily was ambushed by their sniping carousel and Clymythious waved them off in a subtle hand gesture and escorted her through clamoring guests to the balcony of the mansion that shelved the night in staging. Lit by only dim lanterns, its arches opened up into the cool night splendor.

"We must talk my sweet. There is much you might be confused about. Do you not know me? It is I who has always loved you, but you deny me time and time again. Look at you now, although your beauty is unmatched by your predecessors,

it's what you have chosen again. Let me refresh your memory and perhaps your heart will change fate's role. Give up this facade and love for him that not only cannot accept you but has not loved you regardless. This is not Victoria's wrath, but your own lust to please him. Isn't it Ty?"

It's been a long time since someone has called him by that name and made the sound as alluring as any other name. For her, it has come all as one, and she knows that the preference is consciously divisive now under no rule.

"Don't let them taint you my sweet. Yours is a bitter acquired taste that they have never favored, but me on the other hand, am your captive admirer."

Emily did her best to conceal her uneasiness and walked from the ballroom to the adjacent balcony, staring into the night in a full moon's witness and crushed stars through the darkness. She knew that Clymythious was waiting for a reply, but she stalled in his wait. This evening, she not only had to be brave, but she had to have the wit of a warrior and the cunningness of a woman. Night's breeze brushed over her bare shoulders with assurance of what she must do.

"What did he mean by 'Lei che non dovrebbe essere?'" Emily said as a barrage of waiters and elite guests one be one took turns introducing themselves to the isolated couple.

In between the Dukes, Barons, Duchesses, and supposed royal heirs, Clymythious whispered in her ear, *"It means 'she who should not be,'* and winked at her, taking her arm, and leading her to the ballroom floor as an up-tempo waltz played. The guest parted as he escorted her to the center, and she is making every effort to conceal the sword that was under the petticoat. A hush fell on the room as they reached the edge of the checkered polished marble floor. Emily was confident in her ability to waltz, but with all the attention Clymythious commanded, insecurity undermined it. And then there was silence. Her heart was racing, trying to hold her poise. On the sidelines, she could see Navasha, Benoit, and Simon's group led together as if they wanted to kill her right there. Clymythious whispered under his breath,

"Look at all the attention you have. Relax and trust me. I will not harm you."

He bowed to her, and she curtsied as delicate as she could control keeping the sword hidden. The orchestra waited for a nod from Clymythious before beginning the waltz again. By then, everything was a blur of stern faces that were non-friendly in their blank inspective stares. She wasn't sure whether it was because of her color or something else, something she would never understand. There was one that wasn't blank, and its dismay was alone in its rage. There was one that was full of contempt for her dance with Clymythious that he pushed through the guests in unapologetic haste. Only the gasps of the guest in their mouth open shock of witnessing two black men of power in a combative standoff did the two men regain complete attention. Clymythious raised his hand to the conductor without turning his attention away from his approaching adversary and once comrade. The music ceased in tension. The guest backed off to the decorative mirrored walls leaving just the three of them underneath the candlelit crystal chandelier. Closer on the perimeter, irritated and anxious, was Navasha, Benoit, and Simon with swords and weaponry, waiting for the moment to descend on Emily (and Nate to if he intervened). He once was one of them, but since the death over Emily a century ago, they are no longer his alliances, and that betrayal would easily be the same fate as hers.

The two men faced each other in silent snarling expressions with defensive stance. It was only broken by Clymythious' laugh as if he found the entire charade humorous.

"My good friend you are brave and foolish...in many ways. How dare you insult my guests with insolence," he said while dragging Emily by the arm into the adjourning room for privacy. Nate tried to follow, but Navasha's sword at his throat stopped him at the door.

"Foolish Nathaniel! You still love her or him, or whatever he is today." She said trying to infringe on his past prejudices. *"Don't think that our respect for the others here tonight will deter your end if you make one more step!"*

Nate was surrounded by all three of his former comrades- swords, and daggers drawn. The pause in between decision and outcome seemed to slow the moment of action drawing it out to slow ticking seconds. After wise thought, he submitted to their demand.

"That's better, my love," Navasha cooed. *"There's still a chance for you although you gave us the runaround to find her. Let's have some champagne big boy,"* she said flirting with him in distraction and signaling the orchestra conductor to restart the music.

Clymythious had Emily where he wanted her- alone.

"Is this much better my dear. Sit down and make yourself comfortable. Or can you sit in that dress with that sword hidden

under your petticoat? I promise not to harm you. I never have," he rebutted with aloof arrogant candor.

As he excused himself to speak to the guard out front of the library door, she had a moment to see him in his regal stature. She has always seen him as an adversary, but amidst the warmth of the old library in its deep richness and darkness, he was softer spoken and interesting. The room was adorned in oil paintings and antique books in mahogany shelfs that reached from the floor to the ceiling. No one could ever outshine its majestic atmosphere.

Dressed in silken attire, Clymythious not only seemed non-threatening, but ironically alluring in formal dress. Emily relaxed and played on his beguiled field.

"Why have you brought me here Clymythious? You and I have nothing to speak about. Surely, you know my concerns and motives for being here, but I know nothing of yours."

"I have no deception in bringing you here, my dear. I only wanted to compliment the most beautiful and captivating woman in the room alone. By now, I think you know enough about our past to see the relevance of bringing you in here. It is I that have loved you eons and eons and each time you thwart my advances. Can a gentleman just be direct in his admiration?"

There was a quiet rap on the door of the library that interrupted his conversation. He returned with a small velvet box in his hand.

"Close your eyes," he said with assurance. *"I promise that nothing will bite you."*

As he crossed the room, he moved with fitted grace and confidence that he would do as he said and not try anything. When she opened her eyes, he was standing behind her spewing heated breath on her bare shoulders.

"Nothing matches or can come close to rival your beauty this evening, except this necklace, but still pales in comparison," he whispered as he clasped a yellow crusted lemon diamond necklace on her from behind. *"Take this small trinket with no conditions. It should adorn a neck as delicate as yours, my dear."*

In the mirror, she stared at the heavy stoned necklace as it shimmered in the library's light with more opulence than she has ever seen. It fell over her collarbone with droplets of teardrop shaped stones that were framed in smaller ones. Clymythious knew that they had diverted her attention as he grabbed her shoulders and kissed her neck as if sealing the gems on an ebony display.

"I have known you as many, but this last embodiment is the most compelling."

His hands were sleek and far softer than Nate's. They caressed her shoulders in gentle want and endearment, and they trespassed as they fawned, but they were not Nate's. For a moment, she was drunk in it, using recollections Amelia, Frederick, and others she saw and felt in the visions and loves as others. She snapped back to reality still admiring the jewels that laid on her breastbone in dazzling compliment while Clymythious hands were roaming on her trussed waistline. His deception didn't work. When she tried to return the necklace, he grabbed her hands.

"Even if you don't accept me, accept this token of affection. Besides, it matches the little stone on your finger. I assume that it is from Augustus. Must I remind you that you died from his hands once. If credit merits love than I am due. It's hard to believe that you love him so much as to take the form he finds most comfortable. I must say it's the first I have ever seen that kind of power from your predecessors. Young Frederick could have used such a skill, but alas he did not, and it cost him his life. Your coruscant metamorphosis is absolutely amazing my dear, although it makes no difference how you are born. I have loved you regardless. It's your inalienable right."

Just then, there was a banging at the door that rattled the solid oak doors as if they were paper. She could hear Nate's voice from behind them. His voice was angry and distraught.

"*Emily! Emily! Emily!*" He shouted while throwing his shoulder against the double doors.

"*My dear, your friend is worried about you. Perhaps you can calm him with your quelling beauty. Sure, his mind is thinking something horrible has happened to you. Go to your lover,*" he said while turning his back to the door as she ran to it.

She opened the door to find the two guards that were guarding it battered and sprawled in the marble hall. Nate's face was drenched in sweat and panic froze in his eyes.

"*Are you okay honey? I thought...I thought,*" he said drifting his attention on the beautiful necklace that dropped stones into her bosom. "*You didn't? Please say you didn't?*"

Insulted and embarrassed, Emily walked past the now panting in rage Nate. In a glimpse of an eye his emotions have switched from anger to distrust and jealousy. At the end of the corridor stood Benoit, Simon, and Navasha with amused looks on their faces and whispering between each other. The necklace has them intrigued.

"So…whatever you are calling yourself now, we see you and Clymythious are becoming good friends," Navasha said as Emily got closer to them.

In calm aloof disregard, Emily dismissed her with one short eye cutting stare, as if she was above responding to the comment. She raised her hand to Benoit, inviting him to escort her back to the ballroom.

"Emily! Where are you going?" Nate hollered.

"To dance!" She said in the resentment she had for him implying that something else happen between she and Clymythious in the library.

The two men were left alone- Nate wavering in contempt and Clymythious with gloating satisfaction.

"Whisky still your drink?" Clymythious said without turning to face Nate. *"No reason not to be civil."*

Nate stood in the doorway debating whether he should follow Emily to the ballroom or hold his ground with his old comrade and foe. The eventuality of events will happen before nights' end. No need to rush, besides, this conversation is long overdue. He slowly took his hand off his saber and stepped into the library that lingered in Emily's scent. His intentions were for civil behavior, but the past and the dire future urged his tone in aggression and anger.

"Fuck civility! If you think you are going to swoon my Emily into your talons with jewels and suave decorum, you are mistaken. I will kill you right in this spot, you old bastard!"

"Resettle yourself and take company with me before I tire of your contempt and liberties. It is solely my goodwill that allows you breath. True, beauty is vexed by you at the moment. But let's us converse as civil gentlemen and bind your tongue with your saber."

The music in the ballroom livened up and, in its gaiety, Nate's jealousy distracted him in seething malcontent. Laughter and crowded voices seemed to mock him behind the guarded doors.

"If anything happens to her Clymythious, you will feel the fury of my sword and lest not it be as favorable as my feeble tongue."

Clymythious laughed in pleasure that his once liaison honored him in rebuttal. Although the two share centuries of pain and comradeship, the absence and subtle respect only simmered behind its cloaked formalities.

"You do not find fault in my longing to talk with her. It is not I that she has changed who she is. I love her ten times more than I have ever loved her. What say you that command that adoration from such an awakening beauty? To her, I am only a whisper on a flame, while you are a great wind that rages fire to storm. It is I who am at a disadvantaged sir," Clymythious said while passing him a snifter.

He walked as a glide around the perimeter of the room pretending to be interested in the books and artwork that cluttered its archaic walls. He occasionally peered at Nate deliberately holding silence in his uncomfortably- gloating in every tensed second. After a few full circles around the room and Nate, he sat in front of him in a burgundy crushed velvet antique flowered chaise with his legs crossed in aristocrat fashion- upright and stiff. The tights struggled to adjust his long form with grace, his efforts to look at ease failed against them.

"You of all people know this eve well. You dare to blatantly fawn over my beloved as if you had a sentient right and wielding it in pretentious honor? You sir, are the betrayer for you seek what is not yours. You and I have fought many battles side by side. We have altered time with our deeds with righteous blood spilled in immoral virtue on judgmental lure and never has our own penchant been served till her. Can it be that you protest my choice over blind servitude to the Immortali, or do you only want the coldness of a cold bed to be substituted in the blood thirst of what you cannot have or possess?"

"Look about you. You think you have what I want? My how your memory is muddled in inaccuracy. Although she does mirror Amelia, we both know that she is an incarnate of Frederick who we both know suffered from your jealous anger and malevolent hand- or love, whichever way you desire to deviate the truth. It is I that should be the more indifferent in your treachery. You sir are a fraud and a manipulator but let us not spend any more time in past regrets. It only can lead to the eventual, and that is so droll," he said re-crossing his legs and fudging with the leggings.

"Let's make a wager my friend," he paused as if he had already won the odds and merely was baiting Nate into the agreement. *"As you well know, the eve is one that is dire for her. Lay a wager on her choice of whom she chooses. Victor gets the spoils; loser shall be eternally cast in Tartarus and shall never again debate possession of the other's prize. I saw the trinket of a ring on her finger, but by chance did you see necklace that adorns her deserving neck? What can you do for her better than I? I have no idea what spell you have cast on her, but it has bid its time,"* he said waving his glove in the air as shooing a pestilent thought from the thickening air and throwing the locket on the floor in front of Nate.

"Clymythious, why would I ever trust you in such a wager? You could easily in victory or loss, assume a pernicious tide to either outcome. Let say I wager; I am no fool to count fairness as your strong suit. Makes no sense to humor your challenge. If so, be your choice, than as gentlemen we can settle this between us and leave Emily out of it. And that, my ole friend is where we differ. I can never take such a love that God has allowed me to possess more than once over the eons, whereas you see it as a win of betterment over me and not a gain by you," Nate said standing at his feet and pointing at his seated adversary.

"You did not allow me to name the complete terms. Albeit true that in loss you expire by my command, but per chance you win? At the moment, your son and that dogged Elijah are plotting in the woods to seize the festivities. The covenant I speak of does include my associates, for I will keep my word and invite your uninvited companions in to balance and execute the agreement, if by improbable odds she chooses poverty and

uncertainty over heirdom. It could easily occur. She is quite the labyrinthine," he laughed.

"She sir, is my wife, and I thank you not to speak of her as a possession, and if she were a title of possession, it would be mine to behold. This Vessel is no fool to your craft, so I will humor your wager."

"So, I see you have grown in your acceptance of where she lies and is predicated by space, but not obligation. How be it she your wife?"

"Clymythious, you know that she married me last ascension when you killed her over Edison's Cliff. Does that make her by inheritance my betrothed - perhaps not, but she has more secrets than you know."

"My friend I might not know all of her secrets, but I know that in each life cycle she longs to be with you till she is born of the other persuasion and then you not only deny her, but you are the one that cannot accept her then. So now you have found the one that can decide her one persuasion and give it the name 'a secret' to keep what you won't have any other way. Left up to me, she would not have changed a thing and this battle for ascension to free our brethren would be done. If you so love her so much. Set her free. Return her to who she was born…Ty. And another thing, lest not forget whom killed her over those cliffs. It was your hand that dropped her!"

Off balance and heavy in the sentiments that Clymythious barraged him with, Nate had no refuge. No witty reply. Nothing he could say would denounce what he was saying except that he didn't ask Ty to do anything. Ty was asleep most of his life and

Nate never did anything to awaken him except for a kiss, and even that was to help him focus out of danger.

"You are correct in your arrogant assumptions. I prefer the company of a woman, but where you are wrong is what you think my motives are. Not every man can do as you do sir. In fact, your hedonic tastes are unfitting for the Vessel in any form," Nate said while heading to the door and picking up the locket.

"Liar! I find you too funny Nathaniel. If I am hedonistic, than you are a fraud and a charlatan still a prisoner of your own prejudices. Young Fred spoke of how much you disdained him." Clymythious sarcastically interjected in a snipping tone. *"So much so that you detested him every eve till it became the talk of the estate of how you bedded him in your quarters. I think thou detests too much. I did you a favor by taking him as mine, thus allowing you to hide your amorous bedroom secret by doing what you were not man enough to accept, and in jealousy and rage murdered him than to see him free with me. Don't insult me. That young man was more of man than you will ever be. So run and save poor Emily who daunts in a curse. Such a knight in shining armor...as long as it's a damsel of your taste. I'm quite sure she doesn't know about your indomitable parenthetical conditions."*

Before Clymythious knew it Nate had flew across the room, wings extended through the slits in his jacket and hit Clymythious in his mouth with such a force that careened him to the floor. As he laid on the ground, he still had a smirk on his face. He knew where Nate's sensitive areas were, and he deliberately irritated them. Blood trickled from the corner of his mouth and when he smiled in his amusement, his teeth were grinned pink and oozing blood from the assault. Both fairly close in stature and size, it appeared as if two heavyweight fighters were in a ring, with Nate standing over Clymythious panting in rage.

"If you ever mention what happened to Frederick to her it will not be to my disadvantage, but to your detriment Clymythious. Besides, there is far more you don't know than your cavalier tongue thrashes in assumption."

Just as Nate got to the library's door, Clymythious stopped him with one last comment.

"We shall continue later. So, say what of the wager?"

There was no need to reply to anything he said after he attacked Nate's morality and dignity. His blood boiled in an overflow of anger and residual regrets about the past. To turn around would be addressing things that he personally never addressed, and when he did, only Ty knew. He has learned from the past to embrace time and space without explanation. Nothing to lose anymore. For him, Emily/Ty has given him the ultimate sacrifice, and out of it, what Clymythious doesn't know is that it has given a son.

Meanwhile, in the ballroom, Emily is dancing interchangeably with Benoit, Simon, and Navasha. Each one taking turns in shared dance moments amongst the other dancing guests to talk to her.

"Mademoiselle, you are enchanting this evening. Did you understand what I said to you when you arrived?" Benoit said as he whirled her in the dancing rhythm in pomp and circumstance.

"No, I didn't, but Clymythious translated it to me. Am I to take that remark as a threat? I don't think you the kind of gentleman that throws idle threats."

"I am not my dear. It wasn't meant as a threat but more as a remark of reverence. Whereas it might sound as if it was a threat, you are no longer that strange guy who hasn't a clue what is going on. You have blossomed into what you always were. Now, if only we can change you misguided heart."

His embrace said all that the words were saying. It felt as if he was, in an odd way, trying to comfort her as the music from a complete sixteen-piece orchestra ebbed and flowed in lush, sweeping rhapsody through the grand ballroom. It almost seduced her in a trance in their sweet enchantment.

Simon was an entirely different melody; although the same symphonic compositions, they felt forced and obligatory. Even his grasp on her was cold and repulsive to her. His breath upon each of his words to her were rank and just as nauseous as what he said.

"You make a beautiful confusion, boy! If I didn't know any better, boy, you would have fooled me too. So, what does it feel like?" He said, letting his eyes trace over her face as if looking for a string or anything to remove a mask.

"I think this dance is done," she said trying to remove his tight grip from around her waist, but his large hands were inescapable.

"Where do you think you are going boy? You are still technically a boy, aren't you? Perhaps not!" He said, letting his

hands grope down between her legs and tearing the seams that held her bosom.

They had stopped dancing, and he had no concern about what others thought as he assaulted her with no regard. She squirmed and fought the embarrassing investigation to no avail until she slapped him so loud that stopped the whirl of the other dancers. The gaiety in the room came to an appalled stop. From within the crowd, gentlemen who were outraged at her discourteous accosting began to gather. It is not proper etiquette to inappropriately handle a lady in such fashion, even a black one. The men grabbed Benoit from both sides of him and untangled his mangling arms off her.

"No need, no need! I desist and apologize to the lady. Release me," he argued for them to let him go. *"How is this so? He is no a lady! This is a farce! Let me show you!"*

The last comments re-engaged the men, and they apprehended him again. This time, dragging him away from Emily. They thought that he must've been drunk or out of his head. Ironically, the other women did not run to her aid or show any compassion. She, being the only black woman guest, was left alone, stripped of her dignity, divested, and spectacled by the malign whispers in ambivalent stares. Without missing a beat, the orchestra returned to playing as if nothing had happened with stoic grins. The music sounded strained, and tense as arched bows and stiff wooden necks were strangled in tight, disconcerted grips to regain melodic composure.

In the distance, on the far edge of the ballroom, as they towed him out, you could hear him still hollering expletives.

The Book of Emily

"Unhand me! I am an invited guest, and you are removing me for a nigga? A nigga boy at that!" The rumbling voices murmuring through the appalled guests still creating small clusters of spectacle. They had no idea of what it all was about, but they did see that it involved a woman of color and a white man- and that, to them, was unjustified in public. Benoit returned to her with some champagne, but Navasha interrupted, pushing him to the side.

"Your making quite a scene honey. Did you really think you could come here uninvited and blend in?" She said, laughing as she took the champagne glass from Benoit that was meant for her. *"Besides, it's my turn to dance!"*

Navasha took Emily's hand and escorted her to the center of the ballroom and, wrapped her arm around her waist and began a waltz in stubborn lead. It wasn't uncommon for women to dance with each other; nonetheless, it was very uncomfortable for Emily, as it only intensified the ogling of the other guests. Her footing was delicate and commanding as she led Emily in flagrant whirls that spun them in and out through the other guests. One in a beautiful yellow satin blur, the other in crimson and black dominance. Navasha was wearing a crimson taffeta black embroidered gown that buttoned up to her chin. Her auburn hair pinned in a coifed French bun in the back. Her stern appearance equaled in her demeanor. As they danced, she scowled at the other guest in between the low-toned conversation she had in Emily's ear.

"You die tonight, honey and it is a shame. You bring excitement to these ancient ones who are stuck in their dogmatic aristocracy. Smile my dear. I must admit you look ravishing," she said licking her dark plum lips. *" It won't change*

the outcome lest not give them the satisfaction of seeing you distraught. Ignore them and let us dance."

As the dance ended, Emily tried to break away from Navasha's clutches, but she tightly gripped her small wrists and had one more thing to say and was forceful about saying it right at this moment.

"*Dearie, don't get too confused. By the end of the eve, you will be quite dead, and I hope I am the one that has that privilege. You have been a thorn in my side as this last vessel. You think that this great love you have for Nathaniel will save you, but on the contrary, it's that same love that will betray you when the time comes. He might be the one to do it, and if he isn't, I will beg Clymythious to let me do it if you decide not to ascend,*" she said while releasing her wrists with a patronizing kiss on her hand.

The room around Emily felt as if all was frozen in a blur. She tingled from within as she thought about what Navasha was inferring. How could Nate be deceiving her when everything in her being has gotten her this far? She could feel the beginning of energy surge within her.

Just then, Nathaniel appeared from behind her, quelling the rage that ebbed in blue subtle embers from her fingertips. All she knew was that she wanted to release the doubt in fire, right here and right now!

"*Emily don't. I shouldn't have left you alone with them and take off that cursed necklace! You belong to me, and any adornment shouldn't come from them. They are filling your head with confusion. It's a ploy to weaken you and now is not the time to second guess your emotions. I found out that*

The Book of Emily

Clymythious is not as innocuous as he appears, and you are falling right into it. Danger is amiss and we must be ready." he said, dragging her by the arm to the library.

As Emily hobbled in tow to gracefully keep up, he kept talking.

"I didn't come this far to lose you Em. If a showdown is what he wants, then a showdown is what he'll get."

At the huge double doors to the library, Emily stopped. The evening is wearing on her patience with everyone. Each has a manipulative purpose, tugging her in several directions. Steadfast at the door, she wriggled out of his grip and composed herself before she took another step.

"Woman don't play with me! You look fine and I thought I asked you to take that damned necklace off!" Nate screamed in a thunderous rage and ripped it off her neck, scattering gemstones like marbles on the floor.

He stood there in disbelief of what he did without thought, but his expression on his face said that it was something he didn't want, or plan to do. He was making a stand for Emily. In his brutish way, he is using all he has to weaken the insecurity he has over what she might choose. He hoped in his domineering display that she would obey. Tearing the necklace off was only an angered reaction representing the fear that Clymythious planted in his head. She watched as he seethed in regret and impulsive anger, clutching the broken clasped necklace at her bosom. Just as suddenly as he snatched the necklace, she, in reaction, slapped him and took off running down a hall with no idea of where it led to; one hand tossing the broken emerald necklace, the other holding the gown and hidden sword secure as she fled. The halls seemed to taunt her in their mysterious walls that were closing in on her with old stares frozen in ancient smirks that seem to evoke more panic as she traversed them. From behind her, she heard Nate in pursuit, calling her name and pleading her to stop. In the lengthy halls, she couldn't make out what he was saying, but he said the one thing that would stop her. One thing that meant more to her than the emotional carnage.

"I think he has Luke and Elijah captive as hostages to negotiate as a barter for you!"

Emily turned and peered down the dark gas lit hall and all she could see is a large dark winged figure speedily coming in her direction. The calls had ceased, but she had heard enough. No more running, not from Nate, not from Clymythious, and not from herself. She raged in blue ember and vengeance. The figure got closer and closer, and she pulled the concealed sword from underneath her gown. Its handle only magnified her radiated scorch. Her head rang with a personage that she cannot contain or desires to. She let it consume her, and ancient words fell from her lips in possession.

"Portents fury shall come to pass to those who usurp from the sacred. Be warned that so true is the presage that will fulfill in awaited destiny. Be leery to those who approach this vestige path, for it concludes fate's wrath!" She said.

The figure never stopped closing the gap between them. Her heed held his path without reluctance. It was much larger than a normal man and occasionally, the gas light would scintillate a short glimmer upon him until he got closer, but keeping a distance. Her light kept him just out of the blue light but close enough to speak without effort.

It was Nate fully transformed into the beast at his own command in monstrous splendor and sentient rapture. His clothing showed his preparedness in its conformity to the beast, only it was different than its past curse. He could command it, and thus, it wasn't an alternative of himself but a combination of them. He responded to the blazed Emily with careful thought, hoping to appease the wraith that now spoke.

"I know you well. Abide me and veneration shall override discontent. I am here to protect," he said softly while tucking his large wings back into the flaps of his overcoat. *"You know my love. You know my heart that will perish if it is not true to you in any form. We are wasting precious time. Emily you must know your enemies from your heart for it will weaken what you not only want but need. Do this for our son. Do this for Luke. Do this for all the victimized forms whose wake you live in. Lastly, do it for me in forgiveness for failing the others,"* he said kneeling before her as the light dimmed in his words and she returned and eased into the Emily he loved.

The return didn't go unnoticed, but he kept his head down, appearing to be in humility and prayer. Her hand lightly stroked his head, and he lifted his gaze into the bewitching eyes of Emily, and she saw that he was not bowing, or praying. He was subtly weeping.

"Nate, why are you crying?"

"A warrior does not cry! It was the brilliance of the light. I cannot look into it," he said, standing to his feet emotionally emasculated and exhausted in naked candor defensive, but

strong like a frightened broken stallion in a storm. *"We must find where Clymythious is holding the guys while he is busy with the guest and is amused by upper hand."*

Emily's doe eyes would not just accept Nate's dismissal. She locked them into his, and his fight to hide pain that before this moment, she had not realized till then. She wanted answers.

"Why do you suffer in the past? I need to know to release you from yesterday's remorse. I only see visions of it from others. I won't leave until you explain the guilt," she said stepping closer into his space in refusal and defiance.

"There is not enough time to tell you all, but I can tell about the Vessel before you. I was a soldier in the American Revolutionary War in the 1700s, and I was given a command I couldn't do anymore. I have seen many wars, and I have chosen to follow opposing sides of many, but fighting for the British and killing Patriots was just too immoral for me. If it were so righteous a deed, then my heart wouldn't be questioning it so guiltily. I chose to follow my heart's instinct and protect and nourish the very thing I for centuries destroyed without conscious. Now I see a hope for mankind. That hope was in each vessel's eyes as they died- some by my own hands. Each time believing that something was going to save them. Each time nothing did. When I met Emily, I fell for her like a selfish mortal man. I could no longer perform my mercenaries' duties. I began to believe that there was another way; a way that was built on will and love that could change God's plan."

She listened, hinged on every word and in breath's closeness she replied. *"Which is worse, to clearly see the unchanging past, or a future you can change and not see?"*

His face was as still in her closeness that she took ease at the opportunity to lift on her toes and softly kiss him- perhaps the last kiss. He was at least six inches taller than her, but he reserved his inclination to lean in to receive it. Deep inside of him he needed to be assured in feeling that she wanted what he wanted. In that kiss, all doubt erased apprehension in a soft exhale she released as their lips touched. Whatever lies before them will not be weakened by insecurities.

"We must go Em. At the end of this hall is a stairwell that goes to each floor. Maybe we can find Luke and Elijah and figure out how we will make it through this night. If we get separated, follow the path in the back of the mansion to the old mill. Its been abandoned for decades and you can wait for me in safety. Use the back door to get in. There, in a parcel wrapped in an old satchel, is a change of clothes I hid there for you and I."

Nate and Emily took the musty back stone stairwell that twisted in a spiraling descent to the basement floor where they clung to the shadowed walls checking each door along the way, occasionally dipping in its dark rooms when they heard voices. It smelled of mold and cedar dampness with an eerie chill in its air.

Dimly lit by flickering lanterns along old, masoned corridors, this room was locked and looked like it could have been a root cellar at one time. It had a lamp in it lit and seemed the most remote.

"This is the only room down here locked," Nate said while holding his arm against Emily keeping her in the shadow behind him.

His hand unknowingly was upon her breast. He could feel her heavy breathing and quickened heartbeat at his touch though he pretended to not pay any attention to the moment. Things could get intense in these old halls. They needed to find Luke and Elijah, but they needed safety to recompose themselves.

It's old iron lock and latch broke easily as he struck it a couple of times with his saber. The room, except for the light of a small oil lamp, was dark in its cavernous shadows. Whereas the rest of the mansion had a renaissance architecture, this room was unfinished with earth walls and thick with the overwhelming smell of yeast and dirt. The two wandered through its corners and side rooms. Each one seemed larger than the one they exited with small windows where the moonlight beamed through ornamented ironwork. Finally, in the corner of the last room they entered, was a back carved in stone stairwell that went further down into the foundation of the old mansion. They stopped at the bottom of it and the light from above the stairs cascaded around its wound corners and they both wanted a moment to finish what almost started above. Nate put down his saber and approached her hoping to calm her down, only to excite her breathing more.

"You should rest Em. I can feel your heart beating like a frightened dove."

"I am not frightened Nate."

It was obvious for them both why it was fluttering and labored.

"It's been a while my love. If this be the last moment, than I shall drink from it with dry thirst I shall not lose by!" Nate smiled while removing his overcoat.

The Book of Emily

Nate's heightened senses could smell her want. Her breathing synced with his and her loins begged for him to be with her. Tiny beads of sweat prickled on her forehead as she watched him remove his shirt and the top buttons on the leggings. She turned her back to him so that he could unfasten the gown's pearl buttons down her back and it fell to the floor and removed the undergarments leaving her naked before him.

"By the heavens, you are so beautiful," he commented as his eyes swallowed in her beauty from behind.

Emily stood still with her arms crossed over breast still turned from him and allowed him to bask in it in her shyness. Her tiny thin dark ebony frame looked girlish and fragile in the light from the stairs. Nate wanted to ravish her like an animal, but he was afraid of hurting her against the stoney walls.

"Turn around my love. You are so beautiful, and I see you have filled out a little since the birth of our son."

She turned with her arms still crossed over her swollen small teacup breast as if she was hiding them from him.

"Come here and let me drink from your beauty," he said as he stripped off the leggings over the gold trimmed shoes. Emily turned to see that his words understated his excitement. Like a dark stallion he stood before her leaning on the wall in God's nakedness and the devils grin with his hand outstretched to her in wait. His body was muscular and gleaming in the dim light, she could see healed scars of battle on his body as she tried to not stare at his throbbing manhood and trembling hand.

In the dark the two made love and washed away the danger of the moment. Emily has only been with one man before, and it was him then too. Though it was short, the passion seemed to run slowly as she collapsed with her legs wrapped around him against the wall where he held her in strong grip on his hips.

"Is that you crying Em? Am I hurting you?"

"That's not me. It is coming from over there!"

Nate lifted her off his pelvis and pushed her behind him reaching for his saber.

"Clothe yourself Em. It sounds as if an animal is hurt or something," he said stepping into the darkness with nothing but the saber. *"Who's there?"*

Silence and the damp overwhelmed the room as Emily waited to hear something- anything would have been less torture than the dead silence. With her sword also in her hand and gaining the courage to follow, she went into the shadows which soon faded as ignition in her chased the shadows back in blue. Deep in the room, Nate was running in the dark with his saber overhead and about to strike anything that ominously hid. Closer and closer, her light beckoned off dusty cobwebbed boxes and forgotten items stored in the room. Ahead she could see Nate naked in full transformation- wings outstretched and swollen in his beastly reckoning.

"Wait Nathaniel. That's not an animal. Can't you hear them?"

They heard an indecipherable voice echoing just in front of where he was about to strike in the dark.

"We are here Emily," the voice said in the muffled shadows.

Nate didn't hear it, but she did. The voice sounded deep, calm and assured. It was familiar.

"That's them!"

CHAPTER 17

"You two took long enough! Who goes in a dark ass dungeon and get butt ball naked and do the nasty? I had damn rats crawling over me and you too were getting it in. I like a show as well as the next man, but damn! Y'all nasty. That's all I gotta say," Luke said as Nate and Emily untied and removed the gags off them.

Neither paid any attention to their lack of clothes, Emily in a dimming blue haze and statuesque Nate with a saber and with wings folding behind him. It was Nate who turned and looked at Emily as if something is wrong.

"Em!"

Nate snapped her consciousness back when he and all three men stared at her making her feel like Eve in the Garden after a bite of the forbidden fruit, embarrassed and ashamed. She fled to the other side of the room to get her clothes and to hide from their stares.

"Gentlemen we at the crux hour. I don't know how you found us here at Crimea, but your company couldn't come at a better time. Let me ask you something while she is away. How is the child?"

Both Luke and Elijah looked at each other as if waiting for the other to answer. The ordeal of what Emily said happened when Isaiah was born made them leery in trusting anyone. Elijah didn't want to say anything that would divert Emily's attention to the task at hand, and Luke just thought it was none of his damn business where Emily's son is.

"Fuck you wanna know now? Why don't you ask her man. She was good enough to pin on that damn wall a minutes ago, but not good enough to ask how her son is doing? Ye understand that? Don't play me Pop!"

The two men were face to face prepared to back what they were saying. One by a father of two who wasn't going to be talked to like that or be made a mockery of. The other, was frustrated about Nate taking Emily from them and now pretends to care about where his son is. He remembers when he was young how Nate did the same with him after he sent him away on a ship when he was just a child like Isiah. He had residual anger that was waiting to express itself.

"Nigga you ain't never cared about anything but yourself! Let set you straight. I ain't here for you like you wasn't there for me. I'm here because I know what Ty, I mean Emily has been through and I'll be damned if I ain't going to help her end this shit," he said walking away to the other side of the room with Emily, leaving Elijah and Nate uncomfortably in each other's company.

"You are not helping the situation. You have intertwined in both their lives in many ways that are not favorable. The boy needs to work through growing up half human and half Nephilim with no one to explain why he is the way he is.

Although I know what you did and why you did it, one day he will need to hear it from you. As far as Emily and the infant...never make the same mistake twice. You two have had a joint destiny from the beginning and both of you have learned how to return to each other over and over again. The sacred child is my interest and by it being so, Emily, you, and Luke are my charge."

Nate had no response to either of the two men. Besides still being embarrassed about not knowing they were watching him submit to Emily in the basement, there was overwhelming helplessness on all emotional fronts. He would need some time to think things out and now is not the time.

Composed and united, the four plotted the return to the Immortali Ball and Clymythious. To go back upstairs without a plan would be foolish. Every step Clymythious has always seem to know one step ahead of them. The night would hopefully be the end of what has tortured vessel after vessel for centuries. As they discussed different strategies, one important part in all plans involved was Emily. She nonchalantly heard the importance that she played in each one, but kept her input distracted by fixing herself up to return. Despite her tryst with Nate, she was unruffled, from her coiffed hair to her glowing complexion, her disposition was fortified by having all of them together. All the men, they were fascinated how she quickly regained composure and couldn't resist watching her hoist things in place, from her pressed breast to her stockinged legs that harnessed a sword under her gown.

"Em! Whilst you have no reason to cover yourself from us, but have some courtesy for our presence," Nate said, but she gave him a stare that said she had more dire things on her mind.

With a wave of her gloved hand, she walked through them to the staircase leaving each of their mouths gapped in astonishment. She stopped at the bottom of the steps and turned to Nate with her hand held out as if he had lost his manners and gestured for him to escort her up the winding stone steps.

"Oh shit! You better go Pop before she cracks your head with that sword! We will follow and try wait for whatever happens. We got y'all back!"

Emily's hand was trembling as Nate, and she reached the floor where the ballroom was. She might be attempting to be courageous in front of the guys, but her trembling hand said different. She stopped at the doors to the ballroom and asked how she looked. There was a pause in his reply as he had his hand in his pocket to retrieve the locket and return it to back to her bare neck.

"Wait, let me say something," she said clearing her throat. *"Nate you know I love you and have since I was born. It's like I was born to love you. You know that no matter what happens here I will find you again. I love you and I have loved you many times in every form that has been shown me. I have to tell you how much you mean to me and all the others. For whatever reason God has planned for your great love, I am forever grateful for it. Without you I would be still a confused soul victimized by a loop in time. It is your love that gave me the strength to be all of them and combine all their love into one. If I don't survive this, find our son Isaiah. He needs his father to guide him in my failure if it is deemed so. Something tells me he will be a great man. Promise me Nate, and I can walk through these doors with knowing that the future, no matter what, is in God hands. 'Elle ne devrait pas être!'*

The Book of Emily

"When did you learn to speak French?"

"Oh, just something I picked up."

The doors opened by guests exiting and they walked in nodding to those who graciously smiled at them. Many were decorated in military medals and uniforms with impressive ranking and distinction. The ladies too had their adornment hats that also declared their status with huge colorful ostrich plumes and extravagant jewels that was worth more than Emily could imagine. Nate would stop to introduce some of them and introduce her as they weaved through the guest. There was Maharajah with elaborate concubine of women and man servants fanning him and holding wine and platters of fruit. There were princes from regions of Europe Nate spoke of well, but she did not have a clue where it was. Generals, Kings, Viceroys, Dukes, and Earls filled the room with their dignitary air, they were escaping from one side of the ballroom to the other room at least an hour.

"They find you delightful in your mystery. They know who you are, but they have heard so much about you and you live up to everything they have heard in your feminine beauty," Nate said leading her to a quieter place by a large roaring fireplace fixed with a large oil portrait of a scowling aristocrat.

"I will be right back. I'll get you some champagne. Don't hurt anyone while I'm gone," he teased.

Emily had a chance to survey the room in the solitary moment. Large chandeliers adorned beautiful relief panels with depictions of wars and battles in between intricately carved mahogany woodwork that sprawled in Victorian elitism and grandeur. Although they were gas lit, they radiate a warm candlelight glow. Even the floors were layered in colorful oriental rugs that too depicted battles and wars with dragons and mythical creatures. It made her slightly uneasy to see the exhalation of war and death in everything. It felt like the painting over the fireplace was eerily scowling at her.

"That's my son Renault De Gorgious. He built the mansion with his success in Europe developing the rails. He made this his summer home as a tribute to his late wife who died from consumption. That's her over there," he said pointing to a painting on the other side of the room with a regal older woman dressed sitting saddle on a white stallion.

Her expression blank and stoic, she wore riding clothes complete with a leather crop at her side amongst a rural countryside with harvested pastures quilted in barley, wheat, and corn.

"Poor dear never seemed happy. It destroyed Renault with her passing. Some say it was poison; others say that she didn't die but ran off with an Importer from England never to be seen again. It's an interesting story that I am sure bores you," Clymythious said as he entered the room without her noticing it.

She didn't turn or flinch. If he wanted her dead, she would have been. She doesn't know how he crept up behind her, so she acted as if she knew he had.

"No, it doesn't bore me tell me more. I find it interesting."

"Hmmmmmm, it is more than interesting. Shall I tell you what actually happened? Now that is interesting. You see, sweet Clara was a clever girl falsifying her death to run off. When I found out about her deceit, I killed them both- her first, being the more difficult because of her being half human and half sentient like yourself, and then her young companion. They had boarded a train out of town, and I met them on the car and seduce her with a drink that I laced with arsenic and watched her choke as I told her my doings as he searched for a doctor on the train. He was far easier to dispose of. He got off in Pennsylvania, without the train stopping, shall we say," he jovially laughed finding amusement in himself.

"I don't find that amusing Clymythious."

"You don't see the irony?"

A woman of few words, Emily kept her distance from him as she immersed herself in things around the room that could be more entertaining than his macabre humor. Besides, when Nate returns, her placement in the room is all it would take to fuel his jealous anger.

"Have you always found yourself to be a self-righteousness murderer or is it just a characteristic of all you Fallen ones?"

She knows that she has taken a chance and spoken to him in an aggressive tone, but she thinks that playing the game the way he plays it will give her the upper hand, or at least the respect. She approached him as she spoke, stepping just into the center of the room where she had the advantage of his lust for her.

"I see the real you, you know? While you might fool the others with your arrogance and display of power, you can't deceive me," she said while allowing her hand to trace over everything close.

Her mind was resourcefully calculating each move, gesture, and step, she did. Being coy was new and the more comfortable in it she felt using it, the more effective it was. Clymythious was off guard by it. His laugh sounded forced and contrived. Subtle things like a tilt of her head in the light or a slow turn from him urged silent pauses in his rhetoric that always seemed controlled. He moved around the room offensively in step trying to regain his dominance, but she had the control.

"So where is the necklace I gave you?"

"Oh that? It's somewhere. The clasp probably broke, and it is likely somewhere on the ballroom floor. Your buffoons were rather rough on me in their attempts to rile me. Ask them."

Clymythious saw no humor in her newfound arrogance and disregard. Something has changed in her that he couldn't quite put his finger on. Insolence and flagrant dismissal normally would be cause for rebuttal, but he is intrigued by its arrival.

"So, my dear, you don't see the irony that you and your mother share with poor Clara? Your mother was as naive as you and just as beautiful. It was unfortunate that you didn't have a chance to know her as a little boy, and oh how your father wept over her sudden death."

"You know nothing about my mother or my father!"

"On the contrary, I knew her well. And I do mean that in a biblical sense if you allow the pun. She eloped with your father and had you. You don't see the irony? I could have been your father," he said under his breath while buffing his nails incessantly. "Funny that was the disagreement we had all the way to her deathbed. Poor thing."

The hilt on the sword itched at her thighs begging to be withdrawn. It took all the control she had not to react to his accusations about her mother and father. As a child she remembered little about them.

"As you got older it was clear that you resembled your mortal father. It was that hag of grandmother that raised you that hid your ancestry. Powerful woman. You broke her heart with your obsession with men. To her, you were to bring another linage of Vessels in your children. It killed her, but she had no idea of the power you possessed, and I too must have to admit that you fooled all of us. 'Tis a shame to have to extinguish such a unique Vessel as yourself. Of course, we could just make arrangements for you to ascend in the ceremony tonight and you would be all the more powerful and be my bride."

"Surely sir, you don't think that I am gullible enough to believe anything you say. What's funny is that you think that you can tell me on one hand that you murdered my mother and on the other, I would even consider the proposal of marriage with a wretched old disgusting fool as yourself. Per chance you think me the fool?" She chuckled slightly under her breath. *"This from a feeble fallen one who turned his beast from hell loose on someone that he professes to love? I shall destroy you like Raja. All good dogs go to hell!"*

Emily walked away out to glass patio doors to the terrace after her sincere threat and mockery. She wanted to keep him occupied with her and get him out of the library where Nate would soon return. It wasn't so much a plan, but the anger bubbled inside her, welling to compulsive reactions. He didn't directly follow her to the terrace.

"I will join you my dear. Just let me check on my guests," he said leaving the library.

In the foyer, he bumped into Nate who had two glasses of champagne in his hands returning to the library.

"Aw there you are Nathaniel!" Clymythious said as if he was united with an old friend, *"Come with me. You will never guess who is performing in a few minutes. It is our good friend Prunelle du Claire Desuant! She is performing her renowned rendition of "Dante's Inferno" I'm quite sure she will be pleased to see you. Do me the honor of sitting with me."*

The lights in the ballroom were already dimming and the doormen were holding the doors open for Clymythious before shutting them down. As he entered the guest applauded as if he himself was the performance. He held Nate's arm above the elbow tightly in escort through the tables on the outskirt of the room. While Clymythious held a frozen big smile in the applause and appreciation, Nate wasn't smiling. He was being dragged in strong escort to the main table as the room quieted for Prunelle's entrance.

Before she entered the spotlight in the center of the ballroom floor, the orchestra wove a beautiful crescendo of strings accompanied by actors dressed in demonic costumes in theatric white leotards with diminutive wings, encircling themselves as the music swelled with the lighting in alternating hues. Each color was reflected in the captivating movements by the gothic actors ending in total darkness and applause. Out of darkness and sudden silence stood Prunelle in luminescent radiance. Adorned in yards of sheer lace and gray chiffon, she, in solo, sang the Italian composition in dramatic fashion and emotive performance. She sang the hypnotic aria in haunting soprano precision, holding her notes as if she didn't need air. The guests were enthralled and stood on their feet at its exhilarating end, clapping and screaming louder than the now softer orchestra.

"*Bravo! Bravo!*" Clymythious and the other guest roused.

She bowed first to Clymythious who only nodded in appreciation, but when she saw Nate, she touched her hand to her lips in a gentle kiss which brought the first smile the other guest saw on his now almost blushing face. He had a chiseled face that honestly reflected his demeanor not just in rugged grimace, but when urged, in pleased countenance.

"Didn't you two once have a thing? Oh wait, I think it was during the French and Indian War? Aw yes, I remember well as if it were just yesterday. I suppose you don't want to remember how they were going to lynch you for courting a white woman."

Before Nate had a chance to say a word about the incident that happened in Louisiana centuries ago, she was standing in front of them. Her appearance hadn't changed over time. Blond tresses and pale skin, she was breathtaking in all scarlet red. From her crimson satin shoes to her couture gown that trailed in a bustle train behind her, she held her ivory hand out to be kissed by the two overwhelmed gentlemen. Her speaking voice was as velvet as her musical instrument with a strong French accent.

"Did you enjoy the recital," she said, averting her eyes to the seat between them.

Clumsily, both Nate and Clymythious jumped to their feet at her sudden arrival. She smelled sweet as if she had just bloomed in a lost garden of fragrant flowers, Nate thought to himself. It was a calculating distraction by Clymythious, and it was working. Nate sat beside her attempting to not be so diverted in her bewitching beauty.

"Prunelle, you do remember the captain?"

"Yes, I do. Hello Nathaniel. It's so nice to see you after so long. You look like time has done you well."

Clymythious elbowed Nate in his side after a prolonged reply. It wasn't that he was being rude. He was reminiscing in his mind about the last time he saw her. The memory triggered all the moments they were together during the British Resistance movement where she entertained the French troops. It was a time when a black man could fight in the war, but also fought for his equality. Their affections for each other were frowned on by most. He remembers the first time he saw her. She was performing in Hippodrome Theater House for the troops, singing operatic renditions of contemporary songs with a melange of artists from magicians to acrobats. Each night he returned to listen to her mesmerizing classical interpretations. Often the audience were obnoxious and rude, talking amongst themselves in alcohol stupors. It wasn't until one evening that he had had enough of the harsh behavior and rushed from the balcony to address a soldier that heckled her to the others amusement. In that time, negroes had to sit in separate sections of the theater, but that didn't stop him from brawling with the disgruntled soldier which spurred a riot in the theater. When he awoke days later, he was told that she visited him every day. It was her courage to come to the negro hospital and see him that made him visit her at the backstage door after her performance as soon as he gained consciousness. Their special secret affair lasted for months till the Immortali found about it from his then good friend Clymythious who thought he was doing the best thing for him.

"You look well too Prunelle. I hear you conquered Europe. How is it we haven't seen each other in decades?" Nate said as he stared into her marine green eyes.

"You are still very sweet Nate. Will you be here after the ball?"

Clymythious interrupted and interjected that Nate is the guest of honor and must be here for all the festivities. He sneered at Nate sideways as he spoke. For Nate, it was really good to see her, but the conditions couldn't be worse. She excused herself to meet and greet the other guest, but before she left, she kissed on the side of his cheek, nicking his ear drawing a small stream of blood before departing.

Clymythious thought it was humorous and insidiously laughed at the beguiled peck while handing him a handkerchief. Nate assumed that perhaps her jewelry snagged his ear, but it was something in Clymythious' amusement that said that it was much more.

"Aw how sweet! She still has a taste for you Captain."

"What do you find funny? She is not an Immortali, is she?" Nate asked searching for an explanation for his delighted humor.

"No, she is not."

"So how...?"

"She is a night dweller, a ghoul, a succubus, or what many call a vampire. She merely wanted to have a sip of her former lover. She cannot harm you, but if you were mortal, she likely would have ripped your throat out. It happened after you two had long gone separate ways."

"Emily," is the one word that flooded his thoughts immediately. The farce was over and he abruptly left Clymythious at the table still laughing at his dilemma as he followed behind him back to the library.

"Em, I must talk to you," he said bursting in the library with Clymythious close behind.

"I'm sorry I got distracted," he said looking in Clymythious' direction. *"Let us go back to the ball and I will get you some champagne,"* he said sternly as he escorted her from the library.

"You two enjoy yourselves. The hour of truth is upon us soon. Laugh, drink, and be merry."

They scurried out of the grasp of confrontation in the guise of dancing. In the hall waiting just outside of the room was Navasha, Benoit, and Simon looking like they expected a different outcome than this one. Each whispered under their breaths as they passed through them on both sides.

"Traitor"

"Impersonneur féminin"

"Negress," were some of the restrained remarks they murmured.

The hour was getting late and the gaiety of everyone in the ballroom has turned tense and anxious. Discrete eyes followed them through the ballroom, less disguised in the wake of the late hour, but Emily didn't notice. She had everything she thought she could want this evening. Nate's large hands and gentle firm embrace as they whirled on the ballroom floor had all her attention. Whatever ominous future has in store will have to wait for its dance. This dance belonged to them. For these brief quickened steps life stood still, and they ran through it in private moments solitude as lovers can do. Enraptured in each other and oblivious to their surroundings as one, they enveloped themselves as if all was surmounted to this point.

"I love you Nate," she whispered in his ear as they waltzed.

Nate and Emily danced several dances until the orchestra stopped abruptly. Clymythious stood in the center of the ballroom floor concluding and announcing the grand finale to the evening.

"Honored guests, friends, fellow comrades, I hope you have enjoyed the evening. Can I have all the guests head out to the amphitheater for our finale for the evening."

Crimea had an outdoor stoned amphitheater that the original owner had imported from Greece in the center of the estate's garden. Just outside of the large patio doors, a cobbled path aligned in fragrant hyacinths and white dahlia arched through a maze of hedges and marbled statues lit by torches. Overhead fireworks sparkled in the night sky spilling brilliant embers like the tears of stars over the distant amphitheater. The path wound in a downward crooked bend, eventually reaching the sunken masterpiece of Grecian architecture. The large granite stones chiseled in massive blocks stacked into an enormous bowl resembling a gladiator arena.

"So, this is it, isn't it, Nate?" Emily said while holding his arm in escort.

Clymythious stepped out of the shadows and grabbed her free arm, interjecting that it wasn't over and that it is just beginning. Nate's displeased face wrinkled in frustration as Emily was escorted in front of him, her occasional backward glance showed fear of the unknown down the torchlit path. He could only watch from behind. She looked like a goddess in the dress that she held off the ground with one hand and the other traversing the rugged path. Soon the distance between them was lengthy and the labyrinth path hid them ahead of him as it divided and twisted down to the amphitheater. When he reached it, Emily was already seated in the front row with Clymythious straining to turn around and find him with eyes that were afraid. Her delicate face was constrained in fear of what her fate would be.

The flashes overhead of brilliant fireworks exploded in thunderous explosions like cannons in battle. As they ended, Clymythious stood center stage graciously bowing as the guests roared in applause.

"Ladies and gentlemen, it gives me great pleasure to conclude this evening with another song from Prunella du Claire Dusaunt followed by the reason you are all here and what we have been waiting centuries for- 'The Rite of Ascension!' And to make it one you will remember; we have a special treat for you!"

Prunella appeared from the side of the theater diverting the audience attention in spotlight as they followed her as she sang a beautiful Italian aria accompanied by the full orchestra that resounded throughout the granite amphitheater. Her voice, acrobatic and almost shrilling in scaling high notes, ebbed, and flowed as the arena stage was being set up behind her. Her finale was a young boy tied up to a post stripped naked. The last note was ended with a vicious bite to the boy's throat sucking his young lifeblood for all to see.

"*Here, here! Here, here!*" They shouted with applause.

Emily was appalled and could not bear to watch as the boy shrieked in agony before dying, depleted of every ounce of blood and as his now blood-stained body writhed over in death. It was a horrific scene, one that she couldn't watch or want to think about.

"*Who could do this to someone's child?*"

"*Why is no one trying to stop this?*"

"*If they could do this to an eight-year-old child, what might they do to me?*" She thought.

She ran out of the still excited amphitheater mindlessly running in nausea and disgust, not so much running to somewhere, but running from somewhere. Reeling in panic and flight, she somehow got lost in the winding path, ending up at the old Mill that was forgotten and far away from the amphitheater- which is all she wanted. The mill was dilapidated with its huge blades made of decaying sail cloth hand sown and forgotten. Ominous in the dark, it sat alone on the property shrouded in weeds and overgrown ivy that choked it once usefulness. Fate must be with her because she remembered what Nate told her earlier.

"If we get separated, meet me at the old mill. I have a change of clothes theatre, and I will meet you there," she remembered him saying.

In the back of the old mortar and stone building she found the stashed change of clothes as he said and changed into them, only keeping the sword in the change. Night crickets, toads, loud creatures of the night filled the damp air with their songs to an audience of crows. With no shelter from them, she felt they were watching her and singing a song of gloom and night supremacy, but they posed no threat as Clymythious and the Immortali did. She had to go back. Running hasn't given her the upper hand. It only postpones her eventual fate.

The brush and dried bramble cracked as she heard footsteps approaching. The steps were slow and sounded heavy in their step. She drew the sword, and it again gleamed in beckoned hue and the night creature's songs ceased in the tension, blanketing the dark in a dead quiet.

The footsteps stopped and the eerie silence held presence.

"I am not afraid. I know you are out there."

Still nothing.

It infuriated her, and the charge emitted from the sword traveled up her arm and coursed through her body bringing her ablaze in luminescence crackling energy. Whomever was out there hidden in the elm and fir trees never moved until her temper and the fiery discharge revealed their shadow amongst the forest.

The Book of Emily

"So, you are ready to battle?" The voice said.

The voice resounded from all directions of the camouflaged darkness, but the sword chose one and she focused all the fear and anger in that direction, and it spit sparked lightening that struck a tree and splitting it in fire.

"Hold it Em! It is I. If this were a test, you did well," the voice said as a figure stepped from behind the now-burning tree.

Nate slowly walked from behind it, shielding his eyes from her blinding blaze, wings tucked behind his back and bulging in his beast form. Her control was proven, but what she can bring forth doesn't mean that she can retract it. His approach was one of caution.

"Em, we have to go back to the amphitheater. It is with an unfortunate scheme that Clymythious plans to publicly execute Luke and Elijah if we don't return. He has them strapped to makeshift crosses for a bargain and you are the barter. He promised that a vessel will be sacrificed, and he has settled for his blood, although it won't do. It's a plot to get you to commit to it. We have to return. The boy might have quenched Prunella's thirst, but Luke's blood would better suffice her palate. You can run no longer. We have come to a place where your understanding must equal your strength. So far, they have leveraged your weakness in to manipulate what must happen. For every vessel before you, you must balance against those who won't stop until what their want is achieved. Your fate will be their consequence and not the other way around."

His wings arched with each angered word he spoke, outstretched, stiff, and raised above his head in preparedness for confrontation. His body swelled in mass twice his normal size, and as the anger rose, so did the veins that pulled out of each tensed appendage. The more he said, the less light emitted from Emily. Soon, she returned to normal- lightless and deescalated.

"Get up Em!"

Seeing that young boy's eyes filled with fear and his naked young body wriggle to get free from the public humiliation was still burned in her head. The way he screamed just before Prunella attacked him with large fangs that dripped with anticipating saliva. He cried for his mother with shrieks of terror, but it only taunted Prunella to be inauspicious and more frightening to the boy. The last scream the boy had as she ripped into his throat will stay with her forever as she, in terror, watched Prunella find pleasure in his pain and fear.

"Nate, I can't go back there. I just can't. What they did to that boy...was just horrible. I can't. I can't!"

With one flex of his wings, Nate was in front of her as she cringed in the thoughts of what she witnessed. *"This is not a time to weaken. Right now, Luke and Elijah could be being tortured or worse- skinned alive, have their hearts ripped from their chest and eaten. Think about all they have sacrificed to get you this far. Think about all the people that helped you make this journey. Think about that young boy's pleas to go home. That could have been our son! Could you live with yourself if it were? Nothing they can do so far is even close to what their plans are. Get up and be the torchbearer you know you are!"*

The boy's image was still fresh in her mind, and his curdling screams still echoed, but now she could easily see that it could have been Isaiah up there being drained of his blood in some kind of ritual. She could see that same terror on his face. It gave her the strength to get up off the moss she collapsed in and stood up in Nate's awakening points, he mentioned. It was what she needed to hear. Something that kept her focus on everything that has happened not only to her but to centuries of vessels that have suffered in holding on and dying in bravery.

Emily didn't say another word and the sword, in response, reignited along with her entire body into an enraged blue bubbling flame. Nate took off running back to the amphitheater, trampling trees, and catching short spurts of air in gigantic leaps, wings flared, while the engulfed Emily rose to the sky, hovering in belligerent anger over the treetops. Her determination culminated in revenge as she effortlessly glided through the night sky with hundreds of crows behind her, cawing and intertwining in a dark cloud of flapping wings. Her mind was one with all that she had learned and invoked to be the last vessel.

The amphitheater looked tiny from the air, and she could see Luke and Elijah tied to the crosses on the stage that was crowded with at least a hundred of candles flickering on the floor. Gasps from the guests as the crows dived into them in an aerial assault that halted the ceremony with Prunella at Luke's old throat. Whatever they have done to him, they have returned him to the old Uncle Luke for his treachery that he manipulated to get free from jail and help Ty. He looked feeble and very weak, but Elijah looked strong and unlike Luke, they nailed his wings to the horizontal beams of the cross. Both watched as Emily descended from the sky in amazement and surprise. She landed on the edge of the stage with the audience at her back. Her sword in full flame and her eyes were unwavering as she approached Prunella, slaughtering guards that jumped on the stage, killing them in searing discharge from the sword and from direct blows from its sharp blade.

"You must be Emily. We are so glad you decided to return in time for the festivities. We were just about to begin the ceremony, but since you are here, we can perhaps skip their sacrifice and begin with your ascension," Prunella urged as she ran her sharp nails over Luke, who squirmed in painful anguish. *"Ladies and gentlemen, I would like to pause this portion of the sacrifice to introduce the guest of the hour, Emily!"* The crowd stirred. *"She or rather he has done what has never been done before. He is not what he appears to be. He was born as a mortal man and ascended into a complete woman. Look at her beauty, ladies, and gentlemen. She defeated Raja, Hell's guardian dog! And even took part in the beheading of our dear Phillip! She has fought battles with against us and escaped. She is a worthy swordsman and unlike any other before her, this vessel wields the power of all the vessels combined! With her enchanting, bewitching beauty, she has used to coerce others to betray us. For true, she is a worthy adversary!"*

The crowd, now disgruntled, is hissing, and booing louder and louder with each description Prunella boosted. Nate finally broke through the brush like a charged, angered lion but was subdued at the upper perimeter of the amphitheater by Simon and Benoit. He violently struggled to get free from them. They, too, were in their fallen form and arrested him back. Suddenly, a guest jumped from the audience on the candlelit stage with swords in hand. He swings four swords at once as he stood in opposing stance. Emily kept her back to him, never leaving the eye-line from Luke.

"Face me, Emily, and for once, let death escort you into the throws of gods," he said while clashing the sickle-like swords in rapid synchronization. *"I am Azazel. Show your strength lest die in cowardice,"* he said as he froze with all four swords over his head in battle stance as the crowed bellowed,

"Kill her! Kill her!"

She turned and faced him and the zealous audience that once bore friendly faces that are now angry, and many in their true forms. Some had horns; some looked like serpents, and many were disfigured and grotesque. Azazel was large with a breastplate and full armor on his lizard-like skin with gray scales. Where there should be a nose were two slits that opened and closed with his heightening breathing.

Emily rose to the challenge, levitated above the stage edge, and accosted him in sword proximity. Metal on metal clanging filled the arena as the two, in swordplay, sparred against one another- Emily in mid-air, scarlet, blue in a vapor haze, and expressionless on the defense. Azazel's multiple arms flailed in warrior fury, each arm repeatedly swinging in a rotary motion. The gasp from the witnessing guests occasionally would make him smile as she blocked his assault.

"Em!!!!" Nate screamed from the edge of the theater, which diverted her attention and the butt of one of Azazel's swords struck her face, knocking her to the ground in disbelief.

"C'mon Ty! Get up! You can do this! Whip that mutha fucker's ass!" Luke cried out.

Lying on the granite cobbled floor, her hair disheveled and covering her bowed head and still reeling in the hard blow to her head, she rose. Her mind refusing to accept that she might lose this important battle. So many lives depended on what happens here tonight. She could hear Prunella cackling in amusement at her weakened state. As she rose back into the air, she raised the sword to the sky that summoned blinding lightning from swirling clouds overhead. What Azazel and all who were spectating saw was Emily/Ty's duality commanding lightning and thunder. Her image alternating in colorful luminosity from Emily to Ty and from Ty to Emily interchangeably. Emily being sedate in flashing demeanor, but Ty in vengeful anger.

"Now that's what I'm talking about," Luke cheered from his still-bound restraints. *"Y'all done fucked up now!"*

"Enough!" Said the voice of both as a wave of lightening from the sword flung her opponent through the air, still electrifying as he was suspending.

With one enormous, charged thrust, Azazel was hurled into the night skies and the crows descended on him high in the stratosphere by the thousands. Azazel's tortured cries waned as they carried him away in winds that funneled in the charged trajectory. Emily regained her specter composure and dropped the smoldering sword with a weighted thud to the ground, hovering over the crowd, who now was shivering in fear and cowering with each other. Her attention was on Nate, who, in all the diversion, broke free of their grasp.

"Em, I'm fine. Don't worry about me. Help Luke!"

She pitched her hover with her feet now over her head and kissed the top of Nate's head, for he, too, could not look directly into the light.

"Fear not, Nathaniel. Those who trespass on the decreed fate shall fare true to recompense!"

After that gentle kiss on his head, she flew upward into the sky until far out of the view of all who watched. The silence weighed on everyone in anticipation of what was going to occur next, and when nothing happened, they returned to a rambunctious cajole. Nate screamed her name over and over as he single-handily fought through the crowd swinging his sword and cursing. He killed Benoit with a direct blow to the head and wounded Simon in his chest. Unstoppable, it was Clymythious who walked on the stage behind Prunella who stopped his blood fury.

"I'll kill the boy, Nathaniel!" he said.

"If you harm either one of them, I will kill Navasha," Nate replied while holding his sword to her throat.

The amphitheater emptied quickly as the other guest fled leaving only the dead and wounded that were trampled in their hurried exit. Seeing Luke and Elijah tied to the crosses only made him angrier. His large wings stretched out with a loud snap as in an instant he was onstage with Clymythious carrying Natasha by the throat. Without a word he pierced through Navasha's chest running his large blade completely through her and dropped her limp body to the floor. In shock, she winced in pain as the blood soaked her crimson dress into a pool beneath her. All arrogance gone; she looked at Nate as he swole above her getting larger as he destroyed everything in his path but leaving her mortally wounded body as a lure.

"If there shall be blood, let it spill from my sword and if it means that my flesh be exchanged in crushed bones and regret,

so let it be at this moment. I hold no content for your bargaining. The time for reasoning has gone. Free my son and company and penalties will fare well."

 Navasha's body laying at Nate's feet and Benoit's slain body sprawled in the isle steps might have altered Clymythious' plan forcing him to address Nate in battle. Prunella first was going to try, but she would be no match for him in his state of rage. Clymythious removed his evening coat and wig and let his appendages free themselves from his back, ripping the fine silk shirt in the process. Boney ox-like horns sprouted though the top of his head, erupting through, tearing flesh on his forehead twisting upward in a ram like curve. Where once he stood a tall dark lanky gentleman, he grew in size as he held Prunella back, and confronted Nate who held his stance over Navasha. Eminent battle was stifling in the putrid death thickened air intertwined in the burning candle wicks scented smoke that one by one were extinguished from their now large beating wings, all modernity gone. Nate's were black and veined with throbbing muscle with blood pulsing through them, and Clymythious' were large, but they were supported in a boney exoskeleton that arched up to spiked talons on their tips. They stood with duel stance as Luke watched them size each other up- almost grunting as they ballooned to their full size. Nate's size got so much larger that the pantaloons ripped and leaving him naked. His forehead jettisoned from his brow making him appear simian with flared nostrils and chiseled jawline, whereas Clymythious, more dragon-like with his jagged horns, feet like a gargoyle, and now snarling fanged teeth- was nothing remotely close to the eloquent dignitary he presented the whole evening. Gone were the fine clothes and aristocrat flair.

"Aw snap, this going to be good!" Luke yelled.

"Still your mouth Luke. In this battle between the Fallen, no one wins. Dire is the situation," Elijah softly said on the cross nest to him.

"I don't care what you say. Beat the horns off that son of bitch Pop! Break that nigga's wings!"

Prunella had had enough of the old Luke's taunts again grabbed his neck with her claws. She gripped his throat hard enough that he could not talk or barely breath. With one hand, she choked his wrinkled throat, and he had no more words, just spitting and convulsing for air in her strangle. His breaths shortened as foamed saliva oozed from crushed air that has him in seizures as his oxygen deprived body choked in asphyxiation.

"Do not kill him Prunella! We need him for the sacrifice."

She let go of his neck just seconds before he would have been on his last breath and laughed at his labored recovery.

"Punny man! I'll return to you later. We have unfinished business. I'm going to enjoy sucking the last drop out of you fool ass! Say one more thing and I will slice your tongue out and eat it for a snack!"

"Fuck you! You ugly bitch!"

Still in stance, both Clymythious and Nate thrusted themselves in the air with swords drawn. The collision of metal on metal sparked and rained orange embers piercing the night sky echoed in their aerial clanging. Nate grunted with each wield of his heavy steel sword, and Clymythious' war-like cries, made the battle look barbaric in its dance and volatile ballet, yet astounding in the combatant's agility. Aerial battle is a beauty to behold from the ground. The art of riding air currents and protecting the supportive wings resembled two praying mantises in combat with outstretched wings fighting for skies dominance. One wound to the other's wing would be the difference in noble defense in the air, or defeated injury and the unforgiving gravity's dishonorable and disgraceful plummet. Nate and Clymythious' skirmishes were quick like fencing- always returning to guard position before the next confrontation. More than mere swordplay, aerial battle redefines the traditional laws of sword battle. The two men could fight from several planes of battle, unlike fighting on the ground. Most of the advances were hilt to hilt, eye to eye, and a grunting exchange of words as the swords locked intertwined guard to guard in nose-to-nose distance.

"You shall not defeat me, Nathaniel. I am the better swordsman, and you know it. Your betrayal of the Order has its costs, and in this hour, I will redeem them all and your bride in treason."

His eyes, enigmatic and cold with foul breath of a dragon, stung Nate's eyes as he spoke while swords collided in a blade-to-blade stalemate. The two have fought many battles side by side as brethren in war, never on the opposing sides until Emily.

"It is with no honor that I sever our ties in battle Clymythious. Together, the ides of Chronos bides little consequence for valor, or trespass and conspiracy. You will forfeit in eventual truth lest my shadowed eyes death find defeat in love's virtue. See me not as your adversary, but as your executioner. My penance might be pledged in fain of a kiss, but no 'er more potent."

Clymythious broke the sword-to-sword lock with a kick to Nate's groin. He laughed as the pain of an old injury he suffered decades ago alongside Clymythious throbbed in wrenching tenderness. In didn't disable him, but it was enough to give advantage.

"I know your weaknesses, Nathaniel. Each wound, each scar, and even your fixation with empathy for man. It's sickening," he said, still in amusement. *"Not only will I kill your wife, but I will spill your son's blood too!"*

The battle resumed after each had summed their emotions into the other's anger with Clymythious more as the antagonist against an old friend turn foe. Nate, in a turn of events, descended from above him blocking each calculating maneuver simultaneously holding his body with his flapping wings at a diagonal position as not to give his opponent another opportunity to wound him. Clymythious fought with strained difficulty as Nate used the backdrop of night sky to wail down on him from above- each strike forcing out of the upward sky. The upper hand had changed in a flash of a moment as he caught the pommel of Nate's sword, and they wrestled in a spiraling death plummet to the Earth, cursing each other in grip.

"You will not sacrifice my son Luke!" Nate said as he tore at Clymythious' bony leather clenched wing.

Clymythious screamed in anguish as Nate flipped onto his back, punching the back of his head, and trying his best to rip his wing from off him as the ground got closer and closer, ensuring that both would be splattered on the stone amphitheater floor.

"It is not Luke who shall die if you don't release me," Clymythious surrendered. "It is your youngest one that is for certain death if we both die on this eve! Direct your eyes and see your progeny's assured death by your hands!"

Below Nate saw that he had Annie cradling young Isaiah who was screaming swaddled in a blanket, suspended in a cage offstage over a pit of coals and fire. Immediately he released Clymythious' and rode an upward draft to stabilize his descent and contemplate how to rescue both Luke, Isaiah, and Elijah, and Annie. All he saw was things that were not only in his hands, but in ways, his fault.

"It can't end this way," he thought to himself as he landed just feet where Clymythious also landed, but kept his eyes fixed in the first vision he has had of his son Isaiah.

"No Pop! No!" Luke cried as he watched Nate withstand blunt blows from a now retaliating Clymythious.

"I ought to kill both of them now, starting with the old man and then your bastard child! You are a worthless soul, Nathaniel. You betray your brothers. You have never been there for your sons. You yourself dare to judge me who hold allegiance to the Immortali and finally can free the two hundred upon the world...your last vessel has gone in hiding. It's pitiful," he said striking Nate's now human naked form to the ground in repetition as he struggled to get closer to the pit.

"No, Pop, nooooo! Fight that mutha fucker. We gonna die anyway but fight and save Annie and the boy!"

Prunella and Clymythious took turns beating and taunting Nate's now bleeding profusely body as he crawled to the fiery

The Book of Emily

pit's edge. He had no plan of action. Nothing seemed to matter. Emily has gone. Luke and Isaiah are being held captive. Anyone who he alternatively wanted to help are doomed. To him, God has been the one who has betrayed him. Isaiah's cries pierced in his soul as he looked at that tiny, panicked face, and then at Luke's, and it sank within him. Just feet before he reached the pit, he gave up in a flurry of kicks and beatings washed in his own self-pity. His mind drifted in surrender as the salty taste of blood on his lips seemed as if it was a relief from the inner pain.

"Oh no you don't sir. You don't get the option to blackout. Feel the pain. I want you to witness the end of man. All that you thought you could do in some righteous heresy you shall now see with your open eyes," Clymythious said as he held his sword over his head and stabbed it in his back in the left shoulder blade.

"Oh God, I can't take anymore. Forgive me all that I didn't understand and spare my children," Nate cried out loud.

He could smell blood and death as it approached, and he welcomed it as an escape. The infant's screams would not let him drift in the serenity of it. Darkness was seeping in and in it everything froze, and light flushed his dazed senses as all stood motionless, and time stopped. He lifted his head up in the sudden suspended time and he saw Elijah dismount off the cross and walk over to him bathed in all white and aglow.

"This is not the end," he said. *"She is not gone. He is not gone. Get up and follow what has led you this far. Does the universe you know have to make moral sense? He has forgiven you long ago and he used you to keep those who disobey and*

attempt to usurp his holiness," he said pointing to the frozen still Clymythious. *"Behold the child,"* Elijah said with his hand pointing to Isaiah. *"You have shown that it is not destiny that binds you, but an unwavering love and compassion for life,"* he said standing over him in a shroud of brightness.

It then dawned on him that through all of this was an underlining ideology that has bought all this to him. Once he, like them, believed that gods determined his strengths, but God determined his punishment. He has forsaken the deity gods, and in that betrayal for repeated unrequited love, adopted a God that is vengeful and will never let those who believe otherwise thrive. Murder, false idols, ancient mysticism, and centuries of misguided interpretation has led him to here- to this moment.

Battered and invigorated somehow in what Elijah was saying, he stood up to look at the world, still frozen like a captured photograph. First, he looked at Elijah and then at Isaiah as if asking for permission to see him while time was still. Nate hobbled around the frozen flames of the pit to its edge and looked into Annie's protective arms and saw his son. He resembled Luke when he held him over Edison's Edge cliffs. His grimaced face so innocent in her arms. Then he turned and looked at Luke still tied to the makeshift cross, old, and angry.

"What happened to Luke? His whole life had been one of pain and misery. I have not been the father I should have been to him. I ask you for one thing Elijah. Can you give him back his youth that has been taken from him?"

"I cannot," he said. *"He, like Ty, believed that things are controlled by others and in that belief is how they take what he*

considers not his. He must command it like Ty in his love for you commands Emily."

The sky tumbled in a panoramic roar distilled by time being held against its will, and Elijah looked into it as if he heard what it was saying.

"I must let time move on, but I will fight with you when the time comes," he said, walking back to the cross- translucent and still glowing next to Luke. *"Hold strong in your heart and find strength in what you see and feel."*

The pause in time flashed back in real time action in one blink and he turned in time to catch Clymythious' hooves that was about to kick him into the fire. Nate spun him off his feet and into Prunella in surprise- colliding with her to the edge of the theater. He stood magnificent in the moment with the now roaring flames of the pit at his back, and the returned screams of his son over it in the cage in a hostage.

The sky was in a tumultuous rage and rain spilled from it and it's drops washed over his naked form and gave him strength as it dampened out the fire in the pit. Arms outstretched to the night sky, and wings extended to capture every drop, he gazed up into the curling storm clouds as welcomed tears fell in an understanding.

"Thank you, Emily," he said, and picked his sword up from the ground and, with two swings, cut the ropes that held Luke and Elijah on the cross.

"We stand as one Clymythious! I will not let you harm one hair on any one of them!"

The ropes fell from them to the old cobble floor, and they were free in astonishment of Nate's renewed resilience. The tides had turned as quick as the sudden looming storm. The guests were funneling back into the amphitheater, all carrying giant red umbrellas yelling in encouragement.

"Fight! Fight! Fight!"

Fighting was not on his mind. He wanted to get Isaiah and Annie out of the cage, but like his father, the rain soothed him. It could have been the smell of it. It smelled fresh as the wind blew the clean smell of the trees and forest. It could have been the sound of the crashing droplets that sounded like applause from the heavens. It could have been him seeing Luke, or it could be the irony of the cool drops that in an odd way were like Emily's tears. Whichever it was, he had quieted.

"Luke you cannot fight with us. You are too old, and you could get hurt, but you don't have to be. I know you think that the Immortali gave you back your youth, but it wasn't them. It was you. You wanted to help Ty. If you want to fight for Annie, Isaiah, Elijah, and me, you must find that inner power inside of you. Your half my blood and you are more like me than a vessel. Stand with me son!"

The crowd hysterically laughed as Luke tried to stand erect and tall. It wasn't working. His old body just didn't have the energy to fight.

"Sit down old man, before you fall down!" Someone in the crowd yelled, as he fell into collapsed heap in failure. *"Looks like we are too late. He was the walking dead that can't walk!"* Prunella hysterically laughed with crowd.

"He must find reason Nate," Elijah said.

Nate went over to Luke and spoke softly in his ear.

"Alright, Luke the day I saw you after you made a deal with the Immortali to get out of jail, was the day I knew I did the proper thing sending you away. I believed I had a chance to be the father I wasn't. You leaped off a bridge and soared with me side by side. I hid the tears of joy from you at the bottom, but I was prouder than any father could be. You became a man after his father's heart, and you have it. Please for me, stand up and take that inner strength you have and be the son I need you to be. C'mon son!"

Rumbling in the heavens grumbled, and along with the rain, a bolt of lightning bolted down from them and spiked Luke directly in his heart. His body seized and he groaned in the charge of it. Smoke and steam hid him in a vapor cloud. When it cleared, he stood up in his regained youth and the rain peeled the old away in large clumps of decay and leaving him strong and a young spitting image of his father, wings, and all.

"I be God damned!!" He cried on his father's shoulder. *"It wasn't your fault. I was alone in this world for so long and they were the first to make me feel like I wasn't alone, so of course I believed what they said. I spent more than twenty years behind bars as a violent criminal just to avoid being scrutinized and dissected. You know, I always blamed you for not looking for me, but I really should have blamed myself for not looking for you."*

"Fight! Fight! Fight! Fight!" The onlookers cheered, now filling the theater.

Prunella found courage in their excited chants. She and Clymythious were only shortly stunned by Nate's defensive maneuver.

"Aw, this is so sweet. An immortal and a half breed bonding. If I had any emotions, I would be all misty...but I'm not. It's tiring to watch you two."

She closed in the distance between them with speed and agility so fast that she blurred to their eyes.

"Come my sweet," she said speaking directly to Luke. *"Let you and I have a moment, and I can show you so much more than you could ever see."*

Within a flash of a second, she was behind him cooing in his ear and flicking her tongue along his neckline. Her power of seduction held Luke still as he shuttered in her touch.

"I could release you from your mortal bondage right now and you could live forever, but it would be so boring and droll, but if you wanted to, I could make this painless and welcome you to my world of the night. You would like that, wouldn't you?"

Her hands ran along Luke's ribcage, and he was entranced in her lust.

"Yes, I would," was his immediate reply that sounded tranquil and calm.

"Kill him! Kill him! Kill him!" The crowd welled in boisterous approval.

Elijah and Nate did not interfere. While she might have hypnotic presence over Luke, she had none over them. They watched as she played him in her lust, tantalizing him and toying with him. In true theatrical fashion, she led him to the edge of the pit by the hand, swaying her hips and throwing her hair in front of him like a lamb to a slaughter. She was a true enchantress. She ran her finger over his short cropped wooly hair and pulled his head to the side, exposing his neck to the delight of spectators.

"*Wait, my love. I want to see your face when you do it,*" Luke said as he turned around to her. His eyes were fastened in hers.

"*What are you doing my love?*" Prunella said as he grabbed her by her jaw just inches from a kiss.

"*Stop it!*" She cried wriggling in his grasp.

The crowd went eerily deaf. They didn't see that Luke was not under her spell, and that this was not what Prunella intended. Luke's wings raised as he held her eyes in a forced stare.

"*No Luke, no!*" Annie screamed for the cage above the pit.

Annie's pleas were ignored by him- or so she thought. Luke's eyes went from deep brown wells of intimacy and control to fire burning embers that got brighter with each breath. The exchange between them was uncertain as his eyes consumed hers in scorching blaze.

"*Noooooo, Stop it!*" She screamed as he devoured her in light and gently kissed her in completion.

Not any of his friends and family knew what had just occurred. Nate held his hand on the hilt of his sword- prepared to slaughter his own son, and Annie sobbed in the cage, helpless to do anything about it. He gently let her delicate pale face go and the crowd went berserk in excitement. He turned to his father with a smirk on his face and winked.

"I can't see! I can't see!" Prunella cried while stumbling around with her hands outstretched in from her. *"What have you done?*

I will kill you!

I will kill you!"

Realizing what he had done, a hush fell over the just exhilarated crowd. No one tried to help her as she clumsily stumbled over candles and debris, still threatening to kill what she cannot see.

Chapter 18

While Luke was flexing his wings as if he won a prize fight, Clymythious' guards filed on the stage.

"Did you see that Pop? Imma bad brother!" He said while showing off dancing around like a champion boxer taunting the booing crowd. Nate and Elijah discreetly conversed while Luke held them in distraction.

"It is crueller to remove a snake's fangs than it is to put it to death. He must learn to wield his strengths in honorable ways," Elijah whispered.

"Let him get it out of his system. Don't worry about him. I will have a talk with him."

They watched as Luke flapped his new wings in childish bravado until Clymythious' guards filed on stage. Uniformed guards in red overcoats with gold tassels on the shoulders and armed with bayonets and swords. Trailing behind them were Philonious De Canton, who helped Ty and Luke escape out of Baltimore City Jail as a lawyer, and an injured Simon with his left arm in a sling, which simmered Luke down.

Tension has risen and the stage is set for a massacre that is not in their favor. With one command, the guards were pointing the weapons at the three. They were outnumbered by more than twenty men. Upwind past them was rank with the smell of fresh gunpowder jammed in turn-of-the-century muskets. Nate, Luke, and Elijah froze in their steps in the realization that they might not win against an army. They watched as the soldiers took down the cage and released Annie and young Isaiah to

Clymythious and took Elijah's firm grip on Nate's arm to restrain him.

"Oh, there will be a Rite of Ascension tonight, with or without your precious Emily!"

He turned and held the naked infant over his head between his two large horns and the crowd went into frenzied ovation. For them, the night meant a release of their fellow Fallen Watchers from prison against God's orders. It meant that they weren't damned to certain eternity of Hell and endless torture in the Lake of Fire. Isiah's blood spill was only a ploy to get Emily back to do it. Nate could take no more.

"Stop! Clymythious, you know that my son's death gains you nothing. You deceive your people, but if you do not harm him, I will battle you man to man in the flesh, I will commit to getting Emily back. What would you have to lose but the defeat in front of everyone, but if I win you release all of us and we fight another day," he said, throwing his sword at Clymythious feet.

"Very well. Man to man. Warrior to warrior. God against gods it is," he agreed and handed the child to Simon. *"But first..."*

Clymythious didn't throw his sword down, instead shoved it in Annie's abdomen and pulled it out to let her blood run down its blade and over the hilt to his fingers, and then he threw it down. *"This is for Natasha!"*

Luke was so stunned when Clymythious did it that he instinctively ran to her collapsing body where the guards held bayonets at his throat. He cried over her promising that it was going to be alright, regardless of his own safety. All eyes were on Luke and his sorrow, holding her in his arms. No one noticed that Elijah has left to the skies above them. Nate was standing alone now with his palms still open and facing Clymythious.

"*She needs a hospital Pop!*" Luke yelled and stole her unconscious body into the sky with wings that banged the air beneath them in frantic flight.

Clymythious wasn't done. He raised his hands toward the forest and a low buzzing hummed in the brush. The sound rattled the trees as it came closer and closer overhead. Whatever they were, they were in the hundreds and shaking leaves from the treetops as they approached. They swarmed over the amphitheater with large dragonfly wings and amphibian bodies that resemble a tadpole with stingers as tails There were so many that the night sky got darker as they crowded the swirling bulbous clouds above. Clymythious, with a wave of his hand, sent them in pursuit of Luke and they swarmed after them.

"*Clymythious, I thought we agreed that this will be man to man. What gain do you earn by sending them after my son and Annie?*"

"*And man to man it shall be. Annie's life was in exchange of Navasha's death, Luke the cocky one blinded my soothsayer. Did he think that there would be no retribution for his merciless actions? Let's see how cocky and arrogant he will be when they torture and sting him until his carcass is full of their venom and he too can die with his precious Annie,*" Clymythious said while disrobing and transforming into human form and walking towards him. "*Here are the rules. Hand to hand combat with no weapons or ancient magic, form, or assistance. If you defeat me, I will call off my swarm, release your bastard child of abomination, and free..."*

Not until Clymythious noticed that Elijah was gone did anyone else. Guards were frantically searching the perimeter of the amphitheater looking for him. When they reported back that he was nowhere to be found, it infuriated Clymythious. The guards followed his command and made a complete circle around Nate and him. That was four of the five that have found ways to evade him. Emily is gone. Luke took Annie and escaped, and now Elijah has disappeared.

"You enjoy making a mockery of the Order, don't you Nathaniel? So, let's make this charade of a battle more interesting," he said while cracking his neck in preparation for the hand-to-hand duel. *"I will keep my word on what we agreed on- unlike you, but because of your friend's trickery and deception I am upping the ante. Bring the child forth!"*

Simon was let through the circle of guards carrying Isaiah in a cold despondent cradle- his injuries prominent.

"Put the child on the other side of the stage. Here is how this is going to go.. You must fight me with your son's life at stake as well. If the chance allows the opportunity to kill one or both of you, I will not hesitate. Weary is the man who friends abandon him."

Isaiah is now on the cobblestone ground kicking the tattered blanket off him and wailing in anger and discomfort. Nate cannot help but to grieve in the first moments he has to bond with his son shall have to be in this way, but it will have to be quick. He approached the child slowly and calmly staring into eyes that resembled Ty's as he looked like a little infant.

Isiah briefly quieted as he gazed into his father's eyes with his tiny arms flailing as if he wanted to be picked up off the ground and be cuddled in safety. For the first time in the last couple of hours, Nate felt naked and insufficient in what or how to ease his young son. He knelt down to him speaking to him in a low tone as if he understood what the words meant.

"Hey little one. Don't be afraid. The world has you now in it. In this moment I promise you that no harm shall come to you as long as I can prevent it. You came into this world with a family divided by things you are not deserving of. Tonight, unfortunately will be your first battle and I promise you victory, I pray for protection on both of us this eve. Close your eyes and sleep for the battle you inherit is one I will give my life for," Nate said while tying him with the blanket in a makeshift sling.

"I won't endanger my son's life in battle."

Just the joining of his small body resting on his chest, feeling his tiny heartbeat, and looking at his small dark cherub looking face with wispy curly hair, made him stand up to Clymythious and all the guards despite the disadvantage.

"Get me my whip! I think I got me a nigga I have to whip!"

The guards grabbed Nate's arm and turned his exposed back to the crowd and forced him to his knees. He has been whipped and flogged before and his back has the scars to prove it. He looked up at the sky and silently wept in a prayer to give him the strength to endure what is about to happen.

"Em, where are you?"

Far off in the horizon was Luke in desperate haste to follow the halo of city lights that seemed not close enough. Behind him was the swarm like a cloud closing quickly on him. He tried his best to weave and bob in the currents, but they gained in his wake behind him. The first sting from one of them was painful, but he kept his focus on the edge of the city, gripping Annie tight. She hung in his grasp like a rag doll as he dodged through the tops of pines and fir trees bowing their tops as he passed to knock as many off his pursuit in their springy snapback. Each sting on his arms and wings swole in horrific stabbing wounds. His only option would be to land short of the city's edge and as where he might be feeble in the air- the ground would be an ambush he could not win.

"Hold Annie! We are not that far."

But Luke was wrong. The swarm overcame them in ferocity and agitation. Luke's exhausts wings had sustained multiple stings and were tiring from the stings that left jagged numbing barnacled stingers in him. Where once he was soaring like an eagle, he now was barely holding flight. He was falling slowly, a black Icarus who never made it to the sun.

"Let me go Luke," Annie woke up and said. *"We both can't make it, and they are killing you. Go help your father and the baby."*

Sweat was pouring profusely as each tedious beat of his now numb wings exerted everything that was in him. He rode the cross currents to briefly rest in them and focused on the dim twinkling lights that are now close, but so was the swarm. They had engulfed the two of them from every direction. His two-armed carry was now a one man carry as he fought with his extremities, killing as many as he could kill with his feet, wings, two numbed legs, and even his teeth, biting ones that landed on Annie.

"I am so sorry to bring you into my family's shit. I don't think we can make it by air much farther."

Both he and Annie were now in a flying crowd of the toad-like serpents that buzzed and picked on their flesh as the flight descended. She crawled into an embryo ball and Luke wrapped his wings around her and told her how much he loved her.

"I never got the chance to tell you that, Annie. From the first time I laid eyes on you in Elliott City where things were simpler. I will never let you leave me again!"

The two began the plummet out of the night sky wrapped tightly in each other's embrace. From the height they were, they unlikely would have survived the fall.

"I have an idea, but you must trust me," he said, outstretching his wings to slow the chaotic pitch.

Luke grabbed back in a fireman's carry and with all his remaining strength threw her into the sky above so far above him through the swarm that she almost disappeared out of site. All he could hear is her screams dwindling the farther she went up- legs dangling attempting to tread air. Before the swarm could chase her, he burst open his wings yelling and roaring from within emitting a burst of piercing light that one by one fried the ones that were feet away from him. It didn't get all of them, but it killed enough for him to regain his composure and listen for Annie's screams as she began to fall back to Earth. The remaining ones he fought, crushing them in his bare hands and batting them with his wings when suddenly crows appeared from the sky above. They were cawing and swooning down on the swarm ripping their dragonfly wings off with their hard beaks. Behind them was Elijah and Emily out the dark clouds sending the remaining swarm fleeing. He looked at the two of them amongst the murder of crows in the swarming black sky around them.

"I guess I'm supposed to see you Ty, but I'm not. You left me, Isaiah, Nate, and even you Elijah. Now you wanna show up and you think I'm going to be glad to see you? We were there fighting for our lives, and you ran. You ran like you always have. When are you going to stand up for something besides yourself? You left your son, not because you couldn't defend him. You left because you couldn't face Nate! Because of you Annie..."

Right on cue, he heard her returning screams as she fell from the sky from his 'Hail Mary' toss.

"Oh shit!" He screamed as he tried to calculate where she would fall through the night sky, but he couldn't see through the murder.

"Do something Ty! Don't just float there like you can't."

Luke staggered attempting to be under where she would fall to catch her. He was off by yards, and he knew that his miscalculation could mean her death. Neither Emily or Elijah scrambled to help him in his desperate rescue until she was feet away from the ground and far from where Luke could catch her.

"Oh God, what have I done," he cried dragging his numb legs that didn't have the strength or speed to position himself under her hurdling descent.

With a wave of his hand, Elijah froze time.

"Ty, do you see what is happening?"

Emily was unaffected by the stilled scene. She gently descended to the ground and walked over to Luke who is on his knees with hands outstretched. He was covered in welting stings that covered his shirtless frame and even his face was marred by what had to be painful.

"He looks like his father. I have brought him nothing but pain. I didn't inflict all of it, but the Emily that bore him has. I can accept the curse of being the vessel, and he is right in what he said. I couldn't bare Nate rejecting me and I ran. Look at him. He has regained his youth, and he is willing to sacrifice everything for the love of another."

"Share the sorrow that beseeches your soul in truth. Embrace all you are with no appeasement like him, no authority. For with it comes the illusion of control- 'An Angel's Fall.' The fall of Angels is one of control. He cares not that she is mortal. He is brave and has never left your side through this all. What would you give to him?"

Emily looked at Annie who was badly injured. She selflessly protected her and Isaiah without understanding that she was facing the unknown. Her glance before she smashed into the ground was trusting and on Luke.

"Release time Elijah! I cannot let this happen."

Emily's already brighten hue blazed into fire as time resumed.

"Oh God nooooooo," was Luke's last cry as he shifts his eyes to not watch the death of Annie. "I'm so sorry Annie. I failed."

"You have not failed Luke," Emily said as she suspended Annie mid-air.

Luke's mouth wide open, expressed the shock of what Emily could do. No words spilled from them as he could find none that would say all that he should've and maybe retract some that he has.

"I will take her inside for care. It isn't her night's fate this eve. Go with Emily and let your spirit in a victory assured unite and to do what must be done," Elijah said while hoisting Annie from the suspension and carried her off in the direction of the hospital.

"Stand on your own Luke. That what you have charged me with bears no forgiveness. Rise," she said while allowing the blue flames to calm.

"Go without me Ty. I am too weary to travel. I can't feel most of me from the stings of those things. Besides, all that I have said, and all that I felt against you should hold no forgiveness. I misjudged you and you saved my Anna despite what I said to you."

The winds picked up and she turned to him with her hair tangling in the robust wind holding out her small hand to take his. Luke's feeble attempts bound him to the ground no matter how he fought to stabilize his numb limbs.

"I'm telling you to leave me and help them damnit! I would only hold you back Emily!"

"Look at me Luke and take my hand!"

From the ground he could only see her silhouette in her blaze. Something was different in her presence- especially in her face. Emily's eyes meant what they said, they were still the docile eyes of a new Emily that he feels he knows.

"My son, I know you may not recognize me, but your tiny face over the cliffs of Edison's Edge was the last thing I saw face to face with you. Do you not know your mother?"

"No, I don't recognize you. I was too little, but I know who you are Ma. I would know you even if I were blind."

Emily face was the face of the Vessel before Ty. She was just as beautiful with straight wooly hair that in the crosswinds smelled of wild lavender and summer.

"Who are those lights behind you Ma?"

Luke was speaking about tiny orbs of light that bounced around her like lightening bugs in early evening- sleepy and slow. One or two would occasionally land on her shoulder or hand as she still reached out waiting for him to take it.

"They are your brothers and sisters. We all were separated in life, but now you see that we are together, and so are you. Come with me son. Here is one that needs our help."

Luke's trembling hand touched her, and a surge of energy jolted through him washing away the numbness. His whole body healed in her touch, and he laughed as his tiny orb brothers and sisters landed on their joined hands and eventually on him. He could feel them as if he knew them. It was only four, but their joyous touch tickled as they reunited with him.

It was only seconds as he allowed them to know him.

"Hello," he said as they took turns in silently, in unspoken language, welcomed him as a long-lost brother.

"It is time.," Emily of new said as she summoned the sword from a cracked opened sky. *"We must return."*

Hand in hand with a trail of brothers and sisters in tiny lights like the tail of a comet, Emily and Luke took to the sky back to Crimea. Below them above the trees they could see the scourge of crows blackening the reflection of the moon on branches and open fields. There had to be thousands of them swallowing the ground as they swarmed along the way.

There in the distance, still lit by torches was Crimea nestled and centered in acreage of forest. The crows surrounded it but did not swallow it too in their murder blanket. We stopped overhead and could hear Nate's cries as the bullwhip slashed his bareback. His flesh ripped open in gashes on scarred tissue. With each lash drool spewed from his mouth as he yelled through the pain.

"What are we waiting for? He has Isaiah wrapped around him. It's you that Clymythious wants," Luke impatiently said, but when he looked at her, expecting to see his mother, she was gone. Emily had returned to herself and was tearing at the grotesque sight.

"Let me go first Luke. I want nothing of consequence than what is to be. You will know when it is time," she said as she flew off to the back of the Orianda House to the windmill.

Emily didn't want to enter as a well-prepared opponent. She changed back into the ball gown and jewels and wound down the path and through the spectators to the amphitheater. Guests still with red umbrellas overhead parted to let her through. From above, Luke knew it was time by the blood red umbrella's part and the impending thunder behind him. Emily walked on stage with divinity and incredible poise to be witnessing the torture of Nate and the piercing cries of Isaiah.

"And so, you have returned as I knew you would my pet. Have you come to your senses and are ready to complete the Rite of Ascension?"

She said nothing as she gracefully stepped over the carcasses of dead and wounded to approach Clymythious.

"Perhaps you need a better look at your precious Nate. I must admit that he has held up through it and will not submit the half-breed prodigy."

Clymythious ordered the release of Nathaniel, and he knelt to his knees still cradling Isaiah in the sling in front of him as Luke arrived in time to catch him before he fell.

"My, my, the whole family is here! Mommy, Daddy, and sons. Such a quaint affront. You honor me with such a tribute for this celebration. I promise you that you each will die in a historic honor that will be celebrated as the 200 return and devour mankind. You will be stories of folklore for all time!"

"Shut up, man!" Luke said while taking Isaiah out of the sling. *"You run your mouth too much. You know you couldn't beat Pop without that foul shit!"*

Both Emily and Nate told Luke to shut up causing them to notice the first time all four have been together, despite the dire situation.

"He's beautiful Emily," Nate said as Emily took young Isaiah from Luke's arms.

"I know. These wings look good on me," Luke chimes in.

"Shut up, Luke!"

CHAPTER 19

The stage was set, but Nate and Emily only saw each other. Nate's wounds weren't severe enough to stop him from saying things that he felt she needed to hear.

"Emily, I thought you left us because you believed Clymythious' lies. I saw all the vessels interchange within you, and you could never forgive me, lest trust me. I have more than once scorned you into Clymythious' grasp. This too, I believed was another. Stay with me and I will pledge undying love unconditionally, no matter what bestows you."

"Hahahahaha," Clymythious laughed in the background which diverted the private conversation between them. *"Nathaniel, you just never get it. She/he or whatever form she is reborn is mine,"* he walked over to them in assurance that what he said could be proven. *"How many centuries do I have to show you this? Emily my love, come with me again and I will show you the power of Immortali and a kingdom that is prepared to kneel at your feet. This day rejoices as you ascend in your marriage to me. Waste not your time on a man that can only promise a casket full of unsuitable promises to die again and feed worms from your flesh."*

Clymythious gently grabbed her hand as he tried to swoon her over to gifts of darkness. Unshaken, Emily allowed Clymythious' ploy and permitted his escort to the dismay of both Nate and Luke.

"And so, my dear, you can remember that it is not I that deceived you. Many moons and eons, you and I have suffered the sour and the sweet in your previous incarnations, each time

I have loved you. What I offer, I have laid at your feet in hopes that you will be my bride or companion no matter where your heart finding varies. Tonight is the night that it is your choice or your extinguished end. I hope you select wisely."

Clymythious had one flaw in his aloof rhetoric. Initially he held her endearing hand in gentleness uncertainty, but as he escorted and spoke to her, the grip tightens around her small hands. Behind the regal etiquette and proposition, was a man that was gambling for her affection and acceptance of the long night.

The distant chapel annexed to Orianda Manor began to toll the midnight hour in deep-toned, emphatic clangs echoing in the surrounding trees and disturbing the crows out of the spruce and maple trees. All were amplified with a haunting conjoining of crows flapping wings and caws, to heightened lauding from the chaotic spectators that now were fevered pitched with each stroke of the old bell.

"Stay with me as my love, my bride, my queen, and I will spare your sons," he spoke in between the first toll and the impatient second one.

Emily turned to look at Luke and Nate, who was cradling Isaiah. Her heart pounded within her with palpitating bosom heaving against the satin gown in restraint.

"Before the last strike of midnight you must elect a choice," he said while summoning Simon to the front of the amphitheater behind them. *"Gaze at your people that will serve you for all eternity as their queen and I, their king!"*

The faces in the crowd were cheering so loudly amongst the encircling crows cries as the skies swirled raptured clouds and welling thunder. It was hard to focus, or much less breath. Clymythious stood behind her close to her ear to be heard.

"You look ill, my love."

He ripped the fastenings of the gown, and it fell to her shoulders, only supported by her arms that pressed against her breasts.

"There is nothing to be frightened of, my queen," he said at the seventh toll as he removed the sole hairpin that held her coiffed tress and her hair fell on her shoulders as he placed a crown that Simon bought to him on her head.

Emily wasn't frightened or embarrassed about standing half-naked in front of so many. She was more confused as he continued cooing affirmations about her submitting by the final chime. Fear has no home within her after all she has been through. All the presence of all the Vessels past fueled her in defiant consternation. From behind her, Luke's pleading cries struggled as Nate restricted him with a firm one-hand grip from interfering.

"No, Ty! This isn't what you wanted! Don't you remember? You are what I believe in. Your love for Pops is what you want! Not power! Please, Emily, don't do this," Luke shouted over the crescendoing noise.

Hearing his pleas resonated far over the chaos surrounding her. Something came over her as she let the gown fall to the ground grabbing the sword from her thigh harness and raised it to the tumultuous storm overhead. Her exquisite nakedness

The Book of Emily

halted Clymythious as he gawked over her beautiful ebony frame with dewy sweat shining off it, pure and unbridled. Possessed and invigorated, she channeled the lightening from the atmosphere, and it cracked through the charged air with a trembling crack.

"Emily, don't," Nate said as Isaiah shrieked after a startling roaring sound in his father's arms.

She turned her head to Isaiah's cries and lowered the sword which stopped the lightening, now levitating up off the amphitheater floor with her head laid back and arms out at her sides -almost sacrificial. Below her was the crown, the gown and strewn silk slippers. The spectators assumed she was ascending in the Rite of Ascension and all kneeled in respect.

"No longer shall the blood of my ancestors or seed of my loin be persecuted by evil and bloodshed, and you, Clymythious, shall earn the final reward of it," she said to him as she lowered back to the ground.

"Oh, my taciturn goddess, I have waited for this day."

"And you shall have it Clymythious. We shall seal this moment together."

Seeing Emily in royal hue, she incited the spectators to applaud in rejoice over the new queen. She wrapped her legs around his body in a sensuous taunt, still holding the sword.

"Yes, my dear! I have waited centuries for you," he said.

Her enchantment overwhelmed him, and he savored her as she, in her rapture, flickered between the centuries of Vessels before- Amalia, Frederick, Ana, Ty, and more interchanged in flashes.

"Yes! I loved you all. Open the gates of Hell and release my brethren. In this merge, let your power be mine together. We will have the day of redemption at last! The Rite of Ascension is complete," he said to the spectators.

"Hail King Clymythious! Long live the queen!"

"But wait, my King. We should seal the bond in a kiss," Emily said as she kissed him.

Clymythious' eyes closed in assurance that he had gotten all that he wanted and had been waiting for, but didn't expect. Emily rammed the sword through his chest without ceasing the kiss, followed by a huge bolt of blinding lightening that struck them both as Clymythious convulsed in the electrifying conjoin.

"God's wrath is absolute! Your arrogance, deceit, and selfish disdain for power ends now!"

A final bolt struck them with unfathomable brilliance that blinded all who watched in disbelief, leaving a cloud of smoke too dense to see through. The putrid smell of burning flesh and sulphur cleared and on the floor was left a pile of smoldering ashes and a collapsed Emily, still holding the sword as it sparked, still full of energy.

Nate and Luke ran to her still naked body and clothed her in the blanket that was swaddled around Isiah.

"You can't die, Em. You can't leave us," **Nate whispered to her with her head in his lap as the crows landed on the amphitheater stage in tribute, but Emily was somewhere else in

lavender fields in Edison's Edge with young Nate. She let her mind return to a time when Emily knew love. In the clearing at dusk, she and Nate frolicked in the soft meadow, crushing sweet lavender in passion and love unbound. She remembers Nate's touch and his words that filled her complete in that moment.

"If I ever love so more than I am, I surely hath left heaven's boundary for nothing has convicted me more than your love and sweet kisses."

That day was clear in her mind. The smell of his body mixed with the fragrance of twilight, his rough beard and hands on her skin, the gentle breeze, and the enveloping orange tinge sky that pressed their bodies together.

"Nate, I will love you eternally and beyond. You are my reason to live," she remembered saying that spring day.

The memory faded into the past and she returned to the present. Her eyes, full of completion and love, were now staring at Nate and it all felt the same as she lost herself in his moist eyes as her head laid in his lap.

"Remember the lavender?"

"Yes, I do, my love. I remember it all," he said while placing tiny Isaiah on her chest.

Standing over were her were the men she loved with worried faces camouflaged in forced half-smiles.

"We thought we lost you, Em. You surprised us all."

"It is done, Nate. The gates are still sealed, and I have done all I can."

The mysterious storm ebbed away leaving a small gust to sweep the ashes of Clymythious away onto the shocked crowd that ran in fear for themselves. Out of it came Elijah landing by the side of them.

"You have done well, Ty. No er' hath a battle been as fought with more bravery. Luke, Annie is fine, and she will live to fight another day, too. We must make haste to leave this God-forsaken place. There are others who are not finished with you."

"Fight another day? I thought this shit was it. What kind of trick-bag is this? Ty killed that mother fucker! I'm outta here!"

Luke flew off in the direction of the hospital, right past helicopters that were encircling the mansion. They could hear Det. Choo on a bullhorn, carousing the fleeing guest at the entrance.

"Nobody leaves. You are all under arrest!"

Storms of police officers uniformed in riot gear were carousing the panicked guests who tried to escape, handcuffing them in plastic ties as they tried to exit.

"Get them that are up there on that stage! Nobody leaves!"

Detective Choo had experience with Luke and Nate escaping his capture. He ran around in his wrinkled trench coat, ordering officers to let some of the guests go to assist him. "If any of you let them escape, it's your job!"

"Em, we have to go. Choo is going to lock us all up if we don't and who will take care of Isaiah?"

Nate lifted her up in his arms while she cradled Isaiah tightly.

"You are too weak to carry her, Nathaniel. I can slow time down enough for you to carry her into the woods, but it won't last more than a couple of minutes," Elijah said and stretched out his arm towards the barrage of police and they all slowed to an almost standstill, Choo's face frozen- angry and distraught.

"There is one thing you must know," Elijah said as he held time back. *"The life in front of you can only be more difficult than it has. It will take two of you to combat evil and they will hunt you."*

"Why? Haven't we defeated them?"

"No, Nathaniel. You have only wounded them by cutting off their head. As long as Ty is Emily and the boy is connected to her, they will seek them for their nature, but if I remove Emily's power, she can live without pursuit as Tyson- a normal life."

Emily and Nate looked at each other in contemplation of what each thought the other would want to hear, trying their best to be indifferent. It could mean that perhaps they could evade danger and pursuit. It could mean that it would be like a second chance.

"Em, I'm okay if that is what you want. I have guarded you all your lives. I know nothing but you. You have known nothing but pain and a life of heartache and some of it is my own. I stand with you either way. I will never leave your side unless you ask. Your destiny is mine."

She didn't answer what he said. Either way, she would have to live in doubt and identity. She knows what it is like in both choices. There is one thing that encouraged her reply and decision.

"My son..."

Elijah attempted to sound comforting as he told her of his plan to take Isiah and place him in safe hands where he could grow up and one day fight in her place, as he is the vessel to end all. A fluke in fate, it was a relief to know that he would be safe, and she chose the best of solutions. A solution that was so obvious and one that she could live with. She rose to her feet and wrapped her arms around Nate and whispered.

"I choose lavender fields."

THE END

Printed in Great Britain
by Amazon